A WOMAN
OF VALOR

BY ALLAN TOPOL

A WOMAN OF VALOR
THE FOURTH OF JULY WAR

A WOMAN OF VALOR

A NOVEL BY
ALLAN TOPOL

WILLIAM MORROW AND COMPANY, INC.
NEW YORK   1980

Library of Congress Cataloging in Publication Data

Topol, Allan.
 A woman of valor.

 I. Title.
PZ4.T6796Wo   [PS3570.064]   813'.5'4   79-20186
ISBN 0-688-03578-7

Printed in the United States of America.

First Edition

1 2 3 4 5 6 7 8 9 10

I dedicate this book to Barbara, who makes all things possible, and to our children, David, Rebecca, Deborah, and Daniella.

A woman of valor who can find?
For her price is far above rubies.
—PROVERBS

CHAPTER 1

The happiest moments of Leora's childhood came when she reached the age of nine. At the end of the day her mother permitted her to race six blocks across the tree-lined streets of Alexandria from the family's spacious villa to the large brown stone structure that housed the Alexandria Trading Company, the largest export-import firm in Alexandria and a business that her father, Moshe Baruch, had inherited from his own father.

"Go fetch Abba," her mother would say. "Your father never knows when to come home."

Leora treasured that as one of many commands honoring the oldest child.

Off she went, mostly skipping rather than walking, a long-legged gawky girl with long black hair that bounced up and down on her shoulders.

She pushed past receptionists and secretaries, climbing the three flights of stairs to the "Office of the President."

"Only a minute," Baruch called with a smile on his face when he saw his daughter approach.

She made herself comfortable at a desk, leafing through brightly colored catalogs of shipping lines.

Usually they went straight home when they left the office, the giant of a man leaning over to hold the little girl's hand. But sometimes there were those special days when they stopped in a coffeehouse. He ordered her a large dish of ice cream, admonishing her, "It's almost dinnertime, don't you dare tell your mother."

While she enjoyed the ice cream, Abba sipped Turkish coffee and read the afternoon paper. Then they strolled home together.

9

One day in the spring of 1948, Leora sensed that something was different when she arrived to pick up her father. Clerks who usually joked with her were somber and quiet. This time there was no waiting for Abba. He was ready when she arrived.

"We will stop on the way home," Abba said.

Thinking about that dish of chocolate ice cream she would have, she clasped his hand tightly as they walked down the stairs.

In the street they could hear a newsboy shout, "Egypt joins the invasion!" as he hawked his papers. "Farouk vows to capture Palestine!"

She watched Abba hand the boy a couple of coins for a newspaper, telling him to keep the change. Then she watched as intellectuals and merchants gobbled up all of the boy's papers within a few short minutes.

As Leora walked through the streets, holding her father's hand tightly, the sun began setting over the city, its rays glistening on the gently rolling waters of the Mediterranean. The coffeehouses along the beach began filling up.

It was Alexandria.

Founded by Alexander the Great, the city had once been an important center of Greek learning and culture. Physicians prospered and made major developments in its medical center.

It was the city of Euclid, the great Greek mathematician.

During the Greek period it was also the home of Jewish scholars, the greatest center of Jewish intellectual thought outside of the land of Israel.

Everything prospered in Alexandria.

After the Greeks came the Romans. Antony followed in the steps of Julius Caesar.

For centuries it was unrivaled as the commercial center for European trade with Africa and the Far East.

The Moslems followed the Christians as occupiers. Even

Napoleon enjoyed its fruits. Then the British after him. Finally in 1947, the British relinquished their naval base in Alexandria, turning it back to King Farouk and the Egyptian people.

It was this man, King Farouk, who was the center of intense discussion being waged in the coffeehouses that evening early in 1948. For weeks Farouk had listened to the argument raging among his advisers. Should Egypt jump in or stay out? Did the country's ragtag army have enough firepower to join the great Arab struggle?

Finally Farouk decided. Egypt would join. The young colonel Gamal Abdel Nasser was delighted with Farouk's decision.

When Baruch entered the coffeehouse with Leora, they sat down at a table occupied by two men dressed in conservative Western clothes, sitting in silence, each one reading a copy of the late-afternoon newspaper.

Leora recognized them both as good friends of her father. One was a banker, Mohammed Hekel; the other a lawyer, Abdel Rasef.

Baruch greeted the two men, then ordered Leora a dish of chocolate ice cream and a cup of Turkish coffee for himself.

When the ice cream arrived, he told her to be very quiet as he opened the newspaper. She was only halfway through the large dish when Baruch folded his paper carefully, stirred the thick Turkish coffee, then sipped it slowly.

"A very bad decision," he said thoughtfully.

The banker stopped reading and placed down his own newspaper. He stared at Baruch, ready to accept the challenge, his eyes were sparkling.

"Bad. Bad for whom?"

"Bad for business. Bad for the whole country. Just now we have started to achieve some prosperity. And a war will end it all."

The banker was unconcerned.

11

"National pride. That's what we need. That's what we fight for."

"Ah, poppycock," Baruch replied, using the word he had learned from a roommate at school in London twenty years earlier. "You can't feed people with national pride."

Baruch glanced at Rasef, looking for support. The lawyer was still reading. If he had formed any opinion, it wasn't clear from his face.

"We are friends a long time," Mohammed continued to Baruch. "But you are a Jew. You cannot understand the national pride that I talk about."

Baruch's face flushed with anger.

"My family has lived in Alexandria for twenty-two hundred years, since the Greek period. I am as fit as you—"

The lawyer interrupted.

"Gentlemen. Gentlemen. We are all friends. There is no need to reduce the discussion to such a personal level. The real question is whether our army is fit for battle or not."

But Baruch refused to permit Rasef to change the subject so easily.

"That is another question," he said, raising his voice. "First we deal with the other one. Does this nouveau riche banker, one generation removed from a family of peasants, have any right to deny me my opinion of what is good for Egypt?"

There was a certain haughtiness in Baruch's tone that surprised Rasef. Still he tried to make peace. But Baruch resisted.

"An apology is what I demand."

"An apology for what?" Mohammed replied.

Baruch was silent. His views about the war would have been the same if the Egyptians were joining an invasion of Britain or Turkey.

"I see no further point in continuing this discussion," Baruch said, rising sharply.

Leora was startled by her father's tone of voice. She rose and stood next to him.

He placed a couple of coins on the table, making clear his intention to leave. Then he paused for a moment, giving Rasef an opportunity to rise and leave with him. When it was clear that the lawyer was remaining with Mohammed, Baruch grasped Leora's hand, turned sharply, and left the coffeehouse. Behind a great stone face he hid the righteous indignation that had spread to every part of his body.

Three weeks later, Moshe Baruch stood for a long time at one of the third-floor windows in his spacious villa, watching the activity in the streets below.

Everywhere there were soldiers on the move, passing through Alexandria on the way to the Sinai desert. They moved by land and by water as Brigadier Neguib began assembling the Egyptian strike force of ten thousand soldiers, armed with rifles and accompanied by tanks which were to gather in the Sinai at El Arish.

Baruch watched the soldiers milling around with incredulity. They all looked so undisciplined, ill trained, and disorganized. Like so many sheep being led to a slaughter, he thought. Unless, of course, the Zionists were equally disorganized.

Here and there Baruch could hear the shouts of "Holy war! Death to the Jews!" from the masses who crowded the streets watching the soldiers.

Sending the troops through Alexandria had already had a disruptive effect on the city. Baruch's eyes passed over to the commercial port area. Ships that should have been unloaded, loaded, and gone were still sitting idly while a general carnival atmosphere prevailed in the city.

His eyes moved back to the green park below where a speaker was addressing a crowd. If he looked hard enough, he could probably find Hussini, that mediocre clerk, that speck of a man, who had worked for him until two o'clock this afternoon. That clerk had the nerve, the unbridled gall, to say to him, Moshe Baruch, who had physical evidence to trace his background in the city twenty-two hundred years back, "I imagine you'll be going off to Palestine with your people."

He had fired the man on the spot.

Baruch closed the shutters on the window and walked downstairs to the sitting room. Everything was in disarray. Books and papers were scattered on the furniture. Dirty dishes were visible in the dining room. In one of the first-floor rooms a baby was crying.

"It's not possible to clean up this mess, Hannah?" Baruch shouted in Arabic to his wife, sitting on a couch staring straight ahead.

"I've told you that the woman quit. She quit today. I haven't been able to get someone else on short notice."

Leora hid behind the curtains in the sitting room, trying hard to hear every word that her parents said.

"You're still upset over what the woman told you?" Baruch asked.

She nodded weakly.

"So she told you that she didn't want to work for Jews. So what? She's ignorant, illiterate. What does it matter?"

His wife was unconvinced. "You're not realistic. Eighty percent are illiterate. They believe what the government tells them."

The baby started crying louder.

"Feed him, Hannah," Baruch replied in exasperation. "There's no point worrying about this. It will pass. I am convinced it will pass."

Hannah sat motionless on the couch.

"Again I say you are being unrealistic. We sit here with four small children like fools. The Arabs will kill us.

14

This is how they sat in Germany. We are no wiser. We sit like fools." Baruch dismissed her with a wave of his hand. Then he rose to his feet.

"Enough. I said. Go feed Uri. We will manage."

Then Moshe stormed out of the house into the hot sticky evening air of his garden. He sat pensively on a lounge chair in the center of a cluster of palm trees, enjoying the respite from Hannah's harping.

After he sat in silence for a few minutes, his ears detected a slight noise, a rustling in the bushes. He leaned forward, alert, attentive.

"Who's there?" he called sharply.

"Abba, it's only me," Leora replied.

He saw a frightened look on her face.

"What is it, my child? What is it?"

"I do not understand, Abba. I do not understand."

"You are too young. It's not your place."

"No, I am not too young. I must know."

"There is very little to know, Leora." Then Baruch began repeating the story exactly the way his father had told it to him.

"We are Egyptians, and we are Jews. We have lived here for more than two thousand years. Do you know how long that is?"

The child nodded weakly.

"But I heard Mama say that many Jews are moving to Israel."

"Your mother talks too much," he said harshly.

"But why are they leaving?"

The child was persistent. He could dismiss Hannah, but not Leora.

"Those who are leaving are not strong. They are weak. They have achieved little in Egypt. They have not become a part of the culture. Now they leave to seek greener pas-

15

tures. People like us, the strong and powerful, will remain here always. This is our home."

The child walked over and sat on Baruch's lap. He stroked her long hair gently.

"But Abba, once you said I would go to England."

"Yes, you will go to England to attend the university just as I did, and so will your brother and sisters. That is where all of the Egyptian intellectuals go. Then we bring back knowledge to enhance our country. And so it will be with you."

She was quiet. He realized that he hadn't satisfied her fears, only made her forget them for a time. Still, what else could he hope to do the way Hannah had been ranting and raving?

"There are momentous events going on in the world, Leora."

"But what does this have to do with us, Abba? I do not understand."

Her father was silent.

~

CHAPTER 2

LONDON, 1955

What Leora remembered most about the University of London was her enthusiasm for acting that was kindled by the university Drama Society. She joined the society out of a determination to do something to relieve the terrible loneliness that plagued her six weeks into the first term.

Her arrival in London had been filled with anxiety and excitement. After all, she had never before been separated from her family. She was being transported to one of the great capitals of the world. She wasn't even certain whether she had wanted to go. She was going because Abba expected it.

There were two other Egyptian students in the first-year class at the university, both boys from Cairo, children of high-level government officials whose education was being provided by the government. During the first week, they were friendly with Leora, which helped her feel less strange. Then they joined the Arab Students Association. After that, the budding friendship died. They had nothing more to do with her.

Leora experienced weeks of unhappiness. She had always been a bit of a loner. and it was difficult for her to make friends. That was when she saw the notice: "University Drama Society—Organizational Meeting—New Students Welcome."

Leora found that she had talent as an actress. The society decided parts after volunteers tried out. She made up her mind that she would succeed in this competitive system.

Her appearance was an advantage. She was tall, and her features were strong and dark—a contrast from the other girls in the society, who were for the most part smaller and fair. It stood to reason, Leora decided, that she would have the edge for some parts just on looks alone.

Fortunately, early in the second term of her first year, Philip Marks, who was one of the society's directors, decided to do Shakespeare's *Antony and Cleopatra*. Later, Leora guessed that Philip had picked the play because he wanted to work with her. But she didn't think of that at the time. All she knew was that if she really put herself to it, she could land the role of Cleopatra. "I'm a natural Cleopatra," Leora said to herself. The trouble was that Joan Whitney, a third-year actress with considerable experience, had the same idea. They competed for the part, and after a great deal of discussion and handwringing, Philip finally said, "Leora, the part's yours. You'd better not let me down."

17

Philip tried to act like a demanding director, but Leora quickly perceived that he was only playing a role himself. She began to like him.

Antony and Cleopatra played to enthusiastic standing-room-only audiences both scheduled performances as well as an extra one that was hastily arranged. When it was over, Leora started dating Philip, casually at first, more seriously later. When he wasn't playing the role of the director, she found him to be the most sensitive and gentle man she had ever known—except for Abba.

They began sleeping together later that spring. At first Leora felt guilty because she knew that Abba would never approve. But soon the pleasure that she derived from Philip pushed those feelings of guilt from her mind.

Philip begged her to move into his apartment, but she consistently refused, determined to maintain her independence.

It seemed strange to Leora later, but one subject that she and Philip never talked about was religion. Even though they were both Jewish, Philip was British and she was Egyptian, and that was that. Once, Joan Whitney, who wanted a source book Leora had borrowed from the library, sneered at her and called her a "Jewish whore." Leora told Philip about it later, but he laughed it off.

"Don't think anything of it," he said.

But she refused to forget it. When the book was due two days later, Joan came around to Leora's room looking for it. She shoved it under a small ledge above the curtains and told Joan, "Don't know where it is."

Philip was finishing his third year in school that spring, and he began talking to Leora about marriage. Each time he did, she turned him down, telling him that she was much too young for that. She wasn't prepared to tie herself down.

It wasn't that she didn't like Philip. It was just that

18

Leora was beginning to dream about being an actress. All those dreams would go down the drain if she married. Children would soon follow, Leora thought, and that would be the end of her dreams.

London is very far from Alexandria. Just how far, Leora realized in the summer of 1956, when she returned home. Abba wanted her to work in his office, but she enlisted her mother's help to nag him into a one-year dispensation. The family belonged to a swim club in Alexandria, and Leora spent most of the summer lounging at the pool reading books about the theater.

One of the nicest things that happened to her that summer was discovering the private library about the theater that Abdel Rasef, Abba's lawyer, had in his house. He gave her complete access. Sometimes in the evening, Rasef brought her a cup of coffee and joined her in the library to talk about the theater. He called her "Le-le-le." She could sense the lust in his eyes. Sometimes trembling with excitement, she waited for him to take her in his arms, not certain how she would respond. He never did.

By September, she was grateful to return to the civilization of London.

Leora was happy to pick up with Philip again. He was entering his last year at the university, and she knew that he would be pressing her about marriage.

All in all, London in October 1956 was nearly perfect for Leora. Then the war came—the lightning blitzkrieg that the Israelis called the Sinai Campaign, the last dying embers of the grandeur of empire that the British called the Suez War.

Where is it written, Leora wondered much later, that a storm must follow every calm period? And when, oh, when, will the tranquillity return?

CHAPTER 3

"Anthony Eden must go!" The shouting voices filled the chilly night air in Hyde Park. "Down with Eden, the warmonger!"

The protesters covered the grass in the park, waving signs high over their heads. They were young mostly, college students, but there were others too: the local Communist party was out in droves. They had been having a field day ever since the British public had learned that England collaborated with Israel and France in an attack on Egypt to seize the Suez Canal.

The British police, armed only with clubs, had a strategy for handling the protesters. They were prepared to concede supremacy to the shouting protesters inside of a defined area. A solid wall of black coats surrounded that area. Here and there protesters tried to break through the police line, yelling, "March on Downing Street! March on Downing Street!" The police drove back each forward thrust of the crowd.

At the edge of the park next to the Dorchester Hotel, Leora stood with Philip watching the protest in silence.

The gawky, long-legged youth had become a sensuous woman, and the long black hair had given way to a short cut of the type favored by students at the University of London. She was carrying a thick notebook, the script for her part as Lady Macbeth in the Drama Society production that had gone into rehearsal.

On another side, the protesters tried to break through the police line. Again they were driven back. Screams filled the air.

"Kill the fascist pigs!" Philip shouted through cupped hands.

Leora put her arm through his.

"I'm cold, Philip. Take me home."

"Just a few more minutes."

"Your radical politics are showing," she said, pulling the scarf around her face to keep warm.

"Damn right. Eden's a fool. The sooner he goes the better.

"What do you think about it?" he asked her. "You never say."

"I'm cold, Philip. I'm tired from rehearsal. Take me home."

When they were back in his apartment, she fixed two cups of tea. Philip quickly turned on the radio, listening for the late news.

"I love everything about this city except its climate," she said.

He turned off the radio.

"Eden's still not saying anything about withdrawal. They're trying to stiffen his backbone. That should be some job."

She sat in silence, sipping her tea.

"I haven't been able to get you to say anything about it. That in itself astonishes me. I've known you almost a year. You have an opinion about everything."

"What do you want me to say?"

"Want you to say? My God. It's almost funny. You're a Jew, an Egyptian, and living in England. Talk about divided loyalties."

She wondered whether to attach any significance to the order in which he listed her three loyalties.

"I'm apolitical," she answered, trying to sound casual.

"We're not talking about politics. We're talking about people. My father knows some British businessmen whom Nasser kicked out when he took over the Canal. Told them to leave on twelve hours' notice. What will happen to your family?"

21

She looked at him, so serious, so concerned.

"Oh, Abba will manage to walk a tightrope," she said. "I'm not worried."

He was startled by her words. She sounded so cold, so detached. What he didn't know was that deep down she was terrified. She hadn't received a letter in three weeks, since October 27, two days before the attack.

"If I can do anything to help," he said. "If it's money you need . . ."

Maybe she hadn't been able to fool him at all. He knew her so well.

She stroked the top of his hand, gently.

"No, silly, there's nothing you can do."

An hour later when they finished making love, she lay in bed looking at the shadows on the ceiling. Philip was snoring softly. She got up and pulled a robe around her body. Her teeth were chattering.

Then she went into the living room and sat down in a bulky brown leather chair, next to the window, looking out but seeing nothing. She tried to muffle the sobs. But the large tears slid down her face. He found her in that chair in the morning.

Later in the day after classes, she went back to her own apartment to check the mailbox.

She saw the envelope sitting in her mailbox. She carried it up the stairs and tore it open. Immediately she recognized her mother's Arabic scrawl.

Dear Leora:

I have much to tell you that is not pleasant. The Israeli military success has caused bad feeling among our leaders in Cairo, including Colonel Nasser himself. Today, Abba found the doors to his office sealed by order of the government. All of our bank accounts have been taken over by the government, and we have been told that we must leave Egypt within twenty-four hours. It is not only us. Other Jews in Alexandria have been given the same order. There

22

*is some rioting in the streets and burning of Jewish shops.
We are hiding in the house for now.*

*I do not know what we will do. Abba has gone into a
trance since he heard the news, and Rachel, poor little
Rachel, is sick and cries all day. Meantime, I am trying to
make some plans for the family. I have just been told that
there is a ship which will take us to Haifa. The Egyptian
government will permit us to keep enough money to pay
for one-way passage. I think that we will probably take
that ship. I do not know what else we can do.*

*For now we have enough to eat and the trip should not
be long, although I understand that we have to stop in
Cyprus. Your brother Uri has checked the map and does
not understand why this is so.*

*I must ask you to leave London at once and meet us in
Haifa. As you know, I do not have your father's strength.
But he is of little help now, and I do not know how I will
manage without you.*

*I realize now that we were foolish because we did not
leave in 1948 when the others did, but Abba was so certain that it would never affect us. Still I am to blame too.*

*Uri has heard somewhere that in Israel the government
takes care of everyone. I pray to God that will be the case.
I do not know how Abba will start again.*

May God bless you and help you find the way.

Love,
Mama

Leora could hardly believe what she was reading in the
letter. She choked back the tears, took a deep breath, and
read it again.

This time there were no tears, only anger. She was angry
at everyone—at Abba, who had been such a fool, at Nasser
and the Arabs, at the world for permitting this injustice to
occur. Without a coat, she bolted out of the door down the
long staircase and out into the chilly midday air. She took
a long walk around the neighborhood, trying to think
about what she would do.

* * *

23

"You are the most stubborn and pigheaded creature I have ever known," Philip shouted in desperation.

"You didn't say that to me six months ago when we first made love."

He ignored her comment.

"I have told you every possible way. My father would be happy to bring your whole family to England and to support them until they get back on their feet. You could continue at school. You don't have to leave."

She still wasn't moved.

"It wouldn't involve any sacrifice on his part, honest to God."

She remained silent.

"Oh, for Christ's sake, he supports every other Jewish charity in London. Why won't you let him do it?"

"That's the whole point. I don't want your charity."

"Charity," he shouted in despair. "I'm in love with you."

She looked at him. He was so pitiful. Yes, he was in love with her. And he made it all sound so easy. All she had to do was marry him. He would bring them all to England.

She even loved him in kind of a way, she thought. But she could never bring herself to do it. There was such a thing as pride. It was something Abba had pounded into her from an early age. The world is divided into doers and takers. She would stand by herself.

"I will manage fine myself," she said coldly. Her voice had such a ring of finality that even Philip knew that further argument was useless.

That afternoon she withdrew the last two hundred pounds from her bank and closed the account. The following morning, she boarded BEA's flight 612 to Tel Aviv.

CHAPTER 4

Leora was never able to forget the first time she saw Abba in Israel. He was sitting alone on an old metal cot in the absorption center. All of the life, the color that she remembered, was gone. He was a beaten man, subdued, defeated. He gave her a weak greeting, nothing like the large bear hugs she had grown accustomed to.

His only words were: "I certainly managed to ruin our lives." Then he rested his head on the pillow, staring at the ceiling. With large tears flowing down her checks, Leora walked over and stood next to him. He stared at her without seeing anything. He was still thinking about what they had taken from him.

They remained like that for ten or fifteen minutes—father and daughter—until Hannah walked in.

"He's been that way since we left Alexandria. Now you see why I called for you."

Leora looked around the small two-room apartment in the absorption center. At least they were all safe and alive. They had shelter and enough food for the next six months.

She quickly realized that Hannah was unable to cope. Leora decided that she would have to get them on their feet again.

During the first few weeks she didn't give herself the luxury of forming any feelings about what had happened. There was too much to do.

It was Leora who drilled the younger children in Hebrew lessons when they were tired and frustrated from learning a new language that she herself found puzzling. It was Leora who persuaded her mother that the family could start again in new surroundings. And it was Leora who worked on Abba, day and night, attempting to persuade

25

him that he was not too old to start again. That was her most frustrating task. Each time she felt she was making progress, she would be met with a new bout of depression on Abba's part.

But after the first few weeks, strong emotions began taking hold of Leora. She began feeling great waves of anger about the terrible injustice that had been done to them. With the anger came bitterness and hostility. She wanted desperately to get some revenge against those who had been responsible.

And late at night, long after the others were asleep, she lay in her bed pounding her fist into her open hand and vowing that vengeance would be hers one day.

As the end of the six-month period approached, it was Leora who persuaded the bureaucrat from the absorption center that Abba's background could make him a valuable asset to Zim Lines, the Israeli government's entrant in the burgeoning maritime industry. He was hired as an assistant clerk in the administrative branch. And, as for a place for them to live, she was able to obtain a favorable lease from the Jewish Agency on a house in Haifa not far from Abba's new job.

Leora waited until the family was settled into the house on King George Street before she told her parents what her own plans were. Sadly, she reflected on the fact that neither of them had even asked her what she would do. Both were so obsessed with their own individual problems.

She waited until Abba had survived his first week at work without quitting or being fired—a minor miracle in itself. Then she called Abba and Hannah into the living room of the house.

"I have decided to join the army," she said, simply and easily.

"God forbid!" her mother shouted. She looked at Abba, hoping for some encouragement. That hope was forlorn.

He was totally preoccupied with his own problems. His indifference to her may not have been intentional. But it was indifference nevertheless.

"But that is for men," Hannah protested. "A tramp you'll become."

"And what *should* I do?"

"You will continue your studies."

Leora started to laugh. "Where and with what?"

"Tell her she can't do it," Hannah said feebly to Abba.

He remained silent, staring at Leora. He was barely able to handle the daily routine that Leora had arranged so carefully for him.

"Why, why would you do such a thing?" Hannah asked.

"You wouldn't understand, Mama. Really you wouldn't."

She didn't have to attempt the explanation. Hannah didn't press her. It was just as well. She wondered how she could express what she felt inside. All of the bitterness, the anger, and the hatred.

"I want to fight," she said to herself when she left the room.

"Oh, God, how I want to fight. Yes, to fight."

Later that evening, she sat down with a pen and paper, trying to compose a letter to Philip in London. She hadn't written to him since she had arrived.

She tried the letter three different times on three different pieces of paper. But each time she crumpled the piece of paper and fired it into a wastebasket. He could never understand, she decided. She wanted to write, and yet . . .

She reached a compromise. The following day she picked up a picture postcard at the newsstand—one with a picture of the Knesset in Jerusalem.

"Dear Philip," she wrote. "We have all been resettled in Israel. I hope that you are well. I am entering the army next week. Fondly, Leora."

She decided not to put a return address on the postcard. She wanted to burn every bridge to her past.

The army represented rebirth for Leora. It was the great melting pot of Israeli society in those days, taking new immigrants from a score of countries—France, India, Iraq—molding them into a single fighting force. No, more than that, it molded them into a nation.

Basic training was physical. It was outdoors in the desert. At last Leora was free from all of the hassles of family life. She could be her own person again. She enjoyed every minute of it.

Then there were the weapons. In her own mind Leora personalized those cardboard targets used at the range. They were the enemy, the miserable slime of life who had booted her family out of Alexandria, who had taken their home, who had taken Abba's business.

The officers could never understand why she always asked to spend extra time on the firing range, but she did, hour after hour. At first she thought it would relieve some of the anger and bitterness she felt, but it only strengthened these. There was one small fringe benefit, though. She was the first woman in the history of the Israeli army to achieve the award of marksman first class.

Two days after Leora received her medal, the telephone call came. It was her mother. She was frantic and in tears.

"Abba collapsed and was taken to the hospital."

"Don't coddle me," Leora said to the doctor. "I'm a big girl. I've been through a lot. How bad is he?"

The doctor looked at the girl's hardened face. She could take honesty. There was no question about that. Then he glanced at Hannah, standing terrified next to Leora.

"Don't worry about her," Leora said. "She'll never understand what you are saying in Hebrew. I'll translate it and soften it for her in Arabic."

"He's had a stroke that's quite serious. He'll never recover the use of the left side of his body."

"Is he in danger of death?"

"Not at this point, but the paralysis might spread."

The doctor looked for some show of emotion by the girl, but there was none. He left the room unobtrusively, permitting Leora to explain it to her mother.

When Hannah finally grasped it, the first question she asked was "How will we live?"

"I will leave the army and take a job," Leora said. "They have a policy of discharging those who are the sole support of a household. I'll be able to qualify."

"But you like the army."

"What choice do I have?" Leora said, staring into her mother's eyes.

Hannah looked down at the ground, avoiding her daughter's gaze.

❧

CHAPTER 5

Twenty-four hours after Leora submitted her request for a military discharge, she was summoned to the divisional headquarters building.

She was directed by the officer on duty to an empty office and abruptly told, "Wait here. Someone wants to talk with you."

A few minutes later a tall somber-looking man in civilian clothes entered.

"My name is Motti Elon," the man said.

Leora didn't know it then, but by the time she met him in early 1958, Motti was on his way to being a legendary figure.

At that time he was the director of personnel of Shai. He had watched carefully the exodus of Jews from the Arab countries that began after the creation of the state of Israel. They came from every country in the Arab world —from Morocco and Tunisia on the west to Iraq on the east. They were people who were indistinguishable from the Arabs in whose countries they had lived for hundreds of years. Their language was fluent Arabic; their skin and hair were dark; they suffered from the same diseases that afflicted the Arab masses.

As Motti watched them arrive at Lod Airport and the port in Haifa month in and month out, he soon realized that he had a great opportunity that maybe no other country in the world ever had. These arriving immigrants had come from nations at war with Israel. Yet they were indistinguishable from the people in the lands from which they came. Through careful screening, Shai could recruit a large force among these immigrants, train them, and send them back to the countries from which they came as valuable agents to transmit intelligence information back to Israel. He nicknamed the recruitment program Operation Tashuvah, a Hebrew word meaning both return and redemption. There were many in the Israeli government who credited Operation Tashuvah with being the basis for the extraordinarily good intelligence service that Israel developed.

"I am very sorry about your father," Motti said to Leora.

She stared at him, wondering what he wanted.

"I understand you'll be leaving the army."

She nodded weakly.

"What will you do now?"

"What do you think I'll do? I'll get a job."

"I want to help."

She got up and started to leave.

"I turned down one good offer for charity about a year ago. I can do it myself."

30

Motti was amused by her indignation, her show of independence.

He had gathered all of the biographical information he could find out about Leora, but none of it did justice to the strength that he saw in those dark brown eyes blazing at him.

"I wasn't talking about charity. I mean a job."

Leora sat down.

"A job with whom?"

"The Israeli government."

She thought back to the derogatory comments her father always made about government bureaucrats in Egypt. "The dregs of human existence," he used to call them.

"No, I don't think I want to be on the public dole."

"At least listen to what I have to offer."

She was silent.

"I'm the personnel director of Shai, an agency that gathers intelligence for the government in military and defense matters."

"And?"

"And I want to recruit you."

"To man a desk in some dreary and decaying government building left over from the British administration."

"I wouldn't put it that way. What I had in mind is that with your knowledge of Arabic and English, you could be of great value in translating newspapers and other documents for us."

She looked skeptical. Motti knew that he wasn't getting through to the girl.

"Listen, things are bad. But not that bad. I'm not ready to settle for that dreary an existence."

"You'll be contributing to the national struggle. There's satisfaction in it."

"You've got the wrong person. This one's apolitical, and don't talk to me about ideals. I've been suffering since I got here."

31

Motti looked frustrated.

"We pay well. You'll be able to support your family."

"So do London call girls."

He was beginning to lose his patience.

"What do you expect to do?"

"I don't know. I want to look around."

He started to laugh.

"This isn't London. You can't get a job as an actress here in the theater. I'll tell you what you'll find. They need orange pickers in the north, or maybe you want to grow pears in the south. Look, I'm doing you a favor."

"Keep your favor."

She got up and stormed out of the office.

As Motti watched her leave, he realized that he had misjudged the girl. He had underestimated her. She could do much more than translate papers. She had an inner strength that he had never seen before. Suddenly he wanted to recruit her more than he had ever wanted to get anyone else.

For the next month, Leora walked the streets of Haifa, taking interview after interview. Everywhere she went the results bore out Motti's prediction. The huge immigration of Jews from Arab countries in the years since the creation of the state and, most dramatically, since the 1956 war, had swelled Israel's labor force. For the trained and skilled, such as mechanics and engineers, there were abundant opportunities. But for the unskilled and inexperienced such as Leora, the city promised only unemployment—at least in the short run until the new labor force was absorbed.

Agriculture was where the demand for labor was with new kibbutzim (collective farms) being formed by immigrants from Morocco, Egypt, and Iraq. A score of people offered Leora the same advice: resettle with your family in an agricultural kibbutz in the north. But Leora quickly rejected that idea. The collective life was inconsistent with her notions of independence, and in any event she didn't want to spend the rest of her life picking oranges.

After a month of unsuccessful job hunting, Leora began to worry about how she would make the next month's rental payment. She wasn't aware that Motti had been carefully following her progress, or lack thereof, in the job market.

Bitter and frustrated, she sat in the living room of her house one evening when there was a firm rapping on the front door.

"It's open. Come on in," she shouted.

Motti walked in slowly, looking at Leora's worn and haggard face.

"Well, well, what are you selling now," she said sarcastically.

This time Motti was ready for her.

"My dear friend. You can sit around this house and feel bitter and sorry for yourself all the rest of your life. Or you can do something about it."

"Yeh. I can go feel bitter and frustrated behind a desk in some government cell."

"Wrong. This time I'm offering more than that. I'm offering you a chance to gain some of that revenge you're looking for, to go to battle with the people who put you here."

She perked up. Now she was listening carefully.

"Here's what I'm offering. A six-month training program. Then one year at Shai headquarters translating high-grade intelligence papers and teaching us what we don't know about Egypt. If both of those programs work out, we'll put you out into the field—in an Arab country, maybe even Egypt."

"To spy?"

"We prefer to call it gathering intelligence. But there are risks involved."

"I can figure as much."

"I'm serious. We lose people from time to time—mostly the headstrong, like you."

She smiled.

"What about money?"

"There will be enough for your family. We'll see to that, and your father will get what treatment he needs. If anything happens to you, they'll still be taken care of."

"And you're not kidding me? There will be a chance for revenge?"

"That I promise you."

Leora never regretted the decision. The first eighteen months with Shai gave her more than she anticipated. It wasn't the large impersonal bureaucracy she expected. It was small, close knit, almost like a family. Staff meetings frequently degenerated into open discussion. Late-afternoon coffee breaks became the vehicle for formulating policy. In the analysis of documents, Leora quickly became a valuable asset. Her total fluency in Hebrew, Arabic, and English made her unique in the agency.

As the end of the first eighteen months approached, the director general of Shai came to talk with her.

"I want to keep you here at headquarters in Tel Aviv and not send you into the field."

Leora looked distraught.

"I made my deal with Motti when I came with the agency."

"I know that, but I'm asking you to change it. You're too good to send out. Here, you'll move up fast into a policy-making role."

Leora thought about it for a minute. The director general waited in silence, slightly intimidating behind heavy black-frame glasses.

"No, I won't change my mind. I've got to go back into their world, the world that they tossed me out of. I want to destroy it from inside. You can't deny me that chance.

34

I've worked too hard for it the last eighteen months."

He gave a sigh of resignation.

"Motti told me I wouldn't be able to persuade you. I won't go back on his promise. You'll have your go at it."

"Where?"

"Cairo. We've arranged a cover for you with the French Embassy there. You'll be installed as the personal assistant to a member of the embassy staff, Jacques Barot, who happens to be a member of the French Intelligence Service. You'll be a listening post, our ears and eyes in Cairo. Anything worthwhile you pick up, you pass to Barot. He forwards it to Paris, and then a copy comes to us."

She looked puzzled.

"I don't understand how you got me in the French Embassy."

"It's one of our cooperative projects, under our alliance with France. We're doing it in arms development, nuclear research, and scientific development. We decided to try it in intelligence. Oh, they're not doing it out of idealism or because they love the Jews. The whole alliance is a great mutual benefit. They're still at war with the Arabs in Algeria. They need us as much as we need them."

A secretary entered with two cups of coffee.

Leora sipped the coffee slowly, thinking about how good the job sounded. It would be strange being back in Egypt.

"Don't worry too much about being recognized," the director said. "I don't think that will be a problem. We'll rework some of your facial features just enough to change your looks and, of course, you'll be in Cairo rather than Alexandria. Naturally, we'll give you a French name and papers."

"I wasn't worried about that," Leora said. "When do I leave?"

"In about six months you'll fly to Paris, and from there, Cairo. We want to take the time on the physical changes, for a special training course, and also to polish up your

French. You should be out of here by the first of March."

"Just in time for my twenty-first birthday."

The director drained the rest of his coffee. Then he started to leave. He paused by the door, intensely serious.

"Leora, there are two bits of caution I want to give you. First, this is a deadly serious business. You no doubt realize that. If your identity becomes known, we might not be able to get you out under a French diplomatic immunity. We have had other agents captured in Cairo, and their fate was unpleasant."

She nodded, showing acceptance.

"And the second note of caution?"

He hesitated.

"The second is that this fellow Barot is a bit of a rake, even for a Frenchman. He's married, but he chases everything in sight."

"So?"

"I just thought I'd warn you."

"I can take care of myself."

"I don't doubt that for a minute."

❧

CHAPTER 6

CAIRO, JANUARY 1967

Leora gradually taught herself to tell time by watching the movement of the sun through the narrow openings between the bars in her jail window. It wasn't that she was interested in nature or even that it mattered to her what time it was. It was simply something to do to pass the time that never moved.

One of her other frequent activities was going back again and again over the same facts in her mind: What had led to her arrest two years earlier? She was still as mystified about that now as she had been then.

She had had almost five good years in Cairo, gathering information about Egyptian military installations and equipment. In fact, near the end, she had a liaison with an Egyptian general that was producing pearls of information about Egyptian long-term preparations for war. Oh, it had been glorious, feeling that she was actually repaying them for what they had done to Abba. Then they closed down her operation. The Egyptians simply picked her up one evening without any advance notice.

She got up and walked around the cell. She tried to exercise her arm by swinging it, however painful it was. Gradually the life was coming back into that arm. She was happy that there was no mirror in the cell. By the time the Egyptians finished working on her body with those hot coals, a trick they had learned from the Germans, it wasn't much to look at. She felt her face; most of the puffiness under her right eye had receded.

It couldn't have been the Egyptian general who blew the whistle, she decided. He was too dumb to pick up any signals. And she really hadn't made any enemies in Cairo. There had been those run-ins with Barot early in the operation when she had refused to sleep with him, but he seemed to forget it before too long, becoming preoccupied with chasing other women.

When she had been first arrested, she thought that Shai would find a way to get her out. By the end of the first year, however, she lost hope. They've probably destroyed my file in Tel Aviv, she thought.

Day passed to evening and she waited eagerly for the guard to bring her the usual evening mess that passed for dinner. She didn't wait for it because she wanted to eat it; most nights she could do little but take a couple of spoonfuls. She waited because it was a symbolic event. It represented the passing of still another day.

37

She glanced down the hall. There was nothing in sight. Her cell was all alone in a special wing of the prison. As one of the guards once put it, "We don't want you poisoning the minds of our local criminals."

As the sun set, it became chilly in the cell. She moved her toes to keep them warm.

Suddenly she heard a clinking at the end of the corridor as the metal door opened. She saw a solitary figure carrying a dish and a cup on a tray. From the distance, he looked taller, more muscular, than the usual evening guard. Perhaps her eyes were playing tricks on her? Perhaps the regular guard was sick?

Once inside the metal door at the end of the corridor, the man suddenly dropped the tray on the floor and raced toward her cell, shouting in Hebrew.

"Let's go. We're getting you out of here."

He tried half a dozen keys on the ring until he found the one that opened her cell.

"How did you get in?" she shouted with joy.

"No time to talk. Let's go."

He took two small .22 caliber pistols from his pocket and handed one to her.

"Careful. It's loaded and ready to fire."

Quickly he led the way down a dark staircase at the back of the building. When they reached the ground floor, he paused in front of the thick metal door leading to the outside. Slowly, cautiously, he nudged it open with his foot, his finger poised on the trigger of the gun. She stood behind him, watching him, covering him.

Everything was deathly quiet outside of the door. When the door was fully opened, he signaled her with a wave of his hand to follow him. They raced twenty yards to a dark-gray van marked Cairo Laundry Company. He opened the back door, and she followed him inside. Once the door slammed, the van started to move. "Let's bury ourselves," he said, picking up a big bundle of dirty sheets and throwing them over her head.

She lay that way in the sheets for maybe half an hour, nearly suffocating in the foul odor of dirty linen. It smelled from men. The odors were unmistakable—urine and semen. Finally, he picked the sheets off her body and pulled her to a sitting position.

"I'm Dan Yaacobi from Shai," he said.

She nodded recognition. She had never met Yaacobi before, but she had heard the name when she was in Tel Aviv.

Yaacobi had been the head of Shai's Eastern European operation. As she looked into his eyes, she saw something that she had never seen before: a strength, a fierce determination, and yet a warmth that she imagined a man might have. She suddenly felt a deep stirring and a great hunger. Her whole body ached.

She was frightened by what she felt and she dropped her eyes from Yaacobi, looking around the van. The windows were covered with dark curtains. They were traveling at a fast speed.

"Freedom is marvelous," she said. "Even if it stinks."

"We'll have you in Tel Aviv by morning," he said. "We have a rendezvous scheduled with a fishing vessel off the coast at Alexandria. I have a small two-way radio in my shirt pocket. Within the next few minutes, I should get a signal that they're on schedule."

"How did you manage to get me out?"

"Two weeks ago, one of our border units picked up an Egyptian soldier who strayed across the border. They were interrogating him to see if it was an accident or part of an attack. In the interrogation, they learned that his brother was the warden at your prison. You can imagine the rest. We struck a bargain."

"Is he one of ours?" Leora said, pointing to the driver.

"No, but he's a cousin of the warden, which is how he got the contract for the prison's laundry in the first place. He's also being well paid."

Dan pulled the radio out of his pocket, checked to make certain it was working, and then put it back. If he was concerned by the lack of a signal, he kept it to himself.

He reached under the pile of dirty linen and pulled out a small plastic bag.

"Some Arab civilian clothes for you. Take off that monkey suit and put these on."

He handed her the bag and looked away from her toward the side of the van.

"I'm flattered that you think I have any modesty left," she said bitterly, "after what those bastards did to my body."

"Human dignity is a state of mind," he replied, thinking about his own experience with the Germans during the war. "Nobody can take it from you."

She changed clothes quickly. Then they rode in silence along the empty highway. She studied Dan carefully.

Beneath the loose-fitting casual Cairo street clothes, she saw muscular arms, a chest thick with black hair, massive leg muscles. She rubbed her face self-consciously.

"I'm afraid I'm not much to look at."

"You're a helluva lot better than we expected," he said in a matter-of-fact tone.

Suddenly the van stopped.

The driver turned around and whispered in Arabic.

"We're entering Alexandria. Tell me now the rendezvous point."

Dan's mind worked quickly. The plan had been to keep the rendezvous point from the driver until they were in Alexandria. Dan knew it and could direct the driver to take them there.

But he still hadn't received any signal from the ship. Without a signal, it was too dangerous to proceed to the point. They couldn't wait there. Waiting in the van was out of the question. The driver had refused to bargain for more than a quick delivery to Alexandria. If they waited outside along the water, they would be picked up in no time. The place was crawling with Russians.

Leora quickly sensed what was going through Dan's mind.

"We need a safe house in Alexandria?" she asked tersely.

"Something until we get the signal. The ship must have had a problem getting in."

"Will he disclose the point at which he drops us?" she said, pointing to the driver.

"I doubt it. The deal is that the warden's brother isn't released until we show up in Tel Aviv."

She thought about their problem for a minute.

"I have an idea," she said. "It involves some old friends. It's a bit of a gamble, but it may be the best we have."

Dan looked at her carefully. He had never worked with her before. He didn't like having to follow her judgment when he had no basis for assessing it. Still, those who had worked with her in Shai had praised her highly.

"Okay. You know the territory," he said. "Follow your instincts."

"Tell him to drop us at Nasser Boulevard, near the water."

Dan barked the instruction to the driver. Ten minutes later, they came to a dead stop.

"We're here," the driver shouted.

Leora peeked through the cloth over the window, confirming the location. She nodded affirmatively to Dan. He tossed a roll of bills onto the front seat next to the driver.

"Put the gun in your pocket," Dan said.

Then he opened the door and scrambled out of the van. She followed.

"Lead the way," he said. "But walk slowly. Look natural."

It was almost ten o'clock. The streets were largely deserted. She followed Dan's instruction, walking slowly. She looked around cautiously. She hadn't been in Alexandria in over ten years. She remembered well every street and building. She felt no emotion for the cobblestones that her feet had crossed in her youth. If she ever had any emotional sentiments like that when she first returned to Egypt, they had been numbed by her experience in prison.

With some hesitancy she approached the large stone villa. "Hide over there," she said to Yaacobi, pointing to a large clump of hedges.

She carefully examined the brass nameplate on the door: "Abdel Rasef—Lawyer."

Tightly gripping the pistol concealed in her pocket, she rang once. A maid answered.

"I want to see Mr. Rasef. I'm a client who has a serious problem."

The maid looked at her suspiciously.

"It is urgent that I see Mr. Rasef himself."

The maid closed the door.

Come on, she thought. You owe this one to Abba.

It seemed like an hour to her before the door opened. From the way that Abdel looked at her, she knew that he didn't recognize her. And she almost didn't recognize him, he had aged so markedly in the last decade. His hair, then jet-black, was now completely white.

"Mr. Rasef," she said firmly. "I must speak with you about an urgent matter."

He hesitated for a moment. Then he said, "I'm quite busy. But a couple of minutes I could spare."

He led her into a wood-paneled study, then closed the door.

"Who are you? What do you want?" he asked quickly.

"Leora Baruch," she said, pressing the revolver in her pocket.

"Impossible."

"You were the lawyer who handled my grandfather's estate. You wrote letters for me to the University of London. You used to call me 'Le-le-le.' You gave me access to your library in the summer of 1956. What else do you want to know? Ask me anything."

Rasef was shaken. He remembered a beautiful dark-haired young woman of seventeen, sunning herself at the country club swimming pool.

He had never heard any more about the girl, or the rest of the family, since they left Alexandria. He stood in the center of the room, staring at her, frightened by her appearance and frightened by the thought that whatever else, the Egyptian government must be pursuing her.

"Abdel. I will be blunt. I am only asking something simple of you. I want a place to stay here in this house with a friend for a day or two—maybe a little more, maybe a little less. You don't have to ask any questions. I won't give you any explanations. It will be better that way."

"But why should I do it?" he asked skeptically, unwilling to commit himself.

"Because you were our friend once. Because you are a human being."

He didn't move a muscle.

"Because you took over Abba's business when we left," she said, raising her voice slightly. "If you don't feel guilty, you bloody well should."

"I view myself as a caretaker," he said. "Holding it until your father returns."

"Oh, yes. That's why you never tried to find us to send us our share of the profits," she said sarcastically.

"And if I tell you no? What if I pick up that telephone and call the authorities?"

She stared at him coldly. Then she pulled the gun from her pocket.

"I swear by Moses, Allah, and Jesus Christ that I will separate your head from your body."

Her words shook Abdel. He sat down.

"Even if I tell you yes and let you stay tonight, how do you know I won't change my mind and call the police in the morning?"

"You're the lawyer. You know that. You would then be guilty of harboring criminals. No one would believe we forced you to let us stay. You would be implicated, maybe even destroyed. You have too much to lose. You would be better to let us stay the day or two and leave quietly."

"By just coming here, you have put me in a position where I could never clear myself with Nasser's regime." He had a pained expression on his face. "And even if I could, the Russians would never accept that. I have no choice. You and your friend may stay."

She smiled weakly.

"I will put you downstairs."

"No. I want to be able to see out. Give us the upstairs room in the back, the one isolated from the rest of the house, the one your youngest son used."

"You don't have to worry about being seen from someone inside. I am alone now except for two servants. My wife died three years ago."

"I'm sorry to hear that, Abdel."

"I will keep the servants downstairs. Get your friend and come quickly."

Abdel didn't want an introduction to Leora's friend. She didn't provide one.

Silently and quickly, he led the two of them upstairs, pointing to the bedroom at the end of the hall.

It was exactly the same as Leora remembered it when she had last been in the house ten years earlier. It was a large high-ceilinged room that had an adjoining bath. The spread on the large bed and the curtains were made of white lace, hardly fitting for a boy, but Abdel was always sorry that his youngest son hadn't been a girl.

Abdel pushed open the door, then he retreated quickly.

"How do we know that your friend won't go to the police?" Dan asked.

"We don't know for sure. I don't think he will. But we'll have to take that chance. What choice do we have?"

Dan grumbled.

"Do you have a better place to hide in Alexandria while we wait for that bloody boat to get in?" she said.

Dan checked around the room carefully, looking for a hidden microphone. There was nothing. He checked the window.

"It leads to a balcony. We could scramble out the window if we had to."

"Why do you think I picked this room?"

He pulled a wooden chair from behind the desk, placed it near the window, and settled his large frame into it. He checked the radio one more time to make certain it was working. Then, looking tense but fully in control of the situation, he turned back to Leora, sitting on the edge of the bed.

"My advice, Leora, is that you go into that bathroom, take a good long shower, and get rid of the prison grime. Then hop into that bed and try to sleep. It will help blot the memory of the ordeal. I don't need you. I'll wake you when I get the signal."

"What about you? What will you do?"

"Don't worry about me. I haven't spent the last two years in jail. I can keep watch."

"Not now," she replied. "I'm not tired. Maybe later. I've got to know something first."

He raised his hand to silence her.

"Three Russian troops in front of the house."

He watched carefully. They were tossing an empty vodka bottle.

"They're drunker than hell. I don't think they're looking for us."

"I want to know how the Egyptians found out about me. Do they know in Tel Aviv?"

"They know."

He hesitated.

"It's not pretty."

"After what I've been through, nothing could surprise me."

"The French sold you out. The Great Man, Uncle Charles himself, blew the whistle when Nasser was in Paris. The war in Algeria's over. His view of French national interests has changed. It was an easy way to score a few points with the Arabs and teach the arrogant Jews a lesson."

She gave a long low whistle, showing her surprise.

"And Barot didn't go to bat for me?"

"Are you kidding? Barot's moving up fast in the service. He wouldn't do anything to rock the boat. He didn't owe you any favors, did he?"

"Don't be disgusting. I'd sooner take a vow of abstinence. Talk about arrogant."

"I'm sorry. I shouldn't have said that."

She ignored his apology.

"Things have changed in the last two years, then, haven't they?"

"That's not all that's changed. The whole Shai operation is expanding. The section on military intelligence has tripled in size. We're picking up strong signals that the Arabs are getting ready for war again."

"Egypt too?"

"All of them."

"How soon?"

"Later this year. Nobody knows when. Besides that, we've opened up a new section devoted to antiterrorist activities. The M-18 Corps, we call it. This is in response to a rash of airplane hijackings and bombings around Europe —aimed at us and friendly third countries. The prevailing theory in Shai is that the Arab governments are using the terrorists for their own political purposes. This new group will be a small elite strike force. Its job is to hunt and destroy every suspected terrorist. We'll respond in kind— death for death. Once I get back with you, that's my new assignment, with M-18. I'll be operating out of Paris."

"If my old friend Barot doesn't toss you out."

"He'll have to catch me doing something first, the bastard."

There was a gentle knocking at the door. Dan moved quickly to the bathroom, gripping his gun hard. He pointed her toward the door of the bedroom.

"Who is it?" she said, trying to sound calm.

"Abdel Rasef."

"What do you want?" she asked through the closed door.

"I have some food."

"Tell him to drop it and leave," Dan whispered.

"Please leave it outside," she said. "And thank you very much."

They heard the sound of a tray being placed on the floor. Then footsteps on the stairs.

"Go get it," Dan said. "I'll cover you."

She opened the door cautiously. No one was there. She pulled the tray into the room.

It was a large green melon, some cold sliced lamb, chopped eggplant, and two cups of coffee. After two long years of prison slop, it looked good to her. Until she saw the food, she had forgotten how hungry she was.

Dan smelled the food carefully, trying to detect poison. As he looked at her silent pleading face, he knew what she was hoping.

"I can't smell anything," he said. "He's your friend. It's okay with me if you want to take a chance."

"What about you?"

"I ate before I picked you up."

47

She knew that he was lying, but she didn't care as she began tearing into the food. He sat in silence, gazing out of the window.

She looked at his back, so straight, his shoulders so broad, his skin, tough and weather-beaten from desert exercises.

"Are you scared?" she asked.

"Always a little," he said. "Fear has become my normal state. It arouses my senses. Even when I'm off duty, at home on the kibbutz, I'm alert."

"It's funny. I'm not the least bit frightened," she said. "I figure that they've done everything to me that they can. All that I'm left with in life is a desire to repay."

He glanced back at her with a few gentle wrinkles in his forehead.

"The bitterness will pass," he said.

"Never."

"I hope for your sake it does. If not, it will destroy you."

He pulled a package of cigarettes from his pocket, handed her one, and put the pack on the desk. They lit up together, each enjoying the cigarette for a moment.

"When will it end, Dan?"

"When will what end?"

"The war, the killing."

He smiled softly.

"In our struggle there is neither beginning nor end. There are no messiahs and no Armageddons—only the continuing spiral of death and destruction. I have a wife and two small boys back there on the kibbutz. That is the world I hand them."

The coldness of his words shocked her.

"It doesn't bother you to look at the world that way?"

"It's not a question of whether it bothers me. That is the way it is."

When she looked into his eyes, she was startled. There

was a strange inner calm. He was a man who was completely reconciled to the world that was there, who would squeeze the most from it, but who would never try to move mountains to change it.

"You'll never be able to square every wrong that's been done to you," he said calmly, reflectively. "Just when you settle one, there will be others."

She picked up the package of cigarettes and lit another one.

"So what are you telling me to do?"

"Go back to Tel Aviv. Tell the boss you want a good desk job, get yourself a brute of a husband and make love every night till the rooster starts to crow. You'll have a couple of children and the bitterness will pass. You're young and attractive. What's the point of getting your beautiful head blown off."

He made her feel like a woman again. After the long months in prison, she didn't think that was possible.

"You're a bloody hypocrite," she said. "A bloody hypocrite. Why don't you follow your own advice and take a desk job?"

"For me it's a sense of duty. I can't walk away from it."

"And that's a better motive than my desire for revenge, my bitterness?"

He sat silent, staring out of the window. It was quiet on the street.

"I'm going to take that shower," she said as she got up and walked into the bathroom.

The hot water felt good on her sore body. She just stood there for minutes letting it soothe and cleanse her bruised skin. Afterward, drying herself, she opened the bathroom door a little so he could watch her. Then she took a careful look in the mirror. God, I'm an ugly sight, she thought. But I'll come back. You can bet on that.

She put her clothes back on, used a hairbrush she found

on the sink, and returned to the bedroom.

"There was a beautiful body under that dirt and grime," he said tenderly.

She smiled.

"Any signal yet?"

"Nothing."

"I may take that sleep after all."

She pulled down the covers and lay with her damp hair on the pillow watching Dan sitting so intent at the window. Suddenly she was struck with another hunger, the hunger for that man, the strong courageous man who had risked his life to rescue her, who had made her feel like a woman again. She wanted him more than she had ever wanted anything before in her life.

"Come to bed with me," she called. "Oh, come to bed with me."

He got up from the chair, walked over, and sat down next to her, taking her hand. She waited, but nothing happened.

"Don't you want me?" she asked, pleading with him, knowing what the answer was from his eyes.

He began stroking her cheek gently.

"Of course I want you."

"Well?"

"Don't make this so tough for both of us," he said. "Remember, I'm a man of duty and loyalty."

"You mean that wife and those two boys on the kibbutz."

He nodded.

"You're hanging on to those old virtues even in the world you described?"

"Everybody needs something."

She pulled her hand away from his.

"Abba," she said slowly. "I met a strange man, this Dan Yaacobi. He'll give me his life, but not his body."

"It's what I told you in the van," he said.

"What's that?"

"Human dignity belongs to each person. Nobody can take that from you."

He got up from the bed and walked back to the window, resuming his watch. When he peeked at her through the corner of his eye, a couple of minutes later, she was sleeping peacefully.

It was an hour before daylight when Dan heard the steady *beep, beep, beep* from the radio in his pocket.

He nudged the sleeping Leora gently but firmly.

"Let's go, Leora. Let's move."

She jumped out of bed quickly, rubbed her eyes, picked up the revolver that was under the pillow, and announced, "Ready to roll, Commander."

When she looked into his eyes for the first time, she felt like a fool because of what had happened last night. One look at Dan persuaded her that he wasn't thinking about that.

He pulled a small map from his pocket and looked at it for an instant.

"Get us from here to the east port area," he said, "as quickly as possible. Stay off the main roads. When we hit the east port area, I'll be able to find the ship."

The streets were still deserted as they crept out of the house. Her recollections of Alexandria were precise. Twenty minutes later they were scrambling on board the ship. When the first rays of sun shone on the eastern horizon, they were in the hold of a fishing vessel going out for the day's catch. That evening, under the cover of darkness, they jumped from the ship into the Israeli port of Haifa.

A waiting Shai car picked up the couple.

"Where are we going?" she asked Dan.

"Shai headquarters in Tel Aviv. The director general wants to see you first before you have any outside communications."

"Is anything wrong?"

"Routine debriefing as far as I know."

It was cold and damp. A persistent drizzle hit the car window. The steady noise of the windshield wipers put her to sleep. With her eyes closed, she rested her head on Dan's shoulder. She still dreamed about her cell in Cairo.

～❧

CHAPTER 7

"I had no way of telling you that your father died when you were in prison," the director general said to Leora. "Believe me, I had no way of telling you."

He kept waiting for Leora to break down, to cry. But there were no tears, only a blank stare into a distant abyss. Leora's grief was deep and very personal. But if there was one thing she had learned in prison, it was to control any emotions she felt. Now she mustered all of that enormous self-control to avoid showing her grief with the man sitting across the desk from her.

"And Dan Yaacobi, why didn't he tell me yesterday?"

"He didn't know. I swear it. We didn't tell him."

"So he couldn't tell me and risk my going to pieces. Is that it?"

"Something like that," he said, sipping his coffee.

"And the rest of my family?"

"They are all doing well. We have taken good care of your mother. I have seen to that personally."

"Isn't that lovely," she said caustically.

As the thought of Abba's death began to seep in, Leora remembered what Dan had told her last night: "You'll never be able to square every wrong that's been done to you. Just when you settle one, there will be others."

Leora stared coldly at the director general. He had aged markedly in the years that she had been in Egypt.

"I knew that we would get you out sooner or later. I never lost hope. You should know that."

"It turned out to be later rather than sooner," she said as the pain shot through her arm.

"It was a question of finding the right opportunity," he said defensively.

They both sat in silence for several minutes, sipping coffee.

"What happens to me now?" she asked. "Surely you've thought about that too."

"Don't worry about that now. Go home. Spend some time with your family. We'll talk about that in a few days."

"I want to talk about it now," she said emphatically.

"You've had a long ordeal. Please let it wait."

"I can't," she said desperately. "You've got to give me something to dream about."

He hesitated. He was frightened by the terrible look of fury in her eyes.

"Okay, I'll tell you, then. For the next month, I planned to send you and your family to one of the settlements in the south, near Eilat, where it's warm. I want you to rest and relax. Two of our people will be there for intermittent debriefing sessions."

"And after that?"

"After that, I have a place here for you at headquarters in Tel Aviv, analyzing Egyptian documents. There's nobody better than you to do it. If our intelligence information is right, there's another big war on the horizon. We need you to help separate the wheat we're getting from the chaff."

He smiled weakly, hoping for a favorable response.

"I won't do it," she replied grimly.

"You won't do what?"

"I won't take a bloody desk job, that's what."

"Then what do you want?" he said, looking mildly irritated.

"I want to go back into the field. Put me into M-18."

"Yaacobi told you about it?"

She nodded.

He could tell that they were headed on a collision course and he wanted to make one final effort to head it off.

"Listen, you've had an ordeal. Let's talk about it next week."

"No, now," she said.

He sighed deeply.

"Why do you want M-18?"

"Because I want to kill those bastards, to repay."

"It's out of the question," he said firmly.

"Why?"

"Because you suffered enough for Shai."

"I'll decide that."

"Like hell you will. I'm still running this agency."

She played her final card.

"You owe me something for what I've given the last two years. I've paid in blood, my own. This is what I want in return."

"And you don't think that our rescue repays the debt."

"Repays the debt?" she laughed mockingly. "I've spent most of the boat ride back wondering whether you left me in Cairo too long on the intelligence-gathering operation, whether you didn't see some signals and chose to ignore them, squeezing me for every last drop because it was going so well."

His face grew bright red when he heard her words.

"No, dammit, no!" he shouted at her. "We had no reason to believe the French would sell you out. You've got no right to say that to me."

"And you've no right to keep me out of the field."

"I'm running this organization."

She rose to her feet sharply.

"Then bloody well run it without me," she shouted. "Because I quit."

She turned her back to him and walked calmly and deliberately from the office.

The family reunion carried her through the first week back in Israel. She spent long hours at the cemetery standing at Abba's grave, looking into space, seeing nothing. Her mind kept coming back to those early days in Alexandria, to the nine-year-old girl skipping to the office to get Abba, to bring him home, sitting in a coffeehouse eating ice cream. We set our life on a course, she thought, but nothing ever turns out the way we plan it.

She derived some joy from Uri and her two younger sisters those first days at home. But that passed quickly. They had the advantage of coming to Israel at a younger age than she. Fully adjusted, they were caught up in the life of Israeli teenagers in the sixties—parties, rock music, and boy friends.

And as for Hannah, Leora quickly realized that nothing had changed at all. Her adamant and stubborn refusal to even learn Hebrew was symbolic of her unwillingness to make the mental change from Alexandria to Haifa.

There was one thing that the director general had not misled her on. Her family had been well taken care of financially. At the beginning of each month, a check arrived in the mail from a small bank in Tel Aviv. Hannah never asked where it came from. Not only did it provide for the family's living expenses, but Hannah had been able to save a little each month.

Leora's father had executed a will shortly before his death. In appreciation of her support of the family, Leora was named as the beneficiary of all of the stock in the Alexandria Trading Company, his former business that had been taken over by Abdel Rasef. One hundred percent of nothing, she thought. What good is it?

Leora also spent time those first couple of weeks at Hadassah Hospital in Jerusalem. The medical prognosis was that no permanent damage had been done and that her wounds would heal with time, leaving only traces of scar tissue.

By the beginning of the second week, Leora began growing restless, considering what she would do now that she had cut her ties with Shai.

She even contacted the British Embassy in Tel Aviv to inquire about the requirements for immigration to London, thinking that she could get a job in the theater there. That visit to the British Embassy was duly reported to the Israeli Foreign Ministry and then to Shai.

When he heard about it, Motti Elon, who had recently been promoted from director of personnel to deputy director general, exploded. Motti vowed that he would do something about it.

Leora was sitting in the living room playing backgammon with Uri when Motti walked into the house.

"Go chase some girls," she said to her brother. "I think that man wants to sell me something."

Motti walked over and embraced her, kissing her warmly on the cheek.

"I'm glad to see you again," he said. "I was sorry to hear about your father."

"Nothing you could have done," she replied, squeezing his hand. "You've carried out your bargain. You've done well for the family. I'm grateful to you for that."

"I was in Geneva when you got back. I'm sorry I missed your homecoming."

"Some homecoming," she said sarcastically. "Your boss got out a brass band for me."

"I'm sorry about that, really I am."

"Yeh, well, that's how life is, isn't it? Come on Motti, I'll fix you some coffee."

He followed her into the kitchen and lit up a cigarette

for her and one for himself while they waited for the water to boil.

"The stuff you sent back from Cairo was worth a fortune. You were a goddamned gold mine."

"Just tell me one thing, Motti. You're my old friend. Did he leave me in Cairo too long or not?"

He hesitated.

"Don't make me answer that." Then he paused. "Our work isn't that precise. You can never be sure."

"That dirty bastard."

"What happened to the sweet society lady I recruited?"

"That's just it," she shot back. "An awful lot has happened. I'm a long way from that girl."

She poured two cups of coffee.

"Listen, Leora, I'll put my cards right on the table. I'm the number two man in Shai now. When the old man steps down, I should move up to director general. I don't want to lose you."

"Well, go tell your boss that, because I damn well won't be stuck at a desk the rest of my life."

"I've told him that."

"And?"

"And I've worked out a compromise with him."

"I hope you took the bottom half of my body. It's in better shape than the top."

He ignored her comment.

"The deal is that you go through debriefing. Then you take the desk job he has for you analyzing Egyptian documents on a temporary basis."

"How long's temporary?"

"Until after the war that we're expecting. But no longer than the end of this year in any event."

"And then?"

"Then you'll get what you want."

"M-18." She smiled warmly.

57

"Actually it makes sense," he said, feeling satisfaction from her smile and knowing now that she would come back. "You'll be a hell of a lot more useful to us here in a prewar situation than you would be off in Europe."

"How did you sell it to him?"

"I reminded him of your performance in basic training, especially on the firing range. With your hate and bitterness you had all the instincts of a born killer. And that was before two years in an Egyptian prison."

"And he bought that?"

"It took some doing. You made him pretty sore. He's not used to being talked to that way."

"Shame, shame, shame," she said gleefully.

Motti laughed easily with her.

"There is just one thing that worries me," he said. "You're headstrong and you've got plenty of guts. We get our best work from people like that."

"But?"

"But they sometimes take chances that they shouldn't. It's not conducive to living a long and healthy life."

When war erupted in June 1967, Leora was in her office knee-deep in papers with Egyptian military information. They rolled a small cot into her office. It was only slightly larger than the one in her Cairo cell. Six days later, when the war ended, she was still in that same office. Dirty ashtrays and coffee cups were scattered everywhere. She had only been out in the fresh air twice during the week—once for a tour of the Suez front and once to present her intelligence assessments to Levi Eshkol, the Prime Minister.

On July 4, 1967, Motti Elon came into Leora's office and told her it was Independence Day for her as well as for the American people. He handed her a thin piece of blue paper.

"Your orders for reassignment to M-18."

58

He could see the happiness in her eyes.

"You've always done right by me, Motti."

"I try to look out for the people I recruited. Besides, I like you."

Then he thought about his own wife, unable to have children after what the Germans had done to her in Auschwitz. In a rare moment of personal candor, this very private man added: "You're like a daughter to me, Leora, like a daughter."

~⁊~

CHAPTER 8

The mere creation and organization of M-18, which had occurred six months before Leora's return to Israel, was buried in secrecy and mystery. The idea that Israel should be training an elite corps of professional killers, who would murder on command, was anathema to the ideals of the Jewish state. Even its name, M-18, was caught up in this contradiction: "M" was for the first letter of the Hebrew word for death, Mavet; and "18" was for Chai, the Hebrew symbol for life.

It had taken a Herculean effort for the director general of Shai to persuade the Prime Minister to approve the program and then to bury its funding in the agency's general administrative budget.

"I regret it as much as you do," the director general of Shai had argued with the Prime Minister. "But it is the world in which we live. The Arabs send this group of terrorists around the world killing our people, hijacking and blowing up planes. Our friends in Washington and Western Europe raise their voice in mild protest, but nobody does anything of practical significance to curb the growing terrorism aimed at us. It's spreading like a cancer. It will destroy us if we don't act."

"And this new group, M-18, how will that cure the problem?"

"We will send our people into every country of the world where the Arab terrorists hide. When they strike a target, like an airplane, we will thwart their efforts. We will hunt these killers like the animals they are. And, when we find them, we will destroy them systematically and effectively. We are responding to what they have started."

"And the countries in which your people strike? What kind of a diplomatic fury will you create for me?"

"They do nothing on their own. They give in to the Arab blackmail."

"Is that what I should tell them? It is our lawful right to self-defense?"

"Yes, tell them that."

The Prime Minister was silent. He was tired from making hard decisions of life and death.

The director general wanted to keep the discussion moving before the doubts set in too deeply.

"I daresay that some countries may even be happy that we're getting rid of these criminals quietly and without any fanfare."

"But will it be quiet?"

"Absolutely. Nothing will be traced to us. In friendly places our people will operate as agricultural or military attachés at our embassies. In the others, they'll have forged European passports. We will create our own network of safe houses. The countries involved will not be consulted. After all, we are doing them a favor by keeping them out of it."

The Prime Minister tapped his fingers on the table.

"It still worries me."

"With all due respect, Mr. Prime Minister, what other chance do we have to fight the growing terrorism aimed at us outside of our borders? Should we restrict ourselves to saying the Mourner's Prayer and burying our dead each time it happens, just like they did in Europe when you and I were young? Or should we fight and destroy these murderers before they reach us?"

The Prime Minister picked up his pen and scribbled on a blank piece of paper: "It is only with the greatest reluctance that I have approved the creation and funding of M-18."

He handed the paper to the director general.

"Make certain that this paper appears in the organizational files."

"I will see to that personally," the director general said, trying to conceal his satisfaction as he left the room.

A spanking-new Russian bus, painted in dull gray, that Israel had captured intact from Egypt in the Six-day War, dropped Leora and the seven other new M-18 trainees at a dusty base in the Negev desert. The other seven were men in their twenties, officers from the elite paratrooper corps, battle-hardened veterans of at least one and in some cases two wars. They had volunteered to transfer from the army to Shai for purposes of this assignment.

They were a motley-looking crew, caked with dirt from the six-hour bus ride across the hot desert. They wore no fixed uniforms; they had been told that clothes would be provided at the camp.

Dress on the bus was haphazard: cut-off jeans that made no effort to conceal hairy legs, T-shirts that displayed a multitude of antiestablishment symbols, and old battered army boots.

As one of the men quipped after four hours on the road, "We look like we're convicts on our way to prison."

The base had no name on the front—only a cardboard sign on which "M-18" was painted.

What struck Leora most about it on first glance was the barbed wire that was everywhere. The outer perimeter of the camp consisted of ten-foot-high fences with another four feet of electrified barbed wire on top of that.

Everywhere signs were posted in Hebrew, Arabic, and English: "Keep out. Government property. Access prohibited without special permit."

When they filed into the dusty center courtyard, carrying their duffel bags, a half dozen somber figures were waiting, the instructors in the training program. Here and there an instructor recognized a new trainee and nodded in familiarity.

The chief instructor was a man named Yigal, a retired army colonel who had lost an arm in the 1956 war. He stepped forward and told them to drop their bags. They stood around in the hot late-afternoon sun waiting for him to begin. Finally, he was ready.

"I don't know what you've been told. But our job is to put you through three months of brutal hell. You will be using your brains as well as your bodies. Coming so close to the end of the war, that's terribly unfair, I know, but you're all volunteers. We are not cruel or sadistic men, believe me. We earnestly believe that the things we teach you may one day save your lives."

He paused for a moment. The recruits shuffled on their feet.

"Anyone is free to drop out at any time. I'm frankly not expecting all eight of you to make it. Based on our experience with other operational groups, I would say that fifty percent will survive."

Leora thought about Dan Yaacobi. She had not seen or heard from him since he had left her at Shai headquarters after bringing her back from Egypt. She knew from Shai documents that Dan was operating in Paris.

"There is one final thing," Yigal said, looking squarely at Leora. "We've never had a woman in this program before. Well, we do now. I'm not sure why. But we've gone ahead and set up a special barracks for you, Madam, and all that, so the Minister can't say we're not egalitarian. Still, I'm not expecting you to make it, Leora," he added bluntly.

She glared back at Yigal, keeping her silence, vowing that he would choke on those words before long.

The next morning what was to become their camp routine began at five o'clock with the rising of the sun. Mornings were devoted to physical training, exercises, karate, wrestling, judo, weights, and running. There was lunch and a short rest period. The afternoons were devoted to the science of death—to weapons training, use and preparation of bombs and explosives, instruction in poisons, and training in the cruder forms of killing—with the rope, the knife, or the human hands.

After dinner, evenings were devoted to training in communications technology. There were also lectures and movies about the methods utilized by the enemy—the Arab terrorists. Each evening a different Arab terrorist attack was studied, analyzed, and discussed. A psychiatrist examined the thinking of those attacked and the attackers. What had been done? What could have been done?

During the opening weeks of training, Leora's intense motivation began producing rewards. She started to shine in the afternoon and evening sessions. Quickly she saw that her ideas were regarded with respect. It was only in the morning that she was lagging behind. She was a big girl and strong, having regained the weight she lost in prison, but in wrestling or judo she was no match for most of the male brutes she was competing with, well trained and well conditioned from active military duty. Still Yigal had to hand it to her. She was a game one, that woman. No matter how many times someone would put her down she bounced up, no matter how tired she was or how much she hurt, she kept going.

One day Yigal took her aside at noon.

"How in the world did you develop such a high pain threshold, woman?" he said.

She glared at him.

"If you read my file carefully, you'd know where I got it—from those Egyptian interrogations. They put me through their own crash course."

She turned and walked away, thinking to herelf, Don't blow your temper. Yigal would still love to boot you out.

Her best friend in the camp was a trainee by the name of Yitzhak. Although he was from a religious family that could trace its presence in Jerusalem to the Middle Ages, when he was sixteen Yitzhak had decided that God was dead. He had been one of the troops who had stormed Sharm el-Sheikh in the war. In the evenings, when the training was over, he sat in his room and wrote poetry. On Friday evenings, Leora sat with him and listened to the recitation of a week's worth of verse. He wrote about living things, animals and plants and people.

Midway through the program, two men dropped out. One of them got up and made a statement at dinner, his last night in the camp.

"We're not leaving because we can't take it physically. We're quitting because the course revolts us. Death on the battlefield is one thing, but this is another. We don't have the stomach for it."

Two weeks later, another man lost an arm when an explosion went off prematurely.

Then the psychiatrist pulled a fourth man out. Leora heard him tell Yigal, "He won't be able to take it. He'll crack under the pressure."

One week before the course ended, Yigal walked to the front of the mess hall as the trainees were finishing dinner.

"Tonight each of you will be given a simulated mission

assignment," he said, studying their anxious faces. "Everyone's assignment will be different. Each one will take place outside of this base, and each one will be dangerous. You will have to decide how to cope with the danger. One of my officers will come to each of you tonight and explain your assignment."

Leora detected a slight snicker on his face, and she knew that it was directed at her.

Two hours later one of the officers came to Leora's room.

"Tomorrow at sunrise," he explained with great intensity, "a car will take you to Beersheba. You will be dropped in the center of the city with ten pounds of Israeli currency, a Soviet-made gun that is empty, and false Israeli papers, the kind that one of our Egyptian friends might have if he were trying to spy in Israel. Your assignment will be to get yourself into our Shomer army base in the Negev. You will go to the security office on the base. There you will see one of our men, whom you will recognize. Pretend to go through the motions of assassinating that man. Don't tell anyone how you got into the base. Then you must escape from the base, undetected, and return to the center of Beersheba, the original drop-off point, all in twenty-four hours. Any questions?"

"How am I supposed to find the base?"

"We'll give you a map and a diagram of the base."

"Very generous of you."

He gave her a furious stare.

"We're not doing this for our amusement."

He started toward the door. Then he paused.

"Oh, and one other thing," he added almost as an afterthought. "This assignment could be dangerous. No one except our man at the security office will know that you are on assignment with us. If someone else should catch you, you will look like an Egyptian spy, complete with

Soviet gun and false papers. It is just possible that they might shoot first and ask questions later. Of course, if you get into trouble, you can always disclose that you are really on a training maneuver with us. But if you do that, don't bother coming back. We'll send your things."

"You don't have to worry about that," Leora said tersely.

For the next hour Leora paced in her room, trying to think of a plan. Finally, she had an idea.

She quietly made her way to the base communications center.

"I want to call home," she told the operator on duty. "I'm worried about my kid brother."

Two minutes later she was talking to Uri, softly, so no one could hear.

"Uri, wake up. I need some help."

Finally he sounded alert.

"Tomorrow by ten A.M., get yourself to the Zohar Hotel in Beersheba. And bring two things with you: a woman's army uniform that will fit me and an Uzi machine gun. Got that?"

"What the hell for?"

"Don't ask. Do it."

"Where will I get the uniform?"

"Come, come, dear boy. Among all those girls you know who are home on leave now, one must be willing to slip out of her clothes for you. I only need it for a couple of days."

Uri gazed at the naked snoring figure in the bed next to him, then looked at her army uniform draped over the chair and the Uzi on the floor. She'll never even miss them, he decided.

"As a matter of fact, I may just be able to get you the stuff."

The next morning, a car dropped Leora in the center of Beersheba. She raced to the Zohar Hotel, found Uri impatiently waiting, and quickly changed clothes. Then she checked her own clothes with the hotel bellman.

"Come back tomorrow, the same time," she said to Uri. "He'll have your friend's clothes."

"Sure, why not do this drive every day? What am I, a lunatic?"

"Wrong. A devoted brother. And a young man who better beat it back to Haifa before a naked girl wakes up and finds out her clothes are gone."

Leora killed time walking around Beersheba until it was late afternoon. Then she hitched a ride with some tourists from Washington, D.C., driving in the direction of the Shomer base. For a long hour's ride, they threw questions at her about the war and where she had fought. They passed a small Bedouin village, and the Americans asked about it.

She explained that Israel had only recently established this village as an experiment in settling the nomadic Bedouins in a fixed place.

Ten miles from the base, she thanked the talkative Americans, and concealing a great sigh of relief she got out of the car. There she stood at the side of the dusty road looking for cars heading toward Shomer. The sun was beginning to set in the west. In the first half hour, six cars stopped. They contained a score of soldiers, both men and women, returning to the base. Each of the six drivers stopped to offer her a ride. Each time she looked at the driver and declined.

Finally she saw what she had been waiting for. A large black Russian sedan approached her at a great speed. Suddenly, the driver braked in front of Leora.

"Get in," the driver shouted. "I'll take you back to the base."

She quickly studied his uniform. He was a full major, just what she needed. She got into the car.

"Major Zev," he said, touching her hand.

"Batya," she replied naturally, selecting a name different from that on her papers.

"You like my beauty?" he asked, proudly tapping on the dashboard.

He didn't wait for a response.

"She's only got five hundred miles on her. The Russians just left her in the middle of the Sinai and beat it . . . the spoils of war."

"Is that where you fought, Major, in the Sinai?"

"Here and in the north too."

"I was just there in the Golan, on my leave."

They were approaching the camp now. He slowed down the car.

"On your own you couldn't see much. You need an expert guide. Let me take you in a couple of weeks. Tell me when you have a leave again. I'll show you things you haven't seen before." He winked at her.

She wanted to respond, "And your wife? Will we take her too?" But she didn't. She smiled gracefully.

"It's a deal, Major, a deal."

He stopped at the checkpoint at the gate for the base. She held her breath when the guard approached.

The guard immediately recognized the major's new car.

"She's with me, soldier," the major barked, pointing to Leora. "I'm bringing her back."

The guard didn't ask to see her papers. The yellow wooden gate was raised.

Now he'll probably drive to the commanding officer's parking lot, Leora thought, as she remembered the map of the base that had been indelibly imprinted on her mind. That was precisely what he did. When he parked in his reserved space, he jumped out of the car, leaving the keys in the ignition. There was only a tiny sliver of moon in the night sky. The chill of the desert evening was starting to move in.

"Don't forget," he said, "Batya, you come see me when you have leave."

Then he winked again, a nice naughty wink. It was an innocent, harmless flirtation. She wondered what he would have said if she had replied, "Let's go next Sunday."

"Yeh, I'll do that," she said instead, heading away from the car. She walked calmly, trying to appear like she belonged. It was still the aftermath of Israel's lightning six-day victory. The base was chaotic, heady. Captured Russian equipment was everywhere.

The second building on the left is security, she thought as she walked. She was correct. It was an old yellow wooden-frame barracks hut. She climbed one flight of stairs, hid near the door, and peered inside. There he was sitting behind the desk. Yigal himself. Leora was very pleased with herself. She pulled the Soviet-made gun from her pocket and barged into the office, pointing it at Yigal and shouting, "You're a dead man, Yigal, a dead man." She pulled the trigger and nothing happened. The gun was empty, just as she had been told.

Yigal sat at the desk staring at her, devoid of emotion, looking sorry that she had made it.

"How did you do it?" he asked.

She proudly explained about the major and the ride. He listened passively. The compliment she was waiting for never came.

"Okay, you've completed the first half of your assassination. Now try to get back to Beersheba."

He smiled at her weakly, as if she would never make it.

Watch me do it, she thought to herself as she headed out of the door and down the steps.

She never heard Yigal pick up the phone and place the call to Major Zev. She never heard the embarrassed cursing from Zev, when Yigal said, "Major, I have reason to believe you brought an Egyptian spy back with you into the base in your car."

What Leora did hear though were the loud warning sirens that began wailing throughout the base. She also heard shouts over loudspeakers: "Egyptian spy on the base, Egyptian spy on the base. Female. Armed and Dangerous."

Suddenly, Leora knew what Yigal had done. That dirty bastard, she swore as she raced toward the parking lot where the major had left his car. Once inside, she had the engine going, and she was roaring out of the parking lot.

With the great chaos in the base, she made it to the gate without being stopped. There she saw the yellow horizontal wooden bar across the gate, blocking her exit. Next to the guardhouse was the soldier who had waved the major in a little while ago. He was gripping his Uzi machine gun tightly.

Suddenly, the training exercise had taken a grim deadly course. There was only one way out, she decided, as she slammed the gas pedal to the floor. The startled soldier jumped out of her way, and she blasted the yellow wooden bar head on, ripping it off at its hinges with an impact that shattered one of the car's headlights.

Now here comes the fun, she thought. She saw the soldier back on the road ready to open fire with his Uzi. She bent down as far as she could in the driver's seat. Then she began weaving from side to side, watching him through the mirror, trying to dodge his shots. One struck the rear window, but the shattering glass and bullets missed her as she continued driving. The poor major won't love me after he sees what I did to his car.

When she was fifteen miles from the base, she heard the sound of a helicopter overhead. Immediately, she ditched the car at the side of the road and took off on foot. It was getting cool now. She wondered how she would spend the night. Suddenly she remembered the Bedouin village a few miles away. She began walking in that direction, as quickly as she could, knowing that if she reached the village she would be safe. The Israeli army probably wouldn't break into the Bedouin village.

She heard the helicopter move closer, and she quickly dove behind rocks to avoid its spotlight.

She repeated that exercise several more times, showing incredible agility on a difficult and treacherous terrain. Her reflexes were sharp. Each time she managed to elude the spotlight. Then there was a long silence for the last three miles until she reached the village.

The villagers believed her story that her car had broken down, and that she hadn't been able to get back to the base. The next morning they took her into Beersheba on a camel with their produce so that she could hire a mechanic.

She left the Bedouins in the marketplace and raced to the Zohar Hotel to change clothes. She was back at the pickup point in time for her ride.

Yigal was waiting for her at the camp.

"You did a good job," he said proudly. "A very good job."

She glared at him menacingly.

"I could have been killed, you know that?"

"You're the one who made the mistake," he replied.

"Oh, yeh. What?"

"You told me about the major. That let me call him and make him feel like a fool, hell-bent on revenge."

"You asked me how I got in."

"But your orders were not to tell anyone how you got in. You don't follow orders well, do you?"

"I'm not a robot, if that's what you mean."

"Be one, then. Your commander will make the decisions for you."

She glared at him again.

"You'll thank me one day," he said confidently. "Mark my words. You'll thank me one day."

*   *   *

71

On graduation day, Yigal turned out to be both right and wrong on his initial predictions. Only 50 percent made it through the course. His second prediction was dead wrong. Leora was one of the four who made it. Yitzhak was another.

Before they left the camp that last day, each of the four was taken to the officers' hall for a private talk with Motti Elon to receive their orders.

He greeted Leora warmly, kissing her on both cheeks.

"You made one hell of an impression on Yigal."

"He deserved worse."

"And you were careful not to give it to him."

"Exactly."

He smiled.

"I've been incommunicado for three months. Have you made it up to director general yet?"

"Still deputy."

"A pity."

He took a package of cigarettes from his pocket and handed her one. They lit up together.

"I have an assignment for you."

"Don't tell me, let me guess. Someplace exotic? Hawaii or the Canary Islands."

"No one's seen any terrorists there," he said, joking with her. "But it is exotic. Your old stamping ground, London town. You're going over as an assistant military attaché at our Embassy."

She wanted to jump up and down with joy, to show some emotion, but that wouldn't be becoming.

"When do I leave?"

"Four weeks with your family, then two weeks of indoctrination at the Foreign Ministry in embassy and diplomatic procedures. Then we'll ship you out."

He finished his cigarette and pulled another from the pack.

"There is one other thing," he said slowly. "You can say goodbye to Leora Baruch. Since you had the bad judgment to inquire about immigration at their embassy, they have that name in their files. You'll be rechristened, if that's the right word. From now on you're Leora Elon."

"Motti, you old devil. Is that your idea of an informal adoption?"

He started to blush.

"I didn't pick the name. Really I didn't. Someone in documents and identification did it. They never even thought about the coincidence at the time, and by the time they did, all the papers were ready."

"I'll bet," she said, smiling.

"Well, it is a common Israeli name."

"I'm sure I'll see you before I leave for London."

"Absolutely. At the end of the indoctrination."

She squeezed his hand and started to leave.

At the door, Leora turned.

"There is one thing I want to ask you. That man, Dan Yaacobi, who picked me up in Cairo. Did he make it through the course to Paris?"

"He made it okay. I'm not sure how long we'll keep him there, though."

Leora looked surprised.

"What's wrong?"

"I shouldn't really tell you this." He hesitated. "It's all in the family, I guess. Dan has a wife, Zipora, and two kids. He's really quite devoted to them and they've gone to Paris with him. I don't think that Zippy will be able to take it for long off the kibbutz. I promised him we'd re-examine him every twelve months and maybe base him in Tel Aviv. Let him make short trips out of the country."

Leora listened carefully, trying to show little interest in what he was saying. In fact, she was very interested. Ever since that night in Alexandria, she had looked at every man differently. No one looked as attractive as Dan.

"Well, I was just curious," she said. "I feel a debt of gratitude to that man."

She thought long and hard about Motti's words. She understood very well what her adoptive father was trying to tell her.

～

CHAPTER 9

LONDON, AUGUST 1968

It was Leora's first real combat duty. She was just a trifle nervous.

The bulletin came in to the embassy communications room at the end of the afternoon: "Two Arab terrorists are holding an El Al plane and one hundred and twenty passengers hostage at gunpoint at Heathrow Airport. They are armed and dangerous."

In an embassy car, she raced to the airport. Once there, she quickly found the makeshift command headquarters. British troops guarded the perimeter of the field. They were armed, but their orders were to fire only if shots were fired by the hijackers.

She approached Inspector Barnwell, who was in charge. He was biting fiercely on his lower lip, agonizing over what to do, and secretly cursing both the Arabs and the Jews for inflicting this nightmare on him.

"I'm from the Israeli Embassy, Inspector," she said tersely. "I know how to solve your problem."

He greeted her with ambivalence. It was his turf, and he didn't need any foreigners telling him how to run his show. On the other hand, he was relieved to have an Israeli on deck. She could bear some of the responsibility if her

74

countrymen were killed or her country's plane blown up.

"What do they want?" she asked.

He was puzzled by her English. It was as good as his own.

"The release of some Arab terrorists we're holding in prison."

"Which ones? The four you picked up last week, the two men and two women, on the tip from Interpol?"

He looked puzzled.

"Khalid is one of the women. Isn't she?"

"How did you know?"

"It's our job to know. How far from here are they?"

"About two hours."

"You won't turn them over, will you?"

There was a long silence.

"I don't know. There are a hundred and twenty people on that plane."

"And tomorrow, there will be another plane with one hundred and twenty more."

"I just don't know," the inspector said, biting his lip harder.

Suddenly Leora had an idea.

"Why don't you tell them that you'll make the swap, but we won't bring any of the four prisoners here."

"What do we do then?" he asked, puzzled.

"You disguise me to look like Khalid, and I'll get on board in the first exchange. Once I'm in the plane, I can take the two of them."

He hesitated for a minute.

"It's awfully dangerous."

"I speak Arabic. It's my native language."

"I just don't know."

"C'mon, Inspector, it's the best chance we have."

There was a long pause. Her plan reminded him of a trick he had once heard of during the war to obtain the release of two British prisoners from a German field headquarters. One of the British troops, in disguise as a German soldier, was able to remove the prisoners in a German truck with the story that they were being transferred to another location. It had worked then. Maybe it would work now.

"Go ahead," said the inspector, suddenly excited from thinking about his war days. "We'll try it. What do you need from me in the way of support?"

"Have someone get me a recent picture of Khalid, some prison clothes, and the best makeup man in the West End."

She was barking orders now as if she were in charge. "Then get on the telephone hookup with the plane. Tell them we'll swap their friends for the passengers, but we need two hours to get them here. By then it should be dark. And no floodlights on the field."

One hour and ten cigarettes later, Leora was handed a picture of Khalid and prison clothes. The makeup man arrived a few minutes later. As he fixed her hair to resemble Khalid's, she felt as if she were back in the Drama Society at the university. Actually, he had relatively little to do. Leora and Khalid had a close resemblance.

"I'm ready, Inspector," she said once the makeup man had applied his finishing touches.

Barnwell picked up the telephone connecting the plane and the command center and began the speech he and Leora had written.

"Okay," he said, trying to appear calm. "We have your four friends here. We'll send them out one at a time. You get one through the rear of the plane, and we get thirty passengers from the front of the plane. Once those thirty are in the terminal and yours is in the plane, we swap the second."

Leora held her breath, hoping that the hijackers wouldn't balk at this plan. With all four terrorists two hours away still in prison, her plan would have been in deep trouble had the hijackers demanded to see all four before they started the exchange. Fortunately, they were silent, pleased by the thought that they were succeeding.

"All right," the inspector said. "We're ready with Khalid. Get your first thirty passengers."

He put the phone down.

"Good luck, sister."

Slowly Leora walked toward the rear of the plane. Without floodlights, there was a curtain of darkness over the field. Dim cabin lights lit the plane. The hijacker at the rear looked out of the door to make certain that it really was Khalid. He called a greeting to her in Arabic, and she responded, "Praise to Allah, Comrade. Praise to Allah."

Satisfied, he shouted to his colleague in the front of the plane, "It's Khalid. Let the thirty go up front."

Waving his machine gun wildly, the hijacker in the front picked the thirty passengers closest to the front of the plane, and ordered them to get off through the front exit. He carefully watched them walk down the stairs and toward the terminal, making certain that the British police didn't use the confusion on the field as the cover to board the plane.

As the hijacker in the front stood in the doorway watching the thirty passengers walk toward the terminal, Leora climbed the rear stairs into the plane. A surgically sharp knife was concealed in her right hand, most of it hidden from view by the long sleeves of the prison uniform.

When she reached the top of the stairs, the hijacker threw his arms around her in a great joyous bear hug for his released comrade. He had no idea that she had the knife until she plunged its blade straight into his heart. One stab was all she needed. She stared directly into his face as he felt the blade enter his body. Yigal and his friends had taught her well.

She encircled his neck with her left arm, squeezing his throat tightly to silence him. There was no scream, no sound at all. Only the silence of death.

She had never killed before. For an instant her whole body trembled as the realization of what she had done struck her. A slightly nauseous taste welled up in her mouth. Rapidly, she gained control.

The blood squirted on to the floor. She caught his body before it collapsed. Then she placed it slowly down to avoid a loud noise.

She pressed her fingers over her lips, signaling to the passengers to be quiet.

Then she glanced quickly to the head of the plane. The other hijacker was gripping his machine gun tightly, still watching the passengers on the field. The first quarter of the plane was free of passengers.

Speed, she thought, speed. The element of surprise was her greatest asset. She yanked a pistol from her pocket, raised her hand in the air, and began racing up the aisle, shouting in Arabic, "Allah is great! Allah is great!" Her eyes were riveted squarely on the figure in the doorway. He was elated. Khalid was free and racing toward him.

The first shot, she told herself, I have to take him with the first shot or he'll hit some of the passengers.

She was only twenty yards from him when he saw the gun in her hand, when he realized what had happened. He froze for an instant, unable to believe his eyes, unable to raise his machine gun. That was all she needed.

She quickly lowered her arm and fired with deadly accuracy. The hijacker dropped to the floor of the plane in a heap. She continued running toward him. Blood was pouring out of his body. He was moving, crying for help.

Leora lowered her hand and placed the gun against his head. She pulled the trigger again, and still once more. This one won't be in a prison where they can threaten innocent people to buy him back, she said to herself.

A general atmosphere of pandemonium broke out at Heathrow. Gleeful passengers raced out of the plane, relieved, shouting for joy. In the noise and confusion, Leora

walked slowly back to her car. Silently she disappeared
from the airport.

CHAPTER 10

LONDON, 1975

Leora's enormous effectiveness as Israel's M-18 agent in
London was demonstrated during the next seven years.
While there were bloody attacks on Israeli planes, airport
lounges, and athletes engaged in international competition
in cities scattered throughout Western Europe such as
Munich, Athens, Amsterdam, and Oslo, not a single incident of this type occurred in the British Isles.

The British public attributed the absence of these attacks
on English soil to the effectiveness of Scotland Yard. What
they didn't realize was that the Yard had a silent and intensely determined ally. During this seven-year period,
Leora was responsible for the wasting of nine different Arab
terrorists—always disposing of the bodies in isolated areas
where they would not be discovered until years later, or
leaving her target as the apparent victim of an accident,
with his or her body charred beyond recognition.

The secret of Leora's success was simple. She had formed
an alliance with an Iraqi whose code name was Bart. He
was nominally a member of an Arab terrorist organization,
but his real sympathies lay with the Kurds, a fierce moun-
tain people in the north of Iraq who were fighting the
Baghdad government for their independence. The one
thing that the Kurds desperately needed was arms. Once
the Americans stopped being their arms supplier, the Kurds
were forced into the open market. And that took money—
plenty of it. In this seven-year period, Leora paid Bart more

than one million pounds sterling for the information he provided.

Most important, Bart had supplied valuable information to Leora about an Arab terrorist whom Shai called Cherev, the Sword. He was the leader of the assassination unit of the detested Black September movement. While the primary focus of Black September was on terrorist attacks on Israeli civilian targets, the assassination unit had its own operations. It had been trained in Moscow by the KGB, and its primary mission was to systematically track and destroy Israeli intelligence agents who were pursuing Black September members involved in terrorist activities. As one of the Black September documents seized by Shai in a Beirut raid put it, the unit's mission was to hunt the hunters. And so, in a strange procession that was carried on around the world, but mostly in Western Europe, the pursued hunted the pursuer. It was an eerie circular procession. There was neither beginning nor end. Only death.

Cherev's assassination unit had one other role as well. It was available, always at a price, for hire by the radical Arab regimes, who wanted to eradicate a political opponent. The reward for Cherev for these services was far more than monetary. There was a cooperation between the radical Arab governments and Cherev's unit that conferred diplomatic credentials for Cherev's people, assuring easy movement across international borders and access to intelligence information.

In addition, the radical Arab governments served as a front for arms purchases for Cherev's unit—a fact of great importance. In the arms bazaar of Western Europe, extra-governmental purchases faced a myriad of legal hurdles. In contrast, the Defense Minister of any "lawful" regime, regardless of how malevolent, simply had to lend his signature and pay the purchase price. The entire destructive force of modern technology was at his disposal. Cherev took advantage of this "free market," preferring to limit his dependence on his Soviet mentors. And besides, the Soviets were accustomed to telling Cherev which arms he should have; the Western governments offered a supermarket selection.

Cherev was number one on Shai's "get" list, and Leora and her colleagues had been waiting a long time for a good shot at him. As long as Cherev lived, every member of Shai had to live under the constant threat of assassination.

The Israelis had named him Cherev, the Sword, because he left a small black plastic sword at the scene of each one of his assassinations. It was more than a calling card; it was a form of gloating, intended to infuriate members of Shai for their lack of success in apprehending Cherev. And it did precisely that.

Leora's M.O. had another dominant element. She always operated alone. Never trusting anyone, never willing to risk being betrayed, she refused to operate with partners or assistants.

During those seven years, Leora had only slight contact with Dan Yaacobi, who was in Paris. She exchanged with him confidential reports on suspected Arab terrorist activities, as she did with other M-18 operatives in Europe. She also saw him each summer during the one-week staff sessions that Motti Elon, now director general of Shai, had for M-18 operatives at the training base in the Negev. She was surprised that Yaacobi had stayed in Paris so long, but Motti once told her: "We've let him live on a small farm outside of town and that has satisfied Zipora, at least for now."

"I thought you made everyone live close in for security reasons."

"Every rule has exceptions. But it's a security man's nightmare."

Leora always felt strange sensations in her body whenever she saw Dan at these annual sessions. Whatever fires he had managed to light that night in Alexandria at Abdel

Rasef's house still burned. And precisely because the desire had never been satisfied, the flame burned brighter over time.

When they sat together in the staff sessions around a large table in the dining room, their eyes frequently met. On many occasions she thought that she saw a sign, a signal from him that her own feelings were matched by his. But nothing ever happened. Their discussions were always professional, directed to Shai business.

In London, she had half a dozen discreet sexual relationships with other members of the diplomatic corps—harmless dalliances that satisfied sexual appetites but created no emotional commitments. Then too, there were an endless stream of quiet dinners, concerts, and theater evenings when she was the extra woman whose presence was sought by a colleague on the embassy staff.

One afternoon, the Israeli ambassador to London, Ariel Levy, walked into Leora's office.

"Can you join my wife and me for the theater this evening?"

"Not this evening, I'm afraid," Leora responded with a tinge of regret in her voice. "Too much work to do."

Levy wasn't willing to accept her answer. Though the ambassador and Leora had no emotional attachment, the Israeli Embassy in London resembled a large family with Ariel at the head. More than that, he and his wife had become close personal friends with Leora. The ambassador respected her intelligence and dedication.

His wife treasured Leora's companionship, and the ambassador encouraged that relationship, feeling sorry for Leora that she appeared so lonely, so devoid of emotional commitments.

"Tamar will be very disappointed. You're not in a crisis?" he asked, sounding alarmed.

The word "crisis" was their code word for Leora's attacks on terrorists.

"No crisis tonight. Just a lot of paperwork."

"You can't put me off with that," he responded. "I know what you think of paperwork."

She began to laugh, thinking about the efforts of the former director general to confine her to a desk job in Tel Aviv.

"You know, I've never seen you laugh so much in the four years I've known you."

She thought about his words for a minute.

"Maybe it's a sign that I'm aging."

"Or mellowing?"

"Never."

"I won't take no for an answer. Seven o'clock then for the theater. We'll pick you up at your flat."

"You're a persistent man."

"How do you think I got to be ambassador?"

As he started to leave her office, she called to him.

"What are we seeing?"

"*Antony and Cleopatra.*"

As soon as he said it, she was sorry that she had accepted. Then she was furious at herself for having those emotions. You could easily turn into a sentimental old fool, she said to herself.

Leora opened the program quickly. She studied each biographical sketch carefully, thinking that had it not been for events beyond her control, she might be there herself. When she turned to the director, her face froze. There he was, picture and all, Philip Marks. She read slowly.

"*Antony and Cleopatra* represents Mr. Marks' first play in the West End since he left London for the United States in 1960. During this period, he has directed a score of plays on Broadway, as well as a number of movies and an American television series. Mr. Marks was educated at the University of London. He is married to Catherine Ford, the American actress. He has directed *Antony and Cleopatra* once before in the West End, in 1959."

And once before that, Leora thought to herself as the lights went off and the curtain went up.

When Leora looked at Cleopatra on the stage, she saw herself as she had played that role eighteen years earlier. During most of the first act, Leora sat looking at the play but thinking about Philip and their days together in London. She wondered whether she should try to see him that evening after the play or maybe call him tomorrow.

No, she finally decided. No, no, no, a thousand times no. It would produce complications that could only be awkward and maybe even dangerous. It would distract her from the track that she had set her life on.

What's happening to me? she wondered. Why did I even think of calling Philip?

During the second act, she knew the answer to that question. The warrior's life that she had carved out for herself was starting to catch up with her. Being always fearful of forming any emotional attachments had its own emotional toll.

As she looked around the theater at the women sitting with their husbands, at the children with their parents, she wondered what it was in her that made her different. Why wouldn't she ever be able to have a normal life?

She thought about what Dan Yaacobi had told her back in Abdel Rasef's house that evening in Alexandria: "The bitterness will destroy you."

In the darkness of the theater, she clenched her fists hard. What do you know about me, Dan Yaacobi? What makes you an expert on human nature?

When the play was over, she left the theater quickly, walking two steps ahead of the ambassador and his wife.

No, I won't call Philip, she decided.

The ambassador's car was waiting in front of the theater, precisely where he had parked it in an area reserved for diplomats and VIPs. With Leora in the back seat, the ambassador pulled away quickly. A light drizzle was falling over London. The fog was starting to settle in.

"I want to make a short stop at the embassy," the ambassador said.

"Is that really necessary?" his wife shot back, ready to begin a familiar argument. "Why can't we just go for something to eat and take Leora home like normal people?"

"I'm expecting a cable from Jerusalem."

"Tonight?"

"Perhaps. I don't know."

"You always say that."

Leora closed her eyes, tuning out their bickering. If anyone had asked her, she would have said, "Take me home. I want to go to sleep."

But no one asked her.

"A compromise then," the ambassador said. "Mirabelle's, then the embassy, then home for Leora."

His wife nodded assent. With Leora in the car, she didn't want to argue anymore. What good would it do anyhow? He always stuck with it until he wore her down.

It was close to midnight when they left Mirabelle's. It was still raining, and the fog was thicker. Leora relaxed in the back of the car, satiated with food and drink. She closed her eyes as they argued about whether the Scotch salmon was as good as usual.

As the car approached the embassy, the ambassador suddenly saw a dozen flashing lights coming from police cruisers.

"What is it?" she asked tersely. "Can you see?"

Leora pulled the small pistol from her purse.

"Tamar, get down on the floor of the front," she commanded the ambassador's wife. Then, to the ambassador, "Drive slowly."

When the car came closer to the building, Leora saw

police everywhere. They were milling around something on the sidewalk. It looked like a body. None of the police were poised with weapons.

"Wait here," she shouted to the ambassador, as she jumped out of the car.

Quickly, she pushed to the front of the circle.

"Leora Elon, Israeli Embassy staff," she said to an inspector who looked like he was in charge. She showed him her identification badge.

"The ambassador is with me. What happened?"

The inspector pointed to the white sheet on the ground, obviously covering some object. His face looked as pale as the sheet on the ground. He was speaking slowly, slurring his words.

"Somebody dropped it here in front of your embassy," he said. "Apparently they threw it out of a passing car."

"Threw what out? What is it?" she asked, "A dead body?"

"You're partly right."

He smiled nervously.

"What do you mean?"

"It's only the head. We don't know where the rest of the body is." The inspector shook his own head sadly. "I've been in this business for thirty years, and I've never seen anything like it."

"Who was it? Can you tell?"

"We can't identify him."

"Let me look," she said, moving forward.

"How good's your stomach?"

"I'll manage."

"Westfall, show this woman the head," the inspector said, turning away.

She didn't have to look at the face long. The killers had been careful to leave all of the facial features intact. They wanted her to know who it was. That was the whole point. It was Bart, her Iraqi informer.

Even hardened to death as she was, Leora had a sickening feeling in the pit of her stomach as she motioned to Westfall to replace the sheet. She turned around and walked back to the inspector.

"Can you identify him?" he asked her. "He looked like an Arab to me."

"I'm sorry, I can't help you."

The inspector looked skeptical.

"You people aren't playing some more of your war games behind our backs, are you?"

"We wouldn't consider it, Inspector."

"I won't tolerate it in this precinct, ma'am. Really I won't, not from diplomats or anyone else."

She stared harshly at the inspector.

"You should get your priorities straight, Inspector. A man has been murdered. Go find the killer. Don't harangue me."

She walked back to the car and explained to the ambassador what had happened.

"Leave me here, Ariel," she said. "I want to do a little checking of my own."

Then she unlocked the door to the embassy and went inside. She stood next to a window in the dark building, looking out until all the police were gone. Then she came out slowly with a small flashlight in her hand.

She combed the ground in front of the embassy carefully. Finally, she found what she was looking for: a small black plastic sword. "Cherev," she muttered to herself through a tight, grim mouth. So you're in London, my friend.

Suddenly, Leora heard footsteps behind her on the sidewalk, a man's steps. They were getting louder. He was moving up behind her. She pretended to hear nothing. Slowly she reached into her bag for her pistol. When she felt the cold steel in her hand, she whirled around, ready to fire.

"My God, you're tense," Ariel Levy said, as he approached her.

"Please don't walk up behind me like that."

"Okay. Take it easy. I just dropped my wife at home and decided to come back and see if you'd found anything."

She showed him the sword.

"Let's go to Scotland Yard with it. Let them arrest him and get a murder conviction. Let the whole world know what he's been up to."

"It won't do any good, I'm afraid. First they'll never catch him. Second, even if they do, they'll be afraid to try him, and third, even if they try and convict him, they'll release him before long when his colleagues hijack a BOAC plane somewhere in the world. It's useless."

"Then what do you propose to do?"

"Find him and execute him. He's already murdered three members of Shai and a score of civilians."

"Not while I'm ambassador here."

"What do you think I've been doing?"

"I haven't ever asked. I was told to leave you alone."

"Why not follow that same rule now?"

He thought about it for a minute.

"I can't. A man was killed outside of my embassy. I have great respect for you, but I also have certain responsibilities as ambassador."

"Don't you think you should at least call Jerusalem before you take any action?"

"I'm not waking the Foreign Minister in the middle of the night."

"Then wait till morning."

"I'll wait if you'll hold your hand."

"C'mon, Ariel, you know I can't do that. I would lose too much valuable time."

She was furious, but managing to keep her anger under control. In the past, the ambassador had never asked her questions. Why in the hell did he think he was responsible now?

"As long as you're in this country, you're under my jurisdiction."

He said it so intently. Leora recognized that she had become a challenge to his authority. He would never back down without orders from Jerusalem. There was no way that she could get those orders before morning. Valuable time would be lost. Bart had been calling her almost daily on the private telephone in her office, relaying information about Cherev. The telephone had a recorder hookup. It was just possible that Bart had been able to relay some new information about Cherev before his death.

"Well, what will it be?" The ambassador asked.

"You'd better go to Scotland Yard yourself, Ariel. I can't wait until morning. Please try to understand."

He was surprised by her stubbornness. But still he had his own responsibilities.

"Very well, then. I'll go myself."

She turned and walked away from him, heading up the stairs into the building. In the first-floor reception area, she paused to look through the window, watching him get into his car and drive away in the direction of Scotland Yard.

Then she raced up the stairs of the dark building two at a time until she was in her own office. She closed the curtains and turned on the small desk lamp.

Quickly she unlocked the gunmetal-gray file cabinet and pulled out her private telephone with the attached recording device. She punched the play knob. First there were several minutes of silence, then a voice that was unmistakably Bart's.

"I will talk quickly, Leora. They have found out about me, and I suspect they know you are my contact . . . Cherev is in London now. He plans to stop in Paris tomorrow en route to Damascus . . ."

There were several minutes of silence, then background noises, an argument that Leora couldn't discern, and Bart's voice again.

"A meeting has been arranged for Cherev and one of his lieutenants tomorrow afternoon at five o'clock on Montmartre with representatives of Japanese and German terrorist organizations to coordinate their activities. The meeting place is in front of Saint Pierre de Montmartre Church. A black Mercedes, license plate PLN 638, will be parked in front of the church. Barot has given his blessing."

There was another silence.

"Cherev's plan is to drive to Dover this evening. He will be picked up there at three A.M. by a private yacht and then deposited at Calais. A car will drive him to Paris—"

Leora heard screams on the tape, then loud explosions like the sound of firing guns.

"If I do not make it, do not forget my people. The whole world forgets us. We will not be slaughtered. We will not—"
And the machine was silent.

A brave man, Leora said to herself, trying to restrain the emotion welling up in her as the picture of Bart's head flashed into her mind.

She looked at her watch. They were almost at Dover. There was no way that she could still catch Cherev on her own before he left England. If she wanted to stop him before he left the country, she would have to enlist the help of Scotland Yard. They could telephone ahead to Dover and have him picked up.

She thought about it for a minute. If she did that, the chances were the British would drag their feet over red tape until Cherev was gone. Even worse, once they realized they had missed him, they would notify the French Secret Service, never believing that the information would get to Barot, who would tip Cherev off. No, that approach wouldn't work. She had only one way to do it.

She picked up the small red telephone in her desk drawer. She checked the code card and dialed quickly.

When the phone rang in his old farmhouse, Dan Yaacobi had to separate himself from Zipora's curled-up body.

"Allo," he answered sleepily.

"Dan, it's Leora. This is urgent."

Yaacobi snapped awake quickly.

In short staccato sentences, she explained to him what had happened.

Dan needed no explanations. Like Leora, he knew very well that Cherev was number one on Shai's "get" list. He was thinking quickly.

"I have a plan," he said. "You take an early flight over. Then come to my office. In the afternoon, we head for Montmartre."

"I like it. But you'd better get some things ready before I get there."

"What will we need?"

"Lots of dynamite and one of those new radio detonators."

"What else?"

"Oh, one other thing, Dan. I've gotten a reputation of being a bit of a loner. But I think I'm going to enjoy working with you."

"Don't forget an important fact," he said, laughing softly. "We're working in my territory."

"So?"

"That means I'm in charge."

As Leora paused to frame a suitable response, there was a slight clicking on the line, barely audible. Perhaps nothing, Leora thought, but then again maybe Dan's home phone was tapped. She abruptly ended the conversation and listened carefully. There were no other sounds. She placed the telephone in the cradle.

* * *

As Leora began calling airlines to get a reservation to Paris, Ariel Levy was sitting in the office of Chief Inspector Barnwell of Scotland Yard. The inspector was furious at having been brought down so late at night.

"This could have waited until morning, Mr. Ambassador," he said politely but firmly.

"But time is of the essence."

"I really don't see how. Even if this Cherev character is in London, I don't have enough now to go about finding him. I'll have to see what Interpol has, and their information office in Brussels doesn't open until seven o'clock."

Furious that Leora was being proven right, the ambassador tried again.

"But surely you people here have something on Cherev?"

"I've told you before, Mr. Ambassador, we ran the name through our computer. Nothing came up. Maybe he has a different name. I can only learn that from Interpol."

With those words, the inspector rose from his desk. He was tired. He wanted to go back to bed.

"We'll call you first thing in the morning. I promise you that, Mr. Ambassador. First thing in the morning."

They sat in Dan's office in the embassy sipping coffee and looking forward to their confrontation with Cherev.

"Okay," Dan said. "We'll go through it one more time. We go to Montmartre separately. You sit at the outdoor café with a cup of coffee in front of you, like a tourist. At four o'clock I'll go into the church, carrying the brief-case, as if I'm stopping for a midafternoon prayer. You will stay at the table in the café. I'll keep an eye on that little gray box I have in my pocket. It's a two-way signal. You have the other one in your purse. When you press the 'send' button, the red light on mine will start flashing. That's the signal that they're here and in the car. I'll come out of the front door of the church, unobtrusively, and walk toward the street as if I'm looking for a taxicab. I'll place the briefcase near the car and head back inside the church. Once the case is down, you press the detonator button and it will blow. I'll be back inside before that happens—behind the heavy church walls."

Then, thinking of the destruction Cherev had caused, he added: "If you see them move before I'm inside, press the damn detonator anyhow. I'll take my chances. I want him too much."

"And after that?"

"There's a safe house—three blocks down and two to the right—the office of the Anglo-American Steel Trading Company. It has two floors of offices. On the third floor, there's an apartment stocked with enough food to last a week. I'll meet you there."

She sipped her coffee slowly.

"We're making one change, Dan."

"Why now? We've been through it all twice before."

She had a defiant look on her face.

"We're changing jobs. I'm going into the church with the briefcase. You're sitting in the café with the detonator."

"No, dammit. I'm in charge."

"Dan, be reasonable. I agree with you that we may have to activate it before the bag dropper is back in the church. So we both know that there's a pretty good chance that the one in the church will never come out of this alive."

He nodded, looking angry, ready to explode.

"You've got a wife and two children. Let me do it."

"No way. I'm in charge."

She was equally determined.

"Foolish male pride. You've already saved my life once. Give me a chance to even the score."

He was silent.

"You let me go or I'm walking out on you now. Catch him by yourself."

Dan looked at her tensely.

"You wouldn't do that."

"No?"

He thought about it for a minute.

"No, dammit. You wouldn't. I'm calling your bluff. Like me, you want him more than anything else in the world."

She winced. He was the first man who had ever done that to her.

They sat in silence for several minutes.

Finally, she reached into her pocket and pulled out two coins, placing one in each hand.

"Do you know the difference between a French coin and a British coin?" she asked.

He nodded, smiling.

"If you can pick the French coin," she continued, "you'll get the church. If not, you get the café."

He looked into her eyes, trying to read her mind. After a long pause, he agreed to do it. He looked at her two hands carefully. Then he placed his fingers on her right hand, caressing it ever so gently. She opened her fist and showed him: it was a British coin.

"I get the church. It's decided."

He didn't ask her to open the other hand. She wondered if he knew she had placed British coins in both hands.

A few minutes before three o'clock, Dan left his office alone, driving in a rented car. He was dressed like a tourist, gray slacks, knit shirt open at the neck, and a camera bag slung over his shoulder.

At Montmartre he sat down at a corner table at an outdoor café directly across from the church. There was no sign of the black Mercedes. He ordered a cup of coffee and looked around.

The restaurant was only half full—mostly tourists. In front of it on the street, half a dozen artists painted five-minute portraits for tourists anxious to take home a souvenir of Paris.

Everything looks the same as it did when I was up here early this morning, Dan thought.

At four o'clock a taxicab dropped Leora in front of the church. She was dressed like a French lawyer—conservative dark suit over a beige silk blouse. She was carrying a fine leather briefcase. She glanced around the square. Dan was in place at a table at the café, just as they had planned. There was still no sign of the Mercedes.

Standing on one corner was a policeman. She walked slowly into the church, wondering whether Jacques Barot had assigned the policeman to the spot as a protector for the terrorists.

For a long hour she sat on the hard wooden church bench looking at the stained-glass windows. She tried to remember the last time she had prayed in a synagogue. She remembered being there for the funerals of colleagues. But never praying.

She thought about the endless cycle of killing between Jews and Moslems and wondered why, if there really was a God, he didn't let people live in peace.

She studied the large cross in the front of the church, and thought about the bitter religious wars in France between Catholics and Protestants, their cycle of murder and destruction that lasted over centuries, and in some places, like Northern Ireland, had never ended.

She thought a great deal about Abba that hour. How he must have looked for her in vain those final hours of his life.

"And vengeance shall be mine," she muttered to herself, pretending that she was praying.

Back on the street, Dan positioned himself behind a grotesquely heavy American woman whose portrait was being painted. He was partially hidden by the woman. He could see across the street and yet he felt shielded.

At precisely five o'clock, a black Mercedes pulled up. The license plates matched the number Leora had given him. A solitary figure was in the car behind the wheel. He was blond. Could be the German, Dan thought.

Within a minute, another figure walked up the street and got into the front of the car. Number two, Japanese, Dan said softly to himself. Three pedestrians passed on the sidewalk. French students. Dan waited.

The heavy American woman suddenly stood up, partially blocking Dan's view. Her portrait was completed. Just then another car, a blue Renault, stopped and let off two passengers. They quickly got into the Mercedes. They definitely looked like Arabs to Dan. He knew Cherev's face from pictures. But because of the American woman, he couldn't see the faces of the two men before they got in the car. Now all four men in the car were facing each other. He couldn't see any of their faces.

He was at the moment of decision. Was he certain enough that it was Cherev? The whole thing fit precisely what Leora had heard on the tape. Yes, it must be, he decided. He pressed the "send" button to signal her.

A minute later, he saw her come out of the church and walk across the sidewalk as if she were looking for a taxicab. She looked so convincing. She is one helluva good actress, Dan thought. None of the four men in the Mercedes looked up. They were too absorbed in their conversation. She placed the briefcase behind the car, practically under the rear bumper, near the gasoline tank.

Dan watched her walk calmly back into the church. He looked both ways. The street was quiet. He placed his hand on the detonator in his jacket pocket. His fingers were wet from perspiration. Quickly he pressed the button, and a tremendous explosion dwarfed all other Paris street sounds. A huge fireball shot upward as the car exploded, sending debris in all directions. Billowing black smoke followed the flames into the sky.

The heavy American woman shrieked as a piece of flying metal struck her leg. Other bystanders screamed with terror as limbs from the four men in the car hurled into the street. Then the yelling ceased. An eerie silence settled over the area. The policeman who had been on the corner raced to the car to examine the wreckage. As Dan left the restaurant, he saw a waitress, prostrate, crossing herself.

The explosion even shattered the inner calm of the church, sending religious ornaments flying everywhere. An old man on his knees prayed more fiercely. Leora quickly left the church through a side door.

The terrible silence lasted as Leora walked to the Anglo-American Steel Trading Company. When she entered the building, Dan was already there. He threw his arms around her.

"Thank God you're safe."

He squeezed her body close to his.

"That was one helluva command performance you gave walking out of that church."

She smiled softly.

Suddenly the silence was broken. They began hearing sirens one after another as ambulances and police cars proceeded to the scene of the explosion.

From behind the drawn curtains of an upstairs window, they watched policemen combing the area for clues as night began its descent upon Paris. Back and forth the policemen could be seen walking, looking everywhere.

Suddenly a familiar figure caught Leora's eye. He stood on the street corner a block away. She pointed him out to Yaacobi.

"Your old friend Jacques Barot. This really is the big time."

Barot walked down the street toward the Anglo-American Steel Trading Company. He had a furious look on his face. For an instant Dan was fearful that Barot knew about their hiding place and was coming to arrest them. What should they do?

While Dan was thinking, Leora had already decided.

She loaded her gun and took a position at the top of the stairs. Her skirt was pulled up to the top of her thighs. She was down on her knees leaning forward, the pistol poised in her right hand, her bottom thrust behind her, covered only by bikini pants.

One thought kept racing through her mind. Barot could have tipped her off in Cairo before the Egyptians had picked her up. All she had needed was a one-hour head start to escape the country. Political considerations be damned. If he came through that door, she intended to open up firing.

Dan read her mind. He knew that there was no way of stopping her. He watched Barot carefully as the Frenchman continued moving along the street.

Dan gave a great sigh of relief when Barot passed the building, giving it no more attention than any other one on the street.

"He's gone," Dan called to her in the hall. "So you can get up from that compromising position."

"Yes, sir," she replied, gleefully. "Are there any other orders?"

"Just one. It's too dangerous to go out there. We're staying the night. There are two bedrooms, and there's enough food to feed an army."

"There's just one problem, Commander," she said. "I never learned to cook worth a damn."

"Who was expecting you to cook? Don't you think that I've learned something living in France all these years? Go put on the radio. See what they're saying about our little explosion."

She stood in the doorway to the kitchen marveling at how he began assembling food from the refrigerator, examining cooking utensils, and going to work.

"Well, don't just stand there," he shouted. "I said go listen to the radio."

As she walked out of the room, he thought about calling Zippy to let her know he was okay. He decided against it. Chances were that Barot had bugged his phone at home.

"What did you hear about it?" he said when they sat down to dinner an hour later.

"It's very strange. I haven't heard a word."

"That's not surprising. It just means that the government censors have temporarily blacked it out until the government wants them to run it. Don't worry, they'll have it on before long."

She poured two glasses of wine and raised her own glass.

"Here's to cooperation between London and Paris."

"That was one of the best meals I've ever had in my life," she said to Dan when they finished dessert.

"The best I could do on short notice."

"Short notice, hell. When you came up here last night after my call, you stocked the refrigerator."

"Just planning for every contingency."

Her head felt light from the wine. She was completely relaxed. The tension from the afternoon was gone.

"Okay, we change jobs now," she said. "You go in the other room and listen to the radio. I'll clean up here."

"I thought that I was in charge," he said, pouring the last of the bottle of wine into his glass.

"Well, you aren't. Now take your glass and get into the other room."

As she washed the dishes, she began humming a tune to herself, an old tune from her childhood in Alexandria, something girls used to sing when they bounced a ball against the steps of an old stone wall. She could vaguely hear the sounds of the radio in the background.

Maybe it was the wine. Maybe it was being virtually locked up with the one man in life whom she truly felt some emotion for. But for the first time in almost twenty years she felt happy. Suddenly everything seemed so far away—

all of the hatred, the bitterness, their expulsion from Egypt, her torture in Cairo, even Abba's death. What is life really? she wondered—a few snatches of happiness along a route of monotony and suffering.

As she began putting back the dry dishes, she paused to look at herself in the reflection from the glass window.

She unbuttoned her silk blouse and looked carefully. The doctor had been right. All of the scars did fade with time. Only if you looked carefully could you see traces of the scar tissue from the burning coals. The human body heals over time. She had gained back all of the weight she had lost in prison, too. That emaciated look she had then was gone. Her breasts were now full and round.

As she stood in front of the window looking at her body, her blouse unbuttoned, she suddenly saw Dan's figure standing in the doorway. She turned around quickly, embarrassed that her privacy had been invaded. But when she took one look at him, all thoughts of herself vanished. He looked absolutely pale white, terrified, like a man who had just witnessed his own death. His eyes were frozen in their sockets. He just stared straight ahead.

"What is it, Dan?"

He just stood there silently.

"Well, tell me, what is it?"

"I just heard the news on the radio. We didn't get Cherev," he whispered hoarsely. "We didn't get him."

"What do you mean, we didn't get him?" she demanded. "The explosion blasted the bodies sky-high."

"You don't understand. They switched people on us. He wasn't in the car."

"Good God, man, you saw him get in before you signaled me."

He was silent.

"Well, didn't you?"

"I couldn't tell, Leora, I just couldn't tell. Someone

100

blocked my view, a fat American woman. I just couldn't tell."

"Then whom did we get? Did you recognize the names from the radio?"

"All four are low-level functionaries in their terrorist organizations."

"Oh, dammit!" she shouted, suddenly remembering the clicking noise she had heard on Dan's telephone. "They must have tapped your line and heard our call. Then they pulled all four biggies and set up the little toads."

"How could I have been so stupid?" he moaned. "I should have moved so the American didn't block my view. For Christ's sake, I know what he looks like. I should have made sure it was Cherev. What was I thinking about?"

"What about civilians?" she asked.

"Thank God, only three people wounded slightly. They were all treated at the hospital and have already been released. One of them was probably the fat American. I saw her get hit. The radio doesn't say who is suspected of setting off the explosion."

"They don't have to say. Everybody knows. Boy, oh boy, Motti will tee off on us."

He had a pained expression on his face.

"I sure fucked this one up, didn't I? Not making certain it was Cherev. I was stupid to go through with it like a damned mechanical robot."

He looked into her eyes beseechingly.

"I really blew this one, didn't I?"

She just stood there for a minute looking at this powerful man, beaten, humiliated by the defeat that he took so personally. She desperately tried to control her reaction. Her instinctive reaction was to agree with him that they had screwed it up, accepting some of the blame herself and scolding him for the rest. But what good would that do? The death and destruction could not be undone.

Suddenly personal feelings began to overcome everything else. She felt a powerful yearning to be a woman again, not merely an M-18 agent. There were things Dan needed from her, strength that had to be fortified; and there were her own feelings, her own hunger that had always been with her since that evening in Alexandria at Abdel Rasef's home.

She walked over and took his hand. Obediently, like a little boy, he followed her as she led him to the bedroom.

She sat down on the bed, her blouse still unbuttoned, and buried his face in her breasts, warm and soft. She stroked the back of his neck, reassuring him in a soothing tone that the error could not have been avoided. As Motti Elon had told her when she returned from prison, "Our work isn't that precise; you can never be sure."

As the minutes ticked away, he slowly began to overcome his humiliation and feeling of defeat. Gradually some of the life that he had earlier in the evening returned.

It was around midnight that they heard some noise in the street in the front of the building. He got up from the bed to walk to the living room and look out.

"Just some cats outside fighting over garbage," he called to her.

When he returned to the bedroom, she was standing in the center of the room, waiting for him. All of her clothes lay in a pile at her feet. She never gave him a chance to speak. She walked over and pulled off his clothes. Buttons and zippers gave way to her sure, determined hands.

As she led him to the bed, she knew that she was using her own strength to take advantage of his moment of weakness, maybe the only moment of vulnerability in his entire life. She didn't care. She was too consumed in her own passion.

"Let yourself go," she pleaded with him. "Let yourself go."

When he entered her, it was the greatest moment of joy

she had ever experienced. Feelings of strength and weakness, hate and bitterness dissolved in the tremendous force that exploded into her body.

She could feel by the heat of the sunlight on her face that it was morning. She lay on her stomach, afraid to open her eyes. She was fearful that the tremendous joy she still felt would be devastated by the guilt feelings that she thought he might have. To her great surprise, she didn't have to resolve this big dilemma. Before she even opened her eyes, he was kissing the back of her neck, rubbing her legs and thrusting his body on top of her.

He had returned to his normal, self-confident state. When they made love this time, he was in control, tender yet demanding. With Dan, it was different for her than it had been with any other man.

Fully satisfied, they got out of bed an hour later and stumbled into the kitchen. While the coffee was brewing, he turned on the radio. They listened to some music, waiting for the news. All that they heard about the explosion was a repeat of the bulletin from last evening.

She placed some brioches on a plate and poured two cups of coffee, looking at him, so serious, deep in thought, not even listening to the radio. She quickly turned it off.

"Where do we go from here, Dan?" she asked.

He was silent, not knowing how to answer.

"I mean you and I, Dan. Is it a beginning or a little diversion that resulted from the pressures of our business?"

"It's never happened to me before," he protested. "You're somehow different from any woman I've ever known."

"Score three points for me," she quipped.

"I wish that I had met you twenty years ago," he said, ignoring her wisecrack.

"And I wish that I had been an actress in London and that my father was still a businessman in Alexandria."

She drank her whole cup of hot coffee, wanting to feel the pain of the heat against her mouth. Then she refilled her cup.

"But you still haven't answered my question, Dan. Where do we go from here?"

"I just don't know, Leora. Honestly I don't. There are obligations and commitments. I need some time to sort it out in my own mind."

"Well, don't be too damn honest about it, or I know what the answer will be."

They finished breakfast in silence.

Afterward he walked over to the window and surveyed the street carefully. Everything looked normal.

"Do you want to go back to London this morning?" he asked.

"It's not where I want to go, it's where I'd better go. If I'm not back in London soon, my absence, coinciding with the explosion, will look mighty funny."

"Getting out of the country won't be easy. Barot will be looking for our people."

"I'll have to take my chances."

He thought about it for a minute.

"I can get you out. We'll leave separately. You go first, walk about four blocks to the left, away from the scene of the explosion. You'll see a cab stand. Take a cab to the Place Vendôme and wait in the Hotel Ritz lobby. I will arrange to have one of our people pick you up and drive you to the Belgian border. At one of the border points there's a friendly guard, a holdover from the old days of our alliance with France. He says to hell with this business of courting the Arabs, and he lets our people cross. On the other side, they're sympathetic. They won't ask any questions. As for England, it will be weeks before the French even send the details there."

"What will you do?" she asked.

"I'll wait until you leave. Then about ten minutes later,

I'll go. I'd better beat it back to the office. Barot will probably be looking for me."

"What will you tell him?"

"I'll just wink and tell him that a night out of my own bed is one of the bad habits I've picked up in France. But any Frenchman would be proud of my performance."

She snatched a brioche from the table and fired it at him. It struck his naked chest, bounced off, and fell to the ground.

CHAPTER 11

When Leora returned to London, she found a different atmosphere at the embassy. During her years in London, she had always been accepted on a personal basis as a member of the embassy staff, even though it was well known that her activities were on behalf of Shai rather than the Ministry of Foreign Affairs.

All that changed when she returned to London. There was a coldness, an indifference to her that she could easily sense on the part of everyone in the embassy, including secretaries. She was ostracized, treated like an outcast.

Puzzled, she took aside Yoel, the cultural attaché and one of her closest friends.

"What is this nonsense?" she demanded. "What's going on?"

"The ambassador's orders," he responded weakly.

"And you just follow them."

"This is his little empire. He's made it clear that he'll send home anyone who doesn't."

Her face turned red with anger. Furious, she pushed past the ambassador's secretary, forcing her way into his office.

"What the hell is this, Ariel?"

"Don't come in here shouting at me. It's my embassy."

"And you've told everyone to ignore me?"

"You're damn right I have. You're disobedient and insubordinate."

"I don't report to you."

"That's just it. I can't throw you out, but I can isolate you from my people."

"That's a great show of gratitude," she said sarcastically.

He walked over to the credenza and picked up a stack of diplomatic cables.

"Do you see these? Each one contains an official diplomatic protest we've had over the French explosion. Don't tell me you weren't involved. I've confirmed your early-morning Paris flight."

"You've no business checking up on me."

"No. I just have to deal with the diplomatic furor— clean up the mess you leave along the way."

"Nobody told you the job of an Israeli diplomat would be easy. Heaven help us if we start to believe that we will gain anything from the game that you call diplomacy."

He took a cigarette from a package on his desk, and lit it up without offering her one.

"I do owe you a debt of gratitude. Of the three bystanders wounded, none was British. One was American and two were French."

"Look, I regret that. Fortunately they were only superficial scratches. They're probably healed by now."

She sat silently, staring at him defiantly.

"This embassy is not big enough for both of us," he said. "I'm the ambassador. I have no intention of leaving."

She got up and stormed out of his office, cursing about the hypocrisy of diplomats.

Leora expected to hear from Dan shortly after her return to London. When a week went by and the great silence continued, she picked up the red telephone and dialed the number that connected her with his office at the Israeli Embassy in Paris.

A strange voice answered.

"Hello," she said, puzzled. "This is Leora. Whom am I talking to?"

"Moshe Rama, here."

She knew Moshe. He was an M-18 agent, a man younger than she and Dan.

"I want to speak with Dan Yaacobi."

"Dan's not here anymore. He was reassigned to Tel Aviv."

Her facial muscles tightened.

"Are you certain of that?"

"Absolutely. He left three days ago. I was sent to replace him."

"I see," she said softly.

"Can I do anything to help you?"

She never answered Moshe's question. She placed the red telephone slowly in its cradle and sat at her desk in silence, staring ahead.

She tried to persuade herself of possible explanations: that Motti had ordered him home, that Motti had told him not to communicate with her. But she was too much of a realist to believe any of these. Deep down she knew that he was running away from her, running away from an emotional involvement that he couldn't handle, unable to handle the guilt, afraid to cut loose from his obligations to Zipora, unwilling to fly in the face of the loyalty and duty that were the bedrock of his existence.

At first she was angry. Angry at him for not placing her above everything else. Angry at herself for not realizing that he would never come back. But she felt too much love for Dan, the sensation of pleasure was still too fresh in her mind to permit anger to settle in. Who was really the stronger or who was the weaker, she wondered.

Fifteen years earlier, it would have been different. But timing is always critical. The timing had been disastrous for her encounter with Dan as it had been for most other things in her life.

As the afternoon hours passed, no one heard a sound from her office. One of the secretaries became concerned and called a security officer at the embassy. He poked his head in, startled to see Leora sitting at her desk as if in a trance.

"Are you okay, Miss Elon?" he called.

"Very good, thank you," she replied automatically.

He closed the door and reported what he had seen to the secretary who had called him. That report set off a new round of rumors about Leora.

During the next several days, Leora's self-imposed discipline broke down for the first time since she had joined Shai. The letdown after Dan was simply too much for her to bear. She spent several days staring at the walls of her little office and wondering what she could have done differently.

Then she became restless, feeling that she was going stir-crazy. Finally she decided that she needed some change, something different. She picked up the phone to call Gramby's, one of the largest theater agents in London.

This time Leora watched *Antony and Cleopatra* carefully. She wanted to observe the little technical details, those nuances that only someone who knows the play and has had training in the theater can pick up. When you play a part, you always remember a great deal about the play.

She waited until the end of the last act before giving her note to one of the ushers. Then she left the theater quickly, taking a cab to the Hotel Carlton, to wait for him.

She took a table in the corner of the bar, ordered a

Pimms cup, and waited. A German businessman approached her table and asked, *"Ist dieser Platz frei?"* obviously trying to pick her up.

She answered, "No, this seat isn't free. Shove off, Karl."

Ten minutes later, Philip walked through the door. As soon as he saw her, he raced over to the table, squeezed both hands and kissed her once on each cheek.

"Well, I'll be damned," he said, sounding far more American than British, "I wasn't dreaming. I did get that note after all."

She studied him carefully. The American way of life had aged him cruelly. His hair, which she remembered as thick and wavy, was thinning on top and graying on the sides. His lean shape was pushed out in the middle. Too many of those big steak dinners, she decided. His skin was leathery, weather-beaten from the Southern California sun. Despite all that, she had no second thoughts. She had made up her mind. Philip was what she needed now.

"I happened to be at *Antony and Cleopatra* tonight, and as I was looking through the program I saw your name as the director. What a surprise."

"Well, I'll be damned," he repeated.

A waiter approached. Ignoring Leora's drink, Philip said, "Bring us a bottle of good French champagne."

Then he turned to her.

"What are you doing in London?"

"Oh, just visiting for a while," she said, lying easily. "How about you? Are you just here for the show?"

"No. I decided to come home," he replied. "I've left the wife and kids behind for good."

"I'm sorry to hear that."

"Oh, hell, don't be sorry. I've been heading that way for a while. Anyhow, their loss may be your gain." He laughed easily.

The waiter brought over the champagne, opened it and poured two glasses.

"Here's to old times," he said. "And I mean *old times*."

She sipped her drink slowly. She was suddenly very glad that she had never married Philip.

"You know, I was pretty sore at you when I got that card," he said. "Not even a return address."

"Things were difficult then, Philip. Very difficult."

Sipping champagne, they reminisced about their life in London when they were at the university together.

"Let's go get something to eat," Philip said. "I know a good beef place not far from here."

"That sounds like a good idea."

Over dinner he told her about his life in the United States and about making movies and television shows, and about Broadway.

"You've never been in the United States?" he asked incredulously, as if she were the only person alive who had never been there.

"Never been there."

"A pity. Everybody should do it once."

As the waiter cleared the dessert dishes and poured coffee, he looked at her very seriously.

"Will you come home with me tonight, Leora? I've thought about you a lot over the years."

She studied the lines in his face. Did she show up at the right time for him? Was he panicked by the sudden loneliness, she wondered, or did he still feel something for her?

"Aren't you rushing things a little?"

"I'm afraid I've picked up some bad habits over in the States. Americans believe in 'slam bam, thank you, ma'am.' "

They both started to laugh. Then it was her turn to be serious.

"There is one condition, Philip."

"I can look, but I can't touch."

"No, I'm serious."

He stopped smiling.

"I will go home with you, and we will see each other from time to time. But you will never ask me what I do or where I go when I'm not with you. You won't press me about the years since you last saw me. And you'll accept the fact that one day I may simply leave and you may never hear from me again. Now, can you accept all of that?"

Philip was shaken by her words. The color drained from his face.

"What are you? A damn spy for the Russians?" he said hoarsely.

"Can you live with it or not?" she shot back.

He could tell she was serious.

"Yes, of course, I can live with it. I'll swear to it if you want me to. I could live with anything to spend time with you again. I would cut off my right arm, for Christ's sake."

"That better be all you cut off, or we're in trouble," she said smiling.

He started to laugh.

"Well, I'll be damned. You've developed a better sense of humor over the years."

As she walked out of the restaurant, she thought about Motti. She knew that Motti would never approve of what she was doing. "He's a public figure," Motti would say. "There's too much of a security risk. You're taking a chance. You know that the Arabs have a price on your head."

Motti Elon be damned, she decided. It's time I started deciding for Leora Baruch, or Leora Elon, whoever I am.

For the next two weeks, she spent nearly every evening with Philip. They met after the play finished, tried a different restaurant for dinner, and ended up at his suite at the Dorchester. Early in the mornings she went back to her flat, showered, changed clothes, and went to the office.

For Leora it was like a vacation, a badly needed respite from her long years of sole devotion to a single task.

Philip was true to his word. He never pressed her about her work during the day or what she had done during those long years.

Even more than that, he realized that she couldn't be subjected to public exposure.

On those evenings when he had to attend a party related to the play or an important social engagement with someone in the business, he told her what his plans were, invited her to go if she wanted to, but always told her that he would understand if she declined. She always did so graciously.

By the end of the second week, she had no illusions that Philip could compare with Dan. He couldn't. But still, she enjoyed being with him. She enjoyed it enough that, much to her surprise, she actually began considering leaving Shai and moving in with Philip. His divorce would come through soon. They could get married.

She couldn't believe that she actually had these thoughts. But her relationship with Dan, the Paris explosion, the ambassador's conduct, had all combined to create self-doubts that she had never known before.

Then early one morning, when she returned from the Dorchester to her flat, in her long evening dress, she stopped abruptly in front of her door. The thin strip of tape that she always placed over the lock was missing. Someone had been tampering with the lock.

She pulled the gun from her purse silently. Then she placed her own key in the lock, turned it, and waited. Nothing happened. She waited another couple seconds. Then she picked up her long dress above her right knee and kicked the door hard. It opened quickly. She looked around the room, poised ready to fire.

"You wouldn't shoot an old man, would you?" the solitary figure called from inside.

"Motti, how in the hell did you get in?"

"Just because I've become director general of Shai doesn't mean I forgot how to pick a lock."

"You old devil. You've made coffee, too," she said, as the aroma floated to her nose.

"You keep some kind of hours," Motti said. "But then again, according to my watch, it's only midnight in New York, not a bad hour for a girl to come home if she's with an American."

If she had any doubt about Motti's words, his expression made it clear that he had found out about her and Philip.

"I hope that you didn't come all this way to lecture me about my personal conduct?"

"That would be a waste of plane fare. And as for the breach of security, why should I expect you to follow the rules that everyone else follows?"

She was hoping he would smile, but he didn't.

"Are you real angry with me, Father Confessor, or just angry?"

"I'm not worried about that now," he said. "We have other problems. Get out of that outfit and take a shower. I'll meet you in the kitchen. We'll talk over coffee."

"You may be aware of the political storm you and your friend Yaacobi started by your little explosion in Paris," Motti said slowly. "I could take the next twelve hours and tell you about all the grief you've caused me. The French have nearly severed diplomatic relations. Washington is madder than hell because an American citizen was wounded. And the Prime Minister twice threatened to terminate the M-18 program. Fortunately, I've been able to talk him out of it."

"I've heard about some of those things," she said, sipping her coffee.

"Well, there may be some you haven't heard about. The opposition party twice tried to call for a full parliamentary investigation of the whole mess. The Prime Minister has held firm, but it nearly toppled the government."

Motti was so decent, so sincere. She felt sorry for him.

"I should tell you, Leora, I've talked to Dan about it, but I have no intention of cross-examining you or Dan. What went wrong and why, as far as I'm concerned, is not important. You are two of my best people. You made the judgments under fire. If it didn't work, it didn't work. There's nothing we can do about it now."

She wanted him to repeat his words. They made her so happy. She was only sorry she couldn't have heard them weeks earlier, when she returned to London.

"But that's not the problem I came to see you about."

"That was the good news," she said, trying to force some levity.

"The bad news is that your friend Jacques Barot has done some effective intelligence work. He has assembled enough evidence of your involvement in the explosion to persuade the French Ministry of Justice to ask England to extradite you. They want you to stand trial for murder."

She gave a long low whistle.

"Those dirty bastards."

He sat in silence for a minute, making certain his words had sunk in.

"What will the British do? Will they turn me over?"

He got up from the table and paced around the room.

"They're behaving in a typically British way. They don't want to extradite you because of the obvious injustice. The four who were killed were involved in at least half a dozen murders each that Interpol has files on. You've done the civilized world a great favor by getting rid of them. I've been told that in a private conversation by the head of Scotland Yard." He paused to clear his throat.

"But?"

"On the other hand," he continued, "the British don't want to turn France down. The timing's bad. They're pushing hard just now on Common Market tariffs."

"So where do I fit into this little game?"

"The British have told the French that their request for extradition raises novel legal questions in light of your possible diplomatic immunity. They've told Paris that they want a couple of days to research the question. Meantime, they told us that we have forty-eight hours to get you out of the country quietly. They're prepared to look the other way if you go out through Heathrow under a false name. Then they'll tell Paris, 'Terribly sorry, she seems to have disappeared.'"

"What if I don't go?" she asked tensely, without telling Motti that she had actually thought about leaving Shai.

"Oh, they'll muddle around for a while, and we'll protest like crazy. But eventually, they'll ship you off to Paris."

She decided to broach the next subject carefully. Motti was no fool.

"What about Dan? Are they going after him too?"

Motti looked puzzled.

"He's back in Tel Aviv. I just assumed you knew. Oh, they've filed papers with us for extradition. But we've told them to shove off. We even supplied a fancy legal memorandum to justify our position."

She walked to the stove, picked up the coffeepot, and refilled their cups.

"Do you want a roll or something?" she asked.

"No, thank you."

She should have stopped there, she realized. But she had to know for sure.

"You were smart to pull him out of Paris quickly. Before they could grab him."

"I didn't pull him out."

"What do you mean?"

"He called me two days after your little explosion and asked me to bring him home as soon as possible. He had had enough of Europe."

"I see," she said softly, trying to restrain any emotion.

"You remember, Leora. I told you once that he was very devoted to his wife, Zipora, and that she preferred living in Israel."

She stood up and pounded her fist on the table.

"For Christ's sake, Motti, don't twist the knife."

He was unperturbed by her outburst.

"I tried to warn you, didn't I?"

"Yes, you sly old bastard. That you did. But it was still worth it."

"Was it?" he asked skeptically.

The sunlight was streaming through the windows. Motti looked outside.

"Come on, Leora," he said. "Let's go walk around that little park. You need some air."

"That's no park. That's Grosvenor Square."

"Well, whatever."

They walked in silence once around the perimeter of the square. The cool morning air felt good on her face. She was trying to weigh her options.

"What plans do you have for me after London?"

"I'd love to bring you home and make you deputy director in charge of the M-18 program."

"But you know that I wouldn't be stuck at headquarters."

"I didn't think so."

He picked up a small stone and tossed it against a tree.

"So I have formulated plan B. I want to put you into Scandinavia, not attached to any of our embassies, false passport and the works. Your headquarters would be Copenhagen, but your territory would include Oslo and Stockholm as well."

"What would I use for a cover?"

"You would go in as an Israeli journalist. We have a list of safe houses in those countries for you to work from. You'll have one contact at our embassy in Copenhagen if you really get into trouble."

"Why Scandinavia?" she asked, puzzled.

"We're getting reports of increased Arab terrorist concentrations there. They're taking advantage of the less severe controls on movement in those countries."

She was silent, hesitating. Motti led her over to a bench and they sat down together.

"I'll be very frank with you, Leora. Our estimate is that Copenhagen will be the hottest spot for Arab terrorist activity in the next couple of years, including your friend Cherev. By rights, I should order you home after that debacle in Paris, but I'm sending you into the eye of a storm because you're the best I have."

Motti's words made their intended impression. Suddenly she realized how ridiculous she had been to even think of leaving Shai and staying in London with Philip. Even apart from the problems raised by the extradition proceeding, the whole notion was preposterous.

Cherev had to be caught. He would have to be dealt with just as he had dealt with the passengers on the El Al plane from Paris to Tel Aviv, the Israeli athletes in Munich, the Greek children who happened to be in the TWA waiting area at Athens airport, who would be alive and in school if the Arabs hadn't decided to use international terrorism as an instrument of war.

No, Leora's respite was over. She was ready to return to the field.

"Make the arrangements for Copenhagen," she said to Motti. "I need a few minutes to pack."

"Good. Let's go back to your apartment. I can use the phone there."

As they got up from the bench, Motti took her by the arm.

"This assignment has been cleared with the Danish government at the highest level. Please don't embarrass me again."

*　*　*

Except for when he was on the telephone, Motti watched her carefully the whole time she packed her two suitcases.

"I'm not entitled to any privacy," she said.

"That's right."

"Well, do you mind if I make one call?"

"Yes, of course I mind. That's why I've been watching you."

"You don't own me."

"You would be foolish to call Philip. If it came out, it would embarrass the British. You'd better just leave."

"How did you know about him?"

"Ariel Levy has apparently taken an interest in monitoring your activities during the last few weeks. I think that he's concerned about your welfare."

She fumed at the thought of the ambassador checking up on her.

"Well, you could have just told me to break it off cold. You didn't have to stick with me until I was out of the country."

Motti laughed loudly.

"I learned long ago, Leora, that you pick and choose which orders you decide to follow. I've never quite had anyone in the agency as stubborn, as headstrong, and as defiant as you are."

"And you love me for it."

"Yes, sadly enough, I do."

"Why sadly?"

"Because one day it will destroy you."

~❧

CHAPTER 12

A remarkable place, Copenhagen, Leora decided. Having
spent two years with that city as her base, Leora had
formed a tremendous fondness for the Danish people. She
had always heard Israelis talk with great warmth about the
Danes. She had attributed it to the marvelous and heroic
actions that the Danes had taken during the war years to
save Jews from the onslaught of Hitler.

But having lived in Copenhagen, she knew that there
was more than wartime courage to admire. There was a
spirit of freedom in the air. You could feel it. You could
sense it.

Once she had stood at Elsinore along the water with a
Danish security man. He pointed soberly to Sweden across
the water.

"You think our freedom came easily?" he asked her.

"Does anyone's?"

"We fought with the Swedes for many, many years,
more than a hundred years. We thought it would never
end. Like your situation with Arabs."

"But yours ended."

He studied her thoughtfully.

"And yours will too one day. Mark my words."

She was unpersuaded.

"But in the meantime?"

He never bothered to answer her question. He didn't
have to. He knew very well what Leora had been doing
during those first two years in Copenhagen. She had become the repository for information about Arab terrorists
operating in Scandinavia or traveling through those countries. She shared her information with Western intelligence

agents operating in Scandinavia, particularly the Americans.

She made no effort to maintain the semblance of a social life, as she had in London before Paris with Dan. She found no enticement even in the sexual freedom of Copenhagen. She dreamed of Dan during long and melancholy Scandinavian winter nights, still remembering vividly how his strong body felt.

With her comprehensive, almost encyclopedic knowledge about Arab terrorists and their German and Japanese counterparts, she was able to tip off police on a dozen occasions as to possible terrorist attacks in Scandinavia, and elsewhere in Europe. Acting on the basis of Leora's information, the police were able to thwart many terrorist attacks that might otherwise have succeeded with terrifying and bloody consequences.

One of her major accomplishments had been in the area of airline security. She had established rigorous security procedures for SAS and El Al flights to and from Tel Aviv that became a model for Israeli airline security generally.

But none of this success satisfied Leora. For the big one always eluded her—Cherev. Several times he had been in Scandinavia briefly when she was there. But each time he managed to slip through the net she had fixed.

Then, early one damp and rainy morning in October, as Leora sat in her apartment sorting through intelligence messages, sipping the black coffee that she called breakfast, the sound of the telephone shattered the calm. She let it ring three times and then picked up slowly, only listening, not speaking.

"Moshe Rama here," she heard from a frantic voice.

"Where are you, Moshe?"

"The airport in Copenhagen. I followed the big one in on a Lufthansa plane from Paris."

"Cherev?"

"Yes, Cherev."

"And what happened?"

"I never got a shot, Leora," he said apologetically. "I planned to take him after we passed through customs, but he slipped away. Just vanished into the air."

Leora's brain was racing furiously. What day was it? Wednesday. She glanced at the wall clock. It was seven thirty. She thought about airplanes. Perhaps he was planning to blow up an airplane. She had memorized the schedule of every plane between Scandinavia and Israel. Suddenly she relaxed. There was nothing at all this morning between Copenhagen and Tel Aviv. At eight o'clock SAS flight 112 left Copenhagen for Tehran, but there had been a schedule change last week. Now that flight only stopped in Tel Aviv on Tuesday and Friday, and not Wednesday and Saturday.

"He may be just using Copenhagen as a stopover en route to somewhere else," she said tersely.

"What should I do, Leora?" Moshe asked, looking for direction.

"Cover as much of the airport as you can, run from one waiting area to another, looking at passengers. If you see him, you know what to do."

"The police . . . should I notify them?"

"No. Get going. I'll call. Then I'll come out. I'll find you. Don't worry."

Leora managed to dress and grab her pistol while she talked with airport security, relaying what Moshe had told her. She hung up the phone and was out of the door in a single motion. Today's the day, she thought to herself. Today's the day. I'll get the bastard.

Cherev met Khalid outside of the airport coffee shop. She had been quietly released from a London prison one month earlier because the new Foreign Secretary didn't want to risk further attacks against British citizens abroad.

121

She had spent the night in Copenhagen, traveling on an Iraqi passport, as was Cherev.

He began walking quickly along the corridor. She fell in beside him. She was carrying a standard SAS airline bag, loaded with two disassembled machine guns and six grenades. Inside the bag was a tiny sticker that said "Palace Hotel Gift Shop." Khalid hadn't seen it when she purchased the bag, or she would have taken it off. But then again, the attention she was giving this assignment was less than precise. She was overwhelmed by the thrill of working with Cherev again.

"What's the number of the flight to Tel Aviv?" Cherev asked in a hoarse whisper.

"SAS 112."

He glanced at the electronic screen on the wall.

"It says Tehran," he barked.

"It stops in Tel Aviv."

"You're sure?"

"I'm sure. They must leave off Tel Aviv for security reasons."

A sinister smile appeared on his face.

"Yes, that's probably right. They're afraid of us. If we continue, the cowards will even eliminate the stops in Tel Aviv."

Cherev and Khalid walked quickly toward the waiting lounge for SAS 112, next to the gate. Now they were approaching the security checkpoint with the metal detector. The waiting lounge was about fifty yards on the other side of the security checkpoint.

Cherev studied the corridor carefully. There were only two armed guards at the security point. There were lavatories just on this side of the checkpoint. It would be a piece of cake. He couldn't believe that it would be this easy. What he didn't know was that on the days SAS 112 went to Tel Aviv, security was six times greater.

"Shift the bag to my left hand," he whispered.

She quickly obeyed.

"Wait outside of the men's room while I go in."

It was still early morning. The men's room was deserted. Cherev went into a toilet stall, quickly opened the SAS bag and assembled the two machine guns. He stuffed the grenades into his pockets and left the SAS bag in the toilet stall.

Outside in the corridor he moved quickly, handing her one machine gun and then racing toward the security checkpoint. Neither one of the startled guards had a chance to remove his gun from its holster. Mechanically spraying machine-gun bullets, Cherev mowed them both down.

Now there was nothing blocking Cherev's path to the waiting lounge for SAS 112. With Khalid two steps behind, he rushed through the doorway into the waiting lounge.

"Death to the Zionists," he shouted in an insane frenzy, saliva running from his lips. "Death to the Jew bastards."

Later Cherev would learn that only two of the forty people in the lounge were Jewish. Most were Moslems from Iran. The rest were Christian businessmen from Europe.

Unaware of that fact, Cherev and Khalid began spraying machine-gun bullets at random in the lounge. Anguished shouts and cries of helpless terror filled the room. Blood splattered everywhere—on the floor, on the walls.

Then the sound of sirens filled the airport, which was converted into pandemonium.

As the sirens began, Cherev and Khalid jumped into an elevator that lowered baggage to the baggage room. The room was almost empty, deserted by the four regular baggage handlers who had raced for cover once they heard the sirens. Two men remained behind, dressed as baggage handlers. They quickly loaded Cherev and Khalid into two specially prepared trunks, each fitted with air holes and an oxygen supply. Each one was tagged "For delivery to the Palace Hotel, Copenhagen."

Leora and Moshe arrived at the waiting lounge ten minutes after it was over. They paused there long enough to inspect the grim ugly sight.

"No one knows how they got away," a security man said.

Leora and Moshe split up, racing frantically around the airport, looking for some trace of Cherev, but they found nothing.

All day long they searched the airport. They interviewed the few who hadn't been wounded over and over again. They learned that the terrorists had been one man and one woman, that the man's description met Cherev's, and that the terrorists had escaped through the elevator to the baggage area.

But that was all they learned. They combed the lounge again and again, but found no evidence that could help in the search.

They still have to be in Copenhagen, Leora decided. Danish security at every international transit point was tight. They couldn't have gotten out.

As the end of the afternoon approached, the wounded were all being treated at hospitals, the dead had been tagged and removed, and maintenance crews were cleaning the waiting lounge.

Leora sat in the waiting lounge smoking a cigarette, immersed in thought. Somewhere there had to be a clue, somewhere.

"We're finished," Moshe said grimly. "We don't have a damn thing. Let's go home."

"I won't give up," she replied. "I won't give up."

"Let's eat something. Take a break. Maybe we'll get an idea."

"We're not leaving until we find something."

They sat in silence for several minutes.

"At least I'm going to take a leak," Moshe said. She ignored him as he headed toward the men's room.

But a minute later he emerged shouting, "Leora, Leora, quick. I've got something."

He was waving a plastic SAS bag and racing toward her.

He was so excited he could hardly speak.

"It had to be theirs," he blurted out.

"How do you know?"

"Smell it."

She put her nose into the bag. Moshe was right. There were traces of an odor she associated with machine guns and grenades.

Then she saw the tiny sticker inside the bag: "Palace Hotel Gift Shop."

She never even bothered to show it to Moshe.

"Let's go!" she barked. "It's our only chance."

Moshe fidgeted nervously in the car as she drove faster and faster, passing every car on the road.

"When we get to the hotel," he asked, "what do we do then—call the police?"

"Not this time."

"Why not?"

"This is our chance. They'll screw it up. They'll either lose him or take him alive. We need him dead."

Moshe didn't disagree with her conclusion.

"But even if you're right and they are holed up at the Palace, how can we get into their room without the police? The room clerk won't let us see his list. They're under an alias anyhow, and we can't barge into every room."

"We don't have to do that," she said slowly.

"What are we going to do then?" he asked, sounding puzzled.

"We use room service."

"Room service?"

She began driving faster.

"If our friends are there, they'll order lunch and dinner, right?"

"Right," he said, still not sure where she was headed.

"How many people order in two meals a day at the Palace Hotel, with all the restaurants in this town?"

"Aha, but how do we find out their room number?"

She looked mildly disgusted.

"For a man who travels as much as you do, Moshe, you show a surprising ignorance of what motivates room-service waiters."

"Money," he said.

"And plenty of it."

At the hotel she left Moshe in the lobby, and she casually walked into the kitchen, pretending to be in search of warm milk for her sick baby.

She found a friendly waiter, a helpful kindly grandfather type who brought her the milk.

"Can you do one other thing for me?" she said anxiously. "I'll feel better if I can get a doctor to look at the baby. There's one on our tour. He's on his honeymoon, an Arab doctor."

She took a large roll of bills from her pocket.

"Would you know what room they're in?"

"How could I know that?"

"Well, as I said, they're honeymooners, probably eating every meal in the room."

She winked at him, then handed him a roll of bills.

He blushed mildly.

"I guess I could find out for you who has had a couple meals in today," he said. "It is for your sick baby."

He walked to the other side of the kitchen, looked at a list, then returned a couple of minutes later.

"Your Arab doctor must be in room 160," he said.

"They've had lunch and dinner in. They must have slept through breakfast."

She thanked him, handed him some bills, and left the kitchen carrying the warm milk, which she deposited in the first trash can.

It was already dark outside when she returned to the lobby.

She and Moshe walked up the one flight of stairs in silence. The room was at the end of the corridor.

Twenty feet from the door, she stopped and pulled the pistol from her purse.

"Cover me, Moshe," she whispered.

As he pulled his gun, she was already walking down the hall. She tapped gently on the door of room 160.

"Who is it?" a voice asked in French, a voice that she recognized from tapes as unmistakably Cherev's.

"Room service," she answered, trying to disguise her own voice.

"Just a minute," came the reply.

She waited exactly thirty seconds for him to open the door. When nothing happened, she shot at the lock, blowing it off, and forced her way in, holding the gun tightly, ready to fire again.

She was in the living room of a massive suite. But it was empty. She raced toward the bedroom door and tried to push it open. It was locked from the inside. She shot the lock off the door as Moshe raced into the suite.

Then she saw it. A great feeling of disgust covered her face. The window in the bedroom was wide open. They had escaped. So close and still so far away. She rushed to the window and looked out. There they were—Cherev and Khalid—running across the square in front of the Palace Hotel, heading toward Tivoli Park.

She only paused for an instant. Then she was on the window ledge, jumping one story to the ground, and racing after them with Moshe two steps behind.

For the next half hour, Leora and Moshe pursued Cherev and Khalid through the amusement park, losing them, then picking them up, gaining ground, but never getting close enough to shoot without the risk of hitting innocent people.

Finally, Cherev and Khalid stopped near the moving carrousel, pretending that they thought they had eluded Leora and Moshe and that they were resting. In fact they had picked their spot to face their pursuers. They were each gripping a gun in their pocket.

The two Israelis were on the other side of the moving carrousel, one hundred and eighty degrees away, peering through the moving horses at their prey. It was relatively deserted where the Israelis were. The line for the ride was on the other side.

"One shot each is all we'll have," Leora whispered. "I'll go around to the right and get Cherev. You go the other way and get the woman."

"Let me take Cherev," Moshe pleaded.

She hesitated for a minute. He had no right to ask. The privilege should have been hers. Still, at Montmartre with Dan she had insisted on doing it her way, and look how that turned out.

Let him have it, she decided. He's younger, and a good shot. Let youth have it. His reflexes are probably better.

"Take him," she said, "I'll take the woman. Let's start around now. We'll both fire in five seconds exactly."

Slowly they began their separate movements around the carrousel, trying to conceal their weapons. After precisely five seconds they raised their arms in unison and fired. Her shot struck its mark, hitting Khalid in the heart before she could react. But not Moshe's.

Cherev had spotted the gun an instant before Moshe fired. It was that sixth sense he had. He dove for the ground, gripping his own gun and firing toward the gun he had seen.

Screams were heard all around the carrousel as a mad mob scene erupted with people running hysterically toward the exits. Cherev raced into the crowd, disappearing from sight. Leora wanted to pursue him, but she knew it was hopeless in the crowd. Besides, how could she leave Moshe? Cherev's bullet had struck him in the neck. He was bleeding profusely. She rested him on the ground next to their weapons and she shouted, "Doctor, doctor."

Fool, she cursed herself. You fool. You should have taken the shot yourself.

Finally a doctor came accompanied by two burly policemen. It was too late. Moshe was dead.

One of the policemen grabbed Leora tightly by the arms.

She began shouting about Cherev.

"Let me pursue him. Let me pursue him. He is the killer."

But the policemen ignored her words. One refused to loosen his grip on her arms. The other slapped handcuffs on her wrists.

An ambulance came for Moshe.

Then the policemen dragged Leora to their car. She was vanquished. She had neither the will nor the strength to resist.

CHAPTER 13

It was a magnificently clear day in Tel Aviv, with the sun's rays dancing off the Mediterranean, as Motti Elon walked slowly up the stairs in the front of the Danish Embassy. The director general of Shai wore a tired, haggard expression on his face. He had been up most of the night trying to placate opposition leaders in Parliament.

129

The role of a high-ranking civil servant in a democracy is hopeless, Motti thought. I was sixty-seven years old last week. I should have had the good sense to get out at sixty-five, like everybody else.

A secretary ushered him into a small reception area. Motti smoked two cigarettes in rapid succession, lit up a third, and walked over to a glass case that contained some porcelain figurines. He studied the blue-and-white figure of a parent and child reading a book. That Leora will be the death of me, Motti thought.

A secretary appeared in the doorway.

"Ambassador Hansen will see you now."

She led him down a long corridor into the ambassador's office, which occupied a full corner of the red brick building.

Motti walked forward to shake the hand that was extended to him.

"It's good to see you, Lars, even under these circumstances."

"I'm sorry to make you wait. I just now hung up with Copenhagen. They have clarified the facts and given me my instructions."

The secretary walked in and handed each of the men a cup of coffee. Motti lit up another cigarette.

"How bad was it at the airport, Lars?"

"Fourteen dead, twenty wounded, twelve of them seriously. I have confirmed that none of them were Israeli nationals."

"And nobody knows how the gunmen managed to escape from the airport?"

Hansen looked embarrassed. "No one knows, but they did. It was early in the morning. Security was lighter than usual. But no one knows."

There was a knock on the door. A young man, slight, with heavy thick glasses, and carrying a stack of books, entered.

130

"This is Anderson, the embassy's legal officer," Hansen said. "I asked him to join us. I trust that you won't mind."

Motti did mind. He had developed a rapport with Hansen over the years. The ambassador couldn't be as frank with a third party in the room. Besides, Motti had learned long ago that lawyers often complicate and obfuscate problems of international affairs.

Hansen said something in Danish to the lawyer. Motti couldn't understand it. He guessed that Hansen was simply bringing him up to date on what had been said.

"We have a real problem," Hansen said. "Your people didn't make any effort to go to the Danish police. Instead, they decided to battle it out with the Arabs on their own."

"How many of my people were involved?"

"Two that we know of. The man Moshe and the woman."

"Leora?"

"Yes, that one."

The lawyer turned the pages of one of his books, trying to read while he listened.

"There were two dead in Tivoli. Your man Moshe and the Arab woman. The other Arab escaped, and we arrested your woman."

Motti shuffled his feet on the hard wooden floor. Hansen's report was approximately the same as the one Motti had gotten late last night from the Israeli ambassador in Copenhagen.

"Where is she now?" Motti asked. "Our ambassador couldn't find out. No one would tell him."

Hansen looked embarrassed again.

"Yes, well," he stammered. "That was for her own protection. We're holding her at Frederiksberg Prison."

"I want her out today," Motti said emphatically. "How can we arrange it?"

Hansen looked at the lawyer.

"I'm afraid it's not that easy, Mr. Elon. Either she has

committed one murder on Danish soil or she is an accomplice. We won't know until after the ballistics reports are done."

Motti rose to his feet. A lock of gray hair on top of his head was standing up. He ignored the lawyer and directed his comments to Hansen.

"Now just a minute, Lars. She was in Copenhagen under a joint agreement, cleared at the highest levels. Your government was a partner to her activities."

"Some of them. We had no idea that she would open up and start firing guns in the center of Tivoli Park in the middle of the evening."

"For Christ's sake, you knew that she wasn't there for a chess tournament. And besides, don't forget the massacre of innocent civilians that those bastards carried out at the airport."

"We're aware of all that. International terrorism is an unfortunate problem for the Western democracies."

"Surely your government isn't going to put her on trial, is it? Your own people are too decent to tolerate that."

"No. Of course not. We wouldn't do that. We only want to hold her for a short period of time, about four weeks, until the whole thing drops off the front page of the newspapers. Then we will release her quietly, without any publicity."

Motti sat down and puffed on his cigarette, thinking about what Hansen was telling him.

"Where would you hold her?"

"Frederiksberg Prison, a special area reserved for white-collar criminals. She will be comfortable. Don't worry about that. It's not intended to be a punishment. Just something we have to do for political reasons. You understand that."

"Her safety worries me more. There's a price on her head."

"We will protect her well."

Motti was silent, weighing his options. His only real choice was to threaten to go public and embarrass the Danish government with their approval of Leora's work. He didn't want to do that. They had always been so friendly, so cooperative.

The lawyer blurted in.

"We have some legal authority under Danish law for this type of protective custody. We can hold her for four weeks, even if we don't intend to try her. It is perfectly legal. We can supply a memorandum if you want one, Mr. Elon."

Motti ignored the lawyer's words. He stood up again and walked over to Hansen's desk.

"We'll accept what you offered. But only four weeks, no more."

Motti shook hands with Hansen. As he started to leave, Hansen called to him at the door.

"There is one thing, Motti."

"What's that?"

"When we release her, we'll put her on a plane to Tel Aviv. We don't want her back on Danish soil again. Ever. Is that acceptable?"

"Acceptable," Motti said wearily.

As Motti left the building, the final words of the Danish ambassador kept repeating themselves over and over again in his mind. He had heard words like that before, long ago. Suddenly he remembered where.

Back in Poland, when he was a boy, maybe six years old, he and neighborhood kids used to sneak into the local candy store, wait until the old man who owned the shop was busy with a customer, and then quickly stuff their hands into a box of loose chocolate. Once the old man had caught them. As he chased them out into the street, those were his parting words: "I don't want you back in this shop. Ever."

The word "ever" had such a ring of finality that he had never forgotten it.

What did this have to do with Leora? Motti wondered,

surprised at the relationships that his mind was making. I'm just tired, he thought. I really should go home and go to bed.

His car was waiting for him in front of the building.

"Take me to the Knesset in Jerusalem," he said to the driver.

Motti knew that he couldn't possibly go home until he had fully briefed the Prime Minister and the Foreign Minister about Leora.

∾

CHAPTER 14

As Motti sat in the Prime Minister's office, he no longer felt tired. The tongue lashing he received for Leora causing "still another international incident" somehow aroused all of his senses.

Motti knew well from experience that when the Prime Minister was in a state like this you just let him rattle on, then bolt for the door as soon as he finished.

Motti waited on the edge of his chair, prepared to do just that. However, when the Prime Minister finished talking about Leora and the Danish debacle, he sensed that Motti was ready to leave.

"Not yet," the Prime Minister barked. "I have one other matter to take up with you."

Resigned to the fact that this day would never end, Motti leaned back in his chair, lit up a cigarette, and prepared to listen.

The Prime Minister walked over to a small table piled high with papers, snatched a cable from Washington off the top of the pile, and crossed the room bristling with rage. He dropped the piece of paper in Motti's lap.

Then, before Motti even had a chance to read it, the Prime Minister began talking again.

"It's a newspaper column in today's *Washington Tribune*, done by Harper Martin. It has the full list of every major weapon we asked the Americans to sell us. We were told that this list would never be made public."

Motti studied the wire with a worried look on his face. Publication of this list could be invaluable to Israel's neighbors. If they knew what the Israelis wanted to buy, they could guide their own purchases accordingly. Also, publication of the list would increase Congressional opposition to the sale.

"Still another breach of confidence," the Prime Minister shouted. "This isn't the first time. Almost every week someone in the American government releases our sensitive information to the press."

"Washington leaks like a sieve, generally," Motti replied for lack of anything better to say.

"We're going to find out who's responsible for these leaks," the Prime Minister said. "I've told Otzev in Washington to see the Secretary of State and demand a complete investigation. We're not going to let the Americans whitewash this one. I've told Otzev that whoever heads their investigation I want one of your best people from Shai right there in Washington following their investigation. This is top priority. Is that clear, Motti?"

"Very clear, Mr. Prime Minister."

∾

CHAPTER 15

Joshua Otzev, the Israeli ambassador, arrived at the State Department in Foggy Bottom looking wan and pale. He was a heavyset man with thick black hair and a ruddy complexion. With his two bodyguards, he rode up in the private elevator of the Secretary of State. Keith Waller, the Secretary of State, was waiting for him.

"What can I tell you?" Waller said coolly. "We deplore the disclosure. It is an unfortunate incident."

"You must do more than that, Keith. It places me in an untenable position. You tell me to share information, that our special relationship requires full and open disclosure. But for three months now everything we give you ends up in the press."

"It is unavoidable, Otzev. Truly, it is unavoidable. It is not just your information. It is the climate in Washington. We do everything in a fishbowl. I promise to impose more careful controls."

"You must do better than a promise, Keith. I am asking you to arrange an investigation, find out where the leaks are, and punish the wrongdoers."

Waller hesitated. He wasn't a foolish man. He knew that someone had been leaking the Israeli information. But he felt ambivalent about it. While never condoning the unauthorized disclosures, he was persuaded that they could be a valuable aid to policy. They could bring the Israelis to a more flexible position.

Still, he had been troubled by the most recent Harper Martin column. Publication of precise lists of weapons being requested went too far. He was fearful that Israeli-American relations could be strained too much, that the Americans would lose any leverage they had ever had in Jerusalem.

The deadly serious tone he saw on Otzev's face convinced Waller that he had to do something about it. He had to at least initiate an investigation. Punishing the wrongdoers, well, that was something else. He would have to wait to see who was involved.

"I share your concern," Waller said, putting a frown on his face.

"Then do something about it."

"I will do it. I will authorize an investigation."

The Israeli still wasn't satisfied.

"Under whose jurisdiction? The CIA or the FBI?"

"I would like to avoid bringing them in. They don't always solve a problem. Sometimes they make it more difficult."

"Then who will do it?"

"Our own Internal Security Office here at State."

"You mean Jonathan March?"

"Don't dismiss March. Very few people understand how effective March is."

And besides, Waller thought to himself, March had another advantage. He would report his results only to Waller. The Secretary and the Secretary alone could then decide what action to take.

"There is one other matter," Otzev said. "We want to have one of our people in close contact with March, to assist him, to follow what's happening."

The Secretary thought about it for a minute.

"If he keeps a low profile, and if you don't make any public statements about the investigation."

"That is acceptable."

A silence fell over the room as Otzev considered whether he should ask the question that was troubling him the most. Finally he blurted it out.

"What effect will these leaks have on the administration's decision to sell us weapons?"

Waller walked over to a credenza on the side of his office and poured some coffee into a china cup. He took it back to his desk and sat there for a moment, sipping quietly. Otzev studied the face of the Secretary carefully. As usual, it disclosed nothing.

"I could tell you that they will have no effect at all. But we both know better than that. In all candor, I must tell you that they make it more difficult. You know how things are in Washington."

Otzev understood the answer. He would wire back to Jerusalem that Motti should send the best man he had to work with March.

~

CHAPTER 16

Two days later Jonathan March sat at his desk trying to decide how to proceed with his investigation of the leaks of Israeli information pouring out of the American government.

Very few people at the State Department knew precisely what Jonathan March did. To most, he was an enigmatic, mysterious figure—the cripple who insisted on making his own way with a cane through the drab institutional-gray corridors of the Foggy Bottom building. Anyone who watched March pass immediately detected that he was skillfully moving with the combination of a good right leg, a cane, and an enormous amount of self-determination. His left leg was dead; it was carried by his body, not propelling him at all.

March occupied a corner office on the fourth floor. Access was severely restricted. "Division of Internal Security and Research," it said on the door. Those who had never worked with March's unit had little inkling of what that division did. His staff was small: a deputy, Ernest Clay, and a score of clerks, researchers, and field investigators. For the most part he operated solo, not sharing intimate details of his operations with any colleague. Those in the division ate alone in a private dining room on the fourth floor. They rarely mixed with others in the agency.

March had been there as long as anyone could remember. The computerized records in the division's personnel office showed that March had been employed at the State

Department in 1949. What they didn't show was that he had been a creation of Harry Truman's sound instincts for political survival. Truman was constantly fearful that the professionals in the State Department would subvert his moves in foreign policy.

General Hildering had found March in a DP camp in Germany in the American sector. He had been in a Russian intelligence unit when the Germans captured him. They treated him like a civilian and sent him to Bergen-Belsen. The Germans managed to destroy one of his legs, but not his sharp analytical mind, not his near-photographic memory, not his fluency in half a dozen European languages.

And so Truman installed this outsider in the heart of the State Department, an outsider so foreign to those clubby Ivy League grads from the old boys' schools that he would have to be respected, and feared as well. March quickly learned that there was a skeleton buried in nearly every closet at State. It was this knowledge that enabled him to survive each change of administration since Harry Truman left Washington.

After receiving Waller's instructions to undertake the investigation, March had made discreet inquiries at other governmental intelligence agencies in Washington—from the CIA and FBI down to lesser-known private intelligence armies that some congressional committees maintain. But nothing at all had emerged.

March outlined in his mind what he had to do. He had to list every person involved in America's Middle East policy, and then systematically investigate them one at a time. The task would be difficult and time-consuming. Those innocent of this deed would throw up countless obstacles to prevent disclosure of some other wrongdoing with which they were involved.

Then there was Waller's instruction that March should be in close contact with an Israeli. Though March usually preferred working alone, he was not unhappy with Waller's instruction. He had had extensive dealings with the Israeli intelligence service in the past. He had great respect for their people.

The director general of Shai carefully twirled the cable from Otzev in his hand. He walked over to the high windows of his office and looked out at the old city of Jerusalem. The windows were open. He took a deep breath of that unique air that surrounded Jerusalem.

Motti Elon loved October in the city. It was the most beautiful time of the year. A group of schoolchildren were playing ball on an empty lot across from his office. He could hear their joyful shouts through the window, some in Hebrew, some in Arabic. Thirty-two years in Jerusalem, and he couldn't remember an October that wasn't beautiful.

He pressed down on the intercom.

"Get me Dan Yaacobi," he said to his secretary.

A few minutes later she led the tall, muscular Yaacobi into the office.

Yaacobi noticed Motti standing at the window and smoking a cigarette. He settled his bulky frame into one of the battered wooden chairs that were scattered haphazardly through the office. Some said that the furniture was left over from the old British administration in Palestine. Dan expected no personal greeting from Motti. Discussions with the director were always confined to the business at hand.

"You are scheduled to leave Wednesday for Rome?" the director asked.

"Correct."

"How long do you expect to be there?"

"Uncertain. We have an Interpol report that Cherev was spotted at Fiumicino airport traveling under an Algerian passport. There's been no confirmation. It's worth a chance."

"Reuben can go."

Dan winced. Ever since Paris he had been desperately looking for a chance to hit Cherev. He thought about how close he and Leora had been to getting Cherev in Paris, how close Leora had come in Copenhagen. The blood of his colleagues had to be avenged. He was hoping that the end would come in Rome.

Dan was sorely disappointed. But he had no intention of questioning Motti's words. Since Motti had taken over as director general of Shai after the October 1973 war, he had rebuilt from the ground up, demanding a severe military discipline. "In this wonderful democracy of ours," Motti had told the whole agency after he took over, "everyone is an expert on everything. In every government agency each official questions and challenges the decisions made by his superior. We have ultimate democracy—chaos. We will not have it here."

Dan sat quietly waiting for Motti to tell him what new assignment had priority over his trip to Rome. But instead, the director walked across the room from the window to his desk and then, appearing to lose track of his trend of thought, in an almost stream-of-consciousness tone asked Dan, "Do you know Jonathan March?"

"Uncle's director of internal security at the State Department?"

"Yes."

"Three or four times our paths crossed in Eastern Europe in the sixties. Uncle was worried that one of its diplomats was passing information to the Bear. I was running our Vienna operation in the wake of Eichmann. From time to time we stumbled on something worthwhile to them and we passed it on."

Dan was anxious to learn why Motti was so interested in his relationship with March.

"What were your meetings with March like? Any personality conflict? Could you work with him?"

"Professional. We had a job to do. We did it."

Motti then slowly explained to Dan about the leaks of Israeli information that had been occurring in Washington, the Prime Minister's angry reaction, the investigation it produced, and finally March's telegram.

"I want you to go to Washington to follow March's investigation, to assist him if you can," Motti said slowly. "You may be there for a while, so take Zipora and your children with you. We'll give you a diplomatic cover. You're going as an assistant military attaché at the embassy. You'll have diplomatic immunity and the wonderfully inspiring duty of attending cocktail parties four times a week."

Dan wondered to himself what Zipora's reaction would be. She had turned down other chances to travel abroad with him in the last two years since they had returned from Paris. She always said she never wanted to leave the kibbutz again. Still, Motti wanted her to go, to provide the diplomatic cover. He would have to explain it carefully.

"Elizer at the Foreign Ministry is expecting you. He'll give you two days of indoctrination about the embassy organization. Wednesday you leave. You'll report through normal channels, saving the coded telephone for critical intelligence. Is that all in order?"

"In order," Dan replied, accepting his assignment like the good soldier he was.

Dan squirmed awkwardly in his chair.

"What's the news about Leora from Copenhagen?" he asked nervously.

"You were at the staff briefing yesterday, weren't you?" Motti replied sharply.

Dan nodded affirmatively.

"Then you heard what I said. Four weeks or so in a Danish prison. That's all I had to report to the others. What makes you think you're entitled to more information privately?"

142

Dan rose from his chair.

"When I brought you back from Paris," Motti continued, "I told you to forget it with her. Put that behind you. You've got Zipora. You've got two boys. Good God, Dan. I don't mind this agency being like a family—but up to a point."

Dan's face turned bright red.

"Enough. Enough," he said weakly. If he had known that his question about Leora would have led to a thrice-heard lecture, he would never have asked it. This was the only subject on which he had ever aroused Motti's wrath.

As Dan started to leave the room Motti stopped him.

"There is one other thing," the director said with a deadly serious look on his face. "I don't want you taking any weapons with you to Washington. Not even a knife. This is Washington, not Paris or Rome. I don't want a confrontation with the Americans over armed Israeli agents. If it gets to that point, let March call in their own police. Is that clear?"

Dan's hand reached into his pocket and touched the hard cold steel of the small .22 caliber pistol that was standard equipment for every agent of Shai in the field.

"Very clear," he said obediently.

⁓

CHAPTER 17

As Dan's plane flew over the Atlantic with Dan grim-faced and fully engrossed in thinking about the leaks of Israeli information, that same subject occupied two men who met in a small bugproof cubicle in the basement of the Syrian Embassy in Washington.

One of the two men was a Syrian, Major Husni. Though his title was simply "minister," he wore two different hats. There was his public and well-known role as a fully accredited and high-ranking diplomat, party-giver and party-goer—the man who Margarita Bremen, the Washington socialite, claimed was the best Arab between the sheets that she had ever known. Then there was his other role. He was the deputy director of President Assad's private military intelligence network, the most powerful of the three competing intelligence systems in Syria—temporarily stationed in Washington because Israeli intelligence was easier to obtain there than in Jerusalem.

To those who did not know him well, Husni seemed like a debonair sophisticated diplomat. In dress he alternated between his freshly laundered, heavily decorated khaki uniform and conservative American clothes, shopping at Brooks Brothers. He gave the impression of being a cultured gentleman, mixing French phrases he had learned at school in Paris with his heavily accented English.

But there was a brutal and cruel side to Husni that terrified even his colleagues. He had personally directed the so-called interrogation of Israeli pilots who had been shot down and captured during the 1973 war, using the sadistic methods that he had learned from the Russians on an educational mission in Moscow. It was Husni who had ordered these prisoners to be drugged, put into white hospital gowns, carried into hospitals and filmed there for worldwide television consumption. And, finally, it was Husni who, less than twelve hours after the television cameras left, ordered the execution of the prisoners and the mutilation of their bodies so that any future identification would be impossible.

The other man was Douglas Brett, the president of a Washington-based firm called the Douglas Foundation. Officially the firm's business was public relations. Unofficially it was available to discreetly perform, for the right price, a potpourri of tasks which foreign governments needed an American to do for them.

Well connected and well compensated for his services, Brett's face exuded self-confidence as he smiled. His hair

144

was jet-black, thick, and shiny—remarkable for fifty years. One eye was glass, the result of a football injury at the University of Texas. But the rest was genuine: the gray-silk pin-striped suit, the eighteen-carat-gold cufflinks, the polished Errol Flynn mustache and the six-foot-two-inch muscular physique that contained absolutely no fat—the result of monastic dedication to physical fitness.

"You did very well for me this month," Husni said. "More than the usual amount will be deposited in your Swiss bank account this month. There will be a generous bonus as well."

"For the Harper Martin article?"

"Precisely."

The major picked up a package of Turkish cigarettes from the table and lit one.

"May I ask you a question?" Brett said in his East Texas accent.

"Ask. I may not answer."

"Why did you want me to release the information I obtained on Israeli arms purchases to Harper Martin? Why weren't you content to just send it home without letting the Israelis know that you had it?"

Husni thought carefully for a moment about whether he should answer Brett's question. Finally he decided that the answer, even if Brett would be so foolish as to repeat it, could do Husni no harm.

"We have evidence that the coward Sadat is planning a new peace move, perhaps even a trip to Jerusalem. If that happens, Sadat will depend on Washington to push Israel in the peace negotiations. We want to cause a rift between Washington and Jerusalem. If we do that, the Israelis won't listen to the Americans, and the Sadat peace move will fail. It's that simple."

The pungent aromatic odor of the Turkish cigarette filled the small room.

"Now it is my turn to ask a question," Husni said. "How

have you been getting this information? The stuff you have been giving me the last several months and leaking to the press?"

Brett looked uneasy.

Husni immediately understood Brett's reluctance.

"I insist," he said firmly. "You need not worry about a disclosure by me. Where security is involved, I take no risks."

There was something in the way Husni said it that made Brett very uneasy.

"My assistant," Brett said slowly in his East Texas accent, "Michael Holt, obtains the information from an American official. They play tennis together."

"But *who*, Brett? *Who* is the official?"

Brett hesitated again.

Husni squeezed his right hand into a fist and pounded it firmly on the table. He stared harshly at Brett.

"Charles O. Pritchard," Brett said slowly. "The man called Charlie. The President's special assistant for Middle Eastern affairs."

Husni looked satisfied.

"You do very good work, Brett."

As Brett left Husni's office, he tried to guess how large a bonus would be placed in his Swiss bank account. He made a mental note to call Geneva on the first of the month.

Brett never knew why he wanted to accumulate so much money. He had been raised in upper-class comfort in Houston. Yet somewhere along the way he developed what Mary Ellen, his sister, who had her Ph.D. in psychology from Austin State Teachers College, used to call the biggest-oil-rig syndrome.

"Everybody in this land of ours wants to own the biggest oil rig," Mary Ellen used to say. "And, if you build one five hundred feet, someone down the road will build one to a thousand feet. They won't just top yours. They'll try to make it look puny in comparison."

Money wasn't all that mattered to Brett. If it were, he would never have moved to Washington one year earlier. He would have remained in New York, where he ran a lucrative advertising agency.

The new business in Washington offered other rewards for Brett in addition to money. He derived an orgiastic pleasure from manipulating people, controlling them like marionettes. Washington attracted Brett like a magnet. By manipulating people in Washington, he could shape events in the world.

As he crossed the street in front of the Syrian Embassy, Brett only had one concern: perhaps he had met his match in Major Husni.

~<

CHAPTER 18

Charles Pritchard, carrying a battered briefcase and a tennis racket, stopped to talk to one of the guards as he walked toward the west gate of the White House.

"It must be Wednesday night, Mr. Pritchard," the guard said. "You have that tennis racket."

Pritchard tried to ignore the guard's words. They made him very uncomfortable. They meant that his conduct already fit into a recognizable pattern.

Pritchard pressed the button on his digital watch, illuminating the red numbers on the face. It was already eight fifteen. He only had forty-five minutes to get to Bethesda. He should have left earlier. But when he labored in his office in the basement at 1600 Pennsylvania Avenue, he frequently lost track of time. Tonight was no exception. He had been busily formulating still another American proposal to break the logjam in negotiations and get Israel and her Arab neighbors to resume the Geneva Conference.

"It's already eight fifteen," Pritchard said. "Don't I seem like the absentminded professor?"

The guard just smiled politely. White House protocol required that questions like that go unanswered. And anyhow, like most other White House employees, the guard liked Charlie, one of the few professionals working in the executive mansion who wasn't impressed with his own importance, who would stop and say hello.

"Want me to call a cab for you?"

"No. Thanks, anyhow. I'll flag one down on the street," Charlie said, heading toward Pennsylvania Avenue with his eyes alert for taxicab lights.

The guard watched the tall figure with the battered brown briefcase walk along the driveway. He was every bit the forty-year-old university professor, rumpled suit, bushy sideburns that showed the need for a haircut, dandruff flaking on his shoulders, and always in need of a shoeshine.

"Give those two little girls a kiss for me," the guard called behind him.

Charlie smiled and waved his hand high over his head.

Everyone at the White House knew about those two little girls, and most of the city as well. Charlie had been involved in a bitter custody battle with Clarissa, their mother and his second wife.

It had been like a nightmare. His whole world had collapsed. Suddenly he was standing in the middle of a courtroom, the press snapping pictures furiously. "Mr. Pritchard is more fit to have custody," the judge had said, showing his disapproval of Clarissa's style of living. And after the judicial announcement, Clarissa was threatening vengeance in front of the media. On the way out of the courthouse, Charlie's lawyer whispered into his ear: "For God's sake keep clean, Charlie. Her fingers are like swords."

The courthouse had been like a carnival, and why not? It's not often that the responsible newspapers can run

148

stories like: "Presidential assistant testifies to sordid details of wife's life."

He had worried about keeping his job. After all, he was an obscure professor of international affairs from Stanford. Almost by accident he had become the candidate's Middle East specialist. When the candidate became the President, he was given the job of presidential assistant for Middle Eastern affairs.

"I want somebody who will keep a low profile and report directly to me on this issue," the President had said two days after his election. "I can't trust those bastards over at State; and the National Security Adviser is an expert in Soviet relations. He's a novice in the Middle East."

Charlie was flattered.

"The issue is an insider's game," the President said. "Only the experts know the nuances and shades of nuances. You'll be my expert. You've traveled there. You know the languages."

Charlie thought about correcting the record, about telling the President that he had only traveled in the Arab countries, that he knew only Arabic, no Hebrew. But he never had a chance. The President-elect was shaking his hand, pushing him out of the door.

Charlie's appointment went smoothly. He hadn't published enough for American Jewish groups to realize where his true sympathies rested. And there were very few people who knew for certain how much Charlie had the President's ear on Middle Eastern affairs.

Charlie had come to like the young President. Other men would have quickly fired a presidential aide who became involved in a public proceeding like a custody battle shortly after they took office. But he kept Charlie on.

"You're part of this team. We stick together," the President said. "We take care of our own."

When it was over, and Charlie prevailed, the President

149

had called him into the Oval Office and congratulated him.

"Okay, Pritchard. Now that that's over, get your ass in gear. There's work to be done."

There was a large presidential smile that went with that statement. But when they finished their discussion, there was a different, more serious presidential tone:

"Keep out of the papers, Charlie. More than one I can't take."

A taxi stopped. The driver rolled down the window. Charlie saw a woman in the back seat.

"Where you going, mister?" the driver asked.

"Bethesda."

"I'm going the other way." He rolled up the window and pulled away.

Charlie decided to cross Lafayette Park and walk over to the Hay-Adams. You can always get a cab there, he thought. He looked at his watch again.

As Charlie walked across the park, battered briefcase in hand, he wondered how he had made such a shambles of his personal life. At forty, he had already been through two unhappy marriages. His only communication with wife number one was the heavy alimony payments he made each month. That bastard of a lawyer had pushed him into a settlement that was unfit for man or beast. "Eggheads frequently get sucked in like that," a colleague at Stanford had said. And as for Clarissa, he heard from her about every two weeks, another poison-pen letter. Ah, but then there were the girls. Fran and Bea. The six-year-old had a clear notion of what the custody battle was about; the three-year-old understood very little.

Another taxi stopped.

"Bethesda. The Bethesda Indoor Tennis Club."

The driver unlocked the door.

This is the only town in America, Charlie thought, where

the taxi driver has to approve of your destination before he'll take you.

As they drove north on Connecticut Avenue, Charlie nervously reached for the papers he had tucked in the inside of his jacket pocket, right next to his heart. Would this information end up in the newspapers, too, he wondered?

Beads of perspiration appeared on his forehead. How in the hell did I ever manage to get into such a mess? he asked himself. But the question was rhetorical. He knew very well how it happened. He had one person to blame: himself.

It had started on an evening back in the summer, hot and muggy. He could still remember every detail—leaving the White House at nine thirty, riding home in a taxi to his large old wood-frame house in Cleveland Park.

He had slowly walked up the steps to the house across the street from his own.

Sally was sitting on the porch, rocking gently on the glider.

"You look battered and worn," she called.

"Only a little. Probably nothing like the mess you had." She started to smile.

"Look, Charlie, don't start thanking me again. I told you I'd be happy to keep them this week until you got home. I know your housekeeper will be back Friday. Anyhow, it's no big deal. I have to cook for my own two, and with George in Dallas, I don't have a damn thing to do."

Charlie started to blush. Her words were so suggestive. He looked at her stretched out on the glider, her red polyester slacks bulging slightly at places where there had been only straight lines ten years earlier. But still she was attractive. And it had been a long time for him without a woman.

"You're really a trouper," he replied casually, reserving his options.

"What are friends for?" She kissed him gently on the cheek. It was a harmless little kiss, not unlike ones that friends exchange when they get together for dinner.

"Did you eat, Charlie? I'll fix you some dinner."

No! No! No! He couldn't. Christ, not with Sally. They were neighbors. George was his friend. One more personal disaster wasn't what he needed.

Through the large picture window he saw Fran sitting on the floor in her little pink nightgown watching television with Bart, Sally's seven-year-old. How could he do it to them? Even in an age with no prevailing moral standards, each individual had to create standards for himself, had to draw lines, had to separate the tail from the dog.

"I ate already," he said quickly to conceal the lie.

He pushed past her into the house.

"Daddy, Daddy," Fran shouted, jumping into his arms.

Charlie glanced back at Sally. She looked disappointed, he thought. Or maybe he was only flattering himself.

"I'm tired. Daddy, take me home."

"We'll go up and get your sister. Be very quiet."

He carried the still sleeping Bea in his arms across the street. Fran trooped alongside, jabbering constantly.

"It's gunna rain, Daddy. It's gunna rain. Aunt Sally says it's gunna rain."

Charlie put the girls to bed and fixed himself a bologna sandwich and a bottle of Michelob. He wondered what Sally would have cooked for him. He looked at the telephone. It wasn't too late. He could still call her. Hell, no, he thought. He picked up his briefcase and headed for the study. I still have about three more hours of work to do tonight. He began with the Arab newspapers. Each evening he read a half dozen of those from different countries.

As he started reading the newspapers, his mind kept coming back to Sally. Why hadn't he called her? Was it really because of George or their friendship? Or was he afraid of another attachment, the emotional involvement?

Suddenly a bolt of lightning lit the darkened dining room. The roar of thunder quickly followed. He walked out on to the wooden front porch. It was raining hard. The lights were out in Sally's house. She must have gone to bed, he thought. He visualized her stretched out on top of the sheets, restless, unable to sleep, her body damp from the heat, her flesh soft, filled with desire for him. He interrupted his fantasy to watch the rain. It was coming down in heavy sheets. He stood there for several minutes. He walked upstairs and looked at the girls sleeping. Then he fixed a pot of coffee and went back to his Arab newspapers in the study.

The rain continued pounding the roof. There was another crescendo of thunder and then all the lights went out in the house. They came on a few minutes later.

Charlie resumed his reading. Suddenly he heard a frantic pounding on the front door.

He jumped up and raced to the door. Damn fool, he thought. They'll wake the girls.

"Who is it?" he called through the closed door.

"I need help," came the reply. It was a woman's voice. She stopped pounding.

Charlie walked back into the living room to the picture window. He wanted to get a look at the woman before he opened the door.

The first thing he noticed about her was her hair. It was white, pure white, albino white, white as the falling snow. And it was soaking wet and just lying on her head like a horse's mane. She was wearing a tan raincoat that was drenched. Beneath that white hair, she had a round face that looked tense and worried. There were tears in her eyes, or maybe they were raindrops. He couldn't tell. No one was with her.

Charlie slipped the chain off the door and opened it.

"Oh, thank you," she shouted from relief, as she stepped into the house. "Oh, thank you. Your house was the only one in the street with lights still on."

The water flowed off her hair and on to the floor. Her shoes were like sponges, full of water, that someone was squeezing. Her hands were shaking.

"Your telephone. Can I use your telephone?" she asked frantically.

"Yes. Yes, of course. What happened?"

"My damn car gave out up the street. Absolutely dead. The engine must have flooded."

As she spoke, her bright blue eyes expanded. There was red around the pupils. They were bloodshot.

"I've been working since eight o'clock this morning," she said defiantly. "I'm dead on my feet. Damn cars aren't worth a shit."

"Well, that's not so bad," Charlie replied in his usual nonchalant and unemotional tone. "I'll get you a towel. You can dry your head."

He raced upstairs to the bathroom.

"It's not so bad for you, buster," she shouted after him. "Your car didn't go out on you. You don't live way the hell over in Wheaton. And you're not standing here soaked, getting pneumonia."

As Charlie thought about it later, her voice wasn't gentle. It was harsh and rough. She sounded like someone who had a chip on her shoulder. It didn't fit very well with a woman looking for help.

He handed her a towel.

"My name is Charlie."

She took the towel, without responding, rubbed it vigorously around her head and then handed the towel back to him.

"I'm Helen," she replied tersely.

If she had a comb, she didn't use it.

Charlie pointed to a table at the end of the hall.

"There's the telephone. The directory is under the table."

"I need a garage near here. I mean an honest one. Not one of those thieves."

He looked in his wallet and found the card from a nearby Exxon station that a mechanic had once given him. He handed it to her.

"What about a taxi?" she asked. "Who can I call, mister?"

"It's Charlie."

"Okay, Charlie."

"You'll have to find that in the book."

She wandered down the hall without thanking him. Her wet feet made squeaky noises as she left little puddles on the floor.

A few minutes later he heard the phone slam down.

"That's some friend of yours at that Exxon," she shouted at him.

"What happened?"

"He told me to call in the morning."

"What about a taxi?"

"Oh, they'll send one, but they couldn't tell me how long."

She headed toward the door.

"Anyhow, thank you for nothing."

"Where are you going?"

"To wait for the cab." She opened the door. "Where do you think I'm going?"

"You can't wait outside."

"Why the hell not?"

"It's still pouring."

"Look, mister—"

"Charlie."

"I'm soaked to the bone. A little more water won't hurt. I'm a big girl."

Her hands started shaking again. Her face was flushed. She didn't look well, Charlie thought, but he was no doctor.

"You'll get sick."

"Don't mother me," she said curtly.

"Then I'll tell it to you like a big girl. You don't look good. You're a damn fool if you go back outside."

She was silent, hesitating.

"Just wait inside. When the cab comes, you'll hear it. My company isn't that bad."

Suddenly Fran appeared at the top of the stairs, carrying a blanket.

"Who is that, Daddy?" she called, sounding frightened. "Mummy. Is that Mummy?"

"No, it's a woman whose car has broken down."

The little girl walked down to the first landing on the stairs to get a good look at the woman. She wanted to be certain that her father was telling her the truth. She had learned early in life that parents often lie.

Satisfied, Fran went back upstairs.

Helen paid no attention to the little girl. She took her shoes off, and spilled the water outside the door.

"As long as you're going to wait, let me get you some dry clothes," Charlie said.

When he walked upstairs, she glanced around the living room. Then she pushed the door closed to keep out the water. It didn't slam.

He returned a few minutes later carrying an old faded pink housedress, one of the few things that Clarissa had left behind, a red Stanford sweater of his that buttoned in the front, and a pair of white tennis socks.

"The best I could do," he said apologetically, offering her the clothes. "You can change in the powder room."

"Why are you doing this?" she asked.

"Because I'm a do-gooder."

"A do-gooder," she repeated his words and started to laugh.

"Let me hang your coat up."

When she took it off, he saw for the first time that she was wearing a waitress's black-and-white uniform—white blouse with a short black jumper that fell above her knees. Her outfit had gotten wet through the coat. It pressed against her skin, outlining her large full breasts. She looked as if she could take care of herself.

"You work near here?" he asked.

"The Napoli on Wisconsin Avenue."

It was a small neighborhood restaurant. Charlie had passed it dozens of times, but never had gone in. He always wondered what it looked like inside.

She looked at the label on the faded housedress.

"Saks Fifth Avenue. Your wife has rich taste."

"Yeh," he said, neglecting to add that he had bought it for her. She had confined her own shopping to offbeat boutiques.

Helen returned a few minutes later in the dry clothes.

"Look, mister. I still don't know why in the hell you're doing this."

"You wouldn't believe me if I told you."

"Try me," she said defiantly.

"It's sad that people don't help each other more."

"Bullshit," she said. "Pure and utter rubbish."

"You want a drink?" he asked.

She was hesitating.

"Something to warm you. I'll mix it with tea."

She looked at him as if he were crazy.

"Hold the tea, Charlie. I'll take the drink—scotch if you have it."

He walked into the kitchen. On the way back to the living room, he passed the powder room with its open door. Her clothes were neatly hanging on the towel bar, her uniform, her stockings, and her underwear. He walked back into the living room carrying a bottle of Johnnie Walker Red, two glasses and a bucket of ice.

157

He poured the drinks and handed her one. She was sitting on the sofa. He sat down across from her. He watched her take a long sip from the drink.

"You really believe that human-kindness bullshit?" she asked.

"I'm not the only one."

"What is this, a religious movement you belong to?"

"It's not religious. It's decent. Why does it bother you?"

"I just don't believe it," she said. "I grew up in the coal fields of West Virginia. My old man ran away when I was six and my mama drank like a fish. So don't tell me about it."

She talked for a while about her childhood. Charlie listened, trying to mention points of similarity from his own upbringing. He had very little to say. He had been born into a family that had been in San Francisco for a century, nothing wealthy, just some real estate. He had been passed from one prestigious educational establishment to another like a piece of furniture, or a painting. As she talked, the tone of her voice became gentler. She lifted her feet onto the coffee table.

Charlie heard a car outside. He got up and walked to the window, hoping it wasn't her cab. It was just a neighbor coming home.

While he was at the window, she poured herself another drink. She was starting to relax, he thought.

"Are you married?" he asked. As soon as he saw the look in her eyes, he knew it was the wrong question.

"Oh, yeh. I was married okay. For two months. I met him when he was in the Marines at Quantico. They shipped him over to Nam. I got two postcards from him and one telegram from the government. That was the end of my marriage."

A button snapped in the center of the dress. She was bigger than Clarissa. She wasn't wearing any underwear.

158

He tried to imagine what she looked like under the dress.

Suddenly he was filled with a great longing for this woman sitting on his sofa and drinking his scotch. She was a beautiful creature with her pure-white hair. And she wasn't Sally across the street or Martha at the office, who dripped with emotional involvements. She was a waitress at a neighborhood restaurant who happened to land in his house because of a rainstorm. She seemed to like him. He'd be a damn fool not to take advantage of it. It had been so long since he'd been with a woman.

He picked up the bottle of scotch, crossed the room and sat down next to her on the sofa. When he refilled her glass, he gently rubbed her arm. She picked up his hand and held it against her cheek.

"You're a funny man," she said.

She began rubbing the back of his neck where his long hair merged in confusion with the frayed collar of his shirt. That was all he needed, just a small signal. He leaned over awkwardly and began kissing her. She melted into his arms. Soon his hands were reaching under that faded pink house-dress, probing and exploring every part of her body.

"Upstairs," she whispered frantically. "Take me upstairs."

He raced quickly up the stairs, two at a time. I must be dreaming, he thought. This couldn't be happening to me. He looked back. She was following behind, racing up the stairs after him.

It was dark in the bedroom. He was undressing quickly. She tore off the pink dress and turned on the light.

"I want to see you," she whispered.

Then he pushed her onto the bed. He lay in her arms, burying his head in her breasts. He began kissing her again and again. Her head of white hair was moving from side to side. He leaned over her. It had been so long. He was ready to enter her. Suddenly the whole room exploded.

There were bright lights everywhere. There was one man

with a still camera snapping pictures one after another. There was another man with a movie camera that was spinning furiously.

He tried to get up from the bed to find a weapon, to strike out at them, to kill someone. Yes, to kill someone. All he had were his bare hands.

He raised his clenched fist. A furious vengeful cry filled with agony and hatred came from his lips.

Then something came crashing down on his head. His whole world became darkness.

The next thing he remembered was Fran leaning over him, screaming.

"Daddy. Daddy. Get up. I have school today. It's seven o'clock."

He staggered out of the bed and into the bathroom. His head was throbbing so badly that he couldn't stand. He sat down on the toilet, trying to take stock of what had happened. Slowly the events of last evening came back into focus.

It must be one of Clarissa's tricks, he thought, to get the girls back.

It wouldn't work. But why wouldn't it? he wondered. Suddenly he was very frightened.

The brown business-size envelope arrived at Charlie's office at two o'clock, right after lunch. He was sitting at his desk typing a draft of a speech for the President. He frequently typed himself, finding he could think better at the typewriter.

Martha, his secretary, carried the envelope into his office. Later she was able to remember that envelope very well. It was stamped "Personal/Confidential. To be opened only by Charles Pritchard." A heavy layer of Scotch tape supplemented the glue on the envelope.

"Thank you, Martha," he said tersely when she handed him the envelope.

"It must be important," she replied.

She quietly stood next to his desk, waiting for him to open it, curious as to what was that important. He quickly saw what she had in mind.

"Thank you, Martha," he repeated, making it clear with his eyes that he was dismissing her.

When the secretary left the room, he locked the door. Slowly he opened the envelope. It was just what he expected to find: a picture of him with Helen. His first reaction was embarrassment and shame. The picture was so explicit, so humiliating. Then there was anger and fury. The blood surged to his face. He reached back into the envelope, looking for the note from Clarissa. But there was no note. The envelope seemed empty. He poked around in the envelope some more. No, it wasn't empty. He found something—a ticket—a ticket for the Washington Diplomats soccer match that evening. "Washington versus New York, RFK Stadium, 8 P.M."

Now he was truly puzzled. Clarissa knew nothing about soccer. What could she have to do with this? And if it wasn't Clarissa, then who could it be?

Charlie broke out into a cold sweat. He thought of calling the police, but he quickly rejected that idea. There is no such thing as confidential information with the Washington Metropolitan Police department. Everything finds its way into the media. And if it wasn't Clarissa, and she found out, the result would be the same. He'd lose the girls. And if he made it into the media again, he could forget about his job.

He tucked the envelope and its contents carefully into his pocket. His face was now very pale. He moved over to the wastebasket thinking he would throw up, but nothing happened. His head began throbbing again from last night's blow.

No, he wouldn't call the police, Charlie decided. Whatever this was, he would have to deal with it himself.

* * *

161

He went to the soccer match that evening. It happened during the first part of the match, when he suddenly realized that he hadn't eaten all day. He felt hungry and lightheaded as he left his seat and headed toward the refreshment booths under the stands.

The game was still in progress, and it was deserted there. Charlie could hear the clicking of his own shoes on the concrete.

Suddenly he became conscious of the clicking of another pair of shoes. Someone was following him.

"Hey, mister, do you have change for a five?" the man called.

Charlie froze when he heard the voice. He had never heard it before. He couldn't even see the face, but he knew that this had to be the man. He just knew it.

Charlie clenched his fists until they were white at the knuckles. Then he wheeled around.

"I have change. What do you want?"

Pritchard studied the man carefully. He was tall and muscular. He had thick black hair and one glass eye.

"Say, aren't you Charlie Pritchard?" the man asked in an East Texas accent. "I've seen your picture somewhere."

Earlier in the day, Charlie had thought he would want to fight when he confronted his tormentor, tear the man to shreds with his bare fists. But now he had no strength. He felt nauseated.

"What do you want?" he repeated weakly, pitifully.

"Follow six steps behind me," the man ordered. "I'm walking to one of the parking lots to a black Fleetwood limousine. When I get in the car, you follow me inside. Is that clear?"

Charlie nodded weakly.

Following the man was more difficult than Charlie had imagined. The parking lots were only dimly lit because the game was still on. There was very little moonlight. The man moved quickly and gracefully among the rows of cars, knowing exactly where he was headed.

The black limousine was parked in the center of an ordinary row of cars. It almost looked innocuous among so many cars.

The man got in and opened the window that permitted communication with the driver.

"Take a short walk, Mario," he said to the driver.

Charlie wondered if the man was with the Mafia. Maybe it was all a mistake. Maybe he was just after Helen and not really interested in Charlie.

As Charlie sat down in the plush velvet seat, it occurred to him that he should have looked at the license plate. If he had the number, he could identify the man later. He didn't think of it earlier. He'd remember to look when he left the car.

"Who are you?" Charlie asked, trying to sound bold.

"It's not who I am. It's what I want."

"It was a crummy thing to do."

The man ignored the comment.

"Let's talk business, Charlie. I don't have time for foolishness. The girl's name is Helen Hart. She was once an aspiring actress. Now she's a high-priced hooker."

"You bastard. You dirty bastard," Charlie replied. His words came more from frustration than anger.

"She actually liked you. Felt sorry for you."

Charlie's jaw dropped as he listened. He was stuck, really stuck.

"How much will it cost me?" he asked feebly, hoping that the unlikely was possible, that money was the motive, and not Clarissa's vengeance. "I'm not a wealthy man."

"Money you're offering."

The man started to laugh. He took two cigars out of his pocket and offered one to Charlie.

"No. I don't smoke."

"Of course," the man replied. "I forgot how much I know about you."

The man lit up his cigar and opened the window.

"I don't want your money," the man said slowly. "I even want to help you financially, make it easier for you to pay those steep alimony payments to that first wife of yours."

Charlie was startled. He looked apprehensive and suspicious.

"I want to retain your services. I'll explain it simply and bluntly. I want you to provide me with information that you receive about the Israelis, what they are doing politically and militarily, what their plans are, and what they are telling the American government."

At first Charlie thought he would pass out. He was in such anguish. The man just sat there staring hollowly at him, letting the words sink in.

"Treason. You want me to commit treason?" Charlie mumbled as if he were talking to himself. "Treason."

"I wouldn't be that strong. As far as leaking confidential information is concerned, that's not such a big deal. It happens all the time in this town. As far as the other, well, your basic sympathies are with the Arabs anyhow. So it's just a small compromise."

"A small compromise?" Charlie repeated. Those were the words that one of his colleagues at Stanford had used when Charlie announced that he was taking the job in the White House. "Kiss integrity goodbye," his colleague had said. "You'll be forced to make one small compromise after another. That's what happens when a professor takes a job in the government." Charlie had bitterly disagreed, but deep down he knew his colleague was right. And he was prepared for those small compromises that men of intellect and principle are forced to make when they accept a high-level position with the government. But this was different. This wasn't the kind of small compromise that he had in mind.

"I won't do it," Charlie said forcefully. "I just won't do it. I have to live with myself."

The man blew a large cloud of smoke at Charlie's face. He looked angry, his eyes threatening.

"Don't play games, Charlie. I've already made four prints of each picture—one for the *Post,* one for the President, and one for Clarissa. I thought we'd give the fourth set to Fran, deliver it to her when she's in school. The movies we can show at the Plaza Theater. You don't have any choice, buddy."

Charlie was silent.

"I want to think about it," he said weakly.

"You've got the next ten minutes."

There was a long pause.

"Down home in Texas where I come from," the man continued, "we've got a good saying. If a woman knows she's going to get it, she might as well spread her legs and enjoy it. You're in the same boat, buddy. We can do it the easy way or the hard."

Deep down Charlie wanted to resist. He tried to lay out in his mind how the scenario would go if he said no and walked out of the car. But each scenario he envisioned was worse than the one before.

He leaned forward, resting his elbows on his knees and taking his head in his hands. The terrible injustice of it all overwhelmed him. He began to whimper. First muffled sobs. Then large tears.

"Do you want a drink?"

Charlie was silent.

The man opened the small bar that was built into the back of the car, poured a solid measure of scotch into a glass, and handed it to Charlie.

"Drink up, buddy. It'll do you good."

Charlie took a long slow sip. The scotch was rough on his empty stomach. It didn't help at all.

"How long would I have to do this?"

"One year. Then I'll give you back all the prints and negatives."

"How can I be sure you'll stick to it?"

"You can't. But what choice do you have?"

Charlie finished his drink. By now he couldn't even imagine the scenarios any longer.

"Okay, I'll play," he said with a tone of bitter resignation in his voice. "What choice do I have?"

"None at all," the man replied, smirking just a little over his victory.

"Let me turn to the mechanics, Charlie. Listen carefully."

He took a picture of another man, much younger, from his jacket pocket. "Take a good look at this picture. The man's name is Michael. He will be your contact. Each Wednesday evening at nine o'clock, you will play tennis against Michael at the Bethesda Indoor Tennis Club on Rockville Pike."

"How do you know I play tennis?"

"We know everything about you, Charlie."

The way he used the word "we" made Charlie shudder. There were powerful forces behind this man, Charlie thought.

"You and Michael will arrive each week with standard red-and-white Davis covers on your rackets. The information that you have for Michael will be in a brown business-size envelope, concealed in your racket cover. Any message he has for you will be in a brown envelope in his racket cover. When you arrive at the court, you will place your racket cover on a bench next to the court. He will do the same. After the match, you will take the racket cover he came with, and he will take yours. Is that clear?"

Charlie nodded his head. He was stunned. It was a way of communicating that would never arouse any suspicion. Practically everyone in the White House played tennis one evening a week, at an indoor court.

"As I said earlier, you will be paid for your services. Ten thousand dollars a month. It will cover your alimony payments for quite a few months. Give me your bank account number. Deposits will be made on the fifteenth of each month."

Charlie wanted to turn down the money. Somehow that made it worse. Blackmail was bad enough. Bribery was even worse.

He started to say no, but he began thinking of those alimony payments. Christ, he was already breaking every law in the books by going along with the man. Why not take the money? Charlie was rational. He wanted to find some way to rationalize what his instincts told him to do. But he couldn't. Then he stopped trying. He took the easy way out. He removed his wallet from his pocket and handed the man a blank check.

"You can get the number off here," he said in a hoarse whisper.

The man tucked the check in his pocket.

"You'll start next Wednesday," he said. "Court number five, at nine o'clock."

Then he unlocked the door and opened it.

"Go back to the game," he commanded. "Don't leave until it's over."

As Charlie walked in front of the car, he took a quick glance at the license plate, ready to commit it to memory. But again, he was one step too late. The license plate had been removed. Mario would put it back when Charlie was well out of sight.

Charlie didn't look around until he was almost at the end of the parking lot, near the tunnel leading to the stadium. Then he looked back cautiously. He saw a large black Fleetwood limousine heading toward the Benning Road exit of the parking lot. He couldn't see the man in the back seat of the car. But he imagined that the man had a broad smile on his face. He was right.

Even tonight, as he rode in the cab to the Bethesda Indoor Tennis Club, Charlie could still see the face of the

167

man with the one glass eye just as clearly as if the man were sitting next to him in the cab.

As Charlie Pritchard sat in the taxicab wiping the perspiration from his forehead, thousands of miles away, Motti Elon broke into a cold sweat. He tossed and turned in anguish in his bed in Jerusalem. He was dreaming about Leora tonight, as he did almost every night.

Each time the dream was the same. He was standing in the dock of a courtroom—on trial—pleading his cause. Leora was dressed in prison clothes, but she was the prosecutor, pointing a sharp finger at him. In the judge's chair was the vision of God that Motti had had back in Poland when he was a boy.

"You had no right," she was shouting, "you had no right to play God with people's lives."

"The charge?" the judge asked. "What is the charge?"

"Robbery, your Honor," she answered. "Separating us to rob us of our happiness."

"And is that all?"

"No. There is more. He tried to destroy our happiness. Destruction. Murder. The destruction of his own daughter's happiness."

"And the defendant? How does the defendant plead?"

"Not guilty, your Honor. The love was never there to destroy. Dan's primary love is for Zipora and their children."

Looking for understanding, Motti turned toward Leora. She continued pointing a finger, staring at him in harsh condemnation.

∾

CHAPTER 19

Michael Holt was waiting on the tennis court when Charlie got there. He was filled with fear and apprehension when he met Charlie, as he was every Wednesday evening. His eyes kept looking around the club, searching for the figure who would leap onto the court and seize him. He kept trying to formulate what he would say to the government agents as they took him away.

Then there was his peculiar, almost eerie relationship with Charlie. They never spoke to one another except for hello, goodbye, and the verbal exchanges related to the tennis game—love, out, game, etc. That was another one of Brett's instructions to Michael.

"Don't talk to him at all, Michael," Brett had admonished sternly. Michael resented the instruction. He knew what was behind it, a feeling on Brett's part that Michael was too weak, too susceptible, that he would end up befriending Charlie, even feeling sorry for him.

Brett's instruction had another strange consequence. It led Michael and Charlie to communicate with their eyes. There was Michael, who knew every detail of Charlie's life, sympathizing with the agony and anguish the man was going through. And there was Charlie, concerned mostly with his own plight, but occasionally his mind wandered, contemplating what this man Michael, who seemed typically middle-class, was really like, who he was, and what brought them together.

They were two prisoners, held captive by a more powerful force, the man Michael knew as Brett and Charlie knew as a mysterious nameless face with a glass eye in the black limousine. Like two puppets suspended on different ends of the same string, held tightly at the center, they roamed around the tennis court, serving, hitting baseline shots, and running to the net. Michael was the better player, but not by a great margin. Each had periodic lapses in concentration during the game, when the pressure of the real purpose of their silent meeting became overwhelming. Those more often than not decided the winner.

Michael realized that Brett had been quite right in silencing their verbal communication. Even without words, he began to feel an attachment for Charlie. He could see that Charlie had lost weight in the weeks that they had been playing, that there were large bags of flesh forming under his eyes, that his appearance was increasingly unkempt.

When the hour was over, Michael wanted to stop and say to him, "Don't let it eat you up, old man. We do what we have to." Or "How about joining Kate and me for dinner tonight? You look like you could use a good thick steak." But he had his orders. Instead, he gave Charlie a nod and a cursory "See you next week," as each picked up the racket cover the other had brought.

Charlie left the club immediately after the match, still wearing his sweaty tennis clothes as he did every week. Not Michael. He headed for the locker room and a long shower, to cleanse, to purify. Then with the brown envelope still carefully in the racket cover, he drove to Brett's Georgetown house and handed the sealed envelope to Brett. He watched Brett rip it open quickly, then read its contents silently.

"Very good," Brett mumbled from time to time, or "Very good indeed," as he read the document. Brett never shared the information with Michael at the time. Only later, when Brett had disclosed it to Husni and released it to a columnist, did Michael understand that their operation with Charlie was bearing fruit.

Brett would walk into Michael's office with a broad smile on his face. Then he would toss a newspaper article on Michael's desk with a headline such as "Israelis continue to resist American efforts to resume Geneva Conference" or "Internal Israeli memorandum shows no flexibility on West Bank." Brett waited for Michael to digest the essence of the article. Then he lit up. "Your tennis partner, my friend. Keep playing."

And so, on this Wednesday night, like the others, Brett didn't tell Michael what information he had collected from

170

Charlie. "The less you know, the better for all of us," he said tersely.

Brett finished reading the sheets Charlie had given to Michael. Then he dismissed Michael with a wave of his hand.

Michael left Brett's house, walking slowly to his car. A strong breeze whipped the trees in Georgetown. Michael began wondering about his relationship with Brett, wondering where the Douglas Foundation was headed, and wondering whether Brett would be able to control the forces he had set in motion. It wasn't chilly, but the wind made him shiver.

Driving home, Michael realized that he was destined to be Brett's assistant, Brett's lackey and patsy, for the rest of his life.

Twelve years earlier Michael had met Brett, back in New York, when Brett was in the advertising business there, before he started his Washington operation.

During his last year at Yale Michael became interested in advertising. One of his classmates with a father in the business said, "Go talk to Brett and Associates. Brett has just left a big agency with some good accounts. They're bound to be a fast growing operation."

So Michael went down to New York for an interview. The interviewer took him around to Brett's office "to meet the boss of this establishment," as he said. Brett was dictating to a secretary at the time. Two artists were standing by waiting for instructions.

"What the hell do we want with a Yalie?" Brett had snarled at the interviewer while Michael stood awkwardly near the door of Brett's massive office. "Tell him to go into museum curating. There's a great future there—lots of job security."

Two weeks after he started at the agency, Brett called for him.

"I want to see whether they taught you anything at Yale, or whether they filled your head with nonsense."

Brett liked the product, and Michael was launched on his career as "Brett's boy." He was on call twenty-four hours a day, but that didn't bother him. He was a bachelor without many friends in New York. Gradually he found that he lost his own drive and ambition, being dominated by Brett. His own personality and identity flattened out as he merged into Brett's identity.

When Brett moved to Washington, it was only natural that he move with Brett, holding his bags there as he had in New York.

But why was he like that, he wondered? Why was he so eager to take a subservient role, to follow Brett's commands, like a disciplined little boy?

Michael thought about his own childhood back in the Wooster Street area of New Haven. One word came to mind: poverty. The American dream had missed Michael's father in the years after World War II. And so his father hit the bottle for retribution. The more that he drank, the further he moved from the American dream, getting fired from one job after another. Through sheer hard work and a great deal of natural intelligence, Michael had pushed himself to the top of his high school class. He did this while working after school every day and weekends, always hustling something, snatching at odd jobs to provide his mother with grocery money. One force kept driving him: to get the hell out of Wooster Street.

He went through Yale on a scholarship and helped support his family. But when he reached his cherished dream: graduation from Old Eli, something was missing that characterized his classmates, who had never known Michael's poverty. They were eager to go out into the world and take risks to achieve wealth and power in every professional field. Not Michael. He desperately sought one thing: the security that would ensure that he never fell into the abyss of poverty. He was prepared to subordinate himself to anyone who would ensure that security. It happened to be Brett.

Michael took what Brett gave him. Even his wife, Kate, was a discard of Brett's.

No, dammit no, Michael thought. That wasn't right. To be sure, Brett had been married to Kate when Michael met her. But she was twenty years younger than Brett. She was a year younger than Michael. When Brett had found her she was a recent graduate of Smith reading slush at a large New York publishing house. Her marriage to Brett had satisfied her desire for the formalization of what Brett viewed as a harmless fleeting affair. There had been no love or other emotion. Kate had told Michael that often enough. After her divorce from Brett, it seemed only natural that Michael should see Kate once in a while just for friendship's sake. How was he to know that they would fall in love? It was awkward and embarrassing with him working for Brett, but it happened all the same.

Michael had feared Brett's reaction when he told him about his plans to marry the former Mrs. Brett.

"Well, you certainly have my blessing," Brett had said happily.

Michael stood there looking awkward.

"Well, what do I care?" Brett said. "She was the fourth Mrs. Douglas Brett. There may be four more after her."

There was something about the callous way that Brett had said those words that startled Michael, that made Michael think that Brett had changed during the years they had worked together. In the beginning, Michael found Brett an admirable figure—a hard-driving, successful advertising man, the head of his own agency, a giant in his field. But as the business grew, he became more ruthless, not content to be a service to his corporate clients, desperately wanting to exercise the power that they had. Then there had been the representation of a South

American dictatorship anxious to improve its image while selling its raw materials in the United States. That representation persuaded Brett to shift from New York advertising to the world of Washington "public relations." It was a natural for him. Foreign governments could be charged even larger fees than his corporate clients. And in the world of Washington, real power existed. People could be manipulated. Even the course of world events could be affected.

Michael shuddered when he thought of how ruthless Brett had become. Still, he followed blindly.

When Michael approached his house, he suddenly began trembling. Maybe someone was waiting for him, people from the CIA or even one of Major Husni's friends. But there was only Kate sitting at a desk in the study researching and writing her great American novel.

Michael quietly opened the door of the old brick Chevy Chase colonial, trying not to disturb Kate. But she continued working, pretending that she didn't hear him come in.

Only when he walked into the study and gently kissed her head did she acknowledge his presence.

"There's a chicken casserole in the oven," she said curtly. "I waited for you."

"You shouldn't have done that. It's close to midnight."

He sounded apologetic. She hated that tone, wishing he would stand up to her.

"Only the lower classes eat early," she replied, stinging him.

He bit his lip, but refused to take the bait.

"Then we must be really upper. Upper-upper."

Michael walked downstairs to the wine cellar.

"Did you say chicken?" he called halfway down the stairs.

"Yes, chicken," Kate shouted back, wondering what difference it made. He was still absorbed in his Wednesday-evening encounter, present in body but little else.

They were clearing away the dishes when Kate couldn't take any more of the small talk.

"You still won't tell me where you go on Wednesday evenings?"

Michael got a pained expression on his face.

"It's better that way. Really it is."

"At first I thought it was another woman. But then I realized how foolish that thought was. There's barely enough of you for me."

She paused for a moment, letting her words sink in. As far as she could tell, they had no effect. He was in his own world.

"No, it's not another woman. Whatever it is you're ashamed of it and your shame is keeping you silent."

Michael continued washing dishes.

"I would feel better telling you. Really I would. I just can't."

"Oh, bullshit," she said. "Who wants to know anyhow? It's just one of the games that little boys play."

There was a long pause.

"Michael Holt, super spy. Da-da," she said in a mocking tone, trying to imitate a movie advertisement.

Despite her sarcasm, Kate knew deep down that it was probably something serious.

She knew Brett very well. He played for high stakes and took chances. Someone could easily get hurt. Not Brett, because he had the instinct for survival. No, it would be Michael who would get hurt, and with him her and little Michael. Even trapped in a burning building, he wouldn't have the sense to leave until Brett told him he could go.

Still she loved Michael. Yet she was frustrated that she couldn't find a way to drag him away from Brett. It really didn't matter to her if Michael took a cut in pay or if they left Washington.

175

Kate heard the baby starting to cry upstairs. She turned furiously and raced up the steps, stamping her feet as she left the room.

She sat in the rocker holding the baby and trying to pull herself together. She was aggravated. She knew that Michael didn't have the guts to take any kind of risk. She realized that security was what he needed, somebody like Brett to make the decisions. At first that seemed hard for her to understand. She had grown up in middle-class comfort in Winnetka, outside of Chicago. Yet she was prepared to accept Michael even with his obsession for security. She loved him all the same—even more now than when they were first married.

But why did it have to be Brett? It wasn't the personal awkwardness of having her second husband employed by her first. She and Brett had never had any real emotional involvement. She had married him because of the glamorous life he promised. When that turned out to be illusory, he quickly gave her the divorce she wanted. No, it wasn't the personal awkwardness that frightened her now. It was the sinister and secret nature of what Michael was doing for Brett that terrified her.

She put the baby back in the crib and walked into the bathroom. She stood staring at the mirror, looking at her own reflection. She was attractive with perfect white teeth and long brown hair. She carefully watched what she ate, keeping her figure thin for her medium frame. Her breasts were small, her leg muscles fully developed from hours on the tennis court in college.

She decided to go to bed without Michael. Later, when he thought she was sleeping, he crept into the bedroom. She watched him in the darkened room as he climbed into his bed.

"What's happening to us, Michael?" she called across the chasm separating their beds. "Ever since we've come to Washington. He wants to break us. I know he wants to break us."

She was sobbing softly.

"It'll pass," he said, trying to sound reassuring.

He walked over to her bed, stretched out next to her, and began stroking her head.

"It'll pass," he repeated.

She was silent.

"Try to understand, Kate. This is a major project. Once it's finished, things will go back to the way they were. I promise."

"Why can't you tell me what you're doing? Why is it so mysterious?"

"It's just a large public-relations campaign for an Arab government. I can't tell you any more."

"Honor among thieves," she mumbled and buried her head under the pillow.

Suddenly, it struck her that there was something very pathetic about Michael, about his blind subservience to Brett. But how could she ever break it?

Michael returned to his bed, but he couldn't sleep. More stomach pains tonight. He swore to himself. I should forget about those cheeseburgers. Go out for a decent dinner or none at all.

Maybe I should see a doctor. It's been a week now on and off. Give it another, he decided. It's just tension. I'll find something at the drugstore in the morning.

❧

CHAPTER 20

The first couple of weeks in Washington were more difficult than Dan Yaacobi anticipated. Working with March was driving Dan into fits. There were also the personal problems of settling his family of farmers into one of the world's great urban areas, and the endless stream of boring dinners, cocktail parties, and receptions that Dan had to attend to maintain his cover. Then there was the guilt that he felt about Leora—about her being in prison in Denmark, about his irrepressible yearning for her.

March insisted on drawing up a list of all of the people involved in American Middle East policy. There were twelve in all who fell into March's "primary target area" —those with access to most of the administration's Middle East information. March insisted on systematically and exhaustively studying each one, proceeding in alphabetical order.

Dan admitted that there was a certain logic to it. It was the way the Russians did their intelligence work. But Dan didn't like it. He would have proceeded differently. He was a hunch player. By focusing on the specific information that had appeared in the press, and by finding out from Israeli Embassy officials to whom in the American government this information had been communicated, Dan made some instinctive guesses about the most likely candidates. Charles Pritchard was first on his list. He pleaded with March to focus on Pritchard immediately, but March refused to yield to the Israeli. He insisted on doing it his own way. "We'll get to Pritchard in turn," he calmly said.

Dan also urged March to go after Harper Martin— twenty-four-hour surveillance, phone taps, the whole thing.

"After the Nixon mess, we can't operate on the press anymore," March said. "Even if we know they're breaking the law."

In the beginning, Dan made repeated efforts to argue with March about methodology, but soon he gave up in frustration, realizing that they would do it March's way.

At first Dan thought that March was being pigheaded

and obtuse, and Dan was furious. But after the first weeks, he began to face the possibility that March was no longer the intelligence man that he had been ten or twenty years earlier. Natural processes of disintegration were at work. The old man was probably losing his grip. He had been left in his job too long. But who could ever ease him out?

Dan hinted obliquely to March one day that he might want to include Ernest Clay, March's deputy, more actively in the investigation, rather than limiting him to isolated menial assignments.

"He has a good mind," Dan said. "Willing to work hard. He seems discreet. What's the problem with him?"

"I should tell you it's none of your business," March said angrily.

"And you'd be right."

"He's Waller's tool. He owes his loyalty to the sixth floor."

Dan decided not to press the point.

So March moved on, exhaustively, doggedly, investigating each of the individuals on his list of twelve, one by one. March and Dan spent long hours together in March's office. The American treated the Israeli as a trusted confidant, reporting in detail on the course of his investigation and seeking confirmation or assistance as to the extent of contact between those being investigated and the Israeli government.

As the days passed and turned into weeks, March was having no success. Meantime, there were still disclosures in the press. They had reduced in volume, but that was only because the Israelis had drastically reduced the information they were giving to the Americans.

When Dan came home late at night, he was tired and frustrated. He wanted to complain to Zipora about how slowly March was moving, but he was too professional to talk about it at home. And anyhow, she had troubles of her own trying to operate in suburban Washington with fourth-grade English.

Still, she knew it wasn't going well and she told him that.

"What makes you so sure?" he asked in a matter-of-fact tone, neither confirming nor denying her conclusion.

"I can always tell from your behavior in bed."

He began laughing.

"Oh, come on, Zippy. Now you're becoming an amateur psychologist."

"Laugh if you want to. But I can tell."

"How?"

"Because when an investigation is going slow, your frustration turns to passion. You chase me around the bed all night."

"And when an investigation is going well?"

"You sleep contented like a little baby."

He walked over and put his arms around her, squeezing her close to his body.

Still laughing, he said, "Oh, Zippy, we had a very frustrating day today."

Then he began slowly unbuttoning her blouse.

"I hope that you never solve another one of your investigations," she whispered into his ear.

Later, when she was asleep, he lay in bed smoking and thinking about Leora. How were they treating her in prison? Had she changed? He hoped not. He could still remember how her body felt. Had he made the right decision when he asked to be sent back to Tel Aviv? He still wasn't sure.

He loved Zipora. And yet? Leora. Leora. She was always in his mind. He wanted her again. Yes, just one more time. But it wouldn't be only once. He would never be able to stop at that.

Zipora turned over in bed, reached out, and threw an arm around him. The guilt returned. Again the guilt.

* * *

Two days later Dan helped Zipora out of their old battered blue Volvo and walked hand in hand with her along Massachusetts Avenue.

"We really had to go to this reception tonight?" she asked.

"For the third time," Dan replied, sounding irritated, "Rafael Martino is the head of the South American Alliance, the most important single group as far as military procurement by South American countries is concerned. Every military attaché and assistant military attaché from the world's arms suppliers will be here tonight—all of them—the French, the Swedes—all of them. Anyhow, I may pick up something useful for my investigation."

She walked quietly next to him, locking her arm with his.

"Besides, his wife is supposed to be the best hostess in Washington. She gives a good party, so they say at the embassy. She has some reputation, a real beauty, that one."

"And that's why you wanted to come," she said, teasing him.

"Right on the fourth try."

Once they were inside the large gray mansion, Zipora and Dan went their separate ways. She found the wife of another Israeli diplomat and drifted off to the side of the room, talking in Hebrew about events in Israel.

Dan decided to walk around, keeping his ears open. It was a large party. At a reception of this type, with people standing and talking, while balancing a cocktail glass and a plate of hors d'oeuvres, it was easy to move up to the fringe of a small group, remain there and eavesdrop if the conversation seemed interesting, and if not, to move on to another group.

The first hour produced nothing useful for Dan. Almost all of the small groups were discussing the real possibility that President Sadat might visit Israel.

"Imagine an Egyptian President in Jerusalem," one diplomat said in Spanish.

"Inconceivable," another replied. "He'll never go. It's all bluff and gamesmanship."

"I wouldn't like to be that man's insurance carrier," another said.

Dan listened to two Americans and a German discussing Russia's efforts to become an arms supplier to South America. Then he drifted away from that group.

Suddenly he felt a sharp tugging on his sleeve. He heard someone greeting him in French. He turned around quickly.

"Well, well. Jacques Barot," he said.

"All of the world's intelligence men are now going into military sales," Barot said, talking French quickly. "What will be left of the intelligence business?"

"Hey, hey, not so fast," Dan said. "My French isn't that good anymore."

Barot repeated his words slowly, employing the tone that a parent uses with a small child.

Dan had forgotten how much he disliked Barot.

"It's too bad you left Paris so quickly," Barot said. "I had some wonderful plans for you and Leora. The two of you could have been our guests in a French prison— separate cells, of course. I tried to get the Danes to turn Leora over, but they're tough people to do that kind of business with."

Exerting all of his enormous willpower, Dan decided that the best response to that comment was no response at all.

"How long have you been in Washington?" Dan asked, changing the subject.

"Not long," Barot replied.

He was obviously no more eager to share information

about his mission than Dan was. The Israeli couldn't blame him for that.

"Have you met Madame Martino?" Barot asked.

Dan shook his head in the negative.

"You really should. A lovely woman. A true beauty. Pity you never take time to appreciate what life has to offer. You people are too grim and serious."

"And how is Mrs. Barot?" Dan asked coolly.

Barot looked unperturbed.

"Still carrying the honor of France," Dan asked, "from bed to bed with the tricolor sticking out of her ass?"

Dan turned and walked away from Barot, angry at himself for losing his temper. I'm not much of a diplomat, he thought.

Barot deliberately waited until Dan and his wife left the reception before leaving himself. He didn't want to encounter Dan at the door.

He looked at his watch. It was ten minutes since Dan had left. He walked up to the hostess, thanked her, kissed her once on each cheek. Then he disappeared outside. It was a magnificently clear night. He looked up into the sky. He could make out the big dipper, even Orion the hunter.

It was nearly eleven o'clock when Barot returned to his home.

"Monique," he shouted.

No one answered.

The bitch must still be out, he thought.

Barot walked into his study and carefully closed his door. He poured a glass of cognac. Then he took a telephone directory out of a file cabinet and began dialing quickly.

"Major Husni, please," he said to the housekeeper who answered.

"I'm very sorry, sir. He is not available," came the response in poor English.

Barot converted to French, speaking quickly. "It is essential that I locate him immediately. Tell him that it is Jacques Barot and a matter of great urgency."

"I really do not think—"

"You are not paid to think," Barot snapped. "Get Husni the message."

Humiliated and upset, the housekeeper walked upstairs and knocked softly on the bedroom door.

"Major Husni, a call of great urgency," she said meekly.

"Oh, God, not now," a woman shouted. "Tell her to go away."

"Who is it?" Husni called, pulling his body out from beneath her naked torso.

"Jacques Barot," came the reply. Husni started to laugh.

"Maybe he's looking for you, Monique," he said.

She was cursing under her breath.

Husni picked up the white telephone on the small table next to the bed, stretched out on his back resting his head on the pillow, and covered his body with a sheet. He tucked the receiver under his chin.

"No, you didn't disturb me, Jacques," Husni said.

Monique shot a furious look his way.

"I ran into your old friend and mine, Dan Yaacobi."

Husni quickly jumped out of the bed and stood on the floor next to the table.

"Dan Yaacobi," Husni said, repeating the name. There was a long pause.

"What's Yaacobi doing here?" Husni asked.

"Unable to find out. He has some post with the embassy, undoubtedly a cover."

For just a second, a feeling resembling fright raced through Husni's mind. No, the Israelis couldn't be on to the Brett operation. It wasn't possible. Still, that was the kind of assignment that Yaacobi would get.

Monique disappeared into the bathroom, muttering a steady stream of obscenities in French.

"If you hear any more, you'll keep me posted," Husni said.

"Be happy to."

Husni placed the telephone carefully in the cradle, pulled a Turkish cigarette from a gold case, and lit it up.

No sense being rash, he thought. Maybe there's another reason that brought Yaacobi to Washington. Still, this had to be important to the Israelis. He would have to be careful.

Monique emerged from the bathroom, fully dressed.

"So early you're leaving?" he asked.

"The mood has passed," she said furiously.

"Well, you can hardly blame me. You married the man."

"To hell with both of you," she said, slamming the bedroom door.

Husni drove quickly to his office at the embassy. Without even bothering to take off his coat, he barged into the telecommunications room.

"I want to send a cable to our embassy in Copenhagen," he shouted to the operator on duty.

He wrote out the message carefully: "Keep me advised of your location." His intelligence contact in Copenhagen was given clear instructions. The message was to be delivered personally to H-6, the man whom the Israelis called Cherev, the Sword.

❧

CHAPTER 21

Leora was probably the best prisoner the Danes ever had at Frederiksberg. She ate what they gave her. She refused to speak with anyone.

In her first three weeks in prison, she didn't have a single conversation. She didn't utter one word more than what was necessary for food and survival.

Every afternoon the warden brought a different person to talk to her, to make her confinement more pleasant. He brought young women, old women, young handsome men, old fatherly figures. Each one left muttering to himself something like, "She's too tough a nut to crack."

They begged her to let them relieve her loneliness. She refused, "Who needs you?"

They didn't understand that she wasn't lonely. She had her fury and her wrath. They boiled in her. They weren't aimed at her Danish jailers. She wasn't being punished. She realized that. The Danes were only doing what was required politically, and trying to make her comfortable.

No, her anger was directed elsewhere. It was directed at a world that permitted Cherev's organization to exist, that let cruel and fanatic governments bend the rules of civilized society to inflict enormous suffering and death. It was a world that refused to act to stop the bloodshed.

And some of her anger was aimed at dear Motti. She had persuaded herself that he could have gotten her out if he had tried. Instead, he chose to sacrifice her to court political good will. She was confident that it wasn't Motti's idea. But he went along with it all the same. Still more punishment for Paris.

If all Leora had were her anger, then it would not have been enough to alleviate the loneliness.

But she had something else. She had her dream. Her dream was that when she left prison she would capture Dan Yaacobi. She would seize him by the arm and pull him with her to the ends of their little country, to the farthest northern point. By day, he would teach her to be a farmer. And by night they would make love until the roosters began to crow, just as Dan had told her to do back in Abdel Rasef's house. And their lives would belong to only

186

them. Not to Motti, not to the state, not to Zipora. They would discard their obligations and seize time . . . oh, precious time.

For the two years since Paris, Leora had hoped that Dan would have the courage to leave Zipora, to come and get her. She was certain that the fire that burned in her burned in him as well.

But now she understood why he hadn't come. He wanted it as much as she did. But he didn't have the courage to take the first step. Yes, the courage. He was bound by a false sense of obligation.

Now she understood what she had to do. She had to come back to Israel and seize him by the hand.

Then he would come with her. Yes, she was certain that he would come with her. He would choose love over everything else.

Her dream would become their life.

~❧~

CHAPTER 22

Finally, on Thanksgiving Day, March was ready to start the investigation of Charles O. Pritchard.

March asked his secretary, Betsy, to bring him all the preliminary background information that the field investigators, whom March called the clerks, had gathered. March pored through these documents.

That was only the beginning. For the next several days March painstakingly gathered and assimilated more and more information about Pritchard. The objective was formidable—to know every detail of a man's forty years on earth.

There were copies of every speech, every paper, every article Pritchard had published, copies of transcripts from every school he had attended, transcripts from in-depth interviews of friends and associates in California. The profile was complete.

When the week was over, an exhausted March summoned Yaacobi to his office, to report in great detail about what he had learned.

When March finished his report, Dan could barely restrain his glee. Everything March had told him confirmed his original hunch. Pritchard *had* to be the one.

"For the first time we have something," Yaacobi said, his eyes sparkling now with excitement. "I feel it inside. A little voice tells me he's our man."

March looked skeptical.

"You think I'm wrong?" Dan asked.

"I haven't made up my mind yet. I don't get little voices. I have to be more analytical."

Yaacobi frowned. Creases appeared on his forehead.

"Okay, let's talk about what you have so far. On ideology, we know that the man has strong pro-Arab sentiments. No question about that. It drips from his papers."

They talked for a while about Pritchard's basic attitude on the Israeli-Arab conflict. Neither March nor Yaacobi could figure out the reason for his sympathies. The best they could do was tie them to New Left leanings that Pritchard had shown in the sixties.

"But the problem with ideology as a motive," said March, "is that the man just isn't enough of a zealot. And so if he was the one, ideology could make him comfortable with the role, but it couldn't be the motive."

"I agree with you on that," Dan said. "But let's look at the personal side of the man and other possible motives. It's those that make me think he's the one. Money. You told me that he's stuck with steep alimony on wife one. What did that professor at Stanford say? 'Eggheads always get sucked in.' What are his royalties on writing? Nothing. His old man had some dough from the turn-of-the-century

188

real estate that Charlie's grandfather bought. But by the time his father was finished dying three years ago, all Charlie ended up with was four thousand in hospital bills."

"And those were never paid."

"Not one cent. Not even the undertaker. You showed me a few minutes ago the report of the interview that Bruce Nabors, your West Coast man, had with Billy Burns, the undertaker in Palo Alto. The most Burns ever got was his out-of-pocket expenses for the casket. Pritchard still owes Burns for his fee. Burns has been billing him at the beginning of every month for the last three years."

"I thought that my man could have done a better job on those West Coast interviews," March said critically.

Yaacobi started to smile.

"You don't have confidence in anybody, do you? It's a little frustrating. You send out soldiers to gather isolated pieces of information, but you and I are the only two who know what you're doing in this investigation. It's none of my business, but I'll say it again. Maybe we should cut your deputy Clay in."

March grumbled something to himself about "Waller's boy." Then he emphatically told Yaacobi, "It is my responsibility. And one other thing: I don't want you reporting to Jerusalem until we have something concrete. It will get back and we'll be wiped out."

"Okay, okay," Dan said. "Let's move. Take sex," Dan continued. "What have you found there? Wife number two has been bad-mouthing Charlie's sexual prowess all around town. He lived in California, but he never played California games. His neighbor across the street—what's her name? Sally—has the hots for the guy, but can't turn him on. He's knotted up in frustrations."

Betsy knocked on the door and brought in a pitcher of hot coffee. Dan watched her refill the cups, her little nose turned up ever so slightly. Yes, Clay was right, Dan thought, in what he had once said to Dan at lunch. She had assumed some of March's prerogatives. Still, you couldn't hold that against her. Unless, of course, you were March's deputy like Clay.

And what about you, Leora, in Paris? Why did I let you talk me out of going into the church? If I had, everything would not have gone wrong. You wouldn't be in prison now. But would we have spent that night together? Or wouldn't we? Wouldn't it have happened sooner or later? Just as it will happen again, right or wrong.

When Betsy left the room, Dan lit up another cigarette.

"Take another motive. Is he being blackmailed? Look again at the transcript from the interview with Pritchard's secretary, Martha, you told me about. That brown envelope smells like blackmail to me. What else could it be?"

"You're obviously getting that from another little voice. I can't get it from the interview."

Dan ignored the comment.

"If half of what you're telling me is correct," March said, "we should tell Pritchard straight out that we suspect him, show him everything we have, and watch his reaction. Given what we know about his personality, if you are right, he'll go to pieces, disintegrate into a million tiny particles in front of our eyes. Do you agree?"

"Yes. That's precisely what he'll do."

"Then let's get him in here."

Dan thought about it for a minute.

"No, not yet," he said.

"Why not? What can we lose if we're wrong? Just some bad will for this office. I'm too old to care about that."

"I'm worried about what we'll lose if we are right," Dan said thoughtfully. "Pritchard is what you Americans call small fry. We have to find out who's behind him. We have to run the string all the way back. He may not even know. If we have him, we'll plug the leaks, but we'll never find out who was really behind it. Chances are they'll run for cover. They're more important to us than the leaks."

"What are you suggesting, then?" March asked, sounding puzzled.

"We've put a lot of hooks in the water around Pritchard. Let's leave them there for a while and see if we get a bite."

"In the meantime?"

"Why don't you move on to the next candidate to pass the time?"

March leaned back in his chair, closed his eyes and thought for a long time about what Dan had said. It was March's investigation. He alone could make the decision. And he had some real doubts about what Dan was saying.

"At least if we got Pritchard, we'd have something," he said, thinking aloud.

"Very little. Don't settle for that. It's not worth it. Really it's not. Would you have settled for the Cubans in Watergate?"

March thought about it some more. He finally decided to go along with Yaacobi.

One week later they landed a fish.

Betsy barged into the office as March reported to Yaacobi what he had learned about another candidate.

"Bruce Nabors on line two," Betsy said. "From Palo Alto."

March signaled to her to start the telephone recording apparatus.

"Yes, Bruce. What do you have for me?" March said anxiously.

"Remember Billy Burns, the undertaker in Palo Alto?"

"Very well," March replied.

"Burns called me today. Guess what he got in the mail? A check from Pritchard, payment in full."

March tried to disguise his glee. He didn't want Nabors to know how close they were on Pritchard.

"Did you make a photocopy of the check?"

"It's in my hand."

"Read me all the information on it."

Nabors quickly recited the name of the bank—Mar-Wash National Bank—and the account number.

"Put in on the telecopier to me this afternoon," March said.

Yaacobi could scarcely restrain himself when the call was over.

"Our friend has just received an infusion of new capital. Isn't that lovely. Maybe the President gave out Christmas bonuses early. Why don't you get hold of his bank statements, copies of all deposit slips, and then you'll be on your way."

"Take it slow," March said. "Getting those bank statements presents certain problems. Let me worry about that."

Dan realized that they had reached an area where March would have to work alone. He decided to break off their meeting, hoping that alone, March would move quickly. As soon as Dan left the office, March placed the call himself.

"Hiram, this is Jonathan March over at State. . . . Very well, thank you. . . . I would like to meet with you briefly. . . . Yes, this evening would be good. . . . No, I think that your house will be better. . . . I'll see you at nine."

Jonathan March was a man who carefully kept track of the IOUs he had collected in Washington during the last thirty years. It was only as a last resort that he ever cashed one of those. They were like money in the bank. Over time, they matured in value. You could never be sure when you needed one of them.

One of those IOUs had the name of Hiram T. Forrest, Federal Banking Commissioner, written on it.

Ten years earlier, Forrest, then a professor of finance at the University of Wisconsin, had been chosen as the President's designee for the post of under secretary of state for International Monetary Affairs. Because of Forrest's involvement with campus activists, he was painted various shades of pink and red in the confidential reports prepared by congressional staff investigators. March had been given a chance to review the reports before the committee chairman asked the President to withdraw the nomination—a move that would have destroyed Forrest.

March became convinced that the evidence against Forrest was being manipulated because of the man's views on international financial issues. He had persuaded the chairman to give him a month to prove what was really happening. It only took March sixteen days.

In his small wood-paneled den, Hiram spent several minutes rehashing those events from ten years ago. Then he poured two glasses of Amaretto.

March could hear the television blasting in the family room on the other side of the large brick rambler.

"You're one of a kind, Jonathan, you really are. What happens if you ever leave the government?"

March was silent. He never wanted to consider that prospect. Perhaps realizing the lack of tact in his statement, Hiram quickly changed the subject.

"You didn't come here this evening to reminisce, Jonathan. What can I do for you?"

"I will come right to the point. I need a favor. I have to see copies of the bank statements of an individual employed by the government in the executive branch. It may be critical to an investigation."

Forrest squirmed in his chair.

"What's the bank?"

"Mar-Wash."

There was a long pause.

"If you can't do it or if it makes you uncomfortable," Jonathan said, "please tell me that. I wouldn't want to compromise you. I'll find another way to get what I want."

Forrest knew that March meant it.

"I can do it, Jonathan," Forrest said. "I'll have a team of auditors go in to the bank first thing in the morning. We'll call it a surprise audit. All I need is the individual's name. They'll come out with copies of all of his statements for the last five years."

Forrest paused again, thinking about some other reports he had received about that bank from time to time.

"Who knows, they may even come out with something of interest to me. You never know with a surprise audit."

At noon the next day Betsy pushed her way into March's office.

"Our messenger just delivered the material that you were waiting for."

She handed March the envelope and walked back toward the door. He was tearing it open before it was even out of her hand. He spread all of the sheets out on the desk.

There was only one account, a checking account. It had been opened in January 1977, when Pritchard came to Washington. For the first five months, the account never had more than a four-hundred-dollar balance. Twice Pritchard had actually written overdrafts. Each time the bank had paid them as a courtesy to Pritchard in view of his position. Suddenly in June deposits of ten thousand were made into the account on the fifteenth of every month. Then large checks were written each month, to hospitals, real estate agents, finance companies and banks in California.

Undoubtedly to clear up old debts the professor had, March thought.

Then March pulled the deposit slips out of a small brown envelope. He could hardly believe his eyes.

"Pay dirt," he shouted aloud with glee, "pay dirt."

There were eleven ordinary white deposit slips from the beginning of each month covering Pritchard's paycheck from the government. But for the large deposits at the middle of each month since June, there were no deposit slips.

There was something different. Copies of six green-and-white interbank transfer acknowledgments. Each slip contained the name of the transferor bank—the Central Bank of Geneva, Switzerland. There was no identification of the account from which the funds had been drawn in Geneva, only the name of Pritchard's bank and his account number.

March picked up the phone and called Dan at the embassy.

"Get over here as soon as you can," March said. "That little voice inside of you may have been right after all."

Dan was there ten minutes later, enjoying this moment more than he could say.

"You still don't want to haul Pritchard in here?" March asked.

"Even less now. Let's go to the source."

This time March didn't argue. He now shared Dan's view that Pritchard was a little man caught up in something much bigger than himself.

March was on the intercom, telling Betsy to make him airplane reservations to Geneva.

"I'm going alone," he said to Yaacobi. "I'll report to you as soon as I get back."

Dan offered to go with March, arguing that he could be of help because of Israeli contacts. Dan also wanted to use the trip to Geneva as an excuse for a brief stopover in Copenhagen and a visit with Leora. But March quickly rejected Dan's offer.

"With the power of the American government behind me, I'll get what we want."

Three hours later March was on his way to Dulles Airport. Dan was in his office at the embassy checking messages. Betsy was holding the fort when Ernest Clay, March's deputy, barged into March's office.

"Where is he, Betsy?" he asked nervously.

She looked up from her typewriter, glanced at the intruder with bemusement and responded, "Gone to a meeting. Don't know when he'll return."

"The Secretary of State wants him right now for a status report on his investigation."

She ignored Clay and continued typing.

Clay began pacing in the outer office. He was a tall, serious-looking thirty-two-year-old whose thin face was dominated by a thick bushy light-brown beard streaked with gray here and there, and large round glasses with thin metal frames. He wore a conservative dark-blue suit with a vest. There was a thick gold chain across his vest that held a round gold pocket watch at one end—a gift from his grandfather—the founder of the Clay Investment Banking Firm in New York. When he peered over the top of his glasses to look at that watch, he had a bookish appearance, like a professor wondering how much time was left in a class he was conducting.

Clay had been a middle-level bureaucrat in the Criminal Division at the Justice Department, a graduate of Princeton and of Harvard Law School, seemingly preordained to spend a career as a bureaucrat when Waller hand picked him for the job of deputy to March two years earlier. No one was surprised that Waller had selected Clay. The two men came from the same WASPish New York background. What was startling was that March had agreed to accept Clay as his deputy. No one quite knew why. The consensus on March's staff was that the old man was willing to throw what he viewed as a harmless crumb in Waller's direction. He could use Clay to execute minor administrative tasks while freezing him out of information about the larger investigations. This wouldn't be difficult. March was accustomed to conducting major investigations on his own without sharing information with anyone else.

"Well, what should I tell Waller?" Clay asked.

"Tell him you don't know where Mr. March is."

He wasn't satisfied.

"But you know, don't you?"

She continued typing while she talked.

"Do you know what etymology is?" she said playfully. "It's the study of the origin of words. Now the word 'secretary' has its origins with the word 'secret.' That means, of course, that a secretary keeps a secret."

"We're part of the same team, remember?"

"Mr. March does not believe in sharing all of the information with his staff. You know that."

Now she assumed a haughty expression, turning up the little nose on her round face ever so slightly. She pushed back a few strands of light-brown hair that were falling into her eyes.

And why shouldn't she be just a little haughty? At forty-five, she was almost thirteen years older than Clay. And besides, she had been working for March for nearly twenty years. That gave her certain prerogatives over the steady stream of younger men who were attracted by the character of the Office of Internal Security, only to leave a few years later when they learned to their dissatisfaction that March insisted on running a one-man operation. Betsy was confident of her position. She was number two in the department—right behind March. Besides, she knew that March regarded Clay as owing his loyalty to Waller. March would not be disturbed by her rudeness to Clay.

"Waller will be very upset," Clay said, pulling a pipe out of his pocket and lighting it up.

"You'll have to talk to Mr. March about that."

"I know that I'll have to talk to him," Clay said, frustrated. "But I don't know where he is to talk to him."

"Then you'll just have to wait until he gets back."

"The passion for secrecy in this office is unbelievable."

"When you get to be the director, you can run it differently."

He stood in the center of the room, puffing furiously on his pipe, contemplating what response he could make. He knew that they regarded him as Waller's boy, but it wasn't right. He owed no allegiance to Waller. Clay didn't even like Waller. He regarded Waller with some contempt as weak-minded and indecisive.

Clay looked over at Betsy typing quickly, her small round breasts rising and falling in the black sweater as she moved her body. A good bang is what that woman needs, he thought to himself.

Then he stormed out of the office as quickly as he stormed in.

"Thanks for being so helpful."

Had Dan gone to Geneva with March and stopped in Denmark on the way, he would have found Leora sitting at the small wooden desk in her prison cell, lifting the pencil again for the thousandth time.

"Dearest Dan," she wrote. Then she stopped. She tore the white piece of paper into tiny particles and stared at another blank sheet. There had to be a way. There had to be a way to express to him the love she felt, to explain to him that she would be released soon from prison, that she would seize him by the arm, that they would go together to the ends of their country, that—

"Oh, what's the use of writing?" she moaned aloud. Motti will only seize the letter, tear it open, and destroy it. What's the use? Only a few more days, then freedom. Then we'll be together. Then I can explain it to you, dearest Dan.

She had no idea that he was in Washington. She visualized that he was still in Israel, still on the kibbutz, still at Motti's beck and call. Trapped. Yes, trapped between Motti and Zipora. Still shackled by duty. But she knew that he would never forget the magic that they found in Paris.

Geneva has somehow resisted modernization. Its old narrow cobblestoned streets are strangely out of step with the

198

high finance that is transacted in its banks and old-fashioned high-ceilinged small stone office buildings.

During the thirties and forties, Geneva performed valuable banking functions for the Nazis. During the seventies, it was performing other but equally valuable banking functions for the Arabs, who skillfully laundered their massive quantities of petrodollars for reinvestment where their source could not easily be detected. If Switzerland had not existed, those with money and a desire for secrecy would have created it.

When March walked into the Central Bank for his two-o'clock appointment with Heinrich Fuller, the president of the bank, he immediately sensed that he was not welcome. That fact did not surprise March. He expected it. He was an American government official. He knew very well that the one thing that Swiss banks feared more than anything else was the enactment of laws by the American government which would severely restrict the secrecy that American citizens and those with American interests could seek in Switzerland. To date, such laws had not been enacted, but that could change at any time. If it did, Swiss banks would have little advantage over those in London or Frankfurt.

As March expected, Fuller was waiting for him when he entered the wood-paneled reception area that led to the presidential suite. It wasn't simply that Fuller was a punctual man. Surrounded by clocks, how could he be anything but punctual? But it was more than that. Fuller was anxious to hear what March wanted and to send the American on his way as quickly as possible. He had never met March before. In fact, he had never even heard of the man prior to March's telephone call yesterday. After that call, Fuller had made some discreet inquiries. Everything he had heard made him feel very uncomfortable.

When they were alone in Fuller's office, the banker

199

offered March a cup of coffee, but March declined, appearing brusque and businesslike. Fuller was a large heavyset man with an enormous round face, an almost totally bald head, and sagging flesh under his eyes.

"This is an official visit, Herr Fuller. I represent the government of the United States in this matter." March paused.

Feeling ill at ease, Fuller felt the need to fill the silence.

"We have always enjoyed good relations with American officials."

That remark made no impression on March.

"It is no secret, Herr Fuller, that many officials in our government are interested in enacting new laws which would limit the secrecy of your banking operations."

Fuller nodded his large head affirmatively.

"Others have argued that there is no need for new laws. They say that the Swiss bankers always cooperate under the table when we need their help. You are familiar with that whole discussion, I'm sure."

Fuller was still nodding. He wasn't agreeing with March. He was just showing that he had heard what March said. Tiny beads of perspiration appeared on his forehead in the center of his bald head. He was watching March closely.

"Let me come right to the point, Herr Fuller. I need information about an account being maintained at this bank. Each month ten thousand dollars flows out of this account and into a Washington, D.C., bank. I have the Washington account number. I need to know the name of the person or organization who has the account here, the account number, and who is depositing the funds into this account. Is that clear?"

All of the color drained from Fuller's face.

"*Verboten*," he replied with an air of finality. "Absolutely forbidden. It would violate Swiss law."

March brushed aside his words.

"Herr Fuller, you surprise me. I thought you were a practical man, interested in the welfare of your bank and

200

your country's banking community. Perhaps you do not appreciate how difficult it is for responsible government officials to defeat those who are arguing for new laws."

"It is *verboten*," Fuller repeated.

"And if it became known publicly that you resisted cooperating in an important State Department investigation, do you realize what effect that would have on the chances for the legislation?"

Fuller sat silent, staring with contempt at March.

"And it would become known that you were responsible for the legislation. We might even call it the Fuller Act in your honor. Do you realize how that would endear you to your countrymen?"

"You misuse your authority," Fuller protested.

March ignored his comment. Fuller wiped the perspiration from his forehead.

"Perhaps I do not understand you, Herr Fuller. Perhaps you do not think that banking is important to your country. Perhaps your national pride tells you that a great nation can be built with cheese and watches alone. And I shouldn't forget the winter skiing."

"You are a most contemptible man, Mr. March."

"But of course, Herr Fuller. Of course. Life sometimes warps all of our characters in strange ways."

Fuller walked over to the credenza and picked up the pitcher of coffee.

"I might have some after all, Herr Fuller," March said. "Straight black. If you prefer to add some schnapps to your cup, go right ahead. I realize that this is a difficult question for you."

Fuller handed March one cup, reached into his desk drawer, removed a bottle, and added some clear liquor to his own cup.

"The investigation you are conducting," Fuller asked. "What is the purpose of the investigation?"

"I would not trouble you with that."

201

Fuller leaned forward in his chair, not really thinking, just trying to delay the inevitable. Finally he capitulated.

"I will give it to you," he said weakly. "But you are never to say where you got it. Is that acceptable?"

"Absolutely," March said. Then he handed Fuller a small piece of white paper that contained Pritchard's name, the name of his Washington bank and the number of the account.

"Wait here," Fuller said. "I will have my chief clerk get the information you want."

March was startled.

"If it were me," March said, "I would get the information myself."

This was too much for Fuller.

"You may threaten me and blackmail me," he shouted. "But you will not tell me how to run my own organization."

"As you wish, Herr Fuller. As you wish."

During the fifteen minutes that he waited for Fuller to return, March thought about what would have happened if Fuller had contacted the American ambassador or his own ambassador in Washington. What if he had tried to reach someone close to the head of the Swiss government? Waller would have had a coronary on the spot if this had gotten back to him. He would have ordered March to come home without the information and to apologize to the Swiss on top of it.

Fortunately, Fuller did none of those things. He returned with a small piece of white paper in his hand. He placed it at the end of the desk and waited for March to pick it up.

March read it slowly.

"Account number CB-1-071-4269. Account registered in the name of the Douglas Foundation, U.S.A. Deposits made in the name of Valeria Feragamo."

He had never heard of the Douglas Foundation before. That name meant nothing to him. But Valeria Feragamo, that was something different. He raised his eyebrows. Her name was known to March, very well indeed.

March took the piece of paper, creased it under the account number and tore it at that point. The top portion, with the account number, he tucked into his wallet. He removed a package of matches from his pocket, held the lower portion over an ashtray on Fuller's desk and ignited it. He had no need for that portion of the note. He had already committed it to memory. As for the top part, in his youth he would have ignited it also, but he was reaching that point in life when he no longer trusted his memory.

March removed the airplane schedule from his pocket to check the flight time. If he hurried, he could still make the afternoon plane back to Washington.

The chief clerk at the bank gave March a ten-minute head start. Then he feigned a headache and left to go home. Two blocks from the bank, he walked into the office of the American solicitors, just as the man from Texas had instructed him to do if there were any inquiries about the account.

He asked for Mr. Lucas and then for permission to use a phone for a private telephone call to Mr. Brett in Washington.

The miracle of modern communications is never ending. Even before March's plane took off from the Geneva airport, Brett was sitting with Husni in the small metal cubicle in the basement of the Syrian Embassy.

"This man March? Do you know who he is?" Brett asked.

"Yes, of course we know him," Husni replied in a calm tone, hoping that Brett wouldn't become agitated.

"Well, who is he?" Brett demanded to know.

"You needn't worry about March," he replied patronizingly. "He will not interfere with our operation."

But Brett would not be put off so easily.

"I have a right to know," he said angrily.

Husni was surprised. He wasn't accustomed to being talked to that way.

There are some men who prefer to be aware of the danger they face, Husni had learned long ago. And to such men you should disclose at least minimum details. They will not continue to perform if they feel excluded from the decision-making process.

"March is employed with the American State Department," he said slowly. "We know that March has been working with an Israeli by the name of Dan Yaacobi. We have been observing them very closely. They are trembling over the massive developments that our project has caused. But you needn't worry. There is no need for alarm. We have the matter under control."

Brett thought about Husni's words. For an instant, just for a tiny instant, as long as it took Husni to puff on one of his Turkish cigarettes, Brett wondered if maybe he hadn't set in motion forces beyond his control. But that apprehension passed quickly. It was replaced by a tinge of excitement, the excitement that passed through his body when he fully appreciated that he was truly affecting the course of international affairs. He was doing that while banking quite comfortable sums each month. And he was so thrilled by his power and wealth that he persuaded himself to believe Husni when the Syrian said, "You needn't worry, Mr. Brett. We have everything under control. There is no cause of alarm. Your work can go forward."

Much later Brett wondered how a man of his intelligence had reached that conclusion. Man's capacity for rationalization and self-delusion is indeed infinite.

In the limousine on the way back to his office, Brett made up his mind about one thing. He could trust Husni only so far.

He called Michael into his office.

"There are two men. One is Jonathan March, an employee of the State Department. The other is an Israeli by the name of Dan Yaacobi, working in this country. Find out what you can about them in the next twenty-four hours. Do it yourself. Don't use any private detectives or even anyone on our staff. Be as discreet as possible."

Even for Brett it was a curious request. Michael thought about asking what was happening. Brett seemed overly alert, anxious like an animal with ears perked who had just heard a foreign sound in the jungle. What was the point of it? he wondered. He never had a chance to find out. Brett quickly dismissed him.

What are you up to now, Brett? Michael asked himself as he left the office. He no longer felt any of the joy that he used to feel in working with Brett. The admiration was gone. There was nothing to admire—only a ruthless figure —obsessed with his own power, becoming almost sinister with time.

Husni managed to reach Cherev at the Bridge House, a small hotel on the east side of Manhattan that housed the PLO delegation of observers at the UN as well as a number of other militant Arab delegations.

Cherev took the call calmly, without a trace of emotion in his voice. He was a professional, well experienced in his trade, highly paid for every contract, lacking in emotion.

"Anyone besides the Israeli?" he asked.

Husni paused for a minute, thinking about March. No, he decided. His first priority was to ensure the continued viability of Brett's operation. But the second was to avoid antagonizing the Americans. Perhaps March would open his eyes and stop.

CHAPTER 23

Members of Shai are accustomed to living with danger. That is a part of the job description. But if you asked one of the more experienced, like Dan Yaacobi, about it, he would deny it was true. He had become hardened to it in much the same way that a television watcher blots out commercials or the way the body develops immunity to disease.

Yet despite all of this, Dan felt a strange wariness as he and Zipora dressed for the evening.

"Help me with these damn tuxedo suspenders," he finally shouted in frustration.

Still in her underwear, she walked across the bedroom and straightened the twisted black suspenders.

"Are you sure that you have to wear this silly costume?" she asked.

"Of course I'm sure. Dov's secretary gave me clear instructions."

Then he tried mimicking the secretary's shrill voice.

"The senator's dinner parties are always formal. Dov says he's a true friend of ours. Dov tells everyone to dress up. Everyone dresses up."

Zipora wasn't amused.

"Is Dov really sick?"

"I've told you twice, he's in bed with the flu."

"Well, why couldn't somebody else go?"

"There wasn't anybody else. Anyhow, I'm killing time until March gets back. We've been through that. What's bothering you?"

"Nothing's bothering me," she said tersely, pulling a long powder-blue dress over her head. "I just wanted to sit home and enjoy your company one evening. I thought it might be possible with March away."

Dan didn't bother apologizing. He had apologized too much over the years, more in the two years since he had been with Leora in Paris. It was a way of expiating his guilt. His apologies now had a hollow ring. They dressed in silence.

Did she ever suspect about Leora? he wondered. She had never said anything. But she wouldn't. That wasn't her way.

He wondered what March had learned in Switzerland. Dan was uncomfortable about March's trip, and more than a little sorry that he didn't insist on going with him, not just because he had missed an opportunity to see Leora, but because he was worried whether March would get what they needed. How could he have insisted on going with March, though? He would be saying to the old man, "I don't think you can handle it alone anymore."

Still, he was beginning to feel that way. Feeling that March was maybe losing a little of those sharp instincts and ability to isolate every possibility that had been his trademark.

Zipora was standing in front of the full-length mirror, combing her hair.

"I'll behave myself tonight, Dan. Really I will."

"I was never worried about that. Take your time. I'll meet you downstairs."

Dan walked down to the small study on the first floor. As he approached the room, he could hear the sounds of a basketball game on the television set.

"I thought you were studying down here," he said to Roni, his sixteen-year-old son.

"C'mon, Dad. It's the Knicks. Only the first half, I promise. Then I'll hit the books."

Dan put up a mild protest. The boy would never be a student. He lived for basketball.

"Only the first half," he finally said.

They watched together for a few minutes. When the commercial came on, Dan said to Roni, "Listen for the telephone this evening. If a Mr. March calls, give him this telephone number."

Dan handed a piece of paper to Roni.

"Tell March to call me there as quickly as possible. If anyone else calls, tell them I'm out for the evening and unreachable."

"They're talking about snow, Dad. I bought a sled today from a kid at school. It was his older brother's. I've never been on a sled in my life. Did you ride a sled when you were a boy?"

Dan thought about his early childhood in Jerusalem during the days of the British mandate. He wanted to tell Roni about it, but the commercial was over. The game was back on. He had lost his son's attention. Stories from ancient times couldn't compete with the Bullets and the Knicks.

The call came just after they left the table. Senator Johnson's dinner parties fit what the senator viewed as a traditional format. Immediately after dinner the women retired to an upstairs room to "powder your noses," as the senator said in his Mississippi drawl, while the men entered the magnificently wood-paneled study to discuss the affairs of state with cigars and cognac.

One of the team of employees who maintained the Johnson mansion approached Dan unobtrusively.

"There's a telephone call for you, Mr. Yaacobi."

Dan waited a couple of seconds until the Secretary of Defense completed a monologue before excusing himself quietly. The telephone was resting on a small octagonal table in the entrance hall.

"I'm back," the voice at the other end said.

Dan immediately recognized March's voice.

"Where are you?" March asked anxiously.

208

"At Senator Johnson's."

"No, I mean the address."

Dan gave it to him. There was a long pause.

"I want to talk to you. It can't wait," Jonathan continued. "I'm at Dulles Airport now. About fifteen minutes from you. Will you be missed if you leave for about half an hour?"

"I can do it."

"Do it then. Drive up to Glen Falls Road, where it intersects with Route 123. There's a Gulf station and a Seven-Eleven across the street. I'll meet you in the Seven-Eleven parking lot. You'll be driving your old blue Volvo?"

"Regrettably. The Foreign Ministry hasn't seen fit to reward me with anything else."

"I'll see you there," March said and he hung up.

Dan arrived before March. He parked near the road, looked around carefully, saw nothing suspicious and began waiting for March. It was cold in the car. Roni was right. It might snow this evening. The American arrived five minutes later, parked next to Yaacobi, and got into his car.

"I'm sorry for hauling you out here," March said. "I was afraid to talk on the telephone. I had the feeling that I was being followed when I hit Dulles. I think I shook them coming here."

Dan suddenly snapped to attention. The wine he had earlier in the evening had not dulled his senses.

Talking quickly, March gave Dan a full report on what he had learned in Geneva. He had copied the number of the Swiss bank account on a second sheet of paper. He handed it to Dan. The Israeli glanced at the piece of paper and then at March. The old man looked very tired, he thought.

"My suggestion," March said, "is that you fly to Rome in the morning and see what you can do about picking up the trail on Valeria Feragamo. It should lead right to Egypt, where your contacts are better than ours. I'll pursue the Douglas Foundation here, whatever that is. Is that agreeable to you?"

"*Beseder*. In order. I'll communicate with Jerusalem tonight when I get home. I should be able to leave tomorrow."

March looked concerned.

"You have no need to worry about the communication," Dan said. "Our code has never yet been deciphered by the Arabs. It's so complicated that our own people have trouble with it."

March reluctantly agreed.

In the car on the way back to the party, Dan thought about what March had told him. March was experienced and sophisticated. If he thought he was being followed, then he was being followed. Suddenly the whole operation had changed. Whoever they were hunting was now hunting them. And if that was the case, why had March brought the two of them together for this meeting? That didn't make sense. What if he hadn't lost his tail? It was an error of judgment.

Dan thought about Cherev and his organization—all that Leora had learned about them in London. Could Cherev have been called into this act too? And if so, by whom? And who were they after? March? Or Dan himself? He would have to proceed with greater care from now on, he knew that.

Maybe he should have gone to Geneva with March after all, Dan thought. Then he wondered what he would be like at March's age if he remained with Shai that long. No one should ever remain in the same job too long. Inevitably something is lost. Maybe that's what had happened to me in Paris.

Thinking about Paris led Dan to think about Leora. I wanted to stay with her. I wanted to so much, he repeated to himself. Maybe some other time—yes, maybe some other time.

❧

CHAPTER 24

"Parties for diplomats are a great bore," Zipora said, as they walked away from Senator Johnson's house.

"But you liked the idea of coming to Washington," Dan Yaacobi replied, starting the car automatically. "That was only six weeks ago."

Only six weeks, Zipora thought, rubbing her head. She couldn't remember.

A few light flakes of snow began to fall. They appeared suspended in the bright beams of the automobile headlights.

It had seemed attractive then, Zipora thought—life in Washington for a little while. But there were all the problems. Two boys in an American high school. The terrible stiffness of the diplomatic life. She didn't want to be sophisticated.

She wanted to go home, home to the kibbutz, home to the green fields of the Chula, home to the tractors and the pear trees, home.

Zipora rubbed the sides of her head with her long fingers. Oh, God, I had too much to drink again tonight, she thought.

"When can we go home, Danny?"

"Fifteen minutes. By midnight. I promise you."

"No, I mean really home. To the kibbutz."

"Soon," Dan said nervously. "Soon."

He was biting his lip. From what he had learned from March that evening it might be very soon, but he couldn't explain that to her.

211

"Sleep in the car. I'll carry you up when we get to the house."

Dan pushed the button on the cassette recorder. It played Sharm el-Sheikh over and over again. The voice of the Israeli singer filled the car.

Zipora curled up on the seat into a ball, resting her head on his leg.

"Can we go right to sleep when we get there, Danny? I'm tired—so tired."

"I have one call to make to Jerusalem," he said, feeling the paper in his jacket pocket. "I'll carry you up and put you into bed, I promise."

"Why tonight? Can't you call tomorrow?"

He glanced down at her. He was ready to respond, to tell her that tomorrow might not be soon enough. His instincts told him to call tonight. His sense of duty compelled him to make that call, regardless of how tired he was, how enticing the thought of getting into that warm bed.

She was already sleeping. He looked at the little ball rolled up next to him. She had grown rounder with the years.

The snow began falling faster. It was cold in the car. He turned on the window wipers and the heater.

The music was drifting out of the front and rear speakers. He thought about Leora and Paris again. It seemed like yesterday. He could still remember the joy, the pain, and the sadness when he left Paris. What was she doing now in the Frederiksberg prison? he wondered. There was a familiar stirring in his loins—that same yearning that he felt when he thought of her. And the guilt that went with it as he looked at the sleeping figure in the car.

Dan pressed hard on the accelerator, racing the car on to the beltway. He crossed the Potomac River Bridge into Maryland. The snow was picking up.

He studied the rearview mirror. A car had been following him since he got on to the beltway. Maybe a policeman, he thought. He slowed down quickly, cutting into the right lane.

The car passed him. It was no policeman . . . a gray BMW. The driver was talking on a CB radio as he roared past the Volvo.

Dan had no idea that the driver of the BMW was speaking with Cherev, waiting in a dark blue Mercedes near Dan's house.

The music kept playing in Dan's car.

Dan eased the car off the beltway at the Old Georgetown Road exit. There was no sign of the gray BMW as he turned into his subdivision.

When he started down the street, he looked carefully at all the parked cars. It was a habit he acquired when he began working with Shai. Somebody told him it would save his life one day. There was only one car he didn't recognize. It was parked across the street from his house, about three doors away. It was a dark blue Mercedes—license plate RAZ 420. In Paris it had been a Mercedes, too.

Dan stopped his car and flashed his bright lights on the Mercedes. It looked empty. Still, he had to be careful. He got out of his car and cautiously looked into the Mercedes. No, it was empty. It must be someone visiting a neighbor, he thought as he got back into his car and eased it toward his house.

There was about half an inch of wet snow on the ground when Dan pulled into his driveway. He took one look at Zipora sleeping soundly on the seat. He decided to open the door to the house and then come back and carry her up.

Dan left the engine on to keep her warm. It was snowing hard.

He climbed the four steps slowly, trying to find his house key. The snow was caking in his hair. His hands were wet. He pulled out some scraps of paper and a few coins from his jacket pocket. It must be in my pants pocket.

Success. He could feel the cold metal in his hand. He

paused for an instant at the top of the steps as he pulled the key from his pocket.

Just as he did, Cherev rose in the bushes along the side of the house. He was wearing a black diving suit, wet from the snow and shiny. A ski mask covered his face.

Cherev raised his right arm swiftly, his hand holding a black French-made revolver. The barrel was covered with a silencer.

Cherev paused for an instant, then fired twice. One shot struck Dan in the back of his neck, the other in the center of his back. His body lurched forward. Then he collapsed at the top of the steps, his face buried in the snow.

Cherev raced across the street to the Mercedes. He stopped for a moment next to the car, long enough to drop a small black object—a plastic sword, no more than two inches long. It fell through the damp snow and came to rest on the ground in the gutter of the street, next to the sidewalk. Then he jumped in the car. The Mercedes roared away.

The blood began oozing from Dan's body, moving through the pure white snow in strange random patterns.

He wanted to cry for help. The screams never came. Only a single word, barely audible, came out of his mouth: "Douglas."

And then he was dead.

༼

CHAPTER 25

News of Dan Yaacobi's death reached March at six o'clock the next morning when he sipped a cup of black coffee and flipped on the morning news on the radio, a ritual that he performed at six o'clock each day.

214

"The hour's top story: an Israeli diplomat, Dan Yaacobi, was shot and killed outside of his Bethesda home around midnight. Montgomery County police called to the scene of the brutal assassination have been unable to find any trace of the killers. The FBI is expected to be called in . . ."

March was stunned when he heard the report. He just sat there for a few minutes, staring blankly into the black coffee. Guilt was what he felt. Guilt, more than any other emotion. He had led them to Yaacobi. He had no doubt about it.

But that emotion and all others quickly passed. March was a professional. He knew what he had to do. He took a quick glance at the schedule of flights to Geneva that he had practically memorized, called TWA, and threw three clean shirts in the suitcase he had not yet bothered to unpack.

Before he left the house, he looked hard at the telephone. Somebody had to have at least a trace of his whereabouts. He telephoned Betsy, waking her from a sound sleep.

"I'm going back to Geneva," he said tensely. "If anyone asks, I never returned."

The news didn't reach Michael until two hours later, when he was listening to the car radio on his way to the office. He was stopped at a red light on Connecticut Avenue. His mind was wandering, thinking about how he could get Brett the information about March and Yaacobi when he heard the announcement.

"Oh, God, no," he screamed. "Oh, God, no."

Then he just sat there in the car, paralyzed. A furious chorus of horns began honking at him, but he didn't move. A policeman came up and tapped on his window.

"You okay, buddy?"

The officer's voice brought him back to reality. He

began driving again, slowly down Connecticut Avenue.

He was trying to fit the pieces together, but it was a futile exercise. He didn't have enough of them.

The pieces that he did have disturbed him. They all pointed in the direction that Brett was somehow involved with this Yaacobi, and maybe even his death. Why else would Brett have been so concerned about Yaacobi? But how? That he didn't know.

Michael was wan and pale when he barged into Brett's office.

"An explanation's what I want, Brett," Michael said, asserting himself boldly.

Brett just stared at him with an amused expression on his face.

"Close the door," he said calmly.

Brett seemed to have so little concern that Michael wondered whether he had even heard about Yaacobi.

"Did you hear about the Israeli?" Michael stammered.

"You mean Yaacobi."

Michael nodded.

"Of course I heard."

"And?"

"And what?"

"What explanation do you have for me?"

Brett just stared at Michael.

"I don't have any explanation at all for you. Things sometimes happen. People get hurt. I can't make the world just. I didn't create it."

Michael could hardly believe his ears.

"What a crock of shit!" he shouted in frustration. "The state of the world is irrelevant. It's our work that set in motion a series of events that somehow or other—and I'm not sure how—led to a man's death."

"I didn't kill the man, I can assure you of that."

"Chalk one up for our team," Michael said sarcastically.

Brett was annoyed by Michael's tone. It was insolent and disrespectful. But he wanted to let the younger man run his course. The weak were entitled to their emotional outbursts. They never accomplished anything, but they had to be completed before productive activity could resume. There had to be that inevitable hand-wringing, that hollow catharsis.

"And what do you suggest we do?" Brett asked.

"Go to the police, the FBI, the Justice Department. Tell them everything we know."

"That's an excellent idea. We'll tell them how we've engaged in a conspiracy to commit espionage and disclose governmental secrets for the past six months. With two live bodies like us, they won't even have an interest in finding out who killed Yaacobi. No, that is not a very practical idea. As my uncle Jed used to say, 'It just won't fly, my boy.'"

Brett walked over to the credenza, fixed a Bloody Mary for Michael, and handed it to him. Then he poured himself some bourbon and branch water. They sat in silence sipping their drinks. Finally, Michael regained his composure.

"You're not suggesting that we continue with this operation are you—tennis courts and all?"

"And just why not?" Brett demanded.

Michael didn't respond. He sat there, a terrified expression on his face, silently staring into his drink.

Had Brett really reached the point that he was willing to participate in murder if that was the price for expanding his empire? Michael remembered how Brett had dismissed Michael's objections to illegal kickbacks when they were in New York, at the advertising agency. Brett had laughed at Michael, arguing that those who were willing to "step over the line" were the ones who prospered in our society. Those who scrupulously paid attention to every legal requirement ended up drowning in a sea of bureaucratic regulation. "That's the system. Everybody who wants to get ahead does it," Brett had rationalized. "And if we get caught?" Michael had asked.

Brett had ignored the question. Brett never worried about those things. It wasn't that he thought he was above the law. He was just indifferent to it. He didn't understand what it had to do with him.

Once, at a cocktail party, Michael had heard a lawyer talking about some of the Watergate conspirators.

"A reckless disregard for the legal consequences," the lawyer had said. Michael remembered that phrase. He thought at the time that it fit Brett.

But illegal kickbacks were one thing, Michael thought. Murder was quite another. Or was it? Wasn't there a natural progression? Once you decide to step across the line, that magic line that separates the legal from the illegal, can there really be any restraints? Why not a mile? Inescapably one transgression leads to another.

Back in New York before they moved to Washington, Michael had thought that if Brett walked into a deserted room and found a pile of twenty-dollar bills on a table, he would put one or two in his pocket. Now Michael changed his view. Now he believed that Brett would stuff the whole pile into his pocket.

What about himself? Michael wondered. How was he any better? He had doubts, but still he followed blindly, like a child walking after the Pied Piper.

❧

CHAPTER 26

Dan Yaacobi was assassinated on the day before Leora was to be released from Frederiksberg Prison.

Motti took the news about Dan very hard. For several

years he hadn't lost a single agent. Suddenly there were two in the last month: Moshe in Copenhagen and now Dan Yaacobi.

But it was far more than that for Motti. With the exception of Leora, Motti had more of an emotional attachment to Dan than to any of the other Shai agents.

Dan was the only member of the first class of agents who hadn't drifted into other work.

Dan Yaacobi symbolized for Motti the ideal Shai agent. His courage and his intelligence, his obedience to orders, and his sense of duty were the model by which Motti judged other men.

Motti had pieced together very well what had happened between Leora and Dan in Paris. No one had to tell him. He had blamed Leora in the way that God blamed Eve for what happened in the Garden of Eden.

But Motti was also willing to shoulder some of the responsibility. He should have realized, he told himself later, after they returned from Alexandria, that this could happen. He shouldn't have put them into positions where they could have such close contact.

Even if Dan had not asked to come home from Paris, even if there had been no threat of extradition, Motti would have taken Dan away from Leora, one way or another.

Once Motti had pieced together what had happened, he drew one sober and unromantic conclusion: if Dan Yaacobi left Zipora and his children, he would be destroyed as a person—maybe not in a week or two, but sooner or later.

And because he wanted to relieve his own sense of guilt, Motti had done something else. He had made certain that there was no contact between Leora and Dan in the two years since Paris. On those two occasions, when Leora had been in Israel for briefings, Motti had been careful to send Dan on short assignments out of the country.

Motti had also done something to relieve his own guilt

toward Zipora. He had seen that she and the children were well settled on a kibbutz that satisfied them. If Dan should ever be killed in the line of duty, they would at least have some semblance of a life to pick up.

But planning for these contingencies is one thing. Facing them is quite another.

Motti broke down completely when they told him about Dan. A dirgeful wailing sound came out of his mouth. Large tears flowed down the sides of his face. With the strength still left in his bare hands, he tore the cloth of his jacket.

Startled aides and secretaries who had never seen any show of emotion by Motti quickly retreated, permitting him the privacy of his office.

All visitors were kept out as the sobbing behind the thick wooden door continued.

An hour later, Motti walked into the small bathroom that adjoined his office, splashed his face repeatedly with cold water, and opened the door. He was prepared to face some of the hard decisions that would have to be made.

First he called the Prime Minister.

"It is my recommendation, Mr. Prime Minister, that we take no independent action at this time to hunt down and find Yaacobi's killers. I think that you should send a personal note to the American President demanding that the Americans find out who committed this terrible crime. Then we should step back and see what the American government does. They have great law-enforcement resources."

Still painfully aware of what had happened in Copenhagen, he added:

"It's not worth incurring the Americans' anger by striking off on our own. I think that we should wait a decent interval to see if they come to us for our assistance. If not, then we can reconsider the matter of action on our own."

That advice pleased the Prime Minister, who was embroiled with other difficult issues with the Americans relating to arms procurement. He didn't want to risk alienating them further if it could be avoided.

Then Motti dictated a one-page memorandum for all Shai personnel around the world, explaining about Yaacobi's death and the action being taken by Shai. The language was muted in his inimical style of intended obfuscation. But the message was clear: all Shai personnel stay out of the Yaacobi assassination unless you receive specific orders from the director general.

His official actions taken, Motti turned to the personal side. He tried to call Zipora in Washington by telephone, but she was under sedation. She would be returning to Israel late tonight with Dan's body, he learned from an embassy official. The funeral would be tomorrow afternoon.

Finally, there was Leora. She would have to be told today. Motti could not wait until she returned tomorrow and tell her himself. There was too much chance that she would see a newspaper at the airport or hear about it from other Israelis on the plane. Then she would never forgive him for not telling her.

Still, he had to be careful who told her. His guess was that though he had kept them apart for these two years, Leora still cared deeply for Dan. Even for someone as emotionally strong as Leora, Dan's death coming on top of everything else might be too much. It might push her to the breaking point.

She should be told by someone with some compassion, someone to whom Leora could relate.

Motti decided that Yoel, the cultural attaché at the embassy in London, was the right person. He was a novelist, a sensitive person. Also he had been a friend of Leora's in London. Motti checked the airplane schedules. Yoel could be at Frederiksberg by early afternoon.

Motti picked up the telephone and asked to be connected with the embassy in London.

The guard led Yoel down the white-painted corridor. It looked to him more like a hospital than a prison, except for the bars on the windows.

She was sitting at a spartan wooden desk reading a small book when the guard opened the door for Yoel.

"All the way from England," she said sarcastically. "Motti must be worried that I'm going to quit on him when I get home tomorrow morning."

"Let's say I'm an old friend who happened to be in the neighborhood," Yoel replied, trying to add some levity.

"Old friend or not, Yoel, you're taking a real chance visiting me. I may bite you. I'm madder than hell at everybody in the government for leaving me caged up here to suit their political convenience."

Yoel tried to change the subject.

"It hasn't been the same in London since you left."

"Yeh, I'll bet Ariel is pleased that I didn't manage to get Moshe killed in his territory. He doesn't have another mess like the one Dan and I inflicted on him."

Suddenly Yoel realized that he was making a mess of his assignment to break the news to her gently. He just blurted it out.

"He's dead, Leora. I'm sorry, he's dead."

An eerie silence settled over the room. Her eyes stared squarely into his, and for an awful instant he knew that she understood and yet she didn't want to understand. She just stood there in silence.

"Yes, Moshe is dead," she replied grimly. "He died in Copenhagen."

She wasn't making it easy, Yoel thought.

"No. Dan Yaacobi is dead." His voice trembled. He ended with a hoarse whisper, "He was assassinated in Washington last night."

She repeated, "Yes, Moshe is dead. He died in Copenhagen."

She just continued staring at him in silence.

Yoel thought that his profession as a novelist permitted him to look into people's eyes and probe their hearts. When he looked into Leora's, he saw the great love she still had for Dan Yaacobi, and it frightened him.

After a few minutes, Leora turned and walked back to the desk, sat down and picked up one of the books. He could tell that she was looking at it but seeing nothing. She was desperately trying in vain to turn back the clock fifteen minutes to the world that she perceived before Yoel had walked into the cell.

Yoel wanted to help her come to grips with what he had told her, but he realized that it was hopeless. She would have to do that alone.

~~

CHAPTER 27

The Danish police captain pressed the gas pedal to the floor in the small sedan. Five miles back he had turned off the siren. But the blue light on top of his car was still flashing. It was a useless gesture. The early-morning mist was so thick that no one could see the blue light unless he were on top of the car.

The captain looked over at Leora sitting next to him in the front seat. Her eyes were closed, but she wasn't sleeping. He knew that. One thought kept going through his mind. I'll just be glad to get to the airport and get her the hell out of the country.

He was approaching a slow-moving milk truck. The captain began honking furiously. "Move it over, pop," he shouted.

Leora opened her eyes.

"You Danes are terrible jailers," she said in English,

with a strange smile appearing on her face. It frightened him. When he didn't respond, she continued talking.

"No, really. I'm serious. You Danes are the worst jailers. You're too kind. Now the Egyptians, those are people who know how to run a prison. Maybe I should write a book about prisons," she said, rambling on. "Please talk to me," she said. "I don't want the silence anymore. Ever since Yoel was there yesterday, I can't take it anymore."

"Okay, I will talk to you," the captain said. "You asked me to talk. I'll tell you what I think. I've been in this business thirty years. I've never seen one like you. Change your life. You're still a young woman. Meet one of those farmers you have there and settle down in Israel, have some children, grow some oranges."

"They killed my farmer," she said grimly. "Dan Yaacobi, they killed him."

The captain looked at the doors to make certain they were all locked.

"Do you know how old I am?" Leora asked.

"Twenty-five. Maybe thirty."

She laughed.

"You read the reports. You know that I am thirty-nine. If I live until next May fifteenth, I will be forty years old."

She closed her eyes again, lapsing into thought.

Did she blame Dan for refusing to leave Zipora two years earlier? Of course. They could have both left Shai and settled into a normal life. He would still be alive today.

The car stopped at a railroad crossing, waiting for a slow-moving freight to pass. She opened her eyes and saw the first traces of sun starting to appear on the eastern horizon.

"And so why do you continue doing it?" the captain asked.

"For us it is survival," she replied. "Either we will kill them or they will destroy us."

She thought about Dan's words at Abdel Rasef's house a long time ago—"the continuing spiral of death and destruction"—and her voice took on a tone of righteous indignation.

"They pursue us everywhere—in our villages, at airports, even at the Olympics. We have no alternative. One does not have to justify survival. It's like a carrousel at your Tivoli. It goes around and around. One horse always chases another."

"But you, I mean. You personally. Why do you do it?"

She shrugged her shoulders. "Who knows why any of us do anything? There is no such thing as human motive. It is supplied by psychiatrists in after-the-fact rationalizations."

The railroad barriers lifted. The car started moving.

"What will you do when you get back?" the captain asked.

"How the hell do I know? Probably get a paid vacation as a reward for screwing up the best opportunity we've had to catch Cherev."

The captain was silent. He didn't want to talk with her about the case.

Leora closed her eyes once more. A series of blurred and jumbled pictures was racing across her mind. They were all out of focus. It was as if someone were turning the pages of an album faster than her eyes could follow. The pictures were all from Paris: at Montmartre, her and Dan, at the restaurant, in a church, on the street, eating together, laughing together, in bed together.

Motti was waiting for her at the airport. They exchanged no words of greeting. He took her silently by the arm and led her to a waiting car.

It was a damp, chilly day. The car turned onto the highway and began its climb up to Jerusalem.

225

"How did it happen with Dan, Motti?"

"Do you want the story now?" He looked at her skeptically.

"Today I can take it."

He described in a general way the investigation Dan had been involved in and how he had been shot in front of his house in the snow.

"When is the funeral?" she asked.

"Three o'clock today. When we get to Jerusalem, I'll take you somewhere for coffee. We'll kill an hour. Then we can go to the cemetery."

She nodded.

They rode in silence.

When they stopped for coffee, she said, "I suppose I created problems for you because of what happened in Copenhagen?"

He put a finger up to his lips.

"Let's talk about all of that later. It can wait."

It was still raining when they got to the military cemetery —not a heavy rain, just a constant intermittent cold drizzle, like the rain that night when she returned from Egypt with Dan.

She and Motti walked alone on the narrow stone path. It was Jerusalem stone, carved from the hills that housed the cemetery.

Slowly they walked side by side past the small silent markers, each one representing a man or woman who had fallen in one of Israel's four bloody wars.

As they approached the burial site, they could see those who had been at the chapel for the service coming from the other direction.

Four soldiers carried the simple wooden coffin on their shoulders. A blue-and-white flag lay on top, now drenched from the rain.

Three steps behind walked Zipora. A black veil covered her face. It failed to mask the puffy redness under her eyes. On each side of Zipora one of her sons walked, their heads upright, their eyes straight ahead.

Motti walked ahead to meet the procession at the grave. Leora stood back, watching from a distance, trying to fix in her own mind indelibly to last for all time those few moments of happiness that she had shared with Dan Yaacobi.

Her grief was mixed with a terrible feeling of guilt. If only I hadn't let Cherev escape in Copenhagen, she said to herself over and over again, Dan Yaacobi would still be alive today.

A group of twelve soldiers raised their guns into the air and fired blast after blast, signifying the full military hero's burial that Dan Yaacobi was being given.

Then the pallbearers lowered the wooden coffin into the open grave. The cantor began to chant his dreadful dirge, the Mourner's Prayer:

"Magnified and sanctified be his great name in the world he has created according to his will. . . ."

The cantor's voice was interrupted by a piercing shriek from Zipora, followed by loud sobs that even from a distance cut through Leora like a knife. The two boys steadied their mother as she pounded her small fists against her breast.

"May there be abundant peace from heaven, and life for us and for Israel."

When they had covered his coffin with dirt and the others had started to drift away, Motti walked over to Leora, standing as rigid as a tree, and took her by the hand.

No longer was she thinking of her few pleasant moments with Dan. Those were planted on her mind forever. Once again her hatred was reinforced and fortified. Now her purpose was single: to find Yaacobi's killer and to kill him. Leora knew that she would have to be careful to conceal the intensity of her feelings. She had to convince Motti to send her to Washington.

"Now we will go back to my office," Motti said, pulling her away.

"To do what, Motti? To talk, while they bring back the bodies one by one?"

☙

CHAPTER 28

Leora and Motti rode in silence from the cemetery back to his office. Once inside, he slumped down in the chair behind his desk and lit up a cigarette.

She stood in the center of the room ready to take him on.

"You're letting me go to Washington," she said emphatically, "to pick up where Dan left off in his investigation and to punish those who did it."

"Are you asking me or telling me?" Motti shot back, surprised it had come so soon.

"Either way."

"That's not exactly what I had in mind for you."

"Then change your plans."

She picked up the package of cigarettes on his desk and lit one.

"As a matter of fact," he said, "when I first heard about Copenhagen, I had planned to retire you mandatorily. To insist that you take a desk job or quit the agency."

"Because a forty-year-old woman is too slow for this line of work?"

"I wouldn't have put it that way."

She saw that the door was open and she forced her way in.

"But you've changed your plans for me since Dan's death, haven't you?"

"I don't know. I've got to rethink it. The investigation that Dan was on has enormous political importance."

"Oh, sure, the investigation's important. But that's not it. It's Cherev. You've paid with Moshe, and now Dan, the finest of them all. You want him as much as I do, as much as Dan did. You can taste it. If that investigation is sensitive enough that they used him once, then they'll use him again, and I'll be right there."

He got up and walked over to the window.

"I've put up enough clay pigeons," he said pensively. "I just don't know if I want to put up one more."

"Just this one final assignment," she said, pressing him before he could firm up his resolve. "Then I'll go quietly, I promise."

He smiled slightly.

"Do you know what the market value of one of your promises is? Zero, nothing."

"I've never asked you for anything before."

"Not much."

"Okay. Then try it this way. It will be the last favor I ever ask of you."

He was silent looking out of the window. She was afraid that if he decided against it, she would never change his mind.

She decided to play her final card. Her best one, the one that might backfire.

"You owe it to me, Motti. You owe it to me."

He looked at her incredulous.

"I owe it to you?"

"You're damn right. You kept us apart for the last two years. I'm no fool. I know why he was never in the country when I returned for briefings. You didn't trust him. You knew that if he saw me, he would break loose from your hold and hers and snatch a little happiness with me. You

229

had no right to do it. You had no right to play God."

Her tone was bitter, harsh. Her voice was rising.

"You didn't let me love him while he was alive. Now you have to let me avenge his death. You owe that much to me."

Exhausted from her speech, she slumped down in a chair waiting for his answer.

'You don't play very fair, do you, Leora?" he muttered softly.

He walked back to his desk. She could tell from the look of resignation on his face what his answer was.

"Very reluctantly I will let you have it," he said.

She showed no emotion. There was no need to gloat.

"But," he said, "and there is a big but."

"What's that?"

"You will take no action right now. You will cool your heels in Eilat or some other rest place, or go home with Hannah until I tell you we're ready to move."

"That's insane. All the clues will be gone. You know that."

Now he looked angry.

"Insane or not, that's how we're doing it."

"What are we waiting for?" she said gingerly.

'We're going to give the Americans a chance to act first. And if you can't live with that, I'm tossing you the hell out of this agency, regardless of what I owe you."

From the expression on Motti's face, she suspected that he was serious. She had no intention of confirming that suspicion.

Darkness was settling over the city.

"Come home and have dinner with my wife and me," Motti said. "I'll have my driver and take you to Haifa later in the evening."

She nodded, suddenly feeling very hungry and being unable to remember the last meal she had eaten.

* * *

Motti's wife poured two cups of coffee and started to walk out of the dining room, leaving Motti and Leora alone to talk. Leora stopped her at the door.

"I must have eaten everything you had in the house," Leora said. "I've been in Europe a long time. I've never had a European meal like that."

"Okay, now, down to business," Motti said. "This afternoon I told you in a general way about Dan's investigation. Try to keep quiet for the next hour and listen, if that's possible, and I'll give it to you in more detail."

Leora sat quietly and listened very carefully as Motti gave her every detail that he knew about the special investigation that Dan had been conducting with Jonathan March relating to the leaks in Washington.

When he approached the end of his story, Motti poured brandy in two glasses and handed one to Leora. He took a long sip to wet his throat.

"Now there are some loose ends," he said. "Three to be exact." He paused for a minute.

She took a drink. The brandy burned her throat. He was ready to continue.

"One, we know from Zipora that Dan planned to call Jerusalem that night when he got home. From that we have to assume that he learned something important that evening."

She was listening carefully.

"Two, we know from Dan's son that he got a call from March at the party, a call that he had been waiting for. What they said we don't know."

"And three?"

"Three, and most peculiarly, they found this in his jacket pocket."

Motti walked over to his black briefcase sitting on the credenza and pulled out a sheet of white paper. All that it had was the number "CB-1-071-4269" written in the center.

"We don't know what it is," Motti said. "Maybe it had nothing to do with the investigation."

"That's not his handwriting," she replied.

"Treat that piece of paper carefully," Motti added. "The Americans don't know about it. You'll have to decide when to tell them."

She sat in silence finishing her brandy and trying to digest what he had told her. She thought that she had it all.

"And you won't change your mind," she said. "You won't let me go over there now and get started?"

"You always push me," he said. "The answer is still no. There are times when political considerations have to come first for us."

This time she didn't argue.

"On that subject of political considerations," she said, "I heard a lot from the Israelis on the airplane today about the possibilities of peace with Egypt, about Israelis going to Cairo to visit and Egyptians coming here, and this and that. I've been away a long time. I couldn't believe what I was hearing. But what difference do you think any of this will make to our work?"

Motti had thought about her question before. He was ready with his answer. "Peace with Egypt would be wonderful," he said. "I hope for it. If I were religious, I would pray for it. But, unfortunately, the terrorists will never accept it. They will continue, on and on and on."

Suddenly he felt very tired. He looked at his watch.

"My driver is out in front now. Get on your way, Leora, and let an old man go to sleep."

"Yes, sir," she said.

"Oh, and one other thing, Leora. Leave a telephone number with my secretary tomorrow. I'll call you when I'm ready for you."

CHAPTER 29

The stomach pains that Michael Holt had been experiencing on and off for the past several months worsened drastically during that fateful morning on which he learned of the death of Dan Yaacobi. Michael's desk was littered with an assortment of self-prescribed, over-the-counter drugstore products that harried messengers had been sent to purchase. But none of them provided any real relief.

By late morning, Michael left his desk chair in favor of the greater comfort that he felt stretched out on the sofa in his office. But then the pain became too great for him to endure in that position.

Finally, he took the one last step that he had been assiduously avoiding. He called Dr. William Green, an internist, affiliated with George Washington University Medical Center. As Michael hung up the telephone, relieved that the doctor could see him that afternoon, he suddenly felt very foolish for not calling sooner.

Like many other men, Michael was frightened by illness. Being frightened, he responded to it by ignoring it, hoping that eventually the condition would miraculously go away. It never did; it only worsened.

So intense were his stomach pains that Michael could barely walk into the doctor's office.

Following the examination, Michael held his breath, waiting for Dr. Green to return to his study with his prognosis.

The doctor entered carrying some graphs with instrument readings, and what looked to Michael to be a medical textbook.

"I want to put you through some more tests," the doctor said soberly.

"But what does it look like now, Doctor?"

"My judgment is that you have a severely progressed peptic ulcer."

"A stomach ulcer?"

"Probably more than one in an advanced state."

The doctor refused to disclose any emotion.

"What causes it?"

"Severe emotional stress operates on the hypothalamus. Drinking alcohol worsens the situation."

The doctor's diagnosis did little to allay Michael's anxiety and nothing to eliminate his pain.

"What can you do to help me, Doctor?"

"I'll give you a prescription for some immediate relief and a special diet. I'll also warn you to eliminate any conditions of conflict and stress if you can. Then we'll watch it. It may respond."

"And if it doesn't?" Michael asked grimly.

"We'll try surgery. Your case is advanced enough that most doctors would probably go to surgery now. I'd like to avoid it if possible."

"What about exercise?" Michael said, thinking of his Wednesday tennis match.

"In moderation. But not excessive."

Michael construed that as a green light. Then muttered an automatic thank-you as he took the prescription from the doctor.

Standing in the drugstore waiting for it to be filled, he put the facts that the doctor had told him in perspective with his Wednesday tennis matches and the awful stress he had been under since he had moved to Washington.

He desperately wanted to break away from Brett, never again to return to that office, to go home, pick up Kate and little Michael, and get as far from Washington as possible. But Michael knew that he would never do it. He was too weak to break Brett's strong hold.

He suddenly recalled Kate's words shouted at him during

an argument: "You wouldn't have the strength to move out of a burning building. You'd stand there paralyzed until someone pulled you out."

Maybe she was right, Michael thought. Like Brett, she had too much strength for him, Michael decided. Even now she sat at her desk every evening working on that epic she was writing. Maybe he had made a mistake picking her up on the rebound from Brett.

As the druggist handed the small plastic bottle of pills to Michael, he quickly took one and stuffed the bottle into his pocket. He would hide them from her, he decided. She would never know how weak he was.

As Michael walked back to his office at the Douglas Foundation, not more than a mile away, Ernest Clay, March's deputy director in the Internal Security Division of the State Department, sat at his desk puffing on a pipe and stroking his thick beard.

For Clay, it had been a particularly frustrating day. He had been stunned when he heard about Dan Yaacobi's death earlier in the day. With nothing to go on except a lawyer's intuition, Clay decided that Yaacobi's death had to be related to the investigation that March was conducting with the Israeli. He had raced into March's office first thing in the morning to get the boss's confirmation, but all that he found was the stone wall that Betsy erected.

"He's not here, Mr. Clay," she had replied politely.

"But where can I reach him?"

"I'm sorry, but I don't know."

"It's a matter of great urgency," he had said, sounding exasperated.

"Please leave a message. If he calls in, I'll give it to him."

Clay had stormed out. Then he tried checking around the building. He called the guards at the desk in the lobby of the building, the parking attendants, even the housekeeper at March's apartment. No one had seen March. People just don't vanish into air, Clay decided. March has to be somewhere.

As Clay sat in the interior of the self-generated halo of smoke that rose from his pipe, he tried to think of other places he could call to find March. Suddenly he was interrupted by the buzzing of his intercom.

"It's the Secretary of State on line one," a voice said.

Clay picked up the receiver.

"Where the hell is he?" Waller bellowed at him.

"I don't know, Keith. I've been trying to find him myself."

"What do you mean you don't know? You're his deputy."

"Just what I said, Keith. I don't know. His secretary may know, but she won't tell me."

"Well, she won't tell me, either," Waller said, sounding more infuriated as he talked. "Doesn't that bitch know who runs this agency?"

Waller paused. Clay was silent, waiting for him to continue.

"Well, you might as well get your ass up here," Waller finally said. "We'll have to serve you up as a pinch-hitter."

Then the Secretary slammed down the phone.

As Clay rode up to the sixth floor in the elevator, he thought about the man he was going to see. In some ways it burned him up that March and most of the others in the State Department had written him off as "Waller's boy." The truth was that he really didn't like Keith Waller that much at all.

Various members of the Clay family had known Wallers at Princeton, Harvard Law School, the Athletic Club, and over the years in a host of New York public-spirited activities. There was a general feeling passed from one Clay to the next that the Wallers were just a little coarse and crude, a little too pushy, that they never took on civic tasks for the good they generated, but always to move still higher up the social ladder. Clay's own mother, whom Clay himself regarded as a relic from the William McKinley era, once put it this way: "They must have picked up some foreign blood along the way."

The strange thing was that Ernest Clay, who had broken with most of his family's conservative viewpoints and had gone to work with the government, considering himself a liberal Democrat, could never quite shake free of his family's view of the Wallers. It always popped into his mind when he met with the Secretary of State.

Today was no exception.

The Secretary of State was waiting for Clay, pacing his office like a caged tiger.

"The shit has really hit the fan with Yaacobi's death," Waller said curtly. "The President has gotten a letter from the Israeli Prime Minister demanding immediate action. He wants me over at the White House at four o'clock with March, who he knows was heading our investigation on the leaks of Israeli information."

Suddenly Waller stopped talking and cast his eyes over Clay, all six feet two inches of him.

"You're going with me," Waller barked. "You'll sit in for March. We'll tell the President March is out of town on this investigation."

Clay nodded. He had been to two previous meetings at the White House when he had been with the Criminal Division of the Justice Department. He always enjoyed the feeling of power that he had in 1600 Pennsylvania Avenue.

"Oh, and one other thing," Waller said. "Try to keep quiet over there and let me do the talking. Whatever you know about the investigation, I don't want to share with anyone over there, or the White House staffers will try to take it from us and give it to the CIA or FBI."

"You don't have much to worry about," Clay said.

"March and Yaacobi kept it all to themselves. I don't even know whom they were investigating, or what information they had."

"That's S.O.P. with March," Waller said bitterly. "He never shared anything with me, either."

As Clay started to leave, Waller began talking again.

"If you were in my shoes, Clay, the most important thing you would have to worry about is that the White House will take over all the decision-making in the foreign policy area and relegate the Secretary of State to an administrative position. I'm the first strong Secretary of State since Acheson," Waller said proudly. "And I don't intend to hand it over to those little kids the President brought to town."

Except for Charlie Pritchard, Clay recognized everyone at the meeting in the Oval Office. They were all the top presidential assistants who dealt with matters of foreign policy.

Pritchard was introduced to Clay as the President's special adviser on Middle Eastern affairs.

After the President asked one of his assistants to read the short note from the Israeli Prime Minister demanding action in response to Yaacobi's death, there was a great deal of hand-wringing about the deterioration in American-Israeli relations caused by the leaks.

"A number of congressmen have been leaning on me hard," the President said, looking in Waller's direction, "and Yaacobi's death won't help."

"How is March coming on his investigation of the leaks?" one of the White House staffers asked, sounding innocent. "Does he need help?"

Waller jumped in fast.

"March is making good progress. He doesn't need any help. Anyhow, what does one thing have to do with the other? We're dealing here with a separate matter, another one of these isolated acts of international terrorism. It's a homicide, plain and simple. Let the FBI lend some quiet assistance to the Montgomery County homicide unit. Hell, local enforcement is excellent here. I should know. I live in Chevy Chase. We have the highest median income of any county in the country. We ought to buy something with all that money."

"You really don't think the two things are related, Keith?" the President asked, thoughtfully. "The leaks and the assassination?"

"I'd bet on it," Waller replied.

Clay looked down at the thick blue carpet, hoping that the President wouldn't ask him for his own view.

When the President said, "Okay, Keith. I'll do it your way," Clay suddenly felt very guilty for keeping quiet. But then it was too late. They had already moved on to the execution of the decision, of how the FBI could be used to assist the local law-enforcement people. Finally, there was the matter of a formal response to the Israeli Prime Minister's note.

The President called in his secretary and dictated a short response, closing with the words, "And you can be certain that we will spare no effort in finding the perpetrators of this heinous crime."

As they filed out of the Oval Office and a Cub Scout troop from the President's hometown filed in, Clay was suddenly struck by the fact that he and Charlie Pritchard had something in common. Neither one had opened his mouth during the meeting.

∾

CHAPTER 30

Two days after the meeting in the Oval Office, Keith Waller found out where Jonathan March had been.

Shortly after noon, Waller received a telephone call from Ismail, the Egyptian ambassador, who sounded frantic. The Egyptian was seeking an urgent meeting with the Secretary of State.

"How soon is urgent?" Waller said.

"Fifteen minutes," came the grim reply.

"Jesus Christ, it can't be war," Waller said. "You're negotiating with the Israelis."

"It's not war, but it is urgent."

"Come in then," Waller said, thinking about how he would stall the Bolivian ambassador, who had been waiting two days for this meeting.

The Egyptian looked very embarrassed when he took a chair opposite Waller around the small white marble coffee table.

"We regret this, very, very much," Ismail said. "You will have to believe me when I say that our government had nothing to do with it."

Ismail looked tense. He was slurring his words. Waller was surprised. Normally the Egyptian was unflappable.

"Well, what happened?" Waller said.

Ismail had one other prepared statement to make before he told Waller, and he insisted on making it.

"Just now relations between our countries are improving. We hope that an incident of this type will not stand in the way of that improvement."

"For God's sake, what is it?" Waller asked.

"Your Director of Internal Security, the one with the bad leg—"

"Jonathan March," Waller interrupted.

"Yes, March. He was shot by Palestinian terrorists in Cairo last night. He died an hour ago."

Waller could hardly believe what Ismail was telling him. "In Cairo?" Waller said, not trying to conceal his surprise. "What in the hell was he doing in Cairo?"

"We hoped that you could answer that. We couldn't figure it out either. As I told you, it was a gang of Palestinian terrorists. One is dead, and the other two escaped. But we will find them. You can be sure of that."

Waller was silent. Being a God-fearing man, he was ashamed of the thoughts that kept going through his mind. March had always been such a thorn in his side. Obviously he wished harm to no man, but still, his life would be easier without March.

The Egyptian continued apologizing.

"These radicals have gone crazy since our President's visit to Jerusalem last month. We have expelled many. The others will be dealt with harshly."

Waller then patiently assured Ismail that the United States would not blame his government in any way for the death of March.

"There is just one request that I have," Waller said. "Has word gotten out about this yet?"

"Absolutely not. Only I and the chief of police know the man's identity."

"Let's keep it that way," Waller said. "Absolute secrecy. I want the body placed in a simple wooden coffin. Put the coffin into a commercial crate and ship it to the State Department. I will personally supervise a simple burial at Arlington."

The Egyptian was relieved that there would be no publicity, but mystified.

"But what about his family?"

"Jonathan March had no family," he said coldly, as if he were describing the type of stone used in the State Department building.

When Ismail shook his hand and left, Waller stood for a moment near his window, pondering what he should do next.

Waller was no fool. He realized that the deaths of

Yaacobi and March were related. It was obvious that they had been on to something sensitive. But now he had another fear. No longer was he concerned merely about losing control of the investigation. Now he was also concerned that whatever Yaacobi and March were close to might adversely affect his State Department. Now more than ever he couldn't go to the President. He had to keep it under his control at State and have the investigation handled ineffectually in a way that would cause it to die a quiet death. All of these concerns pointed to a single course of action.

Waller decided to keep the Bolivian ambassador waiting a little longer while he pursued that course.

"Get Ernest Clay up here," he barked to his secretary on the intercom.

When Clay entered Waller's office, the Secretary of State was fully in command. He related to Clay everything that the Egyptian ambassador had told him and admonished Clay to keep it all extremely confidential and not to tell another person.

"Our official explanation for now will be that March is out of the country on assignment. You will be appointed acting director of Internal Security in his absence," Waller said. "Keep me posted on your investigation."

Then Waller quickly dismissed Clay, mumbling something about how he had already kept the Bolivian ambassador waiting for an hour.

As Clay left Waller's office, he suddenly had a nauseated feeling in the pit of his stomach. How could Waller have been so cold and unemotional? Clay wondered. To be sure, Jonathan March had some shortcomings as a colleague, but he was another human being—no, much more than that, he was a dedicated and devoted governmental official. He was also a man who had suffered enormously during his life. Was this the end that he really deserved?

By the time he returned to his office, the nausea was gone.

It was being replaced by other emotions. There was grief for March. But something else. There was anger toward Keith Waller.

Ernest Clay quickly saw through Keith Waller. He knew what the Secretary of State was doing. He knew that Waller was playing him for the fool. You've got the wrong man, Clay decided, recalling past investigations he had worked on at the Justice Department. Clay made up his mind that he would find out what really happened to Yaacobi and March.

"You'd better never get a Clay's dander up," his grandfather used to say when he ran the family investment banking firm. Well, by God, Ernest Clay's dander was up!

It wasn't just his feelings toward Waller. Somewhere along the line, with his WASP background and his elitist education, Ernest Clay had developed that sense of decency and fair play that Americans pride themselves upon, yet frequently honor more in the breach than the observance. No, the Israelis weren't his favorite people, Clay thought to himself. But by George, there was something more than a little wrong here. Waller might be helpless, for reasons of personal politics, to find out what it was, but Clay certainly wasn't.

Clay also made up his mind about something else. He wouldn't share a shred of information with Waller. When he had something, he would go right to the top, directly to the President, with it.

~❧~

CHAPTER 31

When Brett walked into the basement cubicle at the Syrian Embassy to meet with Husni the day after March's death, he found the Syrian a trifle nervous. Husni was anxious to see if Brett had learned of March's death. From their opening comments Husni quickly deduced that Brett knew nothing about it, and the Syrian relaxed, lighting up a Turkish cigarette.

"The reason that I wanted to see you," Husni said, "is because I want to go over with you the request for information that your man gives to Pritchard when he plays tennis with him tonight."

Husni then went over the specific items of information that he wanted, all related to Israeli military planning.

"I have the feeling that we're getting near the bottom of the barrel," Brett said.

"Well, it is true that the Israelis aren't giving the Americans as much as they used to. But there's still a lot more there. We just have to be certain that we're getting the best items first."

As Brett rose to leave the room he remarked to Husni, "Was Yaacobi's death really necessary?"

The Syrian had been expecting this question. It was his first meeting with Brett since Yaacobi had been assassinated.

"Necessary, is a relative concept," Husni said slowly. "Let's just say that the only obstacle to a successful operation has been removed. Hopefully we won't have to remove any others as well."

Contrary to what Michael thought, Kate wasn't really making great progress on her novel, despite the hours that she sat at her desk. Much of the time she sat there daydreaming about how rapidly her marriage with Michael was disintegrating.

That thread of communication that binds a married couple together was rapidly becoming severed. They shared a house but not much else. Even the late dinners that they used to eat together were now few and far between. Most evenings Michael worked late at the office, ate in town, and came home after she was already asleep. If she ate dinner at all, it was with little Michael, around five thirty in the evening.

Depending upon her mood, she sometimes placed the blame on Brett for intentionally destroying her marriage to Michael as a punishment to her for divorcing him. In this scenario, she saw Michael as a helpless fragile weakling, trapped in the tentacles of the all-consuming Brett.

Other days, she blamed Michael and got furious at him. Each individual has control of his own life, she thought. If one person permits another to enslave him, well, that is his own decision.

Wednesday evenings always gave Kate the worst trouble. Since she knew that whatever Michael was doing at the tennis court was undoubtedly improper and illegal, she sat in dread each Wednesday evening, staring at the telephone expecting it to ring, expecting someone to tell her that Michael had been arrested. Only when she heard the front door slam on Wednesday evening, knowing that he was safely in the house, did she begin to relax. She became furious at herself for that emotion because she knew what it signified: deep down she still cared for Michael. I must be some kind of masochistic fool, she thought, trying to choke back the tears.

This Wednesday night was no different. The cold December air pushed through the crevices under the bedroom window that should have had storm windows, as Kate tried to bury her body under the blankets while keeping her head on the pillow, her ears listening for the sound of the door. Finally she heard it slam. Then Michael's heavy weary footsteps as he trudged up the stairs.

She lay in bed quiet, pretending to be asleep, not wanting to talk to him, not wanting to hear what he had to say. She could see him through a small opening in her otherwise closed eyes.

He looked so tired, so beaten down, his body so full of

245

aches from the tennis match that he had tried to play with only moderate exertion, as he made his way around the bedroom putting on his pajamas. He looked over at her for a moment to make certain that she was asleep.

Through the small opening in her eyes, she saw him walk over to the jacket that he had hung in the closet, and remove a small plastic bottle. He popped in one of the small pills. Then he rubbed his stomach to ease the pain until the medicine began to operate. He fell into his bed.

She waited until he was asleep and snoring loudly. Then she got up slowly and quietly, groping her way in the dark to his closet. She felt the jacket, next the pocket, and finally she had the bottle in her hands.

She held it up to the window, taking advantage of the traces of street light from outside.

She looked at the date. Only two days ago, she thought. He hadn't even mentioned to her that he had been to see a doctor. There was the name of the drug—a long medical term—that she couldn't understand. Then she saw the name of the physician: Dr. William Green. That name she would remember.

∾

CHAPTER 32

Betsy sat behind her typewriter wiping her eyes, sponging the tears that continued to flow down her cheeks. Finally she put down the handkerchief and raised her hands, stretching out her fingers, trying to think about how many hours they had labored for Jonathan March.

Clay waited patiently for her to absorb the news. As he watched her, it occurred to him that for the first time since he had known her, her little nose was no longer turned up.

"And you are absolutely certain that what Waller told you is correct?" She asked again, her eyes pleading with him to tell her that he had been playing a prank in very bad taste when he had told her about March's death.

"I swear it, Betsy, on my grandmother's grave," he said, in a soothing tone. "I've even checked with the shipping department. They are expecting a large wooden crate from Egypt tomorrow. It is to be logged in as 'relics,' not to be opened unless the Secretary of State personally gives the order."

Finally, she was willing to accept the fact that he was telling her the truth.

"Then why did you tell me about it," she asked, "if Waller told you not to disclose it to another person?"

Clay took the pipe out of his pocket, added some fresh tobacco, and lit it up.

"Because, my dear Betsy, you hold the keys to the kingdom, and I mean that literally. Not only do you know in your head more about what March was doing than I, but you have a set of keys to every one of those locked cabinets in his office."

"In other words, you need my help."

"That's exactly it."

She was silent. Even though March was dead, she would feel guilty giving Clay access to his files. They were personal to March.

Clay sensed her reluctance.

"I'll lay it on the line, Betsy. I'm not asking you to do it because you like me. I don't think you do."

He paused to give her a chance to protest, but she was silent. He began talking in a harsher tone, sounding more self-confident.

"I'm asking you to do it because that's the only hope you have to bring to justice the people responsible for killing that demigod you worshipped."

She picked up her hands, opened them, and looked at

her fingers again. Slowly, hesitantly, she reached into the purse that was sitting under her desk, near her feet, and pulled out a set of keys on a large round hook.

"The keys to the kingdom are yours," she said, tossing them in Clay's direction.

Then they walked into March's private office. Clay didn't dare sit behind March's desk. He slumped his large frame into an uncomfortable small brown leather chair and listened while Betsy described to him what she understood to be the status of the investigation that March and Yaacobi had been conducting.

"So, you see they had pretty well zeroed in on Charlie Pritchard as the one who had been leaking information," Betsy said.

Clay had a quizzical look on his face.

"Well, why didn't they just haul him in? They had enough to get an indictment."

"I heard Mr. March talking about that with the Israeli one day. They wanted to get the source, to find out who was paying Pritchard."

"And that's why Jonathan went to Geneva?"

"Exactly. But I don't know what he did there or whom he saw."

Clay raised his eyebrows. In her own quiet way, sitting behind that typewriter, Betsy had managed to keep track of what March did very well.

"What about Egypt?" Clay asked.

"That I don't know. He must have learned something in Geneva that led him there."

"I didn't think the well would ever run dry," Clay said, trying to add some levity.

Betsy didn't even crack a small smile. She was still too distraught from the news about March's death.

"Okay," Clay said, holding up the ring of keys, "show me which key operates which lock. We'll see what other pieces we can put together."

Betsy's face tightened up. Talking about March's work was one thing, but going through his drawers and files was quite another. She wasn't up to that, not yet at least.

"I'll show you which key fits where," she said. "But then I would like to excuse myself."

Clay understood from her eyes what was going through her mind.

"Yes, of course," he mumbled, feeling guilty that his compelling desire to learn everything he could about the investigation had overcome his sensitivity for her feelings.

After Betsy retreated to her desk outside of the inner sanctum, closing the door behind her, Clay spent the next two hours looking through files, making careful mental notes of what evidence was where, but trying not to disturb anything. He looked over the copies of Pritchard's bank statements. Then he spent a long time studying the detailed reports about Pritchard that the field investigators had prepared.

Clipped to one of the reports was a small photograph of Pritchard. Clay wrapped the picture carefully in plastic and tucked it into his wallet.

Then he emerged from March's office and approached Betsy who was typing furiously at her desk.

"Just some reports for Mr. March that I never had a chance to complete," she said grimly, choking back the tears.

"I'm sorry to disturb you again," Clay said apologetically. "I have only one other question to ask you."

She stopped typing.

"Yaacobi's boss in Israel," Clay said. "What is his name?"

"Motti Elon," she replied, "the director general of an Israeli agency called Shai. He has an office both in Tel Aviv and in Jerusalem."

She resumed typing.

Clay stood next to her, thinking for a moment.

"I'm going overseas for a few days," he said. "If Waller calls, you don't know where I am."

Clay didn't need a response from Betsy. He knew that she would never say anything to Waller again after how he had handled March's death.

Her devotion had been so great to March. He had so dominated her life. Clay knew that Betsy would finish typing his reports, perhaps organize his papers, clean out her own desk, pack her bags, and leave Washington.

∿

CHAPTER 33

Leora paced around Motti's office, cutting and recutting the same path with her feet. The bright red color on her face gave her a healthy look. Motti watched her restlessness with some amusement.

"I told you that a few days at Eilat in the sun would do you good."

"Do me good, I'm going out of my mind."

He smiled weakly, remembering that he had felt the same way when he was her age, but no more. In the last couple of days Motti had made a decision. After this investigation was over, he was retiring. He also planned to make a major effort to have Leora appointed as his successor. He didn't dare mention that to her now, knowing that she would tell him that was ridiculous. But he hoped that when it was over, when she had avenged Yaacobi's death, she might take a desk job if it happened to be the job of director general.

"You're really telling me that I'll have to work with this Clay character?" she said soberly. "Ernest Clay? Ernest, what an odd name."

"Yes, that's what I'm telling you."

"But I don't work well with anyone. You know that."

He raised his hand to stop her.

"We've gone through all that," Motti said. "Let's not start again. This time you have no choice. I'm happy that Clay asked for one of our people to work with him."

"Well, what do you know about him?"

"He's not long on experience. He hasn't been in the field before."

"Oh, thanks. Thanks a lot."

"From what I've been able to learn, he's very bright, a sharp mind, learns quickly." Motti tried to recall the other information he had gathered since Clay's call yesterday. "He's a lawyer and an administrator, first at the Criminal Division of Justice, then as March's assistant."

"That's what I call a background," she said sarcastically.

"Don't laugh. In the United States they think a lawyer can do anything."

She was silent.

"Like I said, he's intelligent, excellent records at Ivy League schools, history degree at Princeton, law degree at Harvard, fine old New York family, and hardworking—a thirty-two-year-old bachelor. What else do you want to know?"

"I'll tell you what I want to know. I want to know why we're saddled with some blueblood Yankee. Why the hell couldn't we have gotten someone good from CIA or FBI to work with?"

"I've already told you that twice," Motti said, keeping his patience and repeating what he learned from his telephone conversation with Clay. "We can pick up with Clay and maybe get something fast, or we can spend the next month bucking the American political system and having Waller throw every roadblock at us."

"It's not much of a choice."

"The world's not perfect," Motti said. "I work with what I have."

"That's what Dan once told me," she said softly.

Motti had heard that statement from Dan, too. He cursed himself for not using more care in his choice of words. He didn't want to get Leora started again.

There was a buzzing on the intercom.

"Ernest Clay is downstairs," the secretary said.

"Go get him," Motti replied.

Then he turned to Leora with a serious look on his face.

"I should tell you no guns in the United States. But I won't."

"Damn right you won't. That's probably what you told Dan. Look where it got him."

He pretended that he hadn't heard her words. Then he began lecturing her.

"But I will tell you, please, not one more international scandal like Paris or Copenhagen."

The first thing that struck Leora about Clay was the physical contrast between him and Motti. The Israeli was aging, heavyset with gray hair. The American was youthful, thin with brown hair, and a large bushy brown beard. He had a serious look on his face. Motti was wearing a plain white cotton shirt open at the neck, no jacket, no tie. Clay had on a blue pinstripe suit, complete with vest, gold chain, and button-down collar. His metal-framed glasses made him seem like a university professor—thoughtful, competent, with a keen analytical mind. He puffed contentedly on a pipe while Motti chain-smoked cigarettes. Motti talked quickly, running his sentences together. Clay spoke slowly, precisely, carefully selecting his words.

Five minutes into the meeting, Clay was still explaining how he had always wanted to visit Israel before, but he had never had the opportunity. I wish he'd get to the point already, Leora thought glumly.

Then Clay turned to Yaacobi's death, describing carefully in minute detail every bit of information he had pieced together about the investigation that March and Yaacobi had been conducting. Despite all of her initial re- actions, as Clay spoke, Leora began to grasp that behind this calm unemotional exterior Clay did have a sharp analytical mind. But how could that possibly make up for his inexperience? The thought of providing on-the-job train- ing to Clay was so loathsome to her that she wondered how she would manage. Still, Motti had made it crystal- clear. Working with Clay was the only way that she could go forward with the investigation of Yaacobi's death. You were right, Dan, she thought, the world is never perfect. We work with what we have.

Motti explained to Clay that Leora would be working with him. The American tried to conceal his surprise that it was a woman, but his bushy brown eyebrows raised on their own in a knee-jerk reaction and he took a deep breath. Leora's senses were sharp. She instantly perceived his reaction. She wanted to interrupt Motti and say that balls have nothing to do with being a good investigator, but she was afraid of Motti's reaction. Motti's tone suggested that it was Be-Nice-to-American Day at Shai headquarters.

Finally, Motti and Clay finished their general discussion, and Motti told Leora to take Clay down to her office. They could decide on their own strategy without him.

There was more handshaking. Then she led Clay down the long barren corridor past old battered wooden file cases that had never found a home. As they walked, Leora de- cided that Clay's beard bothered her. It gave his face a professorial look that contributed little.

Inside her office, Clay began with some more formalities as to how much he thought he would enjoy working with her. Leora quickly dismissed those.

"Okay, buddy," she said. "The question is, Where do we start this thing?"

The term "buddy" bothered him, but he didn't say any- thing to her.

"My suggestion," Clay said tentatively, "is that we start in Switzerland. Let's try to find out whom March was seeing there. Maybe we can pick up the trail and find out what carried him to Egypt."

Leora had her own ideas. She fired back quickly. "There's one thing we better do before we go to Switzerland."

"What's that?" Clay asked, puzzled.

"Let's go back to Washington and check everything there. We may be able to pick up some other evidence that will make our job in Switzerland easier."

"But I've already assembled everything in Washington," Clay protested.

"A second look is sometimes useful," she said, thinking about Motti and trying to be tactful.

Clay was too smart for that.

"You don't think I've found everything. You think I've missed some things."

She looked at him for a minute.

"Yes. If you prefer to put it that way."

He was silent.

"Look, buddy, don't get pissed. It's just that I've been in this business a lot longer than you have. I might see something that couldn't have meant anything to you."

"Please don't call me buddy," he said, politely but firmly.

"What do you want me to call you?"

"Ernest."

"Ernest, then. My instincts tell me Washington first."

Even as she said it, she wasn't sure why she felt that way.

He thought about her suggestion for a moment.

"I'll do it your way," he said, making it clear that he had accepted her idea because it had merit and not out of blind subservience to her experience.

Later when they were ready to leave her office for the airport, Leora suddenly remembered about the piece of white paper with the number that had been in Dan's pocket when he died. She considered telling Clay about it, but decided against it. Maybe later, if he has to know, she thought to herself.

When Clay stopped in the men's room before they left, Leora quickly took the small pistol from her desk and tucked it into her jacket. Motti be damned, she thought. Clay's probably not armed and the two of them would be sitting pigeons. And with Clay's identification no customs agent will ever check for firearms.

When the Boeing 707 touched down at Dulles Airport, the last of the snow that had fallen the night of Yaacobi's death was melting. Christmas decorations were visible everywhere in the airline terminal.

"This was your idea," Clay said to her as they got into his car. "Where do you want to go first?"

"Yaacobi's house first," she said automatically.

He looked puzzled.

"Why there?"

"You wouldn't understand," she answered morosely.

They rode in silence. It was a dreary moody silence. He glanced at her through the corner of his eye. She looked despondent, sticking near the door, her eyes closed.

He turned on the car radio to WTOP, one of Washington's all-news stations. She seemed oblivious to the sounds that it brought into the car. She only opened her eyes and leaned forward when the announcer said:

"Repeating again the hour's top story. The Israeli Prime Minister will definitely be going to Egypt next week to meet with the Egyptian President at Ismailia. The meeting is scheduled for Christmas Day. Already scores of Israeli journalists have begun to invade Egypt. They have been given a friendly welcome at Cairo Airport after the thirty years of bitter war that divided the two countries.

"Now moving along to other items in the news . . ."

Clay could tell that she had been listening. He flipped off the radio.

"What do you think, Leora," he asked, "real peace or not?"

"I'm no politician. And I'm no prophet," she replied curtly. She was in no mood to become embroiled in a long political discussion with Clay.

They rode in silence the rest of the way to Bethesda.

When they reached the house, Clay quickly said, "The police checked the house. They didn't find anything."

He stopped the car across the street.

"Please wait here," she said. "Let me do this myself." Before he had a chance to respond, she was out of the car and slammed the door. He remained behind the wheel, wondering what she hoped to find.

She walked slowly around the house, looking at it from the outside. In the back, she noticed a first-floor window open a crack. It was held by an old rusty lock. She forced it up, ripping the lock from its hinge. Then she climbed inside.

The house was absolutely quiet. But it hadn't been that long. The odors of life were still there. She walked slowly, trying to imagine how he had been when he had lived here, trying to place his physical form in these surroundings. What was she really looking for? she wondered. Was she really looking for some clue to his assassination, or did she have some other purpose in coming to Washington? Was she looking for some small token, some object that confirmed to her that he had remembered her as much as she had remembered him, that he had loved her as she had loved him, some tangible sign that even at the end he had thought about her? She found nothing downstairs.

Slowly she trudged up the wooden staircase, past the boys' room, the basketballs, the posters of football players on the wall, the portable television set, and there at the end of the hall, forbidding, the door to the master bedroom, closed.

The sound of her shoes clicking on the wooden floor sent an eerie sound throughout the house as she walked down the corridor.

She kicked open the door to the master bedroom. It was a small room. The bed dominated it. On each side was a small wooden dresser. He made love here with her, she thought. She looked at the three pictures on the dresser— Dan with Zipora, Dan with the boys, Zipora by herself. Where were the pictures of Dan with Leora in Paris, she wondered, the pictures from the album that she had imagined back in Denmark?

She walked out of the room and kicked the door shut with the back of her heel. It slammed, sending the noise through the house.

She left the house through the window, just as she entered, and trudged across the street. Clay was sitting in the car reading a newspaper.

When she reached the curb across the street, suddenly she saw it lying there. She wasn't even looking for it. It just struck her eye. The small black plastic sword glistened in the bright rays of the sun. It had settled through the snow, lying at the point where Cherev had dropped it.

She picked it up slowly, wiped the dirt off, and tucked it into the pocket of her coat.

"What was that?" Clay asked her when she got back into the car.

"What was what?"

"The thing you just picked up."

"Nothing," she replied softly. "Just an unusual stone. I'm a collector of sorts."

Clay shrugged his shoulders. She's a strange one, this Leora, Clay thought.

At March's office, Leora insisted on looking personally at all of the evidence that Clay had reviewed before his trip to Israel and summarized in Motti's office. She was looking for something, he could tell that, but she stubbornly refused to tell him what it was.

He watched her examine each item of evidence, slowly, carefully, without any emotion, making mental notes, oblivious to his presence. Her thoroughness gave him a kind of admiration for her. She was quickly taking over his investigation, he realized that, using him as a wedge to get into the door; he realized that too. Still, he didn't mind. He could learn a lot from her. She might have some good ideas. After all, he wasn't sure precisely what the next step should be. He knew that they should go to Switzerland, but whom should they see there? That was another matter. Neither he nor Betsy knew what March had done there.

She took an inordinate amount of time, Clay thought, studying the statements from Pritchard's Washington bank and interbank transfer slips. Suddenly her whole face lit up.

"Of course," she said, talking aloud to herself. "That explains the number."

She took the small piece of white paper that Motti had given her from her purse, the paper that had been in Dan's pocket when he was shot, the paper that had the number CB-1-071-4269 written on it.

"Of course," she said, still oblivious to Clay, "CB is Central Bank."

Clay couldn't remain silent any longer.

"Would you mind telling me what you're doing and what that piece of paper is?"

She then explained to Clay about the piece of paper that had been found in Yaacobi's pocket.

"And so, you see, we have the account number. Now we go to Geneva and find out whose account it was and who was depositing in that account. That's our vital link."

His face turned bright red with anger.

"What's bothering you?" she asked. "We've now picked up the trail."

"I'll tell you what's bothering me. We were supposed to be having an open and full working relationship. I shared all of my information, but you never told me about the paper that was found on Yaacobi."

"What difference does that make?" she shot back.

"A lot of difference. It's my investigation. I won't be treated like some type of junior flunky. Either we're doing this together as full partners or not at all."

A look at his face convinced her that he was dead serious.

"Listen, Clay," she said, not liking the sound of Ernest, "I'm used to working on my own. It's strange for me working with someone else. It'll work out."

"What else are you holding back?" he asked.

She thought about the black sword she had picked up in front of Yaacobi's house. No, dammit, she decided, that was personal. She didn't have to share it.

"Nothing," she replied in a matter-of-fact tone.

He wasn't convinced, but he didn't press the point.

"Why don't you call the airplane companies?" she said. "See if we can still get a flight tonight to Geneva."

"Tonight?" he asked incredulously.

"Yes, tonight. Why not?"

Now Clay was losing his patience. He wouldn't be pushed by her any further.

"Because I've already traveled halfway around the world today; because my body hasn't recovered from that trip; because I haven't eaten or slept in God knows how many hours; because I'm dirty and I want to take a hot shower; and because I'm not getting on another airplane until tomorrow morning. That's why."

As he finished his speech, she was preparing to blast back to tell him what was at stake and that time was of the essence. But her better judgment prevailed. Clay would never understand, she realized. He had never had to struggle for his own survival. Decent as he was, he was a man who

259

had never been hungry in his life. How could he possibly understand what a person will do to avoid starvation? Only those who have gone hungry can truly understand that. No man can ever place himself in another man's shoes. No person can ever truly feel another's suffering. A baby falls down a flight of stairs; can even the mother feel the pain that the child is suffering?

"Tomorrow morning then," she said with resignation in her voice.

"Good, I'll make you a hotel reservation for tonight."

Clay eased his car into the driveway of the Washington Hilton. Leora grabbed her small bag, ready to get out.

"I'll pick you up at eight o'clock in the morning," Clay said, stopping the car.

"You'll get the tickets tonight?" she said.

"Is there anything else you want me to do tonight?" he replied sarcastically.

"As a matter of fact, there is," she said, opening the car door. "Shave that ridiculous beard."

She slammed the car door, leaving him cursing to himself. I don't like that woman one bit.

Clay looked at his watch. It was eight o'clock Washington time, and God only knew what time it was for his body. He was so tired. He could hardly move. As he drove to his Georgetown townhouse, he tried to keep awake by thinking about that hot shower, that thick steak he would eat alone with a bottle of Burgundy, and how good it would feel to climb into his own bed.

As Clay finally climbed into bed, Major Husni was about to excuse himself from a Georgetown party only two blocks away.

"The operator is ready with your overseas call," the hostess said.

Husni locked himself in a downstairs study to take the call. He began talking softly to avoid being overheard.

"I've reconsidered the whole subject," he said coldly. "My answer is still the same. We cannot take a chance on Heinrich Fuller."

"And the woman?" the voice at the other end replied. "Valeria Feragamo? What should we do about her?"

Husni paused for a moment, remembering well the pleasures of the flesh that he had enjoyed with Valeria Feragamo when her husband had been the Italian ambassador in Washington, how she had felt, how she had tasted. She was one of the truly magnificent creatures whom God had created.

"Nothing for now with the woman," he said. "Just continued surveillance."

Major Husni then placed the telephone gently in its cradle.

Heinrich Fuller, the president of the Central Bank in Geneva, treasured those three-day holidays when he could escape from the world of banking and finance to the ski slopes near Zurich. He particularly appreciated this holiday because he still had a bad taste in his mouth from his recent meeting with March.

Fuller carefully buttoned his heavy ski jacket and pulled the cloth cap over his ears.

"Do you really have to be the first one out every morning?" his wife called from bed.

"When you have only three days," he replied, "you make the most of them."

"I'll bet you're the only one up this early."

"That's the advantage of it, my little turtle," he replied.

Then he paused to look in the mirror. He should really lose some weight, but he was still healthy and robust. So many of them were like his wife. They came on ski holidays to party, lounge around all day with a hangover, and then begin partying again. But not Heinrich Fuller. He came to ski, and everyone knew that when he was at the lodge you started those lifts early.

As Fuller stepped outside of the lodge, he took a deep breath of the clean morning air. He loved it early in the morning. It was so quiet. Not another skier was out yet.

He made his way on foot, carrying his skis at a fast pace to the lift. Suddenly a black Mercedes pulled out of the parking lot and stopped near him on the road. A woman was driving. Fuller couldn't see anyone else in the car.

She rolled down the window and called to Fuller. "Can you give me some help, my friend? I need some help."

Fuller looked at her with disgust. He didn't easily suffer any interruptions in his early-morning skiing ritual. Still, she was young, a good-looking blond, undoubtedly German from her speech. Even from a distance, Fuller could tell that she was wearing a bright yellow sweater and had the largest pair of breasts that Fuller had ever seen.

It might not be so bad to take a few minutes and aid a woman with a problem, he thought. By the time he reached the car, his organ had already started to rise.

"What is the problem?" he asked, leaning his head into the car, wanting to get good and close.

Just as he did, the woman shoved a damp cloth against his face.

He immediately recognized the sharp odor of chloroform. A few drops trickled into his mouth. It had a sickening sweet taste. He was remotely aware that two men, who had been hiding in the back of the car, jumped out and pulled him in. But that was all that he ever felt.

Clay paused at the airport in Geneva to buy half a dozen different papers.

"I'm compulsive about reading newspapers," he said.

"That and your beard," she replied.

He was happy that she was less grim today, willing to banter with him.

"Yes, I seem to have ignored your advice about shaving it."

She was leafing through the local telephone directory, looking for the address of the Central Bank while Clay glanced at the headlines in his newspapers. He never got past the first page of the *Geneva World*.

"Holy Moley," he said aloud. "Holy Moley." Then his face froze in terror. He dropped the newspapers on the ground.

She heard him across the corridor, just as she found the address she was looking for. She walked quickly back to him.

"What is it?" she asked.

He pointed to the paper on the ground. She picked it up and looked slowly at the headline.

"Mysterious Disappearance of Bank President at Ski Resort."

She read the first two paragraphs and that was enough.

She waited until they were in the cab to bark at him.

"Well, my friend, I hope you enjoyed your good night's sleep last night, because you managed to guarantee Herr Fuller a good sleep from now on."

"It wouldn't have mattered," he protested weakly. "We would never have found him in time, not if he was at the resort."

"Maybe not, but we don't know that for sure, do we?"

They rode in silence. She had no right to tell him that. He felt guilty enough without her words.

"I hope they didn't close the bank today," she said glumly, "because of Fuller's death."

Now they were into a field where Clay could show her that he had greater knowledge.

"This is Switzerland. Banking business stops for no man."

* * *

Clay was right. They were open for business, but that didn't help her or Clay one bit. For two hours they were closeted with Frederich Schultz, the first vice-president of the bank.

Clay politely asked, requested, and cajoled Schultz for the information they wanted: the name of the person who had the account and the name of the depositor. Schultz absolutely refused to divulge any information. He was a little man who had a good idea of what had happened to Fuller, and he was absolutely terrified.

Then they tried it Leora's way. She threatened, insulted, berated, and verbally abused Schultz so badly that he finally stormed out of the office threatening to call the police if they didn't leave the bank in five minutes.

With Clay pulling on Leora's arm and listening to her cursing, they walked out of the building five minutes later. Clay led her into a small outdoor café on the square opposite the bank, ordered two cups of coffee, and looked at her beseechingly to see what ideas she had for their next step.

"We're at a dead end," Clay said grimly.

"Like hell we are."

"Okay, experienced one, what do we do now?"

"We find out where Schultz lives. We go there tonight and threaten to blow his head off if he doesn't tell us what we want. Believe me, he'll tell us. I have never known a man yet who doesn't have more fear of the gun resting against his head than the gun that is far away."

At first, Clay thought she was joking. But as he looked into her eyes, he realized that she was deadly serious. He was incredulous. He would never be a party to conduct like that.

"I won't do it," he said firmly.

"Why not?"

"It violates everything I believe in."

She laughed.

"Good God, man, you're dealing with criminals. They've killed Yaacobi, March, and now Fuller. This isn't a cricket match."

He wasn't persuaded.

"If we adopt their methods, we're no better than they are."

"Don't mix things up in a mass of self-righteousness. I didn't say we should kill Schultz. That's their way. We only threaten him."

"I won't do it."

"This is survival, Clay," she replied.

"Whose?"

"Well, since you're in it now, it's yours as well."

He thought about her words for a minute; they cut deeply. She was right. He had now become a target as March had been. It had not occurred to him before.

Still he refused to yield.

"Think of something else," he said.

She sat glumly stirring her coffee and puffing on a cigarette.

Three cups of coffee and eight cigarettes later, she thought of something else.

"What is it?" he asked hopefully.

"I'm going to the land of my ancestors. Maybe I can pick up something there."

"Israel?" he asked, puzzled. "What do you hope to get there?"

"My dear Clay. My ancestors also were in the land of Egypt."

"You'll never get in," he protested.

"Why not? You heard the radio yesterday. Israeli journalists are going in by scores to cover the Prime Minister's visit. I'll just have to stop in Jerusalem and pick up some press credentials and a couple of other items."

"It's too risky," he said, still sounding negative.

She laughed loudly. "Someday I'll tell you about what taking risks in Egypt is like."

The longer she talked, the more he liked the idea.

"I'll get some plane reservations for the two of us," he finally said.

There was a long silence.

"I think it would be better if I went myself. Just this one time. Please believe me on that."

Her tone of voice was so intense that he decided she had to have some good reason for going alone.

"I'll wait in Geneva," he said. "I'll take a room at the Richmont. Either return here or cable me to meet you somewhere else."

She nodded in agreement, then added wistfully, "If you don't hear from me in a week, tell Motti to ask our new-found friends in Egypt to return my body for burial."

"That's not funny," Clay replied grimly. He was beginning to feel a fondness for this strange creature. He didn't want her to die. "You'd better be careful."

∼

CHAPTER 34

Kate fidgeted with the buttons on her blouse as she waited for the doctor to come into his study. She glanced nervously at her watch. She had been waiting almost an hour. Still, for what she wanted, it was better for her to come at the end of the day.

Finally, he walked into his study, worn out from a day of hospital rounds, seeing patients, and lecturing medical students. Wednesday was always a difficult day.

He was startled to see her sitting there.

"I didn't realize that I had another appointment."

"I'm not exactly a patient," she replied weakly. She looked so distraught. He decided to add some levity.

"Late-afternoon hanky-panky then?"

She never even cracked a smile.

"Okay, young lady, what is it?" Dr. Green said, slumping into the chair behind his desk.

She described her concern for her husband and explained how she had found out about Michael's medicine, and begged the doctor to tell her what was wrong so that she could help him. When she finished, large round tears were flowing down her cheeks.

"I don't usually do that, Mrs. Holt," the doctor replied coldly. "I stay out of marital relations. Whether or not one of my patients wants to share my prognosis with his spouse is his business. I have certain professional confidences to maintain."

"He may be in trouble, doctor," she said grimly, "a lot of trouble. I want to help him. Really I do."

Dr. Green wasn't surprised by her words. As far as he was concerned, Michael's condition was the result of great stress, and in twenty years of practice in Washington he had frequently found that stress of that type flows from wrongdoing in high places. What surprised Dr. Green was the intensity of the feeling in Kate's voice.

"You're a very determined person," he said.

She nodded, feeling that he was leaning toward talking to her.

It just might be possible that she could help him. If she could eliminate some of the stress, his physical condition might improve. The doctor could rationalize telling her, without approval from Michael, as a part of the treatment.

"Let me get the file," the doctor said. "I'll give it to you in all its gruesome detail."

She bit her lower lip, wanting to know and yet not wanting to know what the doctor would tell her.

When Kate left the doctor's office, her inclination was to stop at the first bar and have a stiff martini. It took all of her willpower to squelch that idea.

No, dammit, she decided. He's the one who's weak and fragile. The only way Brett's strong hold will ever be broken is if I do it. I have to be strong. Sooner or later, I'll have my chance.

That evening she waited in a drugstore across from Michael's office building. When she saw his car pull out of the garage, she hailed a taxi and asked the driver to follow him.

At the entrance to the Bethesda Indoor Tennis Club, she asked the driver to stop and wait for her. As inconspicuously as possible, she walked into the deserted spectators' gallery and surveyed the courts below. There was Michael, his back to her, playing against a man she didn't recognize, a sad-looking, tired figure, awkward and disheveled in rumpled tennis shorts that had once been white but were now gray for lack of laundering.

He looks worse than Michael, she decided. She didn't recognize the man. She studied his face carefully and committed it to memory. One day she would find out who he was.

༄

CHAPTER 35

The Alexandria Trading Company still occupied the original brown stone building that had been its headquarters when Moshe Baruch was president of the company. Business had been good during the last four years as the Saudi monarch had been increasingly willing to use his expanded revenues from oil to finance the development of the Egyptian economy.

No longer was the company limited to the single building that Moshe Baruch had found locked in November 1956 by order of the government. On each side of that building, new glass-and-metal structures had been built.

Abdel Rasef, the president of the Alexandria Trading Company, was very proud of those new twin towers. They signified his firm's readiness to share in the new era of prosperity that Rasef hoped would follow if Egypt were able to make peace with Israel at long last. He was waiting anxiously for the meeting that his President would have with the Israeli Prime Minister in two days. He was hopeful that that meeting would lead to commerce and trade between Egypt and Israel that might increase the prosperity of the country, and with it the prosperity of the Alexandria Trading Company.

As Rasef had grown older, he had become more occupied in the accumulation of money. That was one of the few pleasures left for an old man. And so, in recent years, he had given up his law practice, devoting all of his time to the trading company. He even had two of his sons in the business now.

Rasef had decided to work late at his office at the trading company that evening, trying to sift through the myriad proposals that had been flowing in from Israeli firms, when he heard a knock on the thick wooden door of his office.

It must be one of the clerks who had decided to stay late, Rasef thought.

"Come in," he bellowed from behind his desk.

The door opened slowly. Rasef could hardly believe his eyes. Though he was as stunned as he had been when she had come to his house eleven years earlier, he at least recognized his surprise visitor this time.

"Leora," he said, startled, as if he were looking at a ghost.

"Leora, what in the world are you doing here?"

"Well, it seems like it's Israeli week in Egypt, and I thought I would take advantage of the open borders for a brief personal visit. You know, I used to play in this office."

"I doubt if it's pure nostalgia," he said, shaking his head in disbelief.

He walked over to the credenza, took out a large cigar, and lit it up.

"Do you want one?" he asked.

"No," she replied. "But I would like one of those vile-smelling Turkish cigarettes you and my father used to smoke."

The mention of Leora's father made Rasef very nervous. He still had some guilt feelings about how he had bribed an army colonel to give him control of the Alexandria Trading Company. It also bothered him that Moshe Baruch had been his friend and his client. Rasef had rationalized it by telling himself that if he didn't take it over someone else would, and what difference did it make to Moshe who had control?

He pulled a package of cigarettes from his desk, handed her one, and lit it with his gold lighter.

"Since it can't be pure nostalgia," he said, "to what do I owe the honor of this visit?"

"I need some help."

"But my dear Leora, I gave already. Eleven years ago. Now I will admit that it was given at the end of the barrel of a gun, but still, I was motivated to help the child of an old friend. But once is enough."

His face was completely deadpan. His tone was unemotional, but firm.

"No, this time I won't help you," he repeated emphatically. "Find someone else."

Then he sat down behind his desk, watching her carefully. He was in the driver's seat, but still he had to watch her.

"This time is different," she said to Rasef, trying hard not to raise her voice. "This time all that I need is information."

Her statement whetted his curiosity.

"What kind of information?" he asked without committing himself.

"An American was killed in Cairo about a week ago by some Palestinian terrorists. He was an employee of the American State Department."

Rasef raised his eyebrows. It was obvious to her that he hadn't heard of March's death before now.

"I'm not asking you to find out who killed him or what happened to them. I have a good idea about that."

"That's very generous of you," he said sarcastically.

She ignored his comment.

"What I want you to find out for me is what he was doing in Cairo, whom he came to see."

"Even if I wanted to, what makes you think I could get that kind of information?"

"Modesty doesn't become you, Rasef. You are a powerful man in this country. I have no doubt that if you were to travel to Cairo, meeting with old friends and spreading around some of your hard-earned money, you could easily obtain the information in a day or two."

He leaned back in his chair, puffing on the cigar and thinking. He had no desire to argue with her on that point. She was right, of course.

"Yes, I could do it if I wanted to," he replied. "But I won't. I've told you, I gave once."

His tone was firm.

"The lives of other people depend on this information," she replied.

"No, by the word of Allah, the answer is no."

Now he was raising his voice. The line was drawn. Leora was equally determined.

"You will do it," she replied as if she hadn't heard him.

"This time you can't threaten to shoot me. I am too old

for that now. All of the juices have run dry. You have nothing to coerce me with."

She rose to her feet quickly and stared squarely into his eyes.

"Nothing, my friend? Are you certain of that?"

He was watching her closely, fearful of what was coming next. When she reached into her handbag with a dramatic gesture, a look of absolute terror appeared on Rasef's face. He closed his eyes and prayed to Allah, absolutely convinced that she would pull a gun from her bag and shoot him.

Nothing happened.

He waited a full two minutes before opening his eyes slowly. She was standing next to him waving a piece of white paper in each hand. She had a wild look in her eyes, like a woman pushed to the brink of her sanity.

"What are those?" he asked, his voice trembling. It was the voice of a man who had returned from the dead.

"I'll tell you what these papers are." When she began speaking this time, her voice was no longer calm. She was shouting, her voice filled with anger.

"In my right hand I have a copy of my father's will." She threw the document at him. It struck him in the chest and fell into his lap.

"Pick it up and look at it," she commanded.

He raised the paper slowly, fearful of disobeying her. He looked at the outside of the document. The will was in Arabic, but it had been probated in a Tel Aviv court.

"I'll save you the time. Skip to paragraph six. That's what counts. You'll notice that I have been named as the beneficiary of one hundred percent of the stock in the Alexandria Trading Company. In other words, this is my company. You are sitting in my chair."

He laughed nervously.

"Surely you're not serious, Leora. That's a worthless

piece of paper. We both know that. No Egyptian court would enforce that paper to give you control."

By now her voice had calmed down.

"You take me for a fool, Rasef. Of course no Egyptian court would enforce that paper today. I know that. But there is a great deal of talk about the new era of peace and normalization of relations that Egypt and Israel have launched upon. If this normalization does occur in the future, then how can you be certain that five or ten or even twenty years from now when you are dead, when your sons are supporting themselves and their families lavishly from this business, an Egyptian court won't enforce this piece of paper and give me control?"

"I don't think it will ever happen," he said.

"But you can't be certain, Rasef. You can't be absolutely certain."

He was silent.

"You're a lawyer by training," she said. "Lawyers deal in probabilities. We're talking about a legal event. We're trying to predict the chances of an Egyptian court rendering a decision of a certain type in the indefinite future. You can assign some probability to the likelihood of this event. It's small, I will admit. Maybe two in a hundred or one in a hundred. But it's not zero."

He nodded subconsciously. She was right, of course.

"And as long as it's not zero, there's some risk that your children will lose everything."

He leaned forward, listening carefully to what she would say next.

She was waving around her left hand with the second piece of paper, high over her head. That wild, almost insane look had returned to her eyes.

"I want to help you eliminate that risk, Rasef," she said mockingly. "I want to sell you an insurance policy."

She then lowered her left hand and dropped the piece of

paper on his desk. He sat still, not daring to pick it up.

"It's a contract," she said, her voice rising. "You agree to obtain certain unspecified information for me, and I agree to surrender any claim to the Alexandria Trading Company. It's not yet signed, of course. When I get the information, I will then sign the contract and also an acknowledgment certifying that you have given me the information."

When she was finished speaking, she slumped down in a chair and watched him carefully as he picked up the document, which was in Arabic, and began reading it.

Leora was a woman who had lived much of her adult life in complete control of her emotions, but now they were threatening to break out. How bizarre it all was.

Esau had sold his birthright to Jacob for a bowl of porridge. She was selling her own for information that might help her avenge the death of a man whom she had loved as much as life itself. She thought about how happy she had been to come to this very office to pick up Abba, how he had greeted her, how they had left hand in hand for coffee and chocolate ice cream. "Abba, please forgive me," she mumbled to herself, barely choking back the tears, as Rasef continued reading. "But I am at a dead end. This revenge is all that I have left."

Rasef leaned back in his chair and closed his eyes, thinking of the alternatives.

She placed her hand in her purse, gripping the steel of her pistol tightly. She was prepared to resort to the gun if she had to, even to call his bluff when he had said that he wouldn't be coerced that way.

Unaware of her gun, Rasef was weighing the alternatives. There was some risk that he would cause suspicion by getting the information for Leora. It was small, but it was still there. Was it less than the risk of having his children lose the company? It was difficult to determine which risk was greater. But there is a difference, he decided. If I am caught getting the information, only an old man suffers the consequences. The other way, my children and their children will lose.

He opened his eyes.

"Will you do it?"

"Yes, I will do it," he said reluctantly.

She gave a large sigh of relief and let the purse drop to the floor. They sat in silence for several minutes staring at each other.

"I have a confession to make," Rasef said. "That summer when you finished your first year at the University of London and you were at my house in Alexandria using my books, I felt a great sexual desire for you. You were so beautiful then, like a dark-haired princess. I wanted to do much more with you than lend you my books. I was then in the prime of my life. We could have enjoyed so much together."

She wasn't startled by his words. She had suspected something like that at the time.

"But you never said anything to me."

"No. I could never bring myself to do it. You were the child of my friend. And that is why I helped you eleven years ago. It was my own guilt for those feelings as much as your threats." Rasef got up and stood next to his desk.

"I will leave for Cairo in the morning," he said. "Where will you be when I return?"

"I want to stay in your house," she replied. "In the room at the end of the hall that I used eleven years ago when I came with my friend."

Rasef didn't argue. Strangely enough, he wanted her to spend the evening in his house. He wanted to sleep at the other end of the hall, fantasizing what might have happened twenty years earlier if he had had more courage or fewer scruples. What is the harm in a few fantasies? he thought.

As she entered the bedroom at the end of the hall, very

275

much alone, Leora was trembling. I am living my whole life twice, she thought to herself. The second time is even more painful than the first.

Nothing had changed in the room. It had been carefully cleaned by a maid once a week. No one had lived there in the last eleven years. There were the same white linen drapes and spreads, or maybe they had been replaced with new ones identical to the old. Leora couldn't tell.

The chair Dan had sat in that night was still there. She pulled it out and placed it in front of the window where he had sat looking out while she had slept. She went into the bathroom, took a long shower, and opened the bathroom door slightly. She dried herself, looking into the mirror and imagining that he was there watching her. She climbed into the large bed, still looking at the chair in front of the window, waiting for him to walk over and climb into bed with her as he had in Paris. But nothing moved in the room.

And finally, the huge tears began rolling out of her eyes and down her cheeks. She buried her head under the pillow to muffle the piercing cries of anguish that poured out of her mouth. And only when her throat was worn raw and there were no tears left did she finally lie still, fully spent and exhausted.

One day in Cairo was all that Rasef needed. He returned late in the evening.

"Come down to the study," he called to Leora.

She walked quickly down the steps, anxious to hear what Rasef had learned.

He sat down behind the desk, pointing her to a brown leather chair in front.

"I have the information that you wanted," he replied in a matter-of-fact tone. "But how do I know that you will sign it if I give it to you?"

"You will simply have to accept my word for that," she said. "You have no choice."

He thought about it for a minute. Then he started talking.

"The American was named Jonathan March. You are correct that he was killed by Palestinian terrorists. Though you did not ask for it, I will tell you that I learned incidentally that one was killed at the time and two escaped. A search is still on for them."

Everything that he said was consistent with what Clay had told her.

"But why was he in Egypt?" she said, wanting him to come to the point.

"March came to Egypt to meet with a woman. Her name is Valeria Feragamo. She is the wife of the Italian ambassador in Cairo. She is a kind of international jet-setter, a very beautiful woman, wealthy and a celebrity of sorts. I am told that she moves from bed to bed with great ease."

Leora was puzzled. What connection could Valeria Feragamo have with the investigation? Suddenly she had an idea.

"Does she have friends in the Arab world?"

"From what I could learn, she seems to have friends everywhere."

"No, I mean among the oil-rich?"

"She seems to have many friends of that type."

Well, it was a good possibility, Leora thought.

"Is she still in Cairo?" Leora asked. "Could I see her there?"

"She's no longer in the country. The same day that March was killed, she left Egypt suddenly to return to Rome. She told friends that there was an illness in the family. Her husband is still in Cairo."

"Did you find out anything else?" she asked.

He looked disgusted.

"That's plenty. I thought you'd be grateful."

"It is plenty, believe me. I have the contract and the acknowledgment," she said, pulling the document from her purse. "I'll sign them both now."

She placed the papers on his desk and quickly removed a pen from the holder.

"Abba, forgive me," she mumbled to herself. Then she carefully signed both documents, turned and silently walked from the room.

From Rasef's house she walked six blocks to the post office, making certain that she wasn't being followed.

She cabled Clay in Geneva:

"Meet me in Rome at the Hotel Excelsior. Your Egyptian mummy."

∾

CHAPTER 36

The Via Veneto in Rome in the evening is one of the world's great visual treats. Even in the winter, when the outdoor cafés have moved indoors, it is possible to watch the end-less flow of diverse characters—artists and actresses wandering in and out of restaurants, Europe's beautiful people heading to the opera or theater, women in haute couture and men with wide-lapelled continental suits and carefully styled hair, tourists disgorged from large buses, and mixing with all of these, the new class of kidnapper and extortioner that was spawned in the Italian political turmoil of the seventies.

Leora had no time to enjoy any of this scenery as her taxicab drove up the Via Veneto and deposited her at the Excelsior. She asked for Clay's room and was told 615, 617, and 619.

When he opened the door and looked at her, Clay was

visibly relieved. She noticed that he had shaved his beard. He looked completely different. The old professorial look was gone. He had smooth skin, a handsome face.

"What prompted that?" Leora asked.

He looked embarrassed.

"Well, I was worried about you," he replied. "When I was waiting to hear from you back at the Richmont, I said to myself, If she gets out okay, I'm going to shave that beard just like she asked."

Leora smiled, still not understanding Clay, but deciding that she liked him as a person.

"This is one hell of a suite you rented. Is this how Uncle Sam finances his people?"

Clay blushed.

"Actually it's my own money. I thought that two bedrooms connected by a living room would be easier for us to work in."

She kicked off her shoes and looked around. It was a far cry from the antiquated headquarters of the Anglo-American Trading Company that she and Dan had occupied in Paris.

"Now that you've been goofing off for the last couple of days," she said to Clay in a devilish tone, "I've got a terrific job for you."

"Threatening more bank executives?"

"No, this time you're dating a beautiful woman, who's probably too much for you, but do your best."

She sat down and told Clay that they had broken out of their dead end and that she had a new lead, Valeria Feragamo. She didn't tell Clay how she had gotten that information.

"Our first step will be to get into that charming lady's apartment. That may be all we need from her."

"Second-story work is not one of my specialties."

"How about eating fine food and drinking good wine? Is that more fitting for a gentleman of your breeding?"

279

"Yes, as a matter of fact, it is."

"Good, then you're suited for the job."

Clay made the contact through Roger White, the minister at the American Embassy, two blocks from the Excelsior. Roger had been a classmate of Clay's at Princeton. Following Leora's instructions, it actually went easier than Clay had imagined. After two double martinis and a relatively innocuous allusion to cloak-and-dagger activities, White was willing to call Valeria and explain to her how a good friend of his was in Rome, an enormously wealthy American investment banker who was interested in having dinner with her.

Roger's flattery on the telephone with Valeria was so excessive that Clay had to leave the room from embarrassment. Still the objective was accomplished. Roger gleefully said, "Pick her up at nine o'clock at her apartment. She likes to eat at Sabbatino's in the Piazza Santa Maria."

Clay thanked Roger profusely. When Roger handed him her address on a piece of paper, Clay tucked it in his pocket, neglecting to say that he and Leora knew very well where she lived.

As Clay was ready to leave the office, Roger gleefully said, "I didn't believe any of that cloak-and-dagger stuff you told me."

Clay looked embarrassed.

"Then why do you think I want to meet her?"

"That's easy. The woman's a great lay. Everybody in the diplomatic community here knows that."

Clay turned red from embarrassment. As he rushed to escape, Roger called, "Have fun, Ernie."

Leora was right about one thing, Clay thought to himself as he left the apartment with Valeria on his arm. This woman is absolutely beautiful, the long black hair flowing down to her shoulders, the sensuous face with perfect skin, the large rounded breasts, the shapely body. Wearing a black velvet dress with a neckline that plunged in a V nearly to her navel, she was the most beautiful woman he had ever seen. He stroked his hand across her mink jacket just to make certain that he was really dining with this lovely creature.

Leora was also right about something else, Clay decided as they approached her red Alfa Romeo. She handed Clay her key case just as Leora said she would.

He helped her into the car, closing the door gently. Then as he walked behind the car to get to the driver's side, he nervously looked at the brown leather key case. It contained six keys, and only two of them were for the car. Maybe the others would be what Leora was looking for.

He drove quickly across the crowded streets, trying to follow the insane flow of traffic in Rome.

Leora had rehearsed the route with him half a dozen times. He knew exactly where he was going.

"Will you be in Rome long, Ernest?" she asked.

"Only a couple of days more, until I complete my business."

"Oh, a real pity. I'm having a large New Year's Eve party on Saturday. I hoped you could join me."

"If I decide to stay, then I would love to."

She took a cigarette out of her purse and waited for a red light to hand him the gold cigarette lighter. He lit it dutifully and pulled away.

"What about you?" Clay asked. "How long will you be in Rome?"

"Oh, a week or two, then I return to Egypt."

Clay winced. Leora had told him, "Stay away from Egypt and Arabs when you talk to her. We don't want her to get suspicious."

They crossed the Tiber River and entered the strange

281

and wonderful world of Trastevere. Crowds were milling on every corner, residents shopping, tourists, people out for a good time—even balloon vendors.

Clay turned down the narrow street that led to the Piazza Santa Maria. His eyes looked carefully on the right. He saw Leora wearing an evening dress and lounging in the doorway of the shop, looking at the windows filled with leather goods just where she had said she would be. He parked the car as close to that shop as he could. Then he helped Valeria out of the car, locking her door. As innocuously as he could, he announced, "I've forgotten to lock the other door," and he quickly walked around the car, leaving her to gaze into shop windows for a minute.

When he reached the driver's side, he opened the door quickly, placed the key case on the floor, and slammed it.

His eye happened to catch Leora's. She was winking at him.

He walked back around the car, placed his arm on Valeria's, and set off for the restaurant. There was a large clock above the square that tolled out the time at half-hour intervals. It was nine thirty now. Leora had told him that she would need an hour and a half.

Leora waited until they were out of sight. Then she walked quickly over to the Alfa Romeo, scooped up the keys, and raced to her own rented Fiat a block away.

She barreled through traffic heading back to the apartment.

A friendly smile from a woman in an evening dress was all the doorman needed to pass her through.

Leora rode up in the elevator with an elderly woman and her French poodle. The woman was too occupied with the dog to open a conversation. Fortunately, she got out at a lower floor.

Leora studied the keys in the case as well as the door locks as she walked down the corridor. There were only six apartments on the floor. Valeria's was at the end of the hall. By the time she reached the door to the apartment, she had made up her mind which key would open the door.

She was right.

As Leora let herself in, she was struck by the absolute beauty of the apartment. It was filled with luxurious items the likes of which she had never seen before. Oriental carpets covered the floor. Tapestries hung on the wall. A Renoir hung over the marble-topped credenza.

She glanced quickly at her watch. Only half an hour, she said to herself. I'll have to move fast.

First she walked quickly around the whole apartment. There were his and her bedrooms, and his and her studies. That narrowed her options.

The first assumption is that it will be in something that is locked. Only three keys to go, then.

She noticed an antique jewelry box sitting on the chest in Valeria's bedroom. She tried one of the keys. It worked. She carefully looked over the box. It was a crime that the collection wasn't on public display. Only two keys to go.

She walked back to the study. Her eyes immediately came to rest on the desk. She tried to pull open the center drawer. It was locked. She tried the remaining two keys. One of them opened it. She carefully searched the drawer; nothing. She looked nervously at her watch. Only ten minutes left. Only one more key.

She went back into the bedroom and began searching the closet. Buried among dozens of shoe boxes was a thin leather briefcase. She pulled it out quickly. It had a lock. She tried the last key. The case flipped open.

Now she was searching frantically. When she found nothing, she began tapping her fingers nervously on the bottom of the case. It felt funny, hollow, like there was something underneath. She removed a small knife from her pocket and pried up the false bottom. There it was: precisely what she was looking for, a small piece of white paper with a list of Swiss bank account numbers, the person who was depositing, and the owners of each account.

Leora's hunch about Valeria Feragamo was right. She was the banker for some of the Arab oil money. When they wanted to distribute money that could not be traced, they gave Valeria checks, which could pass as gifts, and she in turn deposited them into various Swiss bank accounts.

Her eye glanced quickly over the list until she found the number she was looking for, CB-1-071-4269. Opposite the number was the name of the depositor, an Arab name that she didn't recognize, but she noted mentally. Then on the right side of the paper was the name of the person who owned the account: The Douglas Foundation.

"Pay dirt," she said aloud, "but what is the Douglas Foundation?" She quickly locked the briefcase and put it back precisely where she had found it.

She rode down the elevator and tried to walk slowly as she left the building, smiling at the doorman again.

Walking to the Fiat, Leora had the distinct feeling that she was being followed. She reached into her purse, grabbed her pistol, and began running. It took her only a minute to reach the Fiat. In a single motion, she started the car, causing it to roar out of the space quickly. She saw a black Mercedes in the rearview mirror. Without hesitating, she drove with reckless abandon, even for Rome, racing through alleys and around corners until the Mercedes was no longer in the rearview mirror. If there really had been someone following her, she was confident that she lost him.

Why did Valeria do it? Leora wondered when she approached the Piazza Santa Maria. She finally decided that Valeria probably did it for the extra money. It simply takes a great deal to run an establishment like hers.

As Leora tucked the key case back into the Alfa Romeo, Clay and Valeria were watching the end of an amateur song-and-dance performance that a neighborhood group put on each evening. When the group left, he ordered two cups of cappucino.

"I can't tell you what a wonderful evening this has been for me," Valeria said to Clay. "I spend most of my life with boring diplomats. Your intelligence is very refreshing for me."

Clay smiled weakly. He was feeling a trifle guilty. He rather liked this woman. She was knowledgeable about art, sensitive, and interested in what he had to say about the history of the twentieth century. He believed her when she said that she had done everything possible to make her bad marriage work and that she wanted a life with far more meaning than the rut of frivolity she had fallen into.

The impact of the two bottles of wine on Clay was so great that when he got to the Alfa Romeo, he nearly forgot where the keys were. He picked them up quickly and opened the door for her.

They parked in her garage and rode up in the garage elevator to the lobby. As they were waiting for the other elevator to take them to her door, Clay suddenly announced, "You go up without me, Val, I want to stop in the drugstore next door and pick something up. I'll be right up."

She looked amused.

"You don't need anything from the drugstore," she said. "I'm well protected, really I am."

Clay turned bright red.

"I didn't mean that."

"Go ahead then," she replied. "I'll change into something comfortable."

Inside the drugstore, he quickly walked toward the phone booth. Someone was already talking, a teenage girl, placing a call to her boy friend outside of her parents' house. Clay paced nervously next to the booth, waiting for her to finish—five minutes, ten minutes, finally she was done. He checked a book of matches to make certain that he remembered the number of the Excelsior. Then he picked up the telephone. It was still warm from the teenager's hand.

Leora answered on the third ring, just as they had planned.

"Did you get what you wanted?" he asked.

"Mission accomplished. You can enjoy the rest of your evening, lover boy, and even mix pleasure with business. The Egyptian mummy won't wait up for you."

Clay replaced the phone.

Leora thought about telling him that she might have been followed near Valeria's apartment, but she decided that she had probably been imagining it.

Clay walked slowly back to the apartment, whistling a tune to himself and combing his hair. Suddenly he heard a commotion on the street in front of Valeria's building. A black Mercedes roared away from the building. Instinctively, he tried to see the license plate; but it was moving too fast.

Now he was worried as he rode up in the elevator and raced toward her apartment. The door was open a little. Maybe she left it open for me, he hoped. He let himself in and called, "Val, I'm here." There was no answer. I'm getting too nervous, he decided, working with Leora. Probably Valeria had changed into some thin negligee and was stretched out on her bed waiting for him.

"Ready or not, here I come," he called, dropping his jacket and tie on the floor and heading for the bedroom.

When he entered the bedroom, he came to a complete stop. There on the bed was what was left of Valeria Feragamo. Her naked torso was barely visible in the pool of blood that lay in a large puddle on the bed. Every major artery on her body had been severed. The size of the gashes indicated that those who had done it used butcher knives to mutilate what was left after her death.

Clay began gasping for air. He thought he would pass out completely. Somehow he managed to pull himself to his feet. He was as white as a sheet.

In a reflex action, he picked up his jacket and tie from the living room floor and quickly put them on. He said a prayer of thanks that the doorman wasn't at his post. No one saw Clay leave the building.

∾

CHAPTER 37

The jumbo jet made a screeching noise as the captain lowered the landing gear.

"We're now beginning our final approach into Dulles Airport," the flight attendant on Alitalia announced in her sensuous voice.

Clay closed his eyes with fear as he listened to the roar of the airplane engines, still thinking about the sight he had seen in Valeria's bedroom.

Next to him Leora sat alert and attentive, watching the American through the corner of her eye and wondering if he would be able to continue after Valeria's brutal death. Perhaps he would walk into Waller's office in the morning and dump it all back on the impotent Secretary of State.

It was evening, and she was glad of that. Clay would have ten or twelve hours to pull himself together.

Silently, glumly, they walked into the terminal, past the special customs agent who quickly waved their luggage through when Clay flashed his identification, and into the brightly lit parking lot. She let Clay walk two steps ahead, deep in thought, kicking at the small mounds of snow and ice that lined each lane in the parking lot, like a little boy.

As Clay paid the parking ticket and eased the car onto

the Dulles access road, he announced his verdict.

"Tomorrow morning we'll start moving up on the Douglas Foundation."

She breathed a large sigh of relief.

"We can work out of my office."

"But isn't Waller likely to butt in?" she replied.

He thought about her question for a minute.

"You're right. We'd never keep him out. Let's use the third floor of my house. It has a study that's private. There's also a bedroom up there that you can use. It's clean. You're welcome to stay there, if you want to. We can operate the whole project from the house."

She liked that idea. Without alarming Clay, she wanted desperately to minimize their exposure on the street.

"How do you propose to begin assembling the information about the Douglas Foundation?" she asked.

It was here that his experience in the Criminal Division at Justice would be useful.

"People don't understand how extensive the American government's information is on each person and organization in this country, or even abroad. There are half a dozen government agencies who might have something, IRS, Justice, FBI, Department of Commerce, Export-Import, Trade Commission. I can easily get access to any of their files."

"While we were waiting for our luggage, I checked the phone book," she replied.

"And?"

"Nothing."

"That's not surprising. Even if they had a Washington office, I wouldn't expect it to be a listed number, given what we know."

The traffic was light. Clay raced the car down the George Washington Parkway and onto the Key Bridge.

"Welcome to Washington," he said. "Maybe the end of a long journey."

"Yes," she repeated softly to herself. "Maybe the end of a long journey."

On the morning of the second day of his search, which was Friday, December 30, Clay found what he was looking for. It was buried on microfilm at the Internal Revenue Service—a notation opposite the name Douglas Foundation that said "D.C." To Clay that meant that the organization had been organized under the laws of the District of Columbia.

Quickly, Clay placed his papers in his briefcase and began racing along Pennsylvania Avenue, his coat unbuttoned, perspiring from the run despite the thirty-two-degree temperature, his long legs covering the sidewalk quickly, if not gracefully.

It was almost noon when Clay arrived at the offices of the District of Columbia government. A general holiday atmosphere prevailed in the corridors of the building. The New Year's Eve celebrations had started early. Half of the people who worked in the building had left early. The other half were drinking Cold Duck, beer, or cheap champagne and dancing in the corridors.

Clay nearly panicked when he took a look at the scene of pandemonium that prevailed.

Good God, he thought to himself. If I don't get anything today, we're stuck for the three-day holiday weekend.

Clay looked into the records office. He couldn't see a single person. All that he saw was rows and rows of files. Not knowing where to start and completely exasperated, Clay threw his long arms into the air as if he were praying for help.

It came to him in a strange form. From deep in the shelves of files he heard the soft and uncontrolled sobbing, the barely muffled sound of a woman crying—tears that came from sorrow.

Clay approached the woman cautiously. She was sitting

at a small table, a heavyset woman, her black face buried in her hands, her hair streaked with gray. She was wearing a blue-and-white cotton dress. Clay surmised that she was in her fifties. He was reluctant to disturb her, but he had no choice.

"Can I bother you for a minute, ma'am?" he said tenderly.

The woman stopped crying and looked up at Clay with the largest brown eyes he had ever seen.

"My Ralph was born on New Year's Eve," she said to Clay. "He would have been twenty-eight years old tomorrow."

She desperately wanted to tell her story to somebody. Clay stood there nervously fidgeting with his hands, wanting to extricate himself and yet unwilling to be cruel.

She began talking slowly about how she had come to Washington from Alabama in search of the better life that "you white folks promised."

She told her story of ghetto suffering so full of emotion that tears began to flow from Clay's eyes.

She continued. Her Ralph was drafted into the army "to go over to those jungles to fight somebody else's war."

"Why did my Ralph die in Nam, mister?" she asked Clay beseechingly.

He was silent.

"I want to know why, mister." She was raising her voice.

"It is hard to know the ways of the Lord," Clay said, searching for something that might be comforting.

"Lord, my ass," she replied bluntly, startling Clay. "That was Mr. Johnson and Mr. Nixon sticking their nose into other folks' business."

She wiped her eyes with a handkerchief and stood up, looking at Clay as if he had just appeared.

"You want me for something, mister?" she asked.

Clay explained to her what he was looking for and politely offered to search himself if she didn't want to help him. She was insulted.

"I do my own job," she said. "Nobody does my work for me."

Still filled with emotion, thinking about her son who had died eight years earlier, she began trudging wearily down corridors in the file room, her eyes looking from one identifying marker to the next, while Clay followed two steps behind.

Finally, she pulled a thin pink folder from one of the shelves and handed it to Clay.

"Look at it here," she said, "and put it back when you're done."

With that, she left him standing among the shelves holding the folder. He walked over to the window and placed the folder on the windowsill. All that it contained was the one-page organizational statement, a legal form, the bare minimum required by the law to operate in the District of Columbia.

That form identified a single individual as the principal in the Douglas Foundation. His name was Michael James Holt. It gave an address on K Street as the organization's office and a phone number was also shown. Clay quickly wrote the information in a small notebook that he carried in his pocket and replaced the folder.

In the lobby of the building, Clay went into one of the telephone booths. He dialed the number of the Douglas Foundation slowly, wanting to make certain the number was correct. It rang three times, then a woman answered, giving only the number that he had dialed without identifying the organization.

"Michael Holt, please?" Clay said, holding his breath.

"Mr. Holt is out of town until Tuesday," she replied politely. "Is there any message?"

Clay was tempted to ask where he could reach Holt, but he didn't want to raise any suspicions.

"No message, thank you," he replied.

As soon as Clay placed down the telephone, he immediately began leafing through the telephone directory. Washington has three different directories—District of Columbia, Virginia, and Maryland. He found what he was looking for in the third. There was only one Michael J. Holt. He was in Chevy Chase. Clay copied the address and telephone number in his notebook. He dialed the number, letting it ring a dozen times. There was no answer. He repeated it. Again, no answer. Well, the secretary was probably telling the truth, Clay decided. We'll have to wait until Tuesday to meet Mr. Holt.

∼☙

CHAPTER 38

Leora lit up another cigarette and continued fuming at Clay.

"What the hell do we do for the next three days, Mr. Ivy League?"

Clay tried to be patient, keeping his composure despite her verbal tirade.

"Listen, Leora," he said calmly. "There is no way to find out where Holt is without raising suspicions. You'll just have to wait. Remember, I want this as much as you do."

"I doubt that," she shot back.

He was silent.

"You still haven't answered my question. What do we do for the next three days?"

Clay was thinking. He looked at Leora. So close to the end, she was pacing the floor nervously, like a keg of dynamite ready to explode. He had no intention of spending the weekend caged up with her in his Georgetown townhouse.

"Let's go out to the country," he said finally.

She looked incredulous.

"No, really. One of my aunts owns a country house on the Eastern Shore of Maryland near Oxford. They never use it in the winter. I'll call and make sure it's empty. It'll do you good. Get you outside. You can walk around in the trees. Get back to nature."

At first she thought it was a ridiculous idea, but suddenly it started to sound better. She wasn't sure why.

"Is this place safe?" she asked.

"As safe as we can be."

"Let's go then."

Clay was pleased that she agreed to go. He was feeling a strange attachment to this battle-hardened woman. He couldn't understand his own feelings. It bothered him. When they had started together, he detested her. That was a simple emotion. But now it was something different, more complex. Love? He didn't know. He had always been so reserved, so cold. Occupied in a man's world of Ivy League schools and squash clubs, he had never given himself a chance to find love. But now? No, it was ridiculous. She was older. They were from different worlds.

The next morning, Clay fixed breakfast in the large kitchen of the country estate. When they were finished eating, Leora drained her coffee cup, got up from the table without making any effort to clean the breakfast dishes, put on her brown corduroy jacket and bolted toward the front door.

"I'm walking," she said curtly.

"Have a good time," Clay said, deciding that she wanted to be by herself and hoping that would dispel her moodiness of the last couple of days.

Clay was right. Leora did want to be by herself. She was a warrior preparing for her final siege.

Slowly, she walked over the thick grass, crushing the dead leaves under her feet. It was damp and chilly. She pulled up the collar on her jacket, shivering from the cold.

As she started down a small path, her ears picked up a sound. She paused, alert, listening. She thought she heard the sound again. She stopped walking and pulled the pistol from her pocket. She waited. There was nothing there.

A bad sign, she thought. Now I'm starting to imagine sounds. Maybe Motti was right. I am too old for this business.

The hill ended at a small stream. She stopped there and picked up a handful of twigs. Leaning against a rock, she snapped the twigs into small pieces and tossed them one by one into the stream. They struck the water with a splash, but only for an instant. Then the flow of the water picked them up and carried them downstream. How quickly they were lost.

She stood there for about half an hour—long enough for her whole life to pass before her eyes. She had never reflected like that before. It was like hearing sounds—a sign of advancing years.

She saw Clay approaching from the top of the hill. He was dressed in a sweater and plaid sport jacket. He was only a few years younger then she, but he looked like such a child.

"I thought you got lost," he said, trying to break into her world.

"No, I just wanted to be alone."

He stood next to her for several minutes, silent, letting her think. Then he reached over and gently placed his arm around her shoulder. He tried to draw her close to him.

She was surprised. It was the first physical display of affection he had ever made toward her. His arm was firm. His fingers pressed against her shoulder.

Quickly she pulled away from him and began walking along the stream. He walked alongside of her.

"I don't want to be rude," she said, "but that's not what I need right now."

He was silent. She felt sorry if she had offended him.

"Listen, Clay," she said slowly. "I know that it's a big thing these days for a younger man to take up with an older woman, but I'm not what you need. Get yourself some young debutante. You can do a lot better than this old warhorse."

He shoved his hands into his pockets.

"What about you?" he asked. "What do you do for yourself?"

"I've got one more battle to worry about."

"No. I meant you, yourself."

She thought about his words.

"There stopped being one," she replied.

"A pity. I would have liked her," he mumbled.

They walked along in silence. A few light drops of rain began to fall.

"How long will it continue?" he asked.

"What?"

"The killing, the bloodshed, between Jew and Arab."

She shrugged her shoulders, thinking of Yaacobi's words: "There is neither beginning nor end. This is the world we leave to our children."

"You Americans are so odd," she replied. "You always expect to wrap everything up into a neat little bundle. You can't generate foreign policy in a microwave oven. It isn't instant pudding. Thirty years is a short time in the history of the world."

"Sometimes an outsider brings perspective."

"Is that what you brought to Vietnam?"

"To be sure we failed," he replied soberly. "But our motives were pure—to cure an injustice."

"And your naïveté was staggering."

"Ah, the burden that comes with the power," he replied good-naturedly.

"Then keep the power at home, from sea to shining sea, as you say."

The rain began coming down harder.

"I have an outstanding idea," he said. "Tonight is supposed to be New Year's Eve, although from us you could never tell. My aunt has one helluva good wine cellar loaded with French champagne. Let's go back to the house and get roaring, stinking drunk. By the time we sleep it off, we'll be well into 1978."

She smiled broadly, letting a few raindrops fall into her mouth.

"That, Clay, is one of the best ideas I've heard in a long time."

She began running toward the house. He followed two steps behind.

"Do you know something, Clay?" She shouted as they ran.

"What's that?"

"I've never gotten drunk, really drunk, not once in my whole life."

"And I won't even try to take advantage of you."

"Remember we settled that back there."

She was laughing loudly. He had never seen her laughing like that before.

"I didn't forget. Always colleagues and never lovers."

Not this weekend, he thought. Maybe another time.

∾

CHAPTER 39

As Leora and Clay toasted the New Year in a half-drunken stupor, Kate and Michael Holt sat glumly in a corner of the magnificent high-ceilinged dining room at the Homestead, a resort two hundred miles west of Washington in the mountains of Virginia. The orchestra played songs from the era of the big bands and bejeweled women in long dresses danced around the wooden floor with gray-haired tuxedo-clad men.

This weekend had been Kate's big idea. If she got Michael away from Washington, if she was gentle and patient with him, she could regain his confidence. Then maybe she could help him. Thus far, she had accomplished absolutely nothing.

They went through the motions of talking and being together, but his mind was elsewhere, and his body was in physical pain. That was perfectly plain to her.

The wine steward approached, a gold chain hanging around his neck.

"Some champagne for the New Year?" he announced.

"Yes, of course," Michael said, looking over the list. He had taken a pill late in the afternoon, but already his stomach was bothering him again.

"The Moët," he replied. The steward picked up the list and walked away.

Michael asked her to dance. Kate followed obediently around the floor, the two of them graceless, lacking in enthusiasm.

Back at the table, he played with his salad while she described to him the progress she was making on her manuscript.

The wine steward returned with the bottle of champagne and an ice bucket. He opened the bottle and poured some into Michael's glass.

"You try it tonight," he said, moving his glass across the table. She sipped a little wine, smiled, and announced it was outstanding. The steward filled two glasses without acknowledging her comment and walked toward another table.

She waited until he was gone. Then she drained her glass, refilled it and drained it again.

Choking back the tears and talking through tightly drawn lips, she said to Michael, "You're a damn fool. You're too sick to drink the wine and yet you continue on just like nothing was happening."

"What do you mean?" he protested.

"Please cut the crap," she said, disregarding her vow that this weekend would be free from stress. "I've talked to Dr. Green. So let's start on that level."

He was startled. Then his surprise turned to anger.

"I don't check up on you."

"No, you don't," she replied. "But I have nothing to hide."

"Let's dance," he said, feigning a smile.

"I don't want to dance."

"What *do* you want from me?"

It was like a lob up to the net. She was ready with her answer before he finished his question.

"I want two things from you," she said. "First, I want you to walk away from Brett, just quit the Douglas Foundation. Then, I want you to tell Dr. Green you'll have the operation. After that, we'll take off for someplace far away, California or Arizona. We'll make ends meet somehow."

"A new start," he said weakly.

"Yes, a new start."

He was silent.

"It's not that easy, Kate."

"Why not? Why isn't it, Michael?" She was staring into his eyes, looking very determined.

"It just isn't."

"And killing yourself? That's easy?"

He just sat there looking at her, unwilling to speak.

"You still won't tell me what you're up to with Brett, whom you play tennis with on Wednesdays, will you?"

"No," he replied coldly.

"You really think he's a god, don't you?"

She was raising her voice now. People started to stare at them.

"Please keep your voice down," he whispered.

"No, I won't keep it down," she said loudly. She was so frustrated that she didn't care who was listening. "You probably think he's spending New Year's Eve in the company of presidents and kings, don't you?"

A matronly-looking gray-haired woman in a blue sequined dress, two tables away, leaned toward Kate, straining to hear every word. The woman's glasses were sliding down her nose as she leaned her head toward Kate.

Michael's face was red with embarrassment. He was quiet.

"I'll bet he's not with presidents and kings at all," Kate continued.

Michael looked down at the table, ashamed to look at anyone else in the dining room.

"He's not with presidents and kings at all," Kate said, raising her voice still louder. "He's probably shacked up with that French pussy of his in Georgetown."

There was absolute silence in the dining room. The glasses fell off the face of the woman, two tables away, who was listening intently.

Kate got up, walked over to the woman's table, picked up her glasses, handed them to her, and whispered into her ear.

"I said that he was probably shacked up with that French pussy of his in Georgetown."

Then, very gracefully, Kate walked out of the dining room as the band leader began singing "Should auld acquaintance be forgot . . ."

Happy New Year.

CHAPTER 40

Through the living-room window, Kate watched the black car pass in front of the house as it circled the block for the third time. It paused for just an instant in front of her house, then it pulled over to the curb and came to rest twenty yards away.

Kate was terrified. She had been frightened all day, since the call early in the morning. The caller had sounded innocent enough.

"Is Michael Holt there?"

"No," she had replied. "It's his first day back after the New Year's weekend. He went into the office early. Is there a message?"

"Well, when will he be home?" the caller had asked.

"Seven or eight o'clock," she had replied without thinking.

"Thank you," the caller had said and clicked off.

She had sat for a full hour afterward pondering that call. The voice had been a man's. She didn't recognize it. Yet it sounded suspicious.

Now it was seven o'clock. Michael wasn't home yet, but this mysterious black car was parked near the house. She raced upstairs, got a pair of binoculars, and walked over to the window in one of the front rooms. She could tell that there were two people in the car, but it was too dark to make out anything else.

She thought about calling the police, but what good would that do? she wondered. She was convinced that the people in the car had something to do with Michael and Brett. It would be just as well to deal with them herself. Maybe they could tell her what she was looking for.

She walked into the baby's room and made sure that he

was sleeping. Then she walked down the stairs quickly, very determined. She didn't bother to put on a coat. Instead she headed down the sidewalk in only her black slacks and a loose-fitting blouse. It wasn't much more than twenty degrees, but she didn't feel the cold.

As she approached the car, she could see that there was a man in the driver's seat and a woman sitting beside him. She approached on the woman's side and tapped on the window.

Leora lowered it quickly.

"Are you looking for my husband?" Kate asked.

"Tell us who your husband is," Leora said calmly.

"Michael Holt," Kate replied. Her voice was trembling.

"Yes. We're looking for your husband," Leora replied.

Kate knew from the accent that the woman wasn't an American, but she couldn't tell where she was from. She took a deep breath, summoning all of her courage. Suddenly she was aware of the cold. She was shivering.

"He's not home yet," Kate replied. "Why don't you come inside? It's much warmer."

Leora started to get out of the car. All of her instincts told her what to do. She began walking next to Kate, toward the house. Clay quickly fell in behind the two women.

Once they were inside the house, Kate boldly said, "Who are you?"

Clay flashed his State Department Internal Security identification.

Kate tried not to look frightened. "Well, what do you and your friend want?" she asked Leora.

"To talk with your husband."

"What about?"

"As I said, we want to talk to him. We'll wait until he gets home."

Leora studied Kate carefully. She looked at the wedding picture of Kate and Michael sitting on the mantelpiece.

"I'll get you some coffee while you wait," Kate said nervously. Without waiting for a response, she disappeared into the kitchen.

An idea was running through Leora's mind. It just might work.

"Do you still have that picture of Pritchard that you were carrying around in your wallet?" she asked Clay.

He took out his wallet and handed her the small glossy photograph wrapped in plastic.

Kate walked in carrying three cups of coffee on a tray. She handed cups to Leora and Clay, and picked up the other herself.

"Sit down, Mrs. Holt," Leora said in a sharp tone that made it clear that they were in charge.

Kate retreated to the sofa. Leora was standing in front of her, sipping her coffee. She placed down the cup and lit up a cigarette, making Kate wait.

Leora handed the small picture to Kate.

"Do you recognize that man, Mrs. Holt?"

Leora was watching her carefully, looking for a reaction. Even if she were blind, she would have sensed the terror on Kate's face when Kate recognized the man in the picture as the man who played tennis with Michael on Wednesday evenings. Her hands began trembling. She dropped the picture on the coffee table.

"No, I don't know that man," she said meekly.

Now Leora looked angry.

"Mrs. Holt, I don't have time for games. Of course you know that's Charlie Pritchard, the President's Middle Eastern adviser."

"No, I didn't know," Kate protested.

Clay sat down quietly. He didn't want to interrupt Leora.

Leora began pacing across the floor in front of the couch.

"Your husband is in a lot of trouble, Mrs. Holt."

Kate's eyes followed Leora as she cut a path back and forth across the carpet.

"What kind of trouble?" Kate asked nervously. She was fidgeting with her fingers.

Leora stopped pacing and stared squarely at her. "He's responsible for the murder of two men," Leora said in a cold dispassionate tone.

"Murder?" Kate stuttered incredulously, "Murder?"

"Yes, murder, Mrs. Holt."

"You've made a mistake. You must have made a mistake."

"No, we haven't made a mistake. We have enough evidence to convict him. We're quite certain of that."

Leora resumed pacing. Through the corner of her eye she was watching Kate carefully.

"He's only a pawn," Kate whispered. "Only a little soldier following orders. I swear to God that he is being used. He planned nothing on his own."

Leora stopped pacing and stared at Kate.

"Then who did plan it, Mrs. Holt?"

An eerie silence settled over the room. Leora pulled another cigarette from her purse. The sound of the striking match shattered the silence.

Kate was too frightened to respond. She thought about how awesome Brett could be to anyone who opposed him.

Leora sensed her reaction. She was ready to begin leaning hard on Kate, squeezing her until she would tell them.

Suddenly Clay interjected himself.

"We have something to offer you, Mrs. Holt, an inducement to tell us what you know."

Leora was surprised by Clay's words. What did they have to offer her? Just more grief, maybe even death.

"What do you have to offer me?" Kate asked.

"If you are telling us the truth and if your husband really was a pawn in this game, we will give him immunity from prosecution if we can find out who was really responsible, who planned it all."

Well done, Clay, Leora thought.

303

"But how can I be sure? You're with the State Department?" Kate asked. "How do I know what the Justice Department will do?"

The woman was intelligent, Clay decided.

"Mrs. Holt, I can't give you a guarantee. I used to be at the Criminal Division of Justice. I think that they'll follow my recommendation, but, as I have said, I can't give you a guarantee. I can tell you, though, it's the only chance he's got. If you love him, you'd better not pass it up."

Kate was silent, thinking. She honestly didn't know if she could help Michael by talking to Leora and Clay. She wasn't enough of a lawyer to be able to answer that question. But after a few moments of silence, that question receded. Another thought surged to the center of her attention, obscuring everything else. She suddenly realized that if she were to talk to Leora and Clay, it could have a devastating effect on Brett. Maybe they didn't even know about Brett. Maybe he had rigged everything so that only Michael would be left out front holding the bag if the operation were closed down. Poor Michael, poor Michael.

Suddenly a great surge of hatred for Brett rushed through her body like flood waters after a dam has burst. Every humiliation that he had inflicted on her in both of her marriages, every indignity that she had suffered at his hands, and everything he had done to Michael, interacted to produce this great surge of hatred that burned in her body like a torch. It forced her out of her seat. She rose to her feet dramatically.

She was like a crazy woman, bent on survival and determined to destroy the one person standing in the way of her survival. Yes, destroy. A single impulse flashed through her brain: DESTROY BRETT!

"I don't know everything," Kate said in a loud vindictive tone. "But I will tell you what I know."

Clay pulled a note pad and a pencil from his pocket, preparing to write down what Kate said.

Leora, slowly, painstakingly, began to interrogate Kate, drawing out of her everything that she knew about the Douglas Foundation and about Douglas Brett. Kate explained about the Wednesday tennis matches and identified Pritchard from the picture as the man with whom Michael played.

"Pritchard must pass the information to Michael on Wednesday evenings," Leora said to herself.

"But how do they do it?" Leora asked Kate.

"I don't know. I really don't know."

"Think about it, Mrs. Holt," Leora was screaming at her. "Think about it. You must know."

"I don't know. I swear it. Only Michael can tell you."

Then Kate broke down. She began sobbing violently. The whole exercise was too much for her.

Clay walked over to her and handed her a handkerchief.

"That's enough, Leora," he said. "She's told us what she knows."

Leora stepped back and sat down. She knew that Clay was right. Kate had told them everything she knew. She waited for Kate to pull herself together. Then she began talking to her again.

"Clay and I are going back outside," she said, "into our car to wait for your husband. When he comes home, we'll let you talk to him first yourself, to convince him to tell us what he knows in return for immunity. You have thirty minutes with him to bring him around. If it doesn't work, we'll come in and do it my way. Is that clear?"

Kate stared at her. She was a strange woman, Kate thought, so callous, so unemotional.

"Yes, that is clear," Kate said.

With that, Leora picked up her purse from the coffee table and nodded to Clay. They left the house.

As soon as they were gone, Kate made up her mind about what she had to do. She went upstairs to the attic and got down the two largest suitcases. She placed them both on her bed. Then, quickly, she began filling one of them with her clothes, all of the clothes that would fit. The other suitcase, she filled with the baby's clothes and his toys. They were heavy. With a great effort, she carried them down the stairs one at a time and placed them both near the front door. She went back upstairs and changed into a simple wool suit, the type of suit she would travel in. Then she placed her coat on the sofa, sat down next to it and waited.

Fifteen minutes later, Michael turned his key in the front door and let himself in.

A look of panic fell over his face as he saw the suitcases sitting next to the door, Kate dressed and ready to leave.

"Where are you going?" he asked nervously.

She rose from the sofa to face him. Then she began speaking in a calm, deliberate tone.

"I have very little time," she said. "I'll only explain it once. Listen carefully."

He was stunned by the harshness of her tone.

"There are two people sitting in a car outside," she continued. "Investigators from the State Department. I've told them everything I know about you and Brett."

He collapsed into a chair. A small pitiful "Oh, no," came from his lips as if he were a balloon that had been deflated. She paused for a moment, letting him grasp that fact.

"We made a deal of sorts," she said. "If you and I tell them everything we know, they'll give you immunity from prosecution."

"You had no right to do that," he protested.

"I'm a free person," she shouted, dropping the unemotional tone. "I can do anything I damn well please."

"Well, the same goes for me," he said, moving close to her. "And, I have no intention of talking to them."

She was so sorry to hear his words. He had pushed her into the corner. There was no turning back now.

Slowly, carefully, she put her coat on and began walking up the stairs.

"Where are you going?" he called after her.

"To get the baby. We're leaving you."

She continued climbing the stairs.

"You can't do that!" he shouted.

She stopped halfway up the stairs and wheeled around and faced him.

"And why the hell not?"

"Because I'm sick, very sick. You've been to Dr. Green. You know that. You couldn't be so cruel, so lacking in compassion." Even as he spoke, his stomach began aching again.

"Pity poor weak Michael," she replied mockingly. "You used up my sympathy long ago."

"You forget, woman"—his voice was rising to a scream —"how I took you in after Brett tossed you out. And now that I need help, this is your response."

"Yes, this is my response. I'm doing my best to pull you out of a burning building, since you don't have the sense to get out yourself."

With that, she turned around and began walking up the stairs again. The line was drawn. There was no turning back.

He looked at her helplessly. She was dead serious. He had no doubt about it.

For a full two minutes he hesitated, unsure. It was only when she walked down the stairs clutching the still sleeping baby that he capitulated. He collapsed on the sofa with a defeated whimper, "I'll do what you want."

Still clutching the baby, she raced into the street to get Leora and Clay, fearful that Michael would change his mind.

Kate placed the baby back in his crib. Then she walked slowly down the stairs.

She could hear Leora interrogating Michael in her carefully measured monotone. Michael was sitting on the sofa, talking freely, wanting to get it all out. He had a look of relief on his face.

Kate walked across the room and sat down on the sofa next to her husband, listening to him talk.

Clay was writing it all down carefully in his note pad.

Clay waited until Leora was finished to jump in. Then he gleefully announced:

"Well, that's it. We're finished. We have enough on Brett and Husni to implicate them in both murders. At the very least Brett was a part of a conspiracy to commit murder. We should also be able to get him on quite a few counts of espionage activity and disclosure of governmental information. Your friend Brett will be out of circulation for a very long time."

Clay was so happy that he wanted to jump up and down. Only one thing restrained him. It was Leora, standing rigidly across the room. She didn't share his enthusiasm.

"We're not finished yet," she said.

"What else is there?"

"We should watch them passing information at the tennis courts, take some pictures. That could make our case airtight."

"We don't need it, Leora," Clay protested. "I'm the former prosecutor. We don't need it."

She ignored his words.

"Are you playing tomorrow night?" she asked Michael.

"Yes," he replied meekly with a pained look on his face. He thought that he would never have to go near that tennis court again.

"Then play tomorrow," she said. "Like normal. This will be the last time, I promise you. We'll take movies for evidence."

Michael nodded obediently.

"But we don't need it, Leora," Clay repeated.

She ignored his words. Her thoughts were far away, back in Paris, at the offices of the Anglo-American Trading Company.

"Let's go, Clay," she said. "We've kept these people late enough."

She glanced quickly at her purse sitting on an end table, left it resting there, and started toward the door. Clay followed behind, unwilling to argue with her anymore.

She waited until Clay was in the car, until he had started the engine, then she opened her car door.

"I've left my purse inside," she said quickly. "Keep it running. I'll be right out."

When she looked inside the window next to the door of the house, she saw Michael leaning on Kate's breast like a little baby, sobbing softly.

The door was slightly open. She let herself in. Michael sat up.

"I left my purse," she said, walking over to pick it up.

As she started out of the door, she suddenly turned around and faced the two of them.

"There is one other thing I want from you, Michael," she said tersely. "I want you to call Brett tonight. Right now, while I'm still here."

Michael and Kate looked puzzled.

"Listen carefully," Leora said. "This is what I want you to tell Brett—exactly this, no more and no less. I want you to tell Brett that an Israeli woman named Leora has called and made inquiries, that she must have found out something about Yaacobi and your project, and that she is planning to go to the tennis court tomorrow evening. Tell him that you're afraid she may grab Pritchard and that he'll panic and tell her everything."

"I don't understand," Michael said weakly.

"You don't have to understand," she barked at him. "Just make the call."

Michael looked at Kate. She pointed to the telephone.

Obediently he got up and made the call. A very startled Brett listened carefully while Michael repeated everything exactly as Leora had told him. And then, without uttering a single word, Brett placed the telephone in its cradle.

Leora left the house as soon as Michael had completed the call.

~~

CHAPTER 41

Brett fixed himself a drink after he finished the telephone call with Michael. He knew what he had to do. He had to go see Husni as quickly as possible. He knew that very well. And yet he couldn't get himself to move. He knew how Husni would react, and that began to bother him.

How long a trail of dead bodies would they leave, before they finished? Why was he still in it? he wondered. God knows, he had accumulated so much money that any more didn't matter. Deep down, he still wanted to have the world's largest oil rig. But maybe the price for that was becoming too great, even for Brett.

No, that wasn't it, Brett decided. Shit, man, you're just scared that you'll get caught and that your oil rig will come tumbling down.

With that thought in mind, Brett did exactly what he had to do.

Brett asked his driver to leave him off on Massachusetts Avenue. He walked the remaining three blocks to Husni's house.

The greeting that he received from the Syrian at the door was anything but friendly.

"You know that I don't like to be disturbed here," Husni snapped at Brett.

"It is a matter of great urgency."

Looking exasperated, the Syrian led Brett to an upstairs study.

"Okay. Tell me what it is," he said tolerantly.

Brett explained the telephone call from Michael. Husni wasn't at all surprised. He anticipated that the Israelis would send someone else to replace Yaacobi sooner or later. He also had a complete file on Leora. "A bitch on wheels," Jacques Barot called her.

"Maybe we should pull up our tents," Brett said nervously, "and end this part of the operation."

Husni fixed Brett a large bourbon and branch water to calm his nerves.

Then he announced to the American, "One more evening is all I want, just tomorrow. Then we bail out."

"Why wait until after tomorrow?"

"Because last week we asked Pritchard to get us important military information about Israeli troop deployments in the Golan Heights. I want that very badly. Let your man Holt play with him as always, just one more time."

"But the woman Leora," Brett said.

Husni lit up one of his Turkish cigarettes.

"Don't worry about the woman," he announced calmly. "She will be no problem."

"But?" Brett stammered.

Now Husni looked angry.

"Your man will play tennis with Pritchard one more time," Husni said with the ring of finality.

CHAPTER 42

Several hours before Brett's meeting with Husni, Charlie Pritchard was sitting in his office at the White House and glancing nervously at his watch. It was almost four o'clock. He could make the call now. His fingers were moist with perspiration. He knew very well the importance of the information on Golan Heights troop deployments.

Two rings. No answer. Charlie started to worry. He had waited until today because he knew that Walter Adams, the Secretary of Defense, would be in St. Louis. Another ring. Then the familiar, mechanical-sounding, businesslike voice.

"Department of Defense, office of the Secretary."

"Marge. It's Charlie Pritchard."

The tone changed.

"*Oh*, Charlie. How are you?"

"Fair to middlin', Marge. Fair to middlin'."

"And the girls? How are those girls?"

"Good, Marge. Good."

"A mother's what they need. It's too tough doing it yourself."

There she was, off again, rattling about the advisability of him getting married. He knew that she saw herself as prime candidate number one. It sent chills up his spine. It wasn't her appearance. She was attractive enough in a kind of earthy, farm-girl way—light-brown hair, heavy cheekbones, large round breasts, and good strong legs. Not fat, just muscular—the kind of woman who could have a baby in the morning and head back to work in the fields after lunch. And even at thirty, she looked as if she could still punch out quite a few babies. No, the problem wasn't with her appearance. It's just that she always talked so damn much.

312

"Is Walter there?" he asked innocently, pretending he didn't know the answer.

"St. Louis today, at McDonnell Douglas. Do you want to call him there? He's—"

"No. No. I don't have to call him. It can wait until tomorrow."

"Is it something I can help you with? I can be very helpful. Really I can. Just give me a chance."

He didn't know whether to laugh or to cry.

"Come on, try me," she coaxed.

"Well, as a matter of fact, all I wanted to do was look at some of his files this evening."

Charlie's hand was trembling so badly that he nearly dropped the telephone.

"The President wants an update on some Middle East information first thing in the morning."

"Well, come on over," she said, sounding enticing like one of those bikini-clad girls in the television commercials that airlines run for winter vacations. "I can show you where everything is. You can stay here as long as you like."

He hesitated.

"I'd hate to keep you late. I wouldn't be there for half an hour."

"Oh, no problem at all. My car pool doesn't leave till five. I've got no plans this evening and no one to cook for but myself."

"No, you won't have to miss your car pool."

"It's no problem, really."

"Another time. I'll take you up on it. I'll see you in half an hour then."

Charlie placed down the telephone and gave a great sigh of relief. Then he pressed twice on the intercom.

"Martha. Get me a car and driver from the White House pool. I have to go over to the Pentagon."

"Yes, Mr. Pritchard."

"Oh, you can leave at five. I won't be back until later."

Charlie walked slowly up the long gray staircase at the main entrance to the Pentagon, then through the large double doors.

The guard on duty recognized him immediately.

"Good to see you, Mr. Pritchard."

Charlie walked by the desk.

"I have to see your I.D.," the guard called.

Charlie smiled. It always seemed like a useless act to require identification from someone you knew. Still, he was in no mood to point out that fact. He began searching clumsily through the confusion of cards that were shoved into his wallet.

The guard watched Charlie fumbling with his cards.

"I'm sorry, sir, it's regulations."

Finally he found the bright-green card: "Charles O. Pritchard. Presidential adviser."

"Sign the register and head on up," the guard said.

As soon as he passed through the door marked "Walter Adams, Secretary of Defense," a heavy, disgustingly aromatic odor filled his nostrils. Marge must have taken a bath in perfume, he thought.

After she showed him where the files were, Charlie gazed at the clock on the wall. It was only twenty minutes to five. He decided to wait until she left to begin looking at files. For the next twenty minutes he would have to listen to her chatter.

"You're losing weight," she said. "Working too hard? Not eating well? You should let me cook a good meal for you once."

"Yes, that's a good idea," he replied. "I'll do that. I'll call you when things ease up. Right now I'm working seven nights a week. But when they ease up, I'll call you and take you up on that."

"That's a promise?"

"You bet," he said.

Finally she left. He started opening file drawers. He was trembling. In the past, all of the information he had supplied to Brett had come from his own office. His hands were wet and clammy.

Suddenly the door opened. He was shaking. It was only Marge.

"I forgot my magazine," she said.

Then she walked over to the desk and picked up a copy of *Cosmopolitan* and tucked it under her arm.

"Are you okay?" she asked, looking worried.

"Sure, why not?"

"You don't look well. Your face is pale, ashen."

He wondered where she had picked up the word "ashen." Maybe it was in one of those romantic novels she was reading.

"No. No. I'm fine," he said.

"Lock the door when you leave," she called as she left the office again.

He returned to the files.

It took him about twenty minutes to find the document he was looking for. It contained a summary of Israeli troop deployments in the Golan Heights that the Israeli Minister of Defense had presented to Walter Adams last month when he visited Washington. Charlie had seen it once before in a meeting that the President had with the Secretary of Defense. After that meeting, Walter had taken all of the copies of the document back to the Pentagon.

Charlie thought for a minute about how to copy the document. There was a photocopy machine down the hall.

He tucked the papers into a red file folder and began walking toward the machine, trying to appear nonchalant. As he approached the small room that housed the machine, he could hear the clicking noise that indicated it was in service.

Damn fool, he thought to himself. It's too risky. Do it

the old way, the way it was done before copying machines came along.

He returned to the Secretary's office. He sat down at Marge's desk with a pad of yellow paper and a pencil and began copying all of the information on the document.

He was writing fast, squeezing the pencil hard. At first he thought about the items he was copying. But as he continued to write, his fingers began to ache. His task became mechanical. He stopped thinking about what he was writing. His mind began to roam. How did he end up here, he wondered? How had he managed to squander his promise? Why didn't life ever go the way he planned? Where would he be in another year?

Charlie hadn't been inside of a church for twenty-five years, not since boarding school. Yet sitting in the office of the Secretary, copying the information on the document, he began to pray. "And lead us not into temptation, for thine is the kingdom and the glory forever."

"Oh, God, I want to die," he muttered to himself.

~

CHAPTER 43

Clay walked slowly up the wooden staircase that led to Leora's room and their operation headquarters on the third floor of his Georgetown house.

"Are you sleeping?" he asked softly.

"No, I'm awake," she responded from the darkened room.

He turned on a small lamp and looked at her. She was lying in bed on her back bundled under the covers, her eyes staring at the ceiling. She had an intense, determined look on her face. She was staring off into the terrible void of time and space.

"You did a good job this evening at the house," he said, "with Kate and Michael, I mean. I'll get credit for it, but you did it all. I wanted to tell you that."

She smiled weakly. He wasn't sure whether his words had produced that smile or something she was thinking of.

"Reconsider, won't you, Leora? We really don't need tomorrow at the tennis courts. Let's quit now."

"No, I won't quit now," she said sharply. Her eyes were blazing with fire. He thought that she was sick. He wanted to go over and touch her forehead, to see if it was warm. But he was afraid to. He knew that she was hiding something from him, but he also knew that it was hopeless to try to pry it out.

"You know I was very serious last Saturday, down at the Creek," he said. "It's not too late. You could find a reasonably normal life with me, maybe even a little happiness."

This time he knew that the smile was intended for him.

"You're a very nice man, Ernest," she said, trying to be kind, "but the notion of me as a suburban housewife is preposterous."

He was silent.

"Don't you see what you're trying to promise me?" she said. "An instant happy ending, American style. It won't work for me."

"But don't you ever have any doubts?"

"What do you mean, doubts?"

"Doubts that you're right."

She laughed gently.

"Doubts that you can continue the struggle to the end," he said.

"In history there is neither beginning nor end. We continue to struggle. That is all."

He moved across the room and sat down on the edge of the bed.

"You're telling me that there is no alternative to the continuing death and destruction?"

"No alternative," she replied. "Like the carrousel at Tivoli, it goes on and on, until you reach the point that Dan Yaacobi reached. Then the carrousel stops."

Her eyes blazed as she said his name.

"You loved him a lot, didn't you?" Clay asked.

"Yes, I loved him a lot."

Perhaps it was the way she said it, perhaps it was the look on her face, Clay wasn't certain. But suddenly everything fell into place for him. Suddenly he understood what she had in mind, and he was frightened, more frightened than he had ever been before in his life.

Clay got up from her bed, leaned over, and gently kissed her on the forehead. He turned off the lights and walked downstairs.

He fixed himself a double scotch. Then another. He sat in the brown leather chair of his masculine study, sipping scotch and trying to use the sparks of passion that Leora had ignited to develop a plan and to screw up his courage. By nature he was neither physical nor violent. But, he would have to be both if he wanted to stop her, if he wanted to be left with anything when it was all over, with any chance at all that he could persuade her to start over again with him, and he wanted that very much.

୬ଏ

CHAPTER 44

Leora paced back and forth in the spectators' gallery at the Bethesda Indoor Tennis Club. She alternated her gaze between the long black minute hand on the clock that was fast approaching twelve, Clay sitting in an orange plastic-covered chair, hunched forward, holding a movie camera in one hand and biting a fingernail on the other, and the two tired actors on the court below, who were playing out the final act in their tragedy. When Clay wasn't aiming the camera, he was watching her carefully through the corner of his eye, watching her and waiting.

Leora should have felt some compassion for those two, for Pritchard, whose nerves and emotions were worn to their bitter end by the long months of intrigue and deception, and for Michael, near collapse, periodically stopping the match when the pain became unbearable. Yet Leora felt no compassion for them. They were doing what was required of them for survival, no more and no less. The human condition no longer moved her to compassion.

When the buzzer rang, signaling the end of the hour, Pritchard picked up a ball lying on the ground, tossed it into the air, and smashed it across the court with all of the strength that his frustration could produce. The yellow ball struck a soft foam mat at the other end of the court and fell harmlessly to the ground.

Leora watched Clay carefully as he filmed Pritchard and Michael at the side of the court, each one picking up the Davis racket cover that the other had brought. Those films, coupled with the earlier films, taken when they arrived at the court, were the clearest possible confirmation of the conspiracy.

"Well, that's it," Clay said, putting down the camera. "Even you will have to admit that we're finished now."

Leora and Clay were alone in the room. His words echoed off the wall, creating an eerie hollow sound. She picked up her purse from the floor.

"Wait here," she snapped. "I'm going outside in the parking lot to grab Pritchard."

She had one thought in her mind. Somewhere outside in that parking lot Cherev would be waiting for her. She was certain of that.

But Clay knew precisely what she was thinking. He was ready for her.

"There's no need to do that," he said boldly. "Pritchard

hasn't seen anything that would make him take off. We'll call the FBI and have him picked up."

She started toward the door.

"Wait here, I said. We're doing this my way."

She had a grim look of determination on her face. Clay was equally determined. He had been handed everything in his life on a silver platter. He never had to struggle for anything before. But that didn't mean that deep down he didn't have a reservoir of inner strength.

"No, I won't let you go."

"Wait here, I said."

Clay's face turned red. Beads of perspiration appeared on his forehead.

"I won't let you do it."

Leora was startled by his determination.

"It's my struggle," she shot back.

He started toward the door to stop her.

"I know what you want to do. I won't let you do it," Clay repeated. "I'm not letting you go."

He was only three steps away from her, when she suddenly dropped her purse. With a lightning-fast motion, she tightened her right hand into a fist and drove it into his stomach with all of her force. The wind shot out of his body like a balloon. But he refused to give up. He lunged for her with all of the strength he had left, grabbing her hair and face. He was holding on as if life itself depended on it. Even when she drove him to the ground and fell on top of him, he refused to let go, tearing at her hair, clawing at her flesh.

He could feel the blood from her face flowing under his fingernails. And all the time she was driving her fists into his stomach. He ignored the blows. He knew what he had to do. He had to hold her tight so she couldn't leave that room. His legs, he decided to use them, to wrap them around her like a vise.

Then he felt a great burst of pain as she savagely

smashed her knee into his groin. His whole world disintegrated momentarily as he entered a dazed state of semiconsciousness. Finally, he let go.

She picked herself up from the ground quickly, without even stopping to wipe her face. She grabbed her purse and headed into the corridor.

She had studied the layout of the club carefully when they arrived. The building was shaped like a horseshoe. The outside door nearest the spectators' gallery opened onto the parking lot. Directly across the parking lot was another door that was marked "Players' Entrance."

She paused in front of the outside door, looking out through the small window. The parking lot was well lit. There were a couple of dozen cars scattered around the lot. Everything was quiet outside. There was no sign of anyone coming out of the players' entrance.

She placed her hand inside her purse, clasping the small pistol in her hand. She waited.

A minute later the door across the parking lot opened slowly. She saw Pritchard come out of that door, alone, tired, walking slowly, the tennis racket hanging limply from his hand.

She opened the door and stepped out into the cold January air. Outside it was deathly quiet. The cold air stung the raw flesh of her face where Clay had clawed her. Quickly, resolutely, she began walking across the parking lot toward Pritchard, her eyes roving from side to side.

Everywhere the reflection from the lights on the metal of the parked cars played tricks on her eyes, but except for Pritchard, nothing else moved.

She pulled the pistol from her purse, gripping it tightly, letting the leather bag drop to the ground.

As Pritchard saw her approach, a look of absolute panic appeared on his face.

"Hey, Charlie Pritchard," she shouted. "I want to talk to you."

He froze, paralyzed, unable to run, unable to continue walking.

She continued walking toward Pritchard at a steady pace, her eyes still moving from side to side.

Suddenly, she saw what she was looking for. There was only a slight movement, but it was enough for lights to bounce off the metallic surface of the machine gun. There, crouched behind the front fender of a black Mercedes, was Cherev. She broke her pace and continued walking very slowly. Her eyes were fixed on the Mercedes now, waiting.

She had seen him. She knew that he was there. He realized that.

Suddenly he was on his feet gripping the machine gun in his hands. The awful sound of guns firing shattered the night air.

Leora knew instinctively that her own shot found its mark. She had hit that tiny square on Cherev's body that Yigal called "shoot to kill." She saw his head snap backward. She knew that he would fall, that he would never get up again.

Then she felt the pain, the awful piercing pain as the bullets ripped through her chest, yanking her from her feet. She felt her whole body pulling apart.

"Dan," she mumbled. "Dan."

She collapsed on to the hard cold ground of the parking lot.

Clay heard the shots just as he was getting to his feet, still dazed in the spectators' gallery. He hesitated for a moment, trying to reorient himself. The lower part of his body ached.

"No, no," he screamed.

Then he began racing frantically toward the parking lot, forgetting about his own pain. He saw her lying there in a pool of blood. He ran toward her, desperately hoping, praying that she was still alive. He knelt next to her and gently picked up her head in his arms.

She had a strange look of complete contentment on her scratched face, a look that he had never seen before. It was complete peace for Leora, peace at last.

She was dead.

The Montgomery County police arrived ten minutes later. The first officer at the scene was Lieutenant William Evers, a tall brawny man with a thick brown mustache. The lieutenant took one look at Clay, sitting on the cold ground next to Leora's still body, with large tears flowing down his cheeks.

"She's dead, Officer," he wailed. "She's dead."

The lieutenant walked around the parking lot. He saw a dead man lying next to a black Mercedes. There on the ground next to the man's body was an object that puzzled the lieutenant. It was a small black plastic sword.

∼

EPILOGUE

There was no trial.

Brett decided to plead guilty. He accepted his twenty-year sentence, hoping that with good behavior at Allenwood he could gain an early parole and make a fresh start.

Charlie Pritchard never even made it to the point of having to plead guilty. After he learned that Clarissa had gotten custody of their two daughters, he hung himself in his prison cell at the D.C. jail.

As for Major Husni, he was the subject of great handwringing and long debates at the White House and the State Department. Finally, Secretary of State Waller used a tortured legal analysis prepared by a junior lawyer in the legal office of State to justify the conclusion that Husni's diplomatic immunity permitted him to leave the country quietly, without any charges being filed. Waller sent a mild note of protest to Husni's government.

The day that Waller made this decision, Ernest Clay resigned in protest from the State Department. He forwarded his letter of resignation condemning the hypocrisy of the State Department to *The New York Times*, where it was published on the Op Ed Page. Afterward, Clay traveled abroad for a year, still haunted by the memory of Leora. Then he decided to return to New York and go into the family's investment banking business.

Zipora and her two children went to live on the kibbutz in Israel, just as Motti had arranged. Roni, the oldest child, is counting the days until he can join the army and then volunteer for Shai, just like his father.

Before Clay left the government, he was able to obtain for Michael the immunity from prosecution that he had promised. After a successful stomach operation at George Washington Hospital, Michael moved with Kate and little Michael to Los Angeles. There he opened a small advertising agency that has become quite a success. Michael and his family are thriving now in the sunny climate of Southern California, proving the validity of the great American dream: In real life there are happy endings.

Two years after the move, they had another baby, a little girl. They named her Leora—after a woman of valor.